WHERE MY LOVE LIES
DREAMING

CHRISTOPHER HAWTHORNE MOSS

Dreamspinner Press

Published by
Dreamspinner Press
5032 Capital Circle SW
Ste 2, PMB# 279
Tallahassee, FL 32305-7886
USA
http://www.dreamspinnerpress.com/

Where My Love Lies Dreaming

Cover Art by Paul Richmond
http://paulrichmondstudio.com

Cover content is being used for illustrative purposes only
and any person depicted on the cover is a model.

ISBN: 978-1-62380-637-8
Digital ISBN: 978-1-62380-638-5

Printed in the United States of America
First Edition
July 2013

In memory of my sister, Denise Forest, and my cousins, Randy and Todd Booth, residing now in that Rainbow Pride Parade in the sky.

ACKNOWLEDGMENTS

FIRST and foremost and as always, I acknowledge the love and devotion of Jim, my spouse of the past thirty-one years. He is my Number One Fan and has gone through and supported my choices and changes to a phenomenal degree during our long and loving life together. I hope I give back at least some of what you have given to me.

For their help with the research and writing of this novel, I thank the following:

Anel Viz, author of numerous gay novels, for his savoir français,

"Friar Jak," as ever for his encyclopedic knowledge of battle and war and his good humor,

Jack Russell, skipper of the stern-wheeler *Christine W*,

Linda Laaksonen, the artist who created a Frankie that matched his image in my heart and mind,

Piet Bach, for knowing things about historical costume and décor I had no clue could be known,

Steamboats.org,

Tim Woods, author of *Grant Me Timely Grace*, for his poker know-how,

And my beta group, which included Piet Bach, Alex Hogan, Brian Holliday, Linda Laaksonen, and Lichen Craig, all wonderful authors themselves, with a special thanks to Lichen for being the first, after me, to fall head over heels in love with Frankie Deramus.

PART I
LE BEAU SOLEIL

CHAPTER 1

Chicago, late May 1859

PACKING for his trip to New Orleans, Johnny bustled about his bedroom in his papa's small house in a near south neighborhood in Chicago. He did not hear the knock on the door downstairs and was startled when his papa came to his open bedroom door and called, "Hansi." Johnny turned to see his papa's heartbroken, disappointed expression. "Who is this?" he asked, holding up an envelope. Over their address, it read "John C. Stanley."

Johnny sighed. "You know that's me, Papa."

"But your name is Johann. Johann Steinfeld. Not John C. Stanley."

"Papa, we have talked about this. I need an American name to do business. I can't be going about with a German name."

His papa looked as if he would weep. "Hansi, are you ashamed of being German?"

Johnny wouldn't admit that to his papa. "No, of course not."

"You are ashamed of me, then, your old German papa?"

Johnny walked over to snatch the envelope out of his papa's hand. He knew it contained his railroad and riverboat tickets from the office. "I am not going to get into this argument with you, Papa. You just don't understand how hard it is to make it in this country if everyone thinks you are a foreigner."

"But you are a foreigner, Herr *Besserwisser*. I am a foreigner. Your poor dead mama was a foreigner. Your betrothed, Klara, is a foreigner," his papa lamented.

Being called "Mr. Know-it-all" as much as the mention of Klara's name tipped Johnny over the edge. He shouted, "You are goddamned right she is. And that is why I will never marry her. Get that straight in your head, old man. I am not going to marry any damned *Bauerntrampel*."

His papa's eyes grew moist as he said, "So you are going to find some cheap American girl and marry, I suppose."

Johnny sighed. In English he said reassuringly, "No, Papa. I promise I won't marry a cheap American girl. I'm sorry. I am not ashamed of Klara or you or Mama or the old country." He put his hand awkwardly on his papa's shoulder, such physical comfort being so foreign to them both. "I wish you would stop saying that. I wish you could understand...."

"*Ich verstehe*," his father said. "*Ich verstehe*." Johnny knew from the way he said it, his papa really did understand, all too well.

"I have to go, Papa," Johnny said in a softer voice. "I have to catch the train."

While not Johnny's first journey on behalf of the U.S. Department of the Treasury, where he worked as a clerk, this trip would be the first to someplace as exotic as New Orleans, one of the fastest growing and most prosperous cities in the country. The Treasury oversaw the rapid expansion of the railroads, and many of the most recent lines were private, hastily constructed, and did not meet to create an effective network for transportation. Often someone who needed to travel east or west of the Mississippi River would travel a short distance by rail only to have to disembark and find transportation by horse or cart to another railroad line to continue their journey. Johnny's assignment to survey these disconnections would provide the Treasury with prospects for making rail travel continuous between the North and the South. Ironically, he would travel most of the way to New Orleans by riverboat, but he knew while the riverboats could transport everything the railroads could, the railroads would be able to accomplish it for a fraction of the cost.

So Johnny, bags in hand, headed on foot to the large central rail station at the heart of Chicago's main business district.

It took most of the day to travel by rail to Cairo, Illinois, where he would embark downriver on a grand riverboat with the pretentious name of *Le Beau Soleil*. All that time on the train gave him the chance he most certainly did not want: to think about the constant debate with his papa. Why could he not understand Johnny's reason for striving so desperately to blend into the world in which he worked—the American world? That world was suspicious of and resentful toward newly arrived immigrants from such places as Holland, Scandinavia, Italy, Poland, Ireland, and, of course, the countries made up of German-speaking people. He heard derogatory statements—dirty, ignorant, and untrustworthy—about *micks, Polaks, dagos, and heinies* almost daily. Many people from Johnny's birthplace, Dresden, had fled the suppressed revolutions of the 1840s and brought with them social and political ideas that clashed with supposed American ideals. His papa's friend, Herr Holtzmann, Klara and Kurt's father, would spout radical ideas for hours.

Bad enough they held those ideas, Johnny thought, as the Illinois countryside went by outside the sooty window of the passenger car of the Illinois Central train. Even the properly subdued, neat, and quiet immigrants still gathered in their enclaves and lived as if they had never left the old country, never mixing in American circles, never trying to fit in. Herr Holtzmann insisted they had no choice. "As soon as Americans hear your accent, you are ostracized."

Johnny didn't believe that. He smiled to himself when he thought about how hard he had worked to look like an American, to dress like an American, and to speak like an American. To make it into those circles reserved for native-born Americans, he had to change his name. John Stanley had replaced Johann Steinfeld.

"WAKE up, Mr. Thompson. We're coming in to Branch Junction. Mr. Thompson?"

Startled out of his reverie by the conductor's voice, Johnny pulled into himself as the man leaned across him to touch the shoulder of the occupant of the window seat.

"Mr. Thompson?"

Passengers packed the railway car when it departed from Chicago, which forced Johnny to share the hard wooden seat. When his neighbor, some sort of salesman in a cheap coat and shiny trousers, fell asleep and started to snore, relief flooded Johnny, as he was uninterested in conversation with the talkative man. When the fellow's head tilted over to rest on Johnny's shoulder, he let it stay there rather than risk waking him. Johnny became aware of just how pleasant the feeling was, how comfortable, and finally how it made his mind run to thoughts of such intimacy with a man—he shrugged to dislodge the man's head. After a couple of snorts, the man started snoring again.

Johnny had worked hard to lose his accent and fit in at his job, but he continued to struggle to overcome his unnatural attraction to men. He had to believe he could get past this compulsion, to find an American wife, have American children, and go on as just another American man. He wouldn't marry Klara, though; she had not tried to fit in, had never bothered to learn much English even though she was born in Chicago. If he married at all, it would be to an American girl, but not someone cheap like his papa feared. She would be a proper American girl. The only stipulation with which he agreed was she should be Catholic, like the Steinfelds and the Holtzmanns. But definitely not Klara, who his father was pressuring him to marry. He struggled with the fact, and he certainly did not tell his papa, but he did not want a woman.

German youths traditionally attended a sort of boys' gymnasium where they played sports as the Athenian youths had, quite naked. At the age of twelve, his young prick first began to react when he looked at the other boys. He tried to ignore it, hoping the feelings would go away. They did not abate. In fact, his thoughts took on more specific form. He started to imagine touching the other boys. This made his prick stand up more. *It must be a mistake,* he thought. He tried to stir some interest in the girls he knew, but they did nothing whatever for him. He had no choice but to quit the gymnasium or be found out.

In those days, most immigrant families made use of community groups and facilities like the gymnasium to pool resources rather than either provide them individually or do without. In a city like Chicago, there were public steam rooms, but immigrant populations did not much like sharing them with "Americans." Leaving the gymnasium meant Johnny lost access to the communal steam room. His papa, puzzled at his decision to quit, mostly complained about Johnny's attempts to keep clean with a bucket and a rag. Johnny could not explain to his father that he had made the choice in order to avoid having his secret found out.

He managed a compromise by convincing the priest who ran the gymnasium to let him work there as a menial worker, mopping the steam room and doing odd jobs. He did his best to keep his eyes on the floor and not look at all the wet, slippery bodies. Hardest of all was not looking when the older boys—young men really—bathed. They were so beautiful, so virile, so... attractive. At least when left alone in the evening, he could disrobe and take the steam with no one being the wiser.

He finally left that job because of the daily reminder of his perversion and to avoid the attentions of Father Martin, the priest who ran the gymnasium. At first, Johnny blamed himself for somehow luring the older man. *He must know about me, somehow*, he fretted to himself. One night after hours, when Johnny scrubbed himself in the empty steam room, he happened to look over and saw the man watching him. He tried to laugh it off, but the priest's actions escalated until another night he cornered Johnny in the steam room, put his hand on Johnny's shoulder and squeezed it, and promised him sweets if he would just touch him... down there.

Johnny told his papa he had found a job as a paperboy, which paid better.

As he reached adulthood, Johnny had thought about marrying Klara in hopes that having her, timid and dependent, would help him get beyond whatever this thing was. His confessor had told him to pray, do penance, then find a woman. "Better to marry than burn," the old man had said. Better still to sin with a woman than do the abominable thing with a man.

He took up boxing when he was eighteen, though it meant naked showers again. He found his desires useful in perfecting the manly pursuit of pugilism. If a man attracted him, he hit the man harder. No one had tried to lure him since Father Martin. No one wanted to get close because of the dour, touchy demeanor he'd perfected.

Johnny knew he had to get over this strange aberration. He fought it, he agonized, he did everything he could to hide it from himself, but he had to come to grips with the fact that men—not women—aroused him. He finally pushed it to the back of his mind and chose not so much to deny it as simply to ignore its significance. Perhaps it would pass.

"MR. THOMPSON, you got to wake up." The conductor gave Johnny an apologetic look.

Johnny had given Thompson the window seat so he would not have to climb over the man to get up and stretch his legs. It wasn't like there was anything to see. Through the layer of coal soot from the engine, Johnny could see only trees, trees, and more trees, with an occasional cluster of shacks near a whistle stop or a tiny one-room house and a barn where some fool was trying to farm, just now breaking up the sod in preparation for planting.

"What? What? Branch Junction? I'm not going to Branch Junction, man!" Thompson woke spluttering. He had drool on his chin and on his tie. He dragged a crumpled handkerchief from his coat pocket and mopped at it.

"Yeah, but your ticket says Patoka. You got to change trains here. 'Less you want to go to Cairo."

"Oh. All right. Thanks. How long?"

"Five minutes," the conductor called over his shoulder as he went down the aisle.

Thompson looked at Johnny. "You going all the way to Cairo, Mr. Stanley?"

"Yes, then by riverboat to New Orleans," Johnny reminded him.

"Oh yes, of course, I remember you said that. Some sort of government worker, aren't you?" Thompson dusted himself down in preparation for getting up to retrieve his valise from the net above the seats.

Johnny nodded. "The Treasury. Collecting information on transportation routes."

"Well, that sure is a long trip. But I've heard New Orleans is a beautiful city." He nodded for Johnny to stand so he could move into the aisle. Thompson got up and groaned when he tried to wrest his bag from the sling.

"Can I help you with that?" asked Johnny, since he was taller.

"Oh, yes, if you please. Most kind."

Johnny stood and snagged the bag. As he did, the train swayed abruptly, throwing the two men against each other. Johnny colored deeply, remembering his thoughts about the warm body leaning against him, but Thompson was looking away for a grip to keep upright, so he did not see the blush.

The train whistle blew, signaling to the Branch Junction station.

"Hope I don't got to wait here for my connection too long. I haven't seen my wife in a couple of weeks. She's expecting our first. You married?" After letting Johnny back in to take the window seat, Thompson set his bag on the aisle seat. He stood, looking down on Johnny as he held onto the back of their bench for balance.

"No, but I am engaged." Johnny cringed inwardly at the lie. He'd developed the habit to obscure the truth about himself.

"Oh yeah? She pretty?"

Johnny wished the man would go wait on the platform between the cars. "Klara? Yes, pretty enough."

"You lucky dog. My Muriel ain't real pretty, but she's a damn good cook. You wouldn't know it to look at me." He let go of the seat back to pat his belly, chuckling. The train put on the brakes, and Thompson almost lost his balance. "Well, nice to meet you, Mr. Stanley. You look out for those pretty ladies down South, if you get my drift."

Johnny winced when the man winked, actually winked at him. He smiled and nodded.

FINALLY in Cairo, Johnny stood on the levee, admiring the stately riverboat moored there. It had steamed into the port just as Johnny walked downhill from the train. He felt relieved, since delays at the junction had made him afraid he would miss his connection. As the riverboat came into the mooring, its great side-wheels slowing, Johnny saw its magnificence. *Le Beau Soleil* was one of the "best boats," with four decks and a pilothouse. It could not be called sparkling white, since, like everything else near the levee, soot coated its paint, but the astounding gold-colored sunburst mounted on the grillwork between the smokestacks with its own coating of soot let him see through it to what must have been the real colors. *Le Beau Soleil*, Johnny thought. He had to concede the boat impressed him.

"Steinfeld!" called a familiar fellow just coming down the gangway.

"Lehrer! What are you doing here?" Johnny said, reluctantly greeting his old schoolmate.

Lehrer looked about for a porter. In German he said, "Wait a minute while I get a boy to fetch my bags and take them to the train station."

"Boy!" he called in English to a colored man of at least forty. The man dashed over to them and bowed. Lehrer pointed toward the main deck of the boat where his bags sat and told him to "look sharp" and get them on the Chicago-bound train. He dug in his trouser pocket for change and dropped it in the porter's palm. The man bowed over and over with exaggerated obsequiousness before turning to go up the gangway for Lehrer's things.

"Have time for a drink?" Lehrer asked, turning back to Johnny.

"I don't think the riverboat leaves for another couple of hours. So yes, I think so. In fact, let's get some supper." Johnny looked about for a saloon.

"I couldn't eat. They feed you to busting on that boat. But I do want a whiskey. I've been here before. I know just the place." Lehrer led him off the dock and three doors down the riverfront street to a saloon.

Inside, the dim, noisy saloon smelled of river fish cooking, alcohol, tobacco smoke, and unwashed men. Lehrer found a table and signaled to the barkeep. "I'll have a whiskey. My friend wants something to eat."

"Yeah, well, all we got is fried fish and turnips."

"That'll do," Johnny said with resignation. "And a beer."

Lehrer took a sip of his whiskey when the barkeep set it in front of him. Like Johnny, he was clean-shaven except for a modest mustache, his a dark brown while Johnny's was slightly darker than his blond hair. They were dressed much alike, the new short coat and colorful waistcoat, Johnny's green and Lehrer's violet, each topped with a cravat at the throat. Both wore striped trousers and leather boots.

They had hung their narrow-brimmed hats on the hat tree inside the door.

"Taking *Le Beau Soleil* downriver?" He pronounced the boat's name "Lee Boo Soley." However, to Johnny's relief, he spoke English.

"Down to New Orleans for the Department," Johnny supplied. "Pretty swank boat, eh? I'm surprised they booked me on it. It has to cost a pretty penny."

"You are not kidding. You'd think you were in some kind of palace. Wait until you see the grand cabin. Like Versay or something."

Johnny's fried fish and boiled turnips came, and he hesitated only a moment before he tucked in. "Versay?" he asked.

"You know. That great big palace in France. Where the king who got his head chopped off lived."

"Oh, Versailles," Johnny corrected.

"Yah, that one. Anyway, it's all rich woods and gilding and paintings on the walls. You are traveling second class, aren't you?" Lehrer signaled for a refill of his whiskey.

"Yes, even more surprising. I bet even the poor folks can't be too poor to travel on that thing." Johnny found he enjoyed his supper more than he had expected.

"No doubt. No nigger slaves or Indians being shipped West. That's probably why. But you got to see this statue in a fountain in the dining cabin. Greek or Roman or something and hardly a stitch on. Too bad it's a man."

Oh hell, Johnny thought but said aloud, "Not very decent."

Lehrer chuckled. "No, it ain't. The fellow who owns the boat is some bigwig gambler. A frog and a real *fairy*, if you ask me. Probably gets his jollies looking at that statue. It has some cloth around its balls. He is probably the only one who gets to take a peek under it." He stopped talking abruptly, then went on in a more serious voice. "Not that I'd want to, you understand." He shrugged, then winked at Johnny. "If I want to see a prick, a bigger one than that statue's got, I just look down when I take a piss, right?"

Johnny cleared his throat. "So what are the staterooms like? And you said they really feed you?"

"Comfortable. Like a whore's bedroom, really. I felt like the Prince of Wales, with all that velvet and carpets and paintings on the wall. That is, if the Prince of Wales had to share his stateroom with some other fellow. And yeah, they feed you four times a day, breakfast, supper, dinner, and if you want it, food with your drinks in the saloon. I never want to eat again."

Johnny picked up the last piece of fish, popped it in his mouth, then took out his pristine handkerchief to wipe his greasy fingers.

"They had a singer and this colored piano player too. And of course, there's the star attraction…."

Johnny showed interest. "Oh yeah? What was that?"

"Why, the Nancy!" Lehrer said as though it was common knowledge, which Johnny supposed it could be. "He's a famous poker player. They say he is honest as old Honest Abe, that Springfield politician. Never cheats. I don't believe it, of course."

Johnny snorted derisively. "As though there was such a thing as an honest gambler. He owns the boat? That just confirms it. You don't get that rich by playing straight."

"You said it, Steinfeld." He finished his glass of whiskey and went on. "Hey, we had some excitement on the way north. Somewhere shy of Baton Rouge, we stopped where there was a wreck."

Johnny picked up his mug of beer. "A wreck? What happened? Is that why the boat was late getting in?"

"I suppose so. It was a smaller boat, just a couple decks and a pilothouse, forget the name. It ran into some debris in the river. It wasn't really a wreck. Just stuck. This Deramus fellow, Miss Nancy I mean, pulled it off the sandbar or whatever and waited until they made sure there was no damage, then the little boat went on its way south."

"Well, that's good, I guess," Johnny replied.

TWILIGHT descended before *Le Beau Soleil* left Cairo for points south on the river. Johnny found he shared a stateroom every bit as elegant as Lehrer had described. Johnny relaxed when he met his roommate, a mousy little man with spectacles, a parson or some such.

He made his way to supper in the grand cabin, which he found fitted out like a Paris restaurant. It had a design of fleur-de-lis and sunbursts on the wallpaper, framed paintings of what he assumed to be scenes of New Orleans, and furniture upholstered in the same forest-green velvet as the curtains on the windows. Elaborately carved and gilded doorframes seemed a touch too much even in all this luxury.

Johnny looked up and up at the tall ceiling, at least three decks high, he guessed, and saw the fading light shining through the stained-glass skylight. As a steward led him to his table, he caught sight of the statue in the fountain. The Apollo Belvedere, if he was not mistaken. His cheeks flushed pink at the magnificent physique of the god. The statue's arm extended gracefully. His genitals were, indeed, masked with a white cloth of some kind. Johnny felt drawn to the solemn face, with its marble lips that seemed somehow soft and warm.

At the sound of a cleared throat, he realized the steward had pulled out a chair for him at a table. He thanked the man and sat.

Johnny sat at a table with well-dressed but obviously second-class passengers, two women, mother and daughter, neither attractive, and three men. Instead of a dinner party seating, which alternated men and women, they sat with people they knew or by themselves. Two of the men were obviously friends or colleagues, judging by their familiarity. The third was a middle-aged man whose bald head reflected the light from the elegant chandeliers.

"So, Mr. Hamilton, you going to get in on a game this evening?" one of the younger men, a pudgy fellow in a too-tight suit, asked.

"I might, Mr. Knowles. At least I will have a look. They say Deramus is a cold-blooded fellow, which I guess you have to be to be a cardplayer."

Mr. Knowles's companion, Mr. Casey, who turned out to be a fellow surveyor, joined the conversation. The three talked about what they had heard of Frankie Deramus and how he did not always win, but when he did win—often enough—he always won big.

The older woman pressed her lips tightly together. "Gamblers are the worst sort of people!" she declared. Her daughter, a fork of salad greens on its way to her mouth, stared at her.

"Worse than a murderer, Mrs. Montane?" the bald man said, his lips twisted in a sardonic smile.

"Cheaters, bounders, river slime. Debauchers of innocent women. Catholics," she concluded, adding emphasis to the last word.

Johnny turned to Mr. Knowles, who sat next to him. "Can you point out this Deramus fellow?"

"Sure thing. He's over there, the fellow who needs a haircut, the one with the thin mustache and the big gem in his cravat." He pointed to a table not in front of, but near the scandalous statue. "See him? He's looking over here right now, in fact."

Johnny followed the man's pointing finger straight into coal-black eyes. *That must be Deramus.* The only one at the table of high-class folks who fit Knowles's description, he stared straight at Johnny.

"Must have a sixth sense for attention," Mr. Casey put in. "Knew we were talking about him."

Mr. Hamilton chuckled. "That type always thinks he's the center of attention."

Johnny could not tear his eyes away from that steady gaze. He had no doubt Deramus looked directly at him. Why? Did he have some sort of sign on his forehead? Was the man really what Lehrer had said, a Miss Nancy, and could he see if another man liked other men? Johnny frowned and tried to look away. When he finally started to turn his face, he saw the man smile amusedly and lift his glass of wine in a salute. Johnny felt his face go red.

He wanted to go watch Deramus play cards that night, but he didn't. Instead, he sat in his stateroom and read a newspaper while his mousy roommate studied a Bible.

That night, he dreamed of marble arms coming around him, turning him, and marble lips that were indeed soft and warm on his own. It felt like the statue had grown a thin mustache.

CHAPTER 2

Le Beau Soleil, that same day in late May 1859

FRANÇOIS "FRANKIE" DERAMUS never felt averse to gazing upon a magnificent male figure, but the Apollo fountain had proved to have an unforeseen benefit for his love life. He noticed among the range of reactions the statue received—artistic appreciation, moral repugnance, lewd amusement—there was one more. Occasionally a man would glance over at the statue and quickly avert his eyes. That was not the end of it. The same man would then look again, covertly, and he always looked the same two places: the statue's muscular loins and those marble lips. Frankie wasted no time testing his theory about the amorous inclinations of the men, and so far he had been correct every time.

Frankie noticed the tall blond man with the mustache who came into the grand cabin for supper that night of the departure south from Cairo. The steward led him to a table, but on the way, amid gawking at the high ceiling and the room's admittedly extravagant fittings, the man looked over at the statue. Frankie stood talking to one of his wealthier passengers near the edge of the fountain, and he looked up as the fellow did the typical glance, avert, and sneak-a-look Frankie had come to know and savor. *This one will merit my attention,* he thought, smoothing his mustache with a finger.

Frankie called his purser over to ascertain the blushing man's identity. He had a name now: John Stanley. He could not watch Stanley throughout the meal, having other guests who demanded his attention, guests he could not afford to annoy, but he happened to be looking when he saw the young fellow sitting next to Stanley point in Frankie's direction. "*Merci, mon fils,*" he said under his breath. He had his eyes affixed to Stanley's when that attractive fellow looked up, and Frankie saw pale blue eyes that widened but did not look away. He sensed the surprise, the tension, as if the man were a rabbit frozen by a snake's stare. That was, after all, metaphorically the truth. When the fellow finally tore his gaze away—his face red—Frankie chuckled and toasted him with his glass of wine.

Frankie, an avowed playboy, did not believe in true love. *There were lots of good fish in the sea, so why should I limit myself to just one man?* He sometimes spent time with someone in particular, but with the exception of Michael Murphy, his confidential agent and friend, he had no longstanding arrangement. He had known Michael for years, and whenever they were both in town, they had sex together. Their arrangement was comfortable and reliable, but not stifling.

FRANKIE smiled at the memory of his last visit with Michael, the scene vivid in his mind. He remembered precariously balancing a steaming cup of coffee on one upturned palm as he reached for the door handle with his other hand. The aroma of chicory tickled his nostrils as he executed the two moves without mishap and passed into the darkened room. After making his way to the table on Michael's side of the bed, he set the cup and saucer down. Familiar as he was with this particular bedroom, he had no trouble navigating in the poor light. He could hear Michael's slow, deep breathing from the pillow.

Frankie pulled back the thick drapes. A rosy glow could just be seen in the east, and the weather was cool and dry. It would be a fine day to set out on the river for another trip up to Cairo.

Frankie sat on the edge of the bed, where his hip pressed against Michael's side. He leaned forward and put his lips on Michael's, and he felt and heard Michael awaken at his touch. Michael raised long bare arms from under the covers, wrapped them around Frankie's neck, and pulled him in closer to keep his lips firmly in place. As if the intoxicating smells of bed, sleep, and sex didn't attract him enough, Michael's body gave off the heat Frankie knew so well. Even the crackle of the bed linens as Michael moved tortured Frankie. He felt warmth in his groin as memories of the night before came easily to his mind.

He reached up reluctantly and clasped Michael's arms and gently but resolutely pulled them away.

"No, stay," Michael moaned as Frankie sat up, breaking the kiss.

"Ah, Mick, I can't. We leave for upriver this morning," Frankie said softly.

Michael opened slightly tilted blue eyes made darker and mellower with sleep. "I suppose you must," he pouted.

"I brought you coffee. Sit up so you don't spill it all over yourself."

"But if I do, you can lick it off," Michael said, grinning. He pulled himself up, exposing the broad chest where Frankie had laid his head, contented after their night of energetic lovemaking. "Mmm, that does smell good."

Michael breathed in the aroma of the brew and took a sip. "Perfect." He sighed. "You always know exactly how much cream and sugar to put in."

"I ought to. We've been waking up in each other's beds more often than not these… what is it now? Five years?"

Michael shrugged.

Frankie looked about the room and shook his head. "Look at this place," he said wryly. He pointed to a trail of discarded clothing that began with cravats at the door and ended with drawers by the bed. "I'm surprised I made it from the door to the bed without tripping and spilling your coffee."

Michael chuckled. "But I see you are, as always, impeccably dressed. If those are your trousers over there then how… never mind, I can guess. Charles William?"

"*Oui*, he dropped off my clothes with your concierge, Mme. Lyon, on his way to *Le Beau Soleil*."

Wincing, Michael complained, "You don't think that compromises us just a little? Making it so obvious that you spent the night?"

It was a familiar topic. "Why would Mme. Lyon care? Your sodomitical money gleams like anyone else's."

Michael winced again. "What a cynic you are."

Frankie stood and started to pick up the clothing strewn about. He separated each item by its owner. "Not cynical at all. I know my city. No one in my set worries about such things, not in such a licentious place."

"I hope you are right."

After draping the two sets of clothes over the foot of the big bed, Frankie stood with his arms over his chest and gazed at Michael. "Your association with me damns you from the start. And it hasn't cut into your business, has it?" He glanced about the small but well-furnished room.

Michael set the coffee down on the bed table, and lifting the bedclothes, he swung long legs over the edge so he could sit up. Besides his morning erection, Frankie could not help but notice the long scar on Michael's thigh, made by a bayonet when he'd served in the 1846-48 war with Mexico. How many times had Frankie traced his fingertips along its puckered length, how many times kissed and licked it to make Michael thrill?

"It's less that no one cares you and I fuck each other than that your scores of ne'er-do-well associates need my investigational and bodyguard services." Michael stood and stretched, scratching his well-formed butt cheeks and yawning. "It's not that I'm not grateful. Far from it. I just worry someday you will be too glib with the wrong person." He made his way to a chamber pot discreetly set behind a brocade screen.

"Don't worry, *mon brave*. I know when to be cautious. I just don't see how your concierge could mistake my visits or your nights away at my hotel." He changed the subject. "Speaking of ne'er-do-wells, are you still seeing that Spanish fellow I sent to you?"

Michael's face appeared around the side of the screen shortly before the rest of him. He arched his eyebrows at Frankie. "You mean Carlos? Yes, on occasion. Jealous?"

Frankie barked a laugh. "No, of course not. You and I have no… understanding."

Michael gazed at him. "You don't regret that, do you?"

Frankie strolled about the room idly. "No, I don't. You and I have one… well, two things in common. We don't believe in love."

Michael, still naked, came over to Frankie and took him in his arms. "All that's bright must fade. The brightest still the fleetest. All that's sweet was made but to be lost when sweetest."

Frankie stroked Michael's stubbly jaw. "The Gaelic soul in you, always so dependable." He took Michael's hand and placed a kiss on the palm. "Whose?"

"Thomas Moore. An Irishman."

"*Eh bien*, of course he is… or was?"

Michael shrugged. "Was, I'm afraid." Searching Frankie's dark eyes, he asked, "Will I see you when you return?"

"Probably. Unless I pick up someone especially delicious on the trip south."

"What a wicked man you are," Michael jested. He tightened his arms around Frankie and gazed wistfully into Frankie's eyes. "Ah, Frankie, someday some man will sneak into your heart when you aren't looking, and you will be knocked on your ass in love."

"Men like us don't fall in love."

Michael gave Frankie a pitying look. "That's not true, and you know it."

Frankie put his lips to Michael's and persuaded them to part with a questing tongue. *Damn him for being such a beautiful man.* He felt not only his own cock stirring but Michael's pressing hard against his thigh as well. "No," he said into the kiss. "Michael, I can't," he explained when Michael pulled away with a pout. "I really have to go. You aren't making it easy on me."

"I don't want to make it easy on you." He ground his groin into Frankie's.

"Stop that! And you call me wicked?" Frankie stepped back, laughing. "No, my dear man, I shall never fall in love. The world is my oyster. And I do so love oysters." He straightened his cravat and jacket and turned toward the door.

Michael watched him wearily. "Well, since you're on your way out, I will get ready for my own day."

Frankie laughed. "Discarded, am I?" He smiled warmly at his friend. "Mick, you will be careful, won't you?"

Michael paused in the act of selecting clean linens from a chest of drawers. "With my heart or my hide?"

Frankie sighed. "I have no right to your heart, so just make it your hide."

Michael looked back solemnly. He nodded and said, "I will, I promise." An impish grin crossed his face. "Don't take any counterfeit money, you hear?"

Frankie took inventory in the mirror on the wall next to the door. Repositioning the silver-and-amber sunburst stickpin that held his cravat in place, he approved of what he saw. Black lustrous hair hung down just past his collar, and black eyes with distinct dark eyelashes sparkled back at themselves. His likewise black pencil-thin mustache over well-defined lips gave him a devil-may-care air. His strong pointed chin was clean-shaven. With a last stroke of his long fingers through his hair he replied, "Oh, I will not take any counterfeit money, I assure you."

FRANKIE registered an embarrassment of riches on this trip, for Stanley was not the only man he had caught ogling the Apollo. Another passenger, as dark of hair and eye as himself and whose name turned out to be Henry Armitage, had let his eyes dance about the most alluring bits of the marble. It only remained for Frankie to choose which of the two fish to reel in first.

He scanned the crowd of people who squeezed into the Texas deck saloon to watch him play poker. Armitage had come in some time during the evening. Frankie did his best to catch the man's eye.

The evening's gaming was profitable but not remarkable. The other players were not the professionals he was. Most importantly, they were free with their bets—being three very wealthy men: a banker, a distillery owner, and a private railroad company executive. He got the impression that for them the bets were simply the price for the evening's entertainment. He overlooked the inevitable signs they were trying to catch him cheating. People did not seem to grasp that his entire stock-in-trade was his skill with the game. Being scrupulously honest was a requirement, or no one would think they could best him.

The notorious riverboat gambler George H. Devol could never, as Frankie did, remain in one place for long. Devol's crooked faro and poker games meant he jumped, almost literally, from boat to gambling house to bordello to backwater cabin with rapidity. The man was banned from *Le Beau Soleil* for having been caught cheating some years before, caught by Frankie himself in a private game. No, Devol needed a new set of marks every time. Frankie's honesty meant he could stay where he could be found again.

When the time came for a break, Frankie ordered a round of drinks for everyone squeezed into the saloon, and he personally delivered Armitage's whiskey. As he handed the glass over, he left his fingers on it long enough that the man could not help but touch them with his own. Frankie saw him start at the contact.

Clearing his throat quietly, Armitage commented, "You are an excellent player, *monsieur*."

Frankie smiled, looking directly into his eyes. "*Merci*. It is why people want to play with me. Everyone wants to be the man who beats Frankie Deramus."

"You do lose sometimes," observed Armitage. Frankie had lost several hands this evening.

"*Oui*, but not often and not for long. And I know when to bet high and when not. I may meet a better man someday, but so far I have not." He sipped his wine, looking over the brim of his glass at Armitage, giving the man the full advantage of his own long black lashes. To his satisfaction, he observed Armitage's hesitation, his lips parted, his eyes on Frankie's. "Mr. Armitage, may I call you Henry? And what do you do, Henry?"

Henry smiled and replied, "Why, Frankie, I am a photographer."

Genuinely delighted, Frankie put a hand on Henry's arm and exclaimed, "*Vraiment*? How fascinating. You must tell me all about it."

To Frankie's further pleasure, Henry put his hand on Frankie's where it lay on his sleeve. "I should like to."

Frankie looked at their touching hands. "And are you traveling with your, ah, equipment?"

"Would you like to see it?"

Frankie's smile widened. "Indeed I would. In your stateroom?"

Henry shrugged. "I will need more room than that if you want me to set it up."

"My rooms, then," Frankie responded. "Tell you what. Go to my stateroom. It is on the hurricane deck, the door with the sunburst. Tell my manservant, Charles William, to help you get your photography equipment so you can set it up in my sitting room. I will join you shortly. I have to play a couple of hands with the senator over there." He squeezed Henry's arm, turned, and walked back to the card table.

WHEN Frankie got to his stateroom, he found Charles William alone, looking over some strange items stacked on his dining table.

Henry popped his head around the bedchamber doorway. "Oh good, Frankie, I took the liberty of setting the camera up in here. If I am going to develop any pictures, I think you'd rather not have the smell of the chemicals in your bedroom."

Frankie smiled delightedly. "Very thoughtful of you, my friend. Very thoughtful. Shall I send Charles William for refreshments?"

Charles William, a tall gray-haired man of color, gestured to a small table set up in front of the divan. In a cultured voice, he answered, "I have already brought wine, *monsieur*. Will you want anything else?"

Charles William's face was impassive. He and his wife Dominique had as much as raised Frankie at the Deramus's Lake Pontchartrain mansion. Though Frankie in fact owned the couple, he always treated them as servants rather than slaves.

"You are, as always, one step ahead of my wishes, Charles William." Frankie looked over at Henry with one eyebrow raised, but the man was busily positioning a large wooden box on a small table he had pulled away from the wall. Returning his attention to Charles William, Frankie shook his head. "I think we have all we need. Why don't you go on to your bed? I shan't need your help anymore this evening."

After Charles William bowed and left, Frankie loosened his cravat, then filled two goblets from the decanter on the small table in front of the divan. After taking one in each hand, he moved into the bedchamber where Henry beamed proudly beside the wooden box. Frankie handed the photographer a goblet and lifted his own in a toast. "To modern technology."

Though riveted to Frankie's, Henry's eyes remained guarded. "I hope I did not presume too much…," he began in a tight voice.

For answer, Frankie took the goblet from Henry and set it with his own on the marble-topped washstand. He turned back, took Henry's face in his hands, and leaned forward to bring their lips together softly. As Henry relaxed into the caress, Frankie kept the insistent pressure of the kiss steady for a moment longer, then pulled back. "You don't mind if we look at the camera… after," he murmured. "Do you?"

Henry made an inarticulate noise of assent.

Frankie reached for Henry's jacket shoulders, hooked his fingers inside the collar, and lifted it off and back. It slid with a swish down Henry's arms. He placed it on the back of a handy chair, turned back, and began on the buttons of Henry's waistcoat. Henry's eyes were half closed as he reached to Frankie's own jacket. "No, you first," Frankie murmured against his lips. While continuing to unbutton the waistcoat, he explored first Henry's lips, then his teeth, and finally Henry's tongue in his whiskey-flavored mouth. Finally, he pushed the liberated waistcoat back and reached down for the fly of Henry's trousers. He felt Henry's cock standing erect and long enough to reach almost to his waistband. Henry moaned at the touch. He gave Henry's prick a firm caress, then reached up to push Henry's suspenders off his shoulders.

Henry put his hands to his own shirt, and while Frankie resumed exploration of his mouth, Henry made fast work of the shirt. Not being as fastidious about the discarded clothing, he dropped it on the floor. His voice catching, he begged, "I want to see you too."

Frankie grinned. "Your servant, *monsieur*." He put his hands to Henry's shoulders and pushed gently. Henry let himself be guided back until the edge of the bed hit his legs, and he bent backward. Lying on the counterpane with his lower legs hanging down, he watched Frankie remove one garment after another. His eyes were alternately languorous and round, especially when Frankie's silken drawers hit the floor and he stepped out of them.

Henry's wide eyes made very clear what he thought of Frankie's endowment.

Frankie stepped forward and knelt between his legs. "Let's see yours." He put one hand to the waistband of Henry's drawers, encouraging him to lift up so he could pull the drawers toward him. Being only a momentary obstacle to the removal of the garment, Henry's own considerable endowment was soon bouncing erratically against his belly. "*Merveilleux*," Frankie praised. He reached for the organ and wrapped one hand about it. He pulled it toward his face, kissed the shaft, and ran his tongue from base to tip. Henry jerked and cried out. At the same time, his cock and balls spasmed.

Frankie rose and leaned over Henry on the bed. He was taller, so their faces were at the same level. They explored each other's mouths with their tongues, and reached to stroke each other's faces, necks, hair, chests and shoulders. Neither was a hairy-chested man, but they had the firmness of youth. Frankie nipped first one and then the other of Henry's nipples.

He began to rub his groin against Henry's, feeling the intensely erotic pressure of his and Henry's silken cocks running over and past each other. He felt Henry's hands on his head, pushing him down. He obliged, slid back to his kneeling position, and took Henry's cock into his mouth. Tasting the fluid leaking out of the tip, he put his tongue in the small crevice and licked it up. Henry was moaning and writhing. Frankie let as much of Henry's cock as he could slide into his mouth. It was satisfyingly filling. Putting his fingers on a spot just behind Henry's balls he pressed firmly here and there, not stopping the friction of his lips and tongue, nor the light bites with his teeth on Henry's cock. He could tell by Henry's sudden involuntary jerk that he had found the spot that when stimulated drove any man wild with lust. Henry cried out.

Frankie continued to press his fingertips into that sensitive spot and to suck Henry's now iron-hard prick. He could tell from his shuddering body that Henry was close, so he took the hand he had put on his thigh and gently held his balls. He gauged the moment with precision, pulling Henry's cock out of his mouth just as Henry made a long guttural noise in his throat and spent his semen onto Frankie's face and chest. Frankie rubbed the head of Henry's cock all over his chin and mouth, loving the feel and smell of the hot cream on his lips, cheeks, and chin. Henry's whole body was writhing like a snake's.

As the shudders slowed, Frankie reached to his bed table, took out a cotton cloth, and wiped his face and chest. He pulled himself along Henry's boneless torso. "Taste yourself," he commanded. Henry opened his mouth, and Frankie thrust in his tongue, still tasting Henry's semen. They savored it together, making identical sounds of pleasure.

"I want you to fuck me," Henry said breathlessly.

"Have you done that before?" Frankie asked.

"Yes, a few times," Henry replied.

"*D'accord.*" Frankie moved down the bed and settled on his knees between Henry's legs. He hooked his hands under Henry's buttocks and lifted them. His own prick was hard and hot. He reached to a porcelain jar on his bed table, flipped off the loose lid, and put one finger into the perfumed grease. He rubbed the cream onto his cock and then inserted a finger into Henry's puckered hole, making Henry's prick start to harden again. Henry's moans aroused Frankie even more, if that was possible. Frankie positioned himself and thrust in, slowly but firmly, gauging his partner's comfort by watching his face. From the look of it, Henry was in heaven.

Frankie began to rock his hips, pulling out and thrusting back in, feeling the delicious tightness milking his cock exquisitely. Henry thrust up his groin to meet every forward movement of Frankie's own. Frankie reached out and caressed Henry's belly, making circles that alternated soft and hard pressure. He loved the dip just above a man's thatch of pubic hair, and he put the back of his hand against it, enjoying the tingling feeling he got from the spot.

Frankie knew his cock must be reaching that magic spot inside Henry that corresponded with the one outside that he had stroked before, because Henry moaned louder and louder. He felt Henry's spunk hit his belly as he spent, and the sheer lustiness of the sensation sent Frankie, the more practiced lover, over the edge. Feeling the pressure in his balls and at the root of his cock burst into Henry's hot, moist fundament, he made a wordless cry of ecstasy.

In the end, Henry left the stateroom with two things: a long deep kiss and a promise of a second night of lovemaking. Frankie received an ambrotype: a glass image of himself, fully nude, stretched out along the disheveled bed, a sated smile relaxing his handsome face. He was looking forward to showing it to Michael.

THE next evening, Frankie was looking forward to another night with Henry when he entered the saloon and noticed John Stanley reading a newspaper in the chair outside the barbershop door. He had forgotten all about him. Though he had his hands full for this trip, he remained curious, so he sauntered over to Stanley and extended his hand to be shaken.

"Mr. Stanley? I don't think we have met yet." Frankie turned his devastating smile on him, wanting a better look at the pale blue eyes than he had from across the room.

Stanley looked up. He put out a reluctant hand and let Frankie shake it. "Yes, I'm John Stanley. And you are the Frenchman who plays cards."

Frankie stared openmouthed for a moment before shaking the limp hand and letting out a short laugh. This was too rich, so he pulled over a chair and sat right next to the unfriendly man. "In point of fact, I am Creole and not French. But you are right. I do… play cards.…" He grinned at Stanley, looking amused. "Won't you join me in a game?" He leaned forward, watching as Stanley tried to pull away, but there was no place to retreat since his chair was against the wall. In an intimate and confiding voice, Frankie murmured, "I promise to be gentle."

Stanley's face turned a deep red. "I will not, sir," he shot back firmly. "I am not one of your foppish fools willing to make themselves your victims.… I do not gamble. I especially do not gamble with cardsharps."

Giving him no time to react, Frankie clutched the lapels of his evening jacket and almost lifted him out of his seat. He was no longer amused, and leaning forward, he stated fiercely, "*I. Do. Not. Cheat.*"

Stanley looked startled but then moved quickly. He reached up and took Frankie's wrists in his two hands and clamped down forcefully. Surprised, Frankie loosened his grip and drew his hands off his jacket and away from him, and Stanley let him go.

As he stood rubbing his wrists, Frankie gaped at him. "You are very strong, *monsieur*. Are you some sort of professional athlete?"

Stanley straightened his jacket and growled, "No. I work for the government. And I have no time to waste dealing with fancy fellows like you. You would do me a service by keeping your nancy hands off me."

Anger quickly replaced Frankie's surprise. "This *nancy*, as you put it, owns the riverboat on which you are privileged to be a passenger. If you prefer to switch to another, one most likely owned by a real man, you are welcome to see the purser for part of your passage refunded."

He rose to his feet and leveled a steely glare on Frankie. "Are you throwing me off, *monsieur*?" The last word dripped with sarcasm.

Frankie pulled himself to his full height, realizing as he did that Stanley was still at least two inches taller. "No, sir, I am not. You may do as you please. I shall not touch you again. Be certain about that." He shook his shoulders out, turned on his heel, and stalked away.

Frankie turned back after a half dozen steps to find Stanley seated and lifting his newspaper again. The infuriating man's face showed no sign of disturbance. Frankie was sure his own face was alive with a mix of emotions—fury, confusion, hurt, and damaged pride. Even arousal. He realized this and quickly made his face return to its accustomed mild amusement.

Muttering a French epithet about Stanley's priggishness, "*Sainte-Nitouche!*" he went in search of Henry Armitage. He needed a good hard fuck to take his mind off this idiot.

CHAPTER 3

Le Beau Soleil, that same day in late May 1859

THE moment Frankie walked away, Johnny had second thoughts about how he had reacted to the fellow. He was not by habit rude, though he knew he could be blunt. It had been that insinuating "I promise I'll be gentle" that had provoked him.

Johnny occupied himself with trying to get back to reading the paper in order to get his mind off the stirrings he felt. He took a deep breath, willing his heart to stop racing and ordering indifference back into his loins. He was well practiced. This time it took longer than usual.

Finally giving up, he set the paper aside and decided to walk on the promenade. While warm during the day, on the river at night, even in late May, a chill set in. Perhaps a walk in the chill air would help him forget his arousal.

He went out to the Texas deck promenade and down the stairs to the hurricane deck. *No, not here.* He knew Deramus's stateroom was on this deck, and he most certainly did not want to cross his path. So he headed down the next set of steps and, on impulse, made his way to aft steps he knew would take him to the main deck. If any part of the boat could make him forget the debonair Frenchman—no, Creole, he had said—the main deck would.

The steps did not take him to the part of the deck he had expected—that is, the passenger area. Instead, he found himself behind the galley. Its door was open and light poured forth. The amber light invited him, but the talk and singing drew him in. The heat almost drove him back out. The small cabin was mostly full of massive iron stoves radiating heat and seemed to be the source of a yeasty aroma of baking bread. Wooden tables lined the far wall, and colored men and women—at least eight, maybe nine—crowded the passage between the ovens and the tables. Every last person was busy, moving back and forth in their tasks. They all sang, harmonizing in an upbeat tune— marking time, it seemed, for a sort of dance step that wove in and around each other as they worked.

One of the women, short and very fat, caught sight of him and smiled and winked. Her face was shiny with sweat. She danced over to him and shouted in his ear, "Now you be careful, mister. You don't want to be bumpin' into one of them hot stoves and gettin' yourself burned none."

Johnny nodded and stepped back a pace. He noticed the woman herself had a sizable burn scar on her forearm. She saw him looking and pointed to it. "I had that since I was a girl, sir. Been workin' on these here steamboats since I was that high." She put her palm flat to indicate a height rather shorter than her already diminutive stature.

Johnny glanced about for a door so he could pass through to the foredeck. He saw one on the starboard side and realized the galley was not as wide as the boat. He leaned and shouted to the woman, "How do I get to the other end of this deck?" With a questioning look, he pointed to the door.

The woman followed his pointing finger. "Oh no, mister, that's where we keeps the supplies." She looked about, then shouted, "Here, Lucas, you come show the gentleman how to get forward."

A young man put down the knife he was using to cut bacon and wiped his hands on his filthy apron. "Yes, Auntie," he said, bobbing his head.

He looked at Johnny and narrowed his eyes, examining his clothing. "Excuse me, sir, but you sure you aimin' to go up there to the deckers?"

Johnny gestured out the door. The young man made several quick bobs and followed him out to the bottom of the steps.

After the heat of the galley, the cold air outside was a blessing. Johnny turned to the young man and saw the doubtful look on his rather handsome face. "I want to go forward," he told him. "How do I get there?"

"Beggin' your pardon, but why you want to do that, mister? You from upstairs?"

The question surprised Johnny. He realized he was still in what passed for his dinner clothes. "I just want to get some air."

The young man glanced up at his face and then lowered his eyes submissively. "They be air up on the other decks, mister. Sweeter than with those deckers, if you don't mind me sayin'." He scuffed his feet on the deck boards. "If 'n' you wants a gal, you talks to the purser fella, and he gets you one. Send her to your stateroom, mister."

"Oh no, that's not it. I just want to see the rest of the deck, close up like, you understand."

The glance from Lucas told Johnny he most certainly did not understand. Nevertheless, shrugging, the fellow turned to starboard and walked the short distance to the rail. Johnny followed him and saw there was a narrow walkway that led forward.

"Thank you. Thank you very much." He looked back at Lucas, who would not meet his eye. "This a good boat to work on?" he asked impulsively.

A quick speculative glance from the colored man was replaced with a slight smile. "Oh, yassir. Mr. Frankie real good to us. He takes good care of us, lots more than any other boat do."

"Takes care of you? You mean he pays you? You are not a slave?" Johnny blushed, wondering if he was being too inquisitive, but Lucas's smile just broadened.

"We slaves, but Mr. Frankie got no truck with treatin' slaves bad. On account of that man of his, Charles William. They been friends for years and years, sir. Him and his wife."

Johnny stared. "Mr. Fr... Mr. Deramus is married?" he asked, puzzled.

"Oh no, sir, not Mr. Frankie. Mr. Albright. Mr. Frankie is a bachelor fella. Always been, sir."

Johnny reached into his pocket and pulled out a copper. He handed it to the man, who stepped back. "Oh no, sir, I couldn't," he protested. But when Johnny kept the coin out, he relented. "I thanks you, mister. You can go along there now, just mind your step. You don't want to fall in the river."

Johnny went along the narrow walk, carefully stepping over obstructions on the deck. It took him a little time to come to the point where he had to pass between the wall of the boat and the side-wheel. There was enough of a moon that he could see the sparkle on the water as it splashed up, forward, and down. The wheel was terribly loud, though not as loud as the boilers up on the deck where his stateroom was. Outside his stateroom, that is, for the room was remarkably well-insulated where it shared a wall with the grand cabin. He stayed for a while to watch the wheel turn and then continued his progress forward.

The bales and barrels that lined the rail must have insulated the walkway from the sounds the deckers made, which surprised Johnny when he reached the end of the wall and found himself in the open part of the deck. Someone was playing a fiddle, another a banjo, and yet another seemed to be blowing across the mouth of a large empty jug. He could hear the musicians, but he could not see them through the dancers.

The lower-class passengers gathered in the large foredeck space of the main deck. The colored roustabouts and deckhands standing about the perimeter between stacks of cargo did not join in but watched the white people who either danced or stood and sat around the edges of the activity. Some of those who were not dancing clapped their hands in time with the tune, others smoked pipes made of corncobs, and some, mostly women, either held small children in their laps or kept an eye on older children who clearly wanted to join in the frivolity.

Johnny was glad of the river breeze, having almost immediately detected the odors not only of the livestock penned on one side but also of unwashed human bodies. No wonder the man from the galley had looked at him with puzzlement. He and his clothing were a world away from the rabble that frolicked on this deck. Nevertheless, the noisome throng was having a grand time, away from the more sedate or businesslike upper-deck passengers.

Johnny refused when a young woman with a gap-toothed grin tried to pull him into the dance. She twirled away. He found a place to wedge himself between cotton bales, where he was in shadow so no one would bother him.

He heard a giggle behind him and was surprised he heard it but assumed the cotton bales, which overtopped his height on either side, had funneled the sound. He glanced over his shoulder, and in the faint light from the lanterns on the deck, he saw a man and woman wrapped around each other. They seemed oblivious to him, or to anything else but themselves, for that matter. The girl had her back to the bales, and the young man pressed hard against her. They were kissing passionately. Johnny smiled slightly, but then he noticed the woman's skirts were hiked way up, and her bare thighs were wrapped around the young man's hips. Then Johnny noticed the motion of the man's body, jerking up and down. The girl's giggles changed to sighs. Johnny felt his own unwilling sexual response and shot out from between the bales, almost colliding with dancers who tried to grab him and drag him into the dance.

Johnny frantically pulled himself free and made his way through the throng to the bottom of the grand staircase that led up to the boiler deck. He dashed up the steps. On the balcony at top, he paused to catch his breath.

"Mixing with the riffraff?" came a voice from his right. He looked over to see the lighted end of a cigar.

"Wh-who?" Johnny asked.

A low chuckle came from the smoking figure. "Nobody. Just some nancy."

Johnny watched as Frankie stubbed out the cigar on an iron railing. "Frankie! I mean, Mr. Deramus!" He took a deep breath. "I'm sorry. I was rude earlier. Please accept my apology."

The shadowy figure stood still for a moment, then stepped into the light of the lantern and made a short sharp bow. "Your servant, *monsieur*," he said, spun on his heels, and passed down the starboard promenade.

Johnny stared after him.

IN HIS bunk that night, Johnny lay unable to sleep. His thoughts and feelings would not settle down. He was unsure why the amorous tableau behind him on the main deck had rattled him so. Sex was just part of life.

But Johnny was a virgin. He knew all the other boys with whom he grew up had girls or found willing partners one way or another, but he was always too busy with working at this job. That was what he had told himself; he had places to go and no time for involvements. Oh, he had urges. He was plagued with lust so strong he might have tried to force the matter and find a willing woman, but he feared he would make a fool of himself and the girl would laugh at him and worse, would tell others. So he had never even tried.

He thought about Klara, to whom he was not actually engaged, but who seemed nevertheless slated to be his wife whether he wanted it or not. The trouble with Klara was not just herself. The trouble with Klara was Kurt, her brother. When Johnny's papa had taken him to the Holztmanns' house, there was Kurt. Kurt who was a couple of years older than Johnny. Kurt who had deep brown eyes a fellow could easily get lost in. Kurt who looked at him oddly. Kurt who began to fill his dreams. They were dreams of groping and struggling and rubbing, and he always awoke from them to find his semen on his thighs and the sheets.

Then one May evening at *Fronleichnam*, a German celebration of Corpus Christi, Johnny had too much to drink. The beer had filled his head and also his bladder, and as he looked for a place to relieve himself, he entered the narrow passage between the Holtzmanns' house and the neighbor's. Remembering the incident, Johnny realized it had been much like the couple on the main deck. Two people grappled in the dark. One slid down to kneel on the wooden walk. The other moaned and put his head back against the wall. Johnny, who was in the act of pulling his cock out to piss, recognized the silhouetted profile. Kurt. Surprised, Johnny just stood with his prick in his hand.

Obviously Kurt was letting some girl suck his cock. Johnny's own prick hardened quickly. He couldn't stop himself from stroking.

Kurt's own arousal reached the climax when he looked over and saw Johnny. The two locked eyes, and as Kurt writhed with his spending, Johnny felt his own spunk shoot out of him and onto his hand, the bliss of his own climax making him want to cry out, "Kurt!" Still in the throes of the orgasm and unable to form any thought, he watched as the other person slid back up and put his lips to Kurt's neck. *His*. Rolf, Kurt's best friend. Kurt had just let another boy suck him off.

Johnny cried, "Oh!" Then buttoning up his pants, turned, and dashed out into the street. He had to get away from the festivities. He knew tears streamed down his face. He had to get where no one would see him, would see how rattled he was.

It took him several days to think over what he had seen. He knew about men together. There was Father Martin, after all, and the jokes the other boys made, and then of course his own wet dreams. The Church had taught him it was wrong, a sin. "If a man also lie with mankind, as he lieth with a woman, both of them have committed an abomination: they shall surely be put to death; their blood shall be upon them." *Abomination.* But he wanted it so much. So much that at times he could think of nothing else.

He satisfied his lust with his own hand whenever he could be assured of privacy. Behind his closed eyelids, all he saw was Kurt's face as he spent. After avoiding him for several days, Johnny resolved to go to Kurt and tell him he wanted him. As he turned into the Holtzmanns' alleyway, he felt a hand grab his shoulder; he was swung about and slammed against the wall, hard. He tried to get his fists up to defend himself but then saw it was Kurt. *Mein Gott,* he thought, *is it about to happen?* He felt his cock start to stiffen. He gazed back into those dark eyes and waited for the kiss.

"If you tell anyone, any soul, what you saw, I will kill you. I swear it." Kurt hissed the words through clenched teeth. "You hear me, you little *Scheissgesicht?*"

"But, Kurt! I… I—" Johnny's shocked appeal cut off as Kurt's knee connected with his balls. The explosion of pain in his groin took his breath away. His knees buckled, and he slumped to the wooden walkway. He felt a sharp pain in his kidney and knew Kurt had kicked him. He crumpled into a ball and lay, noiseless, suffering, heartbroken.

Johnny resolved then not to let that perverted side of himself emerge again. There was nothing in it of desire or lust, only degradation and pain.

Now in *Le Beau Soleil*, he couldn't overlook that he, like any other man, had lusts he could not control. That Apollo, Frankie when he stared across the dining salon into Johnny's eyes, then later when he leaned in so close and said he would be "gentle." The couple fucking on the main deck. Frankie's dark eyes, so full of hurt and challenge in the dark. His own cock now rigid in his hand. Dark eyes close in his imagination, hot breath on his face, hard lips on his own. He hoped his stateroom mate slept soundly. In his mind he repeated, *Frankie, Frankie*, as he spent.

THE day they were due to reach New Orleans, Johnny stayed in his stateroom as much as he could. He took a seat at his usual table so his back was to the Apollo and to Deramus. Mrs. Montane was not happy to have to change her seat, but Johnny insisted the light hurt his eyes and he had to change with her. His resolution prevented her from pursuing the topic. Johnny saw Mr. Hamilton smile at him, then to Miranda—the woman's daughter—and back, and wink.

At the levee in New Orleans, Johnny stopped long enough to look at his remaining tickets. He checked to see what boat he was booked on for the trip back north. He groaned. *Le Beau Soleil.* Well, he probably could have it changed. Maybe he would do that. If he remembered before it was time to leave.

He glanced back at the riverboat as he walked to where carriages for hire waited. He saw Deramus on the balcony at the top of the grand staircase. Their eyes met, and Frankie nodded to him cordially, but he did not smile.

CHAPTER 4

New Orleans, June 1859

THE early morning was fair and bright, the air at the levee festive. Johnny, his business in the Crescent City successfully concluded, found himself smiling as he walked, valise in hand, along the levee to where the riverboat's gilded sunburst shone on the waiting passengers like a benevolent totem. He'd failed to find passage on another boat but decided to make the best of the situation.

It must be the weather, he thought. It's difficult not to be cheerful on a morning like this.

Johnny joined the small crowd on the levee, glancing about at the others incuriously. Some appeared to be saying "bon voyage" before separating. He guessed this was the case with one couple standing together just on the other side of the gangway. The man had a valise, but the woman seemed to be without baggage, and the colored man in livery with her was not carrying anything. Johnny concluded the man was on business and was taking leave of his lady fair.

She was indeed fair, one of those New Orleans beauties with just enough Creole to give her face that rosiness of cheek and fullness of lips. Richly dressed—hoopskirt spread about her hips and legs lavishly—and decked out with just enough jewelry to be identifiable as a rich man's wife, she stood with her parasol.

Johnny glanced at her husband, a well-dressed but not ostentatious man with an elegant gold pocket watch. Even the colored man's livery was of the highest quality. The woman stood with her arm tucked into her husband's, looking about as much as looking at him. In fact, it appeared to Johnny that the woman had her eye out for someone in particular.

Johnny thought the picture appealing, the long established happy couple, prosperous, snatching admiring looks from others in the crowd, when he noticed the wife's attention caught. She raised a hand as if to wave to someone, then as quickly dropped it and frowned. Those full lips took on a pout. She turned her face up to her husband's and said something.

Johnny looked to see what had caught her eye. Deramus! He came toward them all with a man on one arm and a woman on the other. The male companion was taller than Deramus and good-looking, with high, chiseled cheekbones and eyes slightly tilted up on the outer corners. Unlike Deramus, he was well but plainly dressed, and he walked with a slight limp.

The woman with Deramus, on the other hand, may as well have worn a sign that read "whore" around her neck. Between the paint, the gaudy baubles, and the alarmingly deep neckline of her already scandalous gown, there was no mistaking a prostitute. All the richness of her accoutrements told one she was a very expensive whore. Her somewhat advanced age—but who could tell with these women— suggested she might just be the madam of a successful bordello. Johnny suddenly understood she was the cause of the elegant woman's displeasure at Deramus's approach.

As they came, the trio chattered animatedly, laughing and enjoying each other's company. Deramus slowed his pace when he looked up and caught sight of Johnny. His smile faltered, and he leaned to whisper to the attractive man whose arm he held. The taller man glanced over at Johnny and back to his companions, and said something that clearly amused them. Johnny looked away, pretending to check his valise was secure.

He relaxed when he heard Deramus call, "Barnet! Madame Julienne! What a pleasure and a surprise. Are you here to wish me and my beloved well on our journey?"

Beloved? Johnny wondered. *Could he possibly mean the prostitute?* A sudden thought made Johnny's stomach clench. He couldn't mean the man with whom he was sharing such intimate closeness. No, of course not. No man would acknowledge another man as his beloved to the world at large. But would one acknowledge a woman like that one? Johnny supposed a studiedly provocative man, like a riverboat gambler, might. But that would mean....

The husband returned Deramus's greeting. "Frankie, how good to see you. And Mr. Murphy, Madame Antoinette, three times the pleasure. You know my wife, of course, Mrs. Barnet."

"Hugh!" A huff of wounded sensibilities came from Mrs. Barnet's lips. She frowned and would meet no one's eyes. Frankie stepped in and broke the tension by lifting her gloved hand to his lips and saying something in a low voice that seemed to please her. He let his coal-black eyes gaze into hers just a little too long for propriety, melting her annoyance. Johnny saw the husband's face harden. Who needed theater in New Orleans? Drama and comedy were center stage on every street corner.

Johnny tried to look bored but managed to watch the rest of the farce from the corner of one eye. Murphy took Mrs. Barnet's hand next and kissed it with a sharp, military-style bow. The madam and the lady did no more than eye each other coolly. Barnet shook Deramus's and Murphy's hands and earned himself a sharp slap on the arm when he made a civil bow to the whore. The gaudily made-up woman smirked.

The quintet continued to play for the others gathered about, Deramus saying to Barnet, loud enough for Johnny to understand, "Hugh, *mon vieux*. Are you and your beautiful wife traveling with us today?"

Barnet shook his head. "No, only I. On my way to Memphis on business. My sweet lady will stay at home to keep the hearth and home ready for my return."

"You are indeed the luckiest of men, my friend, to have such homely pleasures to count on," Frankie purred. "Alas, no warm bed for me on my return."

Johnny caught the exchange of looks between Murphy and Madame Antoinette. It screamed, *Oh really?*

Johnny had already noticed Julienne Barnet only had eyes for Deramus. He had noticed how women on the riverboat gathered about Deramus like bees to a flower, but this was somehow more intimate, more suggestive. Was there history? From the husband's reaction, it looked as if there might be.

Johnny started when he heard Deramus say, "But I hope you will excuse me. I see a friend over here I want Mick and Tony to meet. *Enchanté*, Julienne. *À bientôt*."

Johnny barely kept himself from turning and dashing away as the trio made straight for where he stood.

"Mr. Stanley! You are traveling with us again! How delightful." Frankie had come to him, dropped his companions' arms, and stood pumping Johnny's hand. "You simply must meet my business associates. Ladies first, of course."

Frankie did not have to introduce the madam. She danced up to Johnny, slid a slender hand under his arm, and pressed her dramatically low neckline against it. "Oh, you beautiful man, where have you been hiding? You have not come to Le Coq Rouge during your stay. I know, I should have noticed you." She turned to Frankie. "François, *mon ami*, did you see these eyes? They are so pale a blue they make me shiver to my core!" She put her other hand in Johnny's arm and squirmed against him. "Then they warm me from my toes all the way to… well, you know."

Johnny blushed ferociously.

"Tony, dearest, you are embarrassing the poor man. Mr. Stanley, may I introduce Madame Antoinette. She and I are partners in the ownership of that fine establishment, Le Coq Rouge. There is none better for elegance, distinction, and of course for price. But you look like a man not unwilling to spend where you can be assured of pleasure."

Johnny was sure of the emphasis on that one word, "spend."

The woman pulled a fan from her sleeve and tapped Frankie on the arm. "*Méchant! Est-ce que tu n'as pas d'honte*? You are making the poor man blush even redder."

Frankie smirked back at Johnny. "*Je suis désolé*. Please overlook my clumsiness. Let me introduce you to the very respectable Mr. Michael Murphy, confidential agent extraordinaire and my particular friend."

Michael reached out his hand and shook Johnny's in the most normal and acceptable way. "Good to meet you, Mr. Stanley. My friend, Frankie here, has told me all about you."

Johnny, who had just been feeling a little better, blushed again.

"Not to worry, my dear man, it was nothing but the most complimentary of words," Frankie added.

Johnny cleared his throat. "Mr. Murphy, there's the air of the military man about you."

Murphy smiled and bowed in acknowledgement. "Why, yes. You are perceptive. I served under General Scott in the Mexican War."

Johnny brightened. "Oh yes? My Uncle Peder, um, Peter, was in the Mexican War. He... he...." Johnny's voice trailed off. "Well, he was with the San Patricios."

Frankie and Antoinette looked puzzled, but Murphy gave Johnny a grim nod. "A lot of very good and honorable men served with them. Not a few of my own friends."

Antoinette wielded her fan on Murphy's arm. "What is this, this San Patricios?"

Frankie inquired, "That is Spanish for St. Patrick, *non*?"

"Yes. The San Patricios Battalion was men who went over to fight on the Mexican side. Mostly Irish and Germans. Catholics," Michael added.

Frankie regarded Murphy with his head back, looking at him with narrowed, speculative eyes. "So? And you are Irish and Catholic as well. Were you not tempted?"

Murphy smiled thinly. "Now, Frankie, I don't have to tell you everything, do I? Am I not allowed some mystery?"

Frankie raised both eyebrows in an expression that conveyed, *You think so, do you.* He turned to Johnny. "So this Uncle Peter. He was in the San Patricios? Then was he Irish or German?"

Johnny squirmed. "He was in sympathy with both," he misled.

Antoinette interrupted with a small squeal. "Oh look, they're going to kiss! That is so sweet, *n'est-ce pas*?" She directed their attention to the married couple who were taking leave of each other. Disappointed when the respectable couple did not, in fact, kiss, she grabbed Frankie and threw her arms around his neck. "My darling, how shall I ever live with you gone away from me?" she moaned dramatically. She stood on her toes to plant her lips on Frankie's. He held his arms up for a moment, then let them embrace her, joining in on the kiss.

Murphy looked both amused and annoyed.

Johnny glanced over at the couple in time to see the wife frown at the theatrics.

When the time came to board the riverboat, Johnny did not pay attention to the look Frankie and Michael Murphy exchanged as they shook hands. Frankie said in a leading tone, "Give my regards to Carlos?"

Michael glared briefly at him. "No, not anymore."

Frankie's right eyebrow went up. "I am sorry to hear that."

Michael asked, "Are you? I am not."

Frankie gazed at Murphy's face a moment. "I will see you in a couple of weeks, then. *Au revoir.*" To the madam he said, "I think we have made ample good-byes. I will see you soon, Tony."

Turning to Johnny he said, "Your servant, *monsieur.*" He turned and went to follow Barnet up the gangway, offering Mrs. Barnet nothing more than a wink.

Antoinette noticed someone in the crowd she knew and left Murphy and Johnny alone. As she glided off in the bell-shaped skirts, appearing for all the world as if she were on wheels, Johnny commented, "Well, good to meet you, Mr. Murphy. I may return to New Orleans, but I expect we won't have occasion to meet again."

Murphy did not smile. He took Johnny's hand and held it. "That would be too bad. Yes, it was a pleasure." His gaze returned to Deramus's back, disappearing up the grand staircase on deck.

"May I ask, I overheard Mr. Deramus say something about his beloved. Is that the lady I just met?" Johnny looked in the direction Antoinette had gone.

Murphy's eyes lit with amusement. "Antoinette? No." He laughed. "Frankie's first and only love is *Le Beau Soleil.*" He grew more serious. "And it behooves anyone who gets close to Frankie to remember that. He will never love another." He smiled thinly, made a short bow, then turned on his heel and limped away.

Johnny watched him go, puzzling over what had felt like a warning.

JOHNNY found himself in a new stateroom on the far end of the hurricane deck. While slightly larger, perhaps merely longer, he thought nothing of it. His new roommate was already there—not the mousy parson this time but a dapper young fellow who flashed a smile at him when he toted in his valise. The fellow stood and extended his hand. "Buster Pardee, man about town, at your service, Mr....?"

"Stanley. John C. Stanley, your servant."

"And what sort of business are you in, Mr. Stanley?" the young man asked.

"Government. I am an agent for the Treasury traveling on the business of Mississippi River Valley transportation."

Pardee's eyes widened, but then he gave Johnny a knowing look. "Oh, I get it. Wink's as good as a nod to a blind horse, eh?" And he winked.

"I'm sure I don't know what you mean, my good man," Johnny returned, annoyed at the presumption of... whatever this fellow presumed.

Pardee shrugged extravagantly. "Well, it's no secret Slidell and them fire-eaters are tryin' to stir up trouble with the Northern states."

Johnny stared at him. "Slidell? Who is that?"

"Where you from, Mr. Stanley? The moon?"

"Chicago, and I don't care for your tone, sir." Johnny turned to set his valise on the bunk across from the one Pardee had stood up from.

"Chicago, eh? So you in with Stephen Douglas?"

Johnny turned right around again and gave the younger man a perplexed look. "In with? Listen, man, I don't meddle in politics. I know who Douglas is, but I don't know what you are getting at or who this Slidell fellow is."

The young man's expression changed to incredulity. "Senator John Slidell of Louisiana, the very state we are in, man. He and the fire-eaters—"

"Who are they?" Johnny interrupted.

"Fire-eaters? Why man, you are from the moon. They're that group of proslavery Southerners who are mad as hell so many new states are coming in free. They get along with Douglas on some things, like Cuba, but not on everything."

"Cuba? What has Cuba got to do with anything?" Johnny's patience was evaporating.

"Douglas and Slidell want to make it part of these here United States of America."

"Oh. Well I suppose they do those things." He shrugged. "It's nothing to do with me." He hesitated a moment and then asked, "Mr. Pardee, you haven't said what your line of work is."

Pardee grinned. "I'm speculatin' in cotton."

Johnny gave him a blank look, but nodded. "I see." In fact he felt like he had just been harangued in a language he did not comprehend. *And I have to listen to this buffoon all the way to Cairo?*

WHEN Johnny entered the grand cabin for the midday meal, the steward led him over to the row of tables near the Apollo. He reached to touch the steward's sleeve. "Excuse me, but this must be a mistake. I am not a first-class passenger."

The steward waved Johnny's concern aside. "Yes, Mr. Stanley, but Mr. Deramus has instructed that you be seated at his table."

Johnny slowed his steps for a moment. "He did? Why?"

The steward gave him a *what a stupid question* look and continued.

Johnny's curiosity overcame his momentary trepidation. He let himself be drawn to the table and seated precisely next to Frankie.

Frankie, who had politely risen, took his seat again. "I trust your stateroom is to your satisfaction, Mr. Stanley?"

"It will do, thank you for asking, Mr. Deramus. I am unsure what has passed to gain me this… um… rise in my meal status, however."

Deramus smiled. "What? You mean your seating? No mystery. The diplomat who was to have your seat had to cancel his journey. I thought it would be nice to have a different sort of companionship for a change, that is all." The table steward reached around Johnny to place a bowl of veal bouillon in front of him, then in front of Deramus. "Eat up, Mr. Stanley. Don't let your soup get cold." He lifted his own soup spoon and saluted Johnny with it.

They were not the only diners at the table. Johnny noted the women seated with them flirted with Deramus shamelessly—all but the youngest by far, a daughter of one of the matrons. It seemed she was on her wedding trip with a terribly shy young husband. The other men, presumably the matrons' husbands, were too busy leaning behind their wives to expostulate loudly with each other. Johnny quietly enjoyed the courses, listening to Deramus and the women talk about the weather, fashions, the many weddings taking place now it was June, and about Mr. Buchanan, the President.

"What a scandal," one woman, something of a sage—or so she wanted to demonstrate—said.

Another asked, "Do you mean his... attachment, shall we say, to Mr. King?"

Johnny felt his face pale.

"Ah yes, living together so many years, and you know what Mr. Jackson said of them...," she led.

A third woman, who wore spectacles and a dour look but had nevertheless been just as flirtatious with their host, put her fork down and stared incredulously at the others. "No, I do not. What does he say?"

The second woman, who was richly dressed and coiffed but who had a very ruddy face and bulbous nose, responded sotto voce. "He called them Mr. and Mrs. King. That was, of course, before Mr. King's sad passing."

Johnny almost choked on his mouthful of *Gratin Dauphinois*.

"Nonsense," inserted Deramus. "You know how expensive it is to live in Washington. They were simply frugal. That's what makes Mr. Buchanan such an ideal president."

The first woman shook her head. "Mr. Deramus, then tell me why our Mr. Buchanan has never married."

Deramus paused. "You know, I expect, that his intended did away with herself, back in '19? Oh, dear, excuse me, you were all too young to know of it... assuming you were even born." The comment had its desired effect. The women all giggled and blushed. "Besides, my dears," Deramus went on, "I have never married. You do not think I am...." He let his voice trail off.

The three women all squealed their protest.

The woman seated at Frankie's right put a maternal hand on his arm. "No, of course we do not, dear boy. But someday love will find you. Of that, you may be sure."

Deramus's wistful smile almost appeared genuine. "Alas, my only love is this riverboat. And she is a terribly jealous lover."

The bride, who could be no more than eighteen, looked perplexed. In a stage whisper she asked no one in particular, "But I don't understand. What can two men do? In bed I mean." The three matrons looked either dismayed or amused, but the young husband looked like he wished his chair could plummet through the floor.

Johnny could not help but shoot a look at Frankie, who turned sideways in his chair, his hand to his cheek, hiding his face from everyone at the table but Johnny. He spread his fingers and looked through them at Johnny, so much mirth in those black eyes it was hard to remember the man's accustomed airy hauteur.

"Mr. Stanley, can you explain it?" the young woman asked sincerely.

Johnny sat up and looked her straight in the eye. "I have no idea, madam," he said seriously.

Frankie managed to disguise a snort of amusement as a cough. He could not look at Johnny.

The young woman's nearest neighbor—who could have been her mother—said with a chastising look, "Dear, you know a gentleman cannot speak of such things to a lady." For some reason that set her two companions and then herself off into giggles.

About the time the giggles from this remark subsided, Deramus lifted his glass of wine in salute. "*Mes amis*, our little song sparrow is about to serenade us. *S'il vous plaît*, your attention."

Johnny glanced over at the small dais set along the far wall. A string quintet had provided the atmosphere for their meal, but now a tiny woman in a bright blue gown with wide hoopskirts mounted the dais and waited for the formally attired conductor to raise his baton.

"Her name is Miss Lulubelle Kilpatrick. A sweet thing, as you will soon learn," Frankie offered.

Miss Kilpatrick took a stance with her hands pressed prayerfully together in front of her lacy breast. The conductor lifted his baton, and on his down sweep, the violins took up a sweet lilting introduction. The young woman began to sing in an alto too deep to seem like it should come from such a slender throat.

"Nita! Juanita! Ask thy soul if we should part!

Nita! Juanita! Lean thou on my heart."

Johnny was startled when Deramus leaned toward him, taking advantage of the artificial privacy. "It is not true, you know, what you believe about me."

Johnny stared at him, unsure what he meant or what Johnny could reply. "That you... cheat at cards?" It was the safer choice.

Frankie eyed him speculatively. "Is that what you were told?"

Johnny shrugged. "I thought all gamblers cheated. How else could they be sure they would win?"

Frankie still had a speculative look. He finally said, "That depends. If a player is very good at what he does, he need not cheat to know he will win more often than not."

"And you are that good?" Johnny smiled mockingly.

Frankie's eyes narrowed. "Are you suggesting I am not?"

Johnny glanced at the others at their table, all either attentive to the singer or, in the case of two of the men, still arguing with each other about something. He looked back at Frankie. "I am afraid I will have to watch you play to make up my mind about that."

Frankie stared at him, and then his face cleared. "I am playing this afternoon. Will you come watch me in the saloon?"

Johnny shrugged again. "I can't promise I will know what I am seeing, but yes, I will come watch you play. But don't lose on my account."

"I don't understand. Why would I lose on your account, Mr. Stanley?"

"You might lose, Mr. Deramus, to show me you aren't cheating." Johnny gave him a knowing look.

Frankie's face broke into a delighted smile, and he laughed. "*Touché, monsieur*. But you need not fear. I never lose... on purpose that is. I shall see you in the saloon then, shortly after our sparrow has finished her performance."

With this assurance, Frankie stood, made polite bows to his guests, and took his leave.

CHAPTER 5

Le Beau Soleil, that same day in June 1859

"WHAT'S got you smiling, Frankie?"

Making his way out of the grand cabin, Frankie was brought up short at Hugh Barnet's words. Hugh stood with his shoulder against the promenade wall, his hands in his pockets, and one leg bent at the knee. "Why, Hugh, you are not inside enjoying the music?"

"I was," Barnet said, "but I saw you get up and wanted to intercept you. I want a word with you, Frankie." Barnet stood straight, putting both feet flat on the deck boards.

Frankie eyed him warily. "That sounds ominous. Should I be afraid?"

Barnet shook his head. "We used to be such friends, Frankie. What came between us?"

Frankie frowned irritably. "What did not?" He considered his childhood chum a moment. "Shall we get a drink? I am to play this afternoon, but I can spare you a few minutes."

Frankie led Barnet up the two flights of stairs to the Texas deck saloon. He indicated a stool at the bar.

Barnet shook his head. "Let's sit over there," he suggested, gesturing with a tilt of his head to a small corner table.

Frankie sighed. He turned to the bartender and ordered, "Bring a bottle of the bourbon from my private stock and two glasses, won't you, Lou?" He slapped his palm on the bar and turned and went to where Barnet had taken a seat. He sat, leaned back, and crossed his legs. "So what is this all about, Hugh? What have I done now?"

Lou brought the bottle and glasses and waited for Frankie to instruct him to open it.

"Your own stock, is it?" Hugh asked sardonically. "Am I supposed to be in your debt?"

Frankie rolled his eyes. "Go ahead and open it, Lou."

The bartender opened the bottle after tilting it so Barnet could see the intact seal of paper. At Frankie's dismissive wave of his hand, Lou poured two fingers of whiskey into each glass. "Make it four," Frankie said. "I can tell this will take a while."

"Shall we make a toast to Mme. Julienne?" Frankie saw the frown on Hugh's face and smiled without mirth. "I thought she was probably part of whatever has your nose out of joint. What is it this time?"

Hugh took the glass and, without lifting it in toast, took a sip. "As if you don't know, you provoking scoundrel."

Frankie started to drink but put down his glass. "I can honestly say I don't know what the hell you are going on about." His voice had grown tighter and harsher by the end of the sentence.

Hugh grimaced at the vulgarity. "That little display on the levee. First, you insult my wife by introducing your whore. Then you put on that comedy right in front of her. You know better than to treat a decent woman that way."

Frankie's eyes danced with humor. "Oh, Antoinette didn't mind."

Hugh slammed his free hand down hard on the tabletop, making Lou and the other customers look over. "Damn you, Frankie!"

Frankie's eyes flashed. "Behave yourself, Hugh."

"Do not provoke me, then," he warned through clenched teeth. "You know I meant my wife. Antoinette is hardly a decent woman."

"You were the one who introduced Julienne to Tony." Frankie pushed down a chuckle.

Frankie wondered how much Hugh knew about his wife Julienne's indiscretions. Oh, she had never been loose in the full sense, as far as Frankie was aware. But she had been unchaste and—as far as Frankie knew—was still a notorious flirt, and there had been gossip about a couple of men. She had even once set her cap to seduce Frankie.

The three had grown up together. Their relationships had been a never-ending love triangle, though neither Hugh nor Julienne had known Frankie's position in it. Hugh had wanted Julienne. Julienne had wanted Frankie. And Frankie had wanted… Hugh. The memory of that bittersweet longing made him wince now.

"I see, sir, that you are quite aware of your offense."

Frankie's eyebrows shot up at Hugh's statement. His mind had traveled along to the triangle, but he realized a moment later Hugh's mind was still on the affront to his wife's respectability.

"I know, Hugh, and you are right. I should have left Murphy and Mme. Antoinette and come over to greet you alone. It's just that…." He paused, looking for the words. "It's just so much fun to ruffle your feathers." He waved his glass of bourbon. "Yes, yes, it's as you say, provoking. And entirely unforgivable. Yet I ask that you do pardon me, for old times' sake. Won't you?"

He offered the bottle again. Hugh set down his glass, indicating his assent. Frankie brought the level of liquor back up to four fingers.

When Hugh said nothing more, Frankie sighed. "What do you want me to do, Hugh? How can I make up for something I never did?"

"You expect me to believe that? That you never tried to cuckold me in my own house?"

Frankie put down his glass, sat back, and put the heels of his hands on his eyes. "We have been over and over this, Hugh. I did not, I repeat, did not try to make love to Julienne. Not then and never. I never will. On my honor as a gentleman of New Orleans, I swear it." He looked up into Hugh's face.

Hugh glared back. "*I saw you*," he stated firmly.

Frankie stood up suddenly. "I don't know what you saw, Hugh. All I know is that I have never tried to take Julienne from you, never will, never would. I… I…." He stopped himself. His frustration was so acute he wanted to tell Hugh why the trespass he so insisted he had witnessed could never have occurred. But he couldn't. As much as he wanted to be himself in every way, to live his life as it made sense to him, he knew he mustn't share his preference for other men's bodies with someone like Hugh. Half of his society, the *demi-monde*, allowed him at least some liberty. But the penalty was too great in the world he shared with Hugh. The least of it would be awkward in the extreme, affecting the legitimate side of his businesses. The worst would be a lifetime at hard labor in a prison somewhere if somehow he was caught.

"I'm not finished with you yet," Hugh barked. He started to stand.

"But I am finished with you," Frankie shot back furiously. "Keep the bottle, with my compliments. I have a show to put on."

The crowd had gathered in the room where the card table was set up. Brand-new, unopened decks of cards sat on the bar waiting to be brought over and inspected. Frankie signaled to Lou to bring him a clean glass and a fresh bottle of whiskey. He proceeded to the table where the game would commence in a few minutes.

He saw Johnny Stanley enter the saloon. He smiled dryly and bowed to the man, then watched him take a chair nearby.

"Who will take my challenge for some high-stakes five-card stud?" The game was quite new, a variation on five-card draw, but by the summer of 1859 was familiar to anyone who played regularly on the river.

A murmur went through the crowd of those who stood and sat about the saloon. High stakes were usually reserved for late-night games on *Le Beau Soleil*, and it was afternoon. As more people filed into the saloon, they sensed the tension and whispered, wanting to know what was going on.

Three men made their way to the bar, bought into the game for two hundred dollars' worth of chips each, and took their seats at the table.

Once the table was full, the men sized each other up. Names were exchanged with quick nods and bows, but no handshakes. No point feigning friendship.

Frankie calmly looked the three men over. Like any other professional gambler, Frankie was prone to superstition. Some men wore special stockings, others carried a rabbit's foot, yet others found the prettiest woman in the room and kissed her. Frankie had started a tradition of giving his opponents secret nicknames based on something he observed about them. He glanced at the long-nosed, beady-eyed man to his left and christened him "The Weasel." The man who sat across the table was a rather fat, red-faced man with an expensive pearl stickpin. Frankie had played him before, but knew he was not a professional. He also remembered something else about him, the body odor that had given him the nickname, "The Stinker." To Frankie's right was a young man who was making eyes at him. He looked like the son of a wealthy man, richly dressed, bejeweled, and feigning indolence. Frankie felt fingertips on his knee and, though intrigued, moved his leg out of reach of the man's caresses. He had seen the man earlier that same day. He was handsome, with a tanned, clean-shaven face, strong features, and lustrous curling black hair. He wore a plum-colored waistcoat under a fine, gray wool suit. Frankie noticed he had stared at the Apollo appreciatively, his gaze traveling down the figure and stopping at the drape of white silk. Frankie had also been pleased to see the man turn and look him straight in the eye—signaling a shared desire. Frankie knew he had to push these thoughts away if he wanted to concentrate on the game. He named the man "The Mouthful."

Frankie signaled Lou to bring over the four decks of cards arranged on a pearl-inlay tray. He gestured for one of the other men to select one of the decks.

The young man, the Mouthful, clumsily removed one deck, but before he could break the seal, the Weasel grabbed them from his hand and said, "I'll check these."

The Weasel proceeded to break the seal on the cards and remove and count them. Then he riffle-shuffled them. Frankie knew he was making sure the cards shuffled without any hitches, the quickest way to detect mechanical markings on the cards. He watched the Weasel examine the fine design on the backs of the cards. Covering just a few tiny dimples was a crude way to mark a deck, but it still happened.

Now the Weasel sorted the cards by suit. The two other players frowned impatiently. The Stinker made a comment about the man going overboard. But Frankie was not vexed. He knew what the Weasel was up to. His careful opponent was checking the tiny white margins between the decorated backs of the cards and the card's final edge. This was a sophisticated way to mark a deck without having to physically damage it.

Frankie smiled patiently at the Weasel, giving his assent to this time-consuming exercise to make sure the game was honest, but it made the other players ill at ease. All fine with Frankie. An opponent's discomfort was simply another advantage.

Unlike notorious Mississippi River cardsharps, Frankie's success at card games was not the use of sleight of hand or marked decks. He never cheated. He knew the games and the odds, but more than that, he knew people. He could watch them without seeming to, find their "tells," and recognize when their heartbeats sped up or they felt threatened and showed weakness. He also knew how to influence others with his own card play. Poker was about winning and making opponents think they were beaten. Like all great poker players, Frankie could win with bad cards. Still, Frankie was a conservative player and never allowed his emotions to dictate his play. He knew steady, relentless play would pay off.

He also had a phenomenal memory. He was not a card counter, but he did track cards as they were revealed. Whenever he sat at a poker table, he remembered how each man played a given hand—how he modified his play, raised, called, folded, and which cards his opponents revealed after every play.

The deal went around the table twice, giving Frankie his first sample of how these men played. He studied them rigorously.

He glanced at Johnny, who sat with one leg crossed over the other, his hands on the chair's arms, his head cocked at an angle that suggested he had more on his mind than cards. Frankie assumed he was watching him, his face, his reactions, more than his card play. He caught Johnny's gaze, held it, and was amused to see color come up in Johnny's cheeks.

The Stinker's odor started to take over the room after an hour of engaging but unspectacular play. There was such a crowd in the saloon that any number of their audience may also have contributed to the aroma.

Frankie had long since discounted the Mouthful as a serious player. He had not quite decided about the Stinker or the Weasel. The Stinker was a good player, but given his misplay of the last three hands, Frankie began to dismiss him as a real threat. As suggested by his card examination at the game's beginning, the serious player was the Weasel, who though seemingly calm had the singular focus of a tightly wound man.

Like all high-stakes games, it all came down to one hand. The Mouthful was dealing.

Without appearing to do so, Frankie kept a close eye on all the other players, even glancing quickly beyond them to detect if anyone was sending a player clues as to his own hand and play. He was satisfied no one had a confederate among the watchers, and as play continued he focused more and more on the Weasel. His assessment proved right when the game came down to a showdown between him and the sharp-faced man. The cards on the table told spectators the game could go either way. Those who knew Frankie's style were not fooled by the fact that he was calm and cool while the other man seemed honed to a sharp point. No one knew Frankie was in fact growing nervous when after he drew a useless deuce, the Weasel exclaimed "Yes!" as he drew his next card.

Frankie saw the slight muscle twitch in the Weasel's jaw. He watched the man count the rest of his chips, not nearly enough to avoid folding for lack of funds. The Weasel frowned, reached into an inner jacket pocket, and pulled out a gold pocket watch. "My daddy gave me this on my twenty-first birthday. Will the bank accept it?"

Frankie gestured to Lou, who came over and took the watch. He examined it carefully, flipped up the cover, listened to the works, played with the winding mechanism, then clapped it shut. He placed the watch on the pile of chips and nodded to Frankie, who looked over at the Weasel.

The Weasel, looking at no one and nothing, sat back and waited, making everyone at the table and the spectators stew. Of course, he was betting the last of his money. He just wanted everyone to wait on his great play, to savor besting the Mississippi's greatest poker player.

"I presume you're calling, sir," Frankie asked as calmly as if he were asking for the man's calling card.

Sweat broke out on the Weasel's temples. He glared at Frankie. He frowned at his cards. "Try and beat 'em," he said.

Frankie considered. His opponent had either caught the winning hand or had just executed a perfect bluff. The Weasel had played his hand strongly on each card, betting and raising like he knew he would inevitably catch the winning hand.

Frankie picked up and sipped his bourbon, glanced at the watch crowning the mountain of chips, then looked back at the Weasel. "You certainly seem confident, *monsieur*."

The room grew silent. Frankie continued to stare at the Weasel. There it was again. The tight jaw accompanied by the pursed lips. But more than these possible tells, Frankie reminded himself, the chances of the Weasel catching the perfect card at the end of the hand was improbably high, even with no other diamonds showing.

Frankie knew the odds favored his two pair despite the Weasel's reckless betting. He called.

"Damn you!" the Weasel protested. No one would call against those show cards. Disgustedly, he flipped his hole card over, a feckless five of spades. He had nothing.

As Frankie leaned forward to sweep his winnings from the middle of the table, the Weasel abruptly stood up. "Now just you wait. Just you wait. I want to see your hand."

Frankie sat back. "You know I don't have to show you. Anyway, my show tens beat your knave high."

The man shook furiously. "You will, if you know what's good for you," he hissed.

Frankie eyed him. "If it will keep the peace, *voilà*." He turned over his hold card, showing the full winning hand, knaves over tens.

The man stared at them. Then he looked up at Frankie. "Why, you copperhead!" he shouted. He pushed the chair behind him so hard it crashed to the floor. He darted around the table with his fists clenched.

He grabbed Frankie's jacket lapels. "I wanna see what you got hidden up your sleeves." In surprise, Frankie didn't resist. "Nobody wins that many times in a row." The Weasel started to rifle through Frankie's coat and waistcoat pockets, even reaching down to feel in the waistband of his trousers.

Johnny, who had been watching, got out of his chair, shot forward, grabbed the Weasel's arm, and yanked him back. The Weasel whirled, swung his clenched fist and connected with Johnny's face. The thwack was audible to the whole room. Blood started to drip from Johnny's nose.

Johnny roared with fury and delivered a blow to the man's jaw, lifting him off his feet. The man flew backward and struck his head on the edge of a wooden chair. He crumpled to the floor, insensible.

"He's dead," someone exclaimed.

Another man, kneeling at the Weasel's side, said, "No, he's not dead. He's just out cold."

Frankie stood slowly, his eyes on Johnny's face. Then he turned to the crowd. "Take the bastard to his stateroom and get him a doctor." He walked up to Johnny and stood close, gazing into his face. He put up a hand but did not quite touch the growing bruise on Johnny's cheek. Tenderly, he said, "You're hurt." He reached into his jacket for his handkerchief. "Your nose is bleeding." After wadding up the cloth, he pressed it under Johnny's nose.

Johnny took the cloth and held it in place. "I'm all right."

"Oh, Charles William, good," Frankie said as he saw his servant. "Help me get Mr. Stanley to my stateroom. We need to look to his injury."

Frankie paused just long enough to reach for the watch that sat on the summit of the chips pile. He carried it over to where the Weasel lay on the saloon floor. Squatting to slip the watch into the man's jacket pocket, he said softly, "Wouldn't want your daddy to think you threw it away." He stood and returned to Johnny.

Tut-tutting Johnny's protestations, he took Johnny's arm and draped it over his shoulders. Jocularly he told him, "I've known Charles William since I was born, and he always appears when most needed. Like a guardian angel."

Background voices filled the room.

"Did you see that?"

"One good blow!"

"That Frenchie is lucky that fellow was in the room."

"What happened? Did he cheat?"

Frankie guided Johnny out of the saloon and down to the lower promenade where the air came cool off the river.

CHAPTER 6

Le Beau Soleil, that same day in June 1859

"IN HERE. Go on. Yes, it's my stateroom." Frankie herded Johnny into his sitting room. Johnny had Frankie's handkerchief to his nose, so his protests were muffled. "Charles William, get some soapy water and towels."

"Yes, Mr. Deramus. Won't take me a minute."

Frankie ushered Johnny to the divan. "Sit down. Take your coat off."

Johnny sat staring, seemingly transfixed as Frankie removed his own jacket, took out his onyx cufflinks, and rolled up his sleeves. Pulling a small table in front of him, Frankie bent down. "Let me see that."

Johnny flinched when Frankie reached to his face and took hold of the handkerchief.

"I am not going to hurt you," Frankie said. He drew the handkerchief away and examined Johnny's nose. "Oh good, it's stopped bleeding." He gently fingered it. "Your nose isn't broken. We just have to clean you up. You'll have a hell of a black eye."

A quiet tap on the door heralded Charles William's return carrying a tray with a porcelain bowl and small linen towels. He set the tray on the small table. "The soap is mixed into the water, Mr. Deramus."

"Excellent. Hand me a damp towel."

As Charles William dipped one of the fine linen towels in the water and squeezed it out, he gave Johnny a look of sympathy. "Oh my, Mr. Stanley. That looks like it smarts. How are you feeling, sir?"

Johnny returned a baleful look. "The bastard must have been wearing a big ring."

Frankie started dabbing at the blood on Johnny's chin. "Charles William, why don't you take this shirt and see if you can get the bloodstains out. The waistcoat too." He waved the damp towel to cool it and put the towel in Johnny's hand. "Hold that against your nostrils. It should be cool. That's good." He proceeded to unbutton Johnny's waistcoat and carefully drew it off one arm and then the other, then he did the same with Johnny's bloodstained shirt.

Throughout the disrobing, Johnny sat rigid, his eyes staring but his lips quivering.

Frankie let Charles William bundle up the waistcoat and shirt and motioned him to take Johnny's coat as well. "See what you can do. Thank you. I think we have all we need here. I'll call if we need you."

Charles William bowed to each man in turn, went to the door, and as he was about to close it behind him, asked, "Do you want the door locked, Mr. Deramus?"

"I don't think that's necessary. The Weasel won't be looking for any more fights." The nickname was now an apt commentary on his attacker's character, and Johnny and Charles William both seemed to know exactly who he meant.

Johnny sat rigidly as Frankie took a clean towel, dampened it, and wiped more of the blood away. "I can't thank you…," Johnny began.

"Then don't. It's the least I can do. Thanks to you my own pretty face is unscarred." He grinned and glanced up at Johnny. "That was, well, impressive." He mimed a left hook. "Never knew what hit him." He peered at the growing bruise on Johnny's cheek. "Keep the towel there while I get fresh water."

Frankie took another towel with him to the sideboard and wetted it with clean water from a pitcher. "I thank you. I don't think anyone has ever jumped to defend me before. It was… nice."

He returned to Johnny, then bending at the hip, leaned over him. He pulled the cloth away from Johnny's cheek and nodded. "Let's see that hand." He reached for Johnny's left hand and turned it over to examine the knuckles. "Bruised. Nothing worse."

Frankie let go of Johnny's hand and looked into his face. He felt his own face go slack, and his heart thudded madly in his chest as he leaned toward Johnny and half closed his eyes. Their lips touched, and he felt Johnny jerk in surprise.

Suddenly Johnny reached out and grasped Frankie's arms near his shoulders. He pulled Frankie closer and mashed their lips tightly together. Frankie's arms were pinned to his sides by the elbows, his lower arms and hands powerless. He dropped the towel and returned Johnny's intense kiss.

JOHNNY had felt his body coming alive ever since Frankie had taken charge and started to treat his wounds. Their closeness alone would have stirred him, but Frankie's genuine concern tipped him over the edge. The feel of gentle fingers on his face, holding it steady while Frankie dabbed with the cloth, had sent a shiver through Johnny's very core. Perhaps it was the shock, but he felt unable to control his actions.

A memory flashed in his mind of a darkened passageway in Chicago, of Kurt's beautiful face intense and hungry as Rolf took his cock in his mouth. Johnny's prick was already hardening, but the recollection of Kurt's look at him as both of them spent took hold of Johnny now. His sudden intense need focused on the tableau, and all he could think of was how much he wanted to be the man sucking Kurt's cock.

Johnny pushed Frankie away, but only to gain access to his trousers. He frantically clawed at the trouser buttons, popping one off onto the floor in the process. When he had Frankie's placket undone and hanging open, he pushed Frankie's trousers down, then his silken drawers. He glanced up at Frankie.

With his arms away from his body and his pants around his ankles, Frankie stood looking down at Johnny's frantic ministrations.

Johnny slid forward onto his knees in front of Frankie, and his mouth dropped open as he stared at Frankie's quickly engorging cock. He made a low moan and took Frankie's taut member into his mouth. He heard Frankie's moans echo his own.

Johnny put his mouth around the head of Frankie's cock. He was not sure what to do, other than what he had rehearsed in his fantasies. He found that when he let the prick go deeper into his mouth, it triggered his gag reflex. He pulled back quickly to disguise the reaction. Perhaps if he just sucked and slid his lips on the end of Frankie's prick it would be good enough. All he knew was he did not want to stop. He could taste the drops of semen from Frankie's prick on his tongue and savored it. It felt every bit as wonderful as his imagination, in spite of the pain in his bruised cheek.

Johnny barely registered when Frankie reached for the hem of his shirt and pulled it up above his waist, permitting him full access to his cock. "Oh...," he heard Frankie moan as he began to thrust forward into Johnny's mouth.

FRANKIE had been so stunned by Johnny's lustful assault he could only react in kind. While he knew his stateroom door was unlocked, he could not move to correct that. He could tell Johnny was unpracticed, but the fact Johnny seemed to be focused so hard on his own hunger just made being on the receiving end that much more astonishing.

"Say my name," Johnny demanded, pulling away just long enough to say the words and then engulfing Frankie's cock again.

Gasping, Frankie managed, "What is it?"

Johnny pulled his mouth off Frankie's cock. "Johnny."

"Oh yes, Johnny, Johnny, Johnny!" Frankie said obligingly as the heat of Johnny's mouth closed around him once again.

Johnny reached around, grabbed an ass cheek in each hand, and squeezed hard enough to make Frankie cry out.

The sudden onslaught, the unexpected ferociousness of Johnny's lust, had Frankie ready to spend. The pressure built in his groin more intensely than he had experienced in some time.

A faint tap came at the door. Frankie instinctually called out, "No!"

"Deramus?"

Hugh Barnet!

"Later. Please," Frankie begged. "Don't come in." He moaned. "Oh Johnny…."

There was no further noise outside the door. Frankie, his eyes tightly closed, pounded into Johnny's throat, hearing Johnny's own rising vocalizations. He spent voluminously into Johnny's mouth.

Johnny had pulled his mouth off Frankie's cock and was gagging on his semen. He coughed and spit out a large glob of Frankie's seed. Frankie tried to help him wipe it away.

"I'm sorry. I'm sorry," Johnny spluttered.

"No, no, it's all right," Frankie reassured.

To his surprise Johnny leaned in and put his forehead against Frankie's abdomen. His shoulders seemed to be shaking. Frankie thought he was still gagging but all at once realized Johnny was weeping.

"*Mon petit, mon pauvre*," he sympathized. "No, no, it's all right." Frankie slid down to kneel in front of Johnny and took him in his arms. "Shhh, shhh, it's all right. What's wrong?"

When Johnny continued to sob, Frankie pulled him up to standing in his arms. "Here, let's have you lie down. It's all right." Awkwardly, Frankie kicked his trousers and drawers off his ankles, then guided a sobbing Johnny to his bedchamber door and opened it. Frankie led him to the large bed and pushed him down onto it. "Let me take off your shoes."

Johnny covered his face with one arm. Kneeling at the bedside where Johnny's feet hung, Frankie untied and pulled off each shoe, leaving Johnny's stockings and garters in place. He carefully lifted Johnny's legs and pulled them up and forward so his body was stretched out on the bed. Frankie jumped up to pull out a pillow from under the counterpane and lifted Johnny's head to tuck it under. After toeing off his own shoes, he dashed around the bed to climb up and lie alongside the still weeping man.

While pressing up tight against Johnny, Frankie put his arms around him. He maneuvered the blond head onto his shoulder and tenderly cradled it there. "Shh, shh, it's all right. Johnny, Johnny, whatever is wrong? It doesn't matter if you couldn't swallow. I don't mind."

Johnny clutched Frankie to him desperately. He moaned into his chest. "That's only part of it. I... I... have not done it before. I have tried so hard to resist."

Frankie did not question Johnny's grief. He was not ignorant of the self-recrimination most men had when they made love to another man for the first time. Hell, even men who preferred women were known sometimes to experience regret and guilt after their first time. He held Johnny tighter and hummed a soothing Creole tune as he rocked him. "It's all right. I have you. I won't let anything happen to you." He felt such a strong need to stroke and cherish the man in his arms. It startled him. He had never felt this way before.

Johnny's sobs turned slowly into hiccoughs. Still crooning, Frankie rubbed Johnny's back and brushed his chin across his head. He eventually felt Johnny's quaking ease. He glanced down to see Johnny's red eyes looking up into his face.

"It's Frankie, right?" Johnny asked.

Frankie could not help but let out a laugh. "Yes, it's Frankie. Your servant, *monsieur*." He looked down at Johnny with genuine concern. "I am so sorry what we did upset you. You know, it's the most natural thing in the world."

Johnny looked doubtful. "Is it?"

"*Je crois que oui, mon ange.* I believe so, my angel."

The tears in Johnny's eyes welled up anew.

"What? What did I say?" Frankie asked, clutching him tighter.

Johnny shook his head. "You are just so sweet and kind. And I was so awful to you before."

Frankie hushed him. "I've heard worse." He felt Johnny stiffen. "No, really, it is all right."

"No, it isn't. You are accustomed to insulting words. I can't face it."

Frankie frowned. *So that was it.* He did not want to be one of "them," to be part of a reviled group. A Miss Nancy. There was nothing Frankie could say. All he could do was soothe. He shifted up on his elbow and let Johnny's head down slowly onto the pillow. He gazed into Johnny's miserable face, came close, and kissed him tenderly. The kiss was salty with tears. Frankie reached down to put his hand on

Johnny's belly. He pressed hard on it, then drew his hand up to Johnny's breast.

Johnny reacted just as he hoped he would. Arousal took over for grief. Frankie reached down to unfasten Johnny's trouser buttons.

Johnny started. "Stop!"

Frankie paused. "If you don't want me to touch you there, I won't."

"That's not it. It's just that I...." He turned his face away. "I spent in my drawers."

"Nothing to be ashamed of. It just means I was so irresistible you couldn't wait."

"You have an answer for everything," Johnny said with a wistful smile.

"Damned right I do," Frankie assured him and leaned in for another, deeper kiss. He continued to unbutton Johnny's trousers. "I want to make love to you," he said.

Johnny looked back. He smiled and nodded. "But... but I don't know what to do."

Frankie stroked his cheek. "I will teach you."

WHEN he woke late that afternoon, Frankie was pleased to find Johnny naked in his bed. Johnny started at first and then relaxed back into Frankie's arms.

Frankie purred, "Mmmmm.... You are so nice to cuddle. How are you feeling?"

"I'm starving," he confessed.

Frankie stretched languorously. "It's probably almost time for supper. We should get dressed.

Johnny rested his chin on Frankie's chest. "I have no clothes."

Frankie grinned. "I noticed. You look wonderful."

Johnny asked, "Really?"

Frankie nodded solemnly and kissed him.

They made love again, rubbing against each other and kissing and licking everything they could reach. When Frankie drew himself down Johnny's body and took his cock in his mouth, he could tell Johnny would probably spend right away. He was certain if that happened, Johnny would be ashamed of it—so he went slowly, raising up to kiss the man's lips, softly stroking his belly and thighs. He brought Johnny to orgasm slowly.

JOHNNY lay sated, marveling at the past couple of hours. His irresistible impulse for raw sex had, in as little time, shifted to so much more. What was it about this tender man's touch that not only aroused him so but soothed him, made him feel cherished? It was the last thing he expected.

When Frankie sat up on his side of the bed, he said, "Oh good, Charles William must have gone to your stateroom and gotten some of your clothes." A full suit of evening wear hung on a "silent valet."

Johnny sat up fast. "He came in here?"

Frankie put a hand on his bare leg. "It's all right. Charles William is discreet. Hell, he's known me since he changed my diaper when I was a baby. There's nothing about me he doesn't know."

"But he saw us? Lying here, naked?" Johnny was horrified.

"Probably not. He doesn't look."

"But he knew."

Johnny stiffened when Frankie reached for him. "I will instruct him never to come in when you are here," he tried to reassure.

Johnny stared at him dumbfounded. He started to exclaim, "It's a little too late for that!" but then something else in Frankie's words pushed past the protest. "This… will happen again?"

"Do you want it to?" Frankie asked.

Johnny gazed back. "I do, very much. I do want to… do this… with you, again and again."

The look of childish pleasure on Frankie's face told Johnny the afternoon had been special for him as well. At least until they parted at Cairo, they would be together.

LEAVING the stateroom, Frankie was as expansive as ever, but he noticed how shy Johnny had suddenly become. As they took their places for dinner, he leaned to him. "They can't see it, you know."

Johnny started and asked, "See what?"

"How we spent our afternoon. You don't look any different than you did this morning." He gave Johnny an appraising look.

"Well, the way I feel right now it will be hard to imagine I spent the afternoon innocently...." Johnny glanced down.

Frankie was puzzled, and then he understood. "I'm flattered. Try to think about something else. It will be a long evening."

Johnny gaped at him. "I can't think of anything else. Does it have to be a long evening? Can't we go back after dinner?"

"No, I have to be in the saloon. Especially after your act of heroics... more people than ever will want to watch me play."

The soup arrived, and the conversation paused. Johnny became aware the ladies at their table were gossiping furiously in low tones.

"They aren't talking about us," Frankie reassured.

At that very moment one of the women turned and looked straight at them.

"They aren't, eh?" Johnny blushed scarlet.

"They probably heard about the fight. That's all."

Sure enough, one of the three matrons leaned to address Frankie. "Oh, Mr. Deramus, it is all over the boat. Some nasty man tried to attack you. How dreadful! Are you uninjured?"

Frankie glanced at Johnny. "It happens from time to time. You know how some men simply cannot bear to lose."

The four women nodded and chuckled conspiratorially between them, giving their bemused husbands significant looks.

"The brave man who prevented the attack was injured, however," Frankie continued.

The women looked blank. The sharp-faced woman shook her head. "I had not heard about him. Who was it? A bodyguard?"

"Why," Frankie began, stopping to look at Johnny. Frankie put his hand on Johnny's shoulder. "Why, this young man. Don't you see his black eye?"

Johnny flinched when Frankie touched him. When Frankie looked into his eyes, he saw not fear, but desire.

The women and their husbands all looked at Johnny as if they had not even realized anyone was sitting in his chair. His face deepened in color.

"He is modesty itself," Frankie purred. "He is a boxer." His tone expressed his pride, which made Johnny even more uncomfortable.

The women made approving noises, then turned back to Frankie. They peppered him with questions. He finally stopped trying to include Johnny in his answers, since the man seemed not to want to be included and the women showed no sign of any interest in his part in the events of the day.

When the attention finally diverted to some other focus, Johnny rasped under his breath, "Can we go? This is torture."

Frankie involuntarily glanced at Johnny's crotch, but managed to keep his head in motion in an attempt to cover what he had been about. "I can't, but do you want to go back to the stateroom? You can wait for me there."

Johnny pleaded, "Come with me."

Frankie looked about distractedly. "Oh, all right. But I will have to come back."

Frankie made his excuses and rose. He stood waiting for Johnny, who appeared to be frozen. "Well?" he asked.

"Just a minute. I can't stand up just now."

Frankie could not help but chuckle, earning himself a sharp glare from Johnny. "Just button your coat," he suggested.

Johnny managed to get up and clasp his frock coat around him. He followed Frankie to the entrance to the grand cabin. They had almost made their escape when Frankie stopped, making Johnny run into him.

Hugh Barnet once again stood in front of Frankie. All at once Frankie remembered the knock on his stateroom door. *Merde.* Barnet's face glowed with an odd mixture of confusion and disgust. *Merde, merde*, Frankie repeated silently. He turned to look over his shoulder at Johnny. "Why don't you go on ahead, Johnny? I'll be right along."

Ducking his head down, Johnny nodded and danced around them and out the door.

Frankie watched him go. He turned back to Hugh. "What can I do for you this time?" There was nothing friendly or gracious in his voice.

Barnet's eyes had widened when Frankie spoke to Johnny, using his name. He also followed Johnny's retreating form. His eyes when they came back to Frankie were full of fury. "Mr. Deramus, had I known just how low you had sunk—"

Frankie grabbed his arm, saying, "Let's talk somewhere less public."

Barnet jerked his arm away but followed Frankie onto the promenade.

"We seem to meet out here so often, I should probably just put out a desk and a sign that says 'Office,'" Frankie said.

Barnet snapped, "Can you never be serious?"

"I try not to," Frankie replied with a long-suffering look. "What is it, Hugh?"

"I came to talk with you after that fracas in the saloon this afternoon. I heard you."

Frankie glared at him. "Heard me what?"

"I think you know."

Frankie studied his former friend. "No, I have no idea. And neither have you." He smirked. "You ought to be relieved, though. At least now you know I never made love to your wife."

Barnet flared up and reached for Frankie.

"Why, Hugh, I never knew you cared," Frankie said in a simpering voice.

As Barnet pulled back his arm to smash Frankie in his face, Charles William suddenly stood next to them, his hand on Barnet's arm. "Begging your pardon, sir, but I would not do that were I you."

Barnet glared at the big colored man. "Do you know what this man is? What he does… with other men?" he demanded.

Charles William stood without replying.

Barnet turned back to Frankie. "You think you are immune, but you aren't. Somehow, someday you will make a mistake, and I will see you dragged off to jail like the dog you are. I swear I will." He spat at Frankie's feet, spun, and walked away down the promenade.

Frankie let out a deep breath. "That was rather unpleasant."

Charles William slipped out of his deferential pose. "Frankie, will you ever learn to be careful? You think the world is your teacup. It isn't. You have to try to be more circumspect."

Frankie did not bridle at his words. He frowned, but he nodded. "I know I went too far this time. But when Hugh was outside my door, I was in no position to be careful." He looked up at Charles William's grim expression and attempted to project a look of boyish ingenuousness.

The bigger man shook his head. He slipped back into his servile demeanor. "May I be of some service to you, Mr. Deramus?"

Frankie sighed. "Yes, please go to my suite and tell Mr. Stanley I was unable to join him. Tell him I will have a late supper brought when I am finished with tonight's bit of cards. Ask him… to wait there for me."

"Very good, sir" came the reply, but the look on Charles William's face showed he did not think it "very good" at all.

CHAPTER 7

Le Beau Soleil, that same day in June 1859

JOHNNY recognized the man who had intercepted Frankie on their way out of the dining hall. It was the man from the levee, the one whose wife had been flirting so blatantly with Frankie. Johnny's first reaction upon remembering the two women was angry jealousy. How dare they? Then he thought *they must not know about... Frankie's nature.* In fact, the only one who had given Johnny the impression of knowing anything about it was the fellow with the Irish name, the one who had fought in Mexico. The memory of that fellow, and of his striking good looks, made Johnny seethe with jealousy anew. He shook the sensation off. That was, he tried to.

He reached Frankie's stateroom door and wondered how he was to get in. He tried the door latch, and, surprised to find it unlocked, he pushed at the door and went in. Being in the sitting room alone felt strange. He looked around it, realizing he had not paid much attention before, when he had first come in after the fight. The spaciousness surprised him—the room was at least the size of two of the medium staterooms. He saw that Frankie's trousers, which he recalled had been left in the sitting room when they went to bed, were now gone. He had to sit down, so he went to the divan where Frankie had cleaned his face, but he was no less aroused there. He could remember vividly the feel of Frankie's cock in his mouth. He could feel the moment when his own climax came, seconds before Frankie filled his mouth with choking semen. He remembered the feel of Frankie's arms around him, comforting and caressing him as he sobbed.

The memory of his breakdown caused his growing tumescence to subside and made his face grow pale. He was as surprised by his overflow of tears as what he had done to Frankie. The sweetness of

Frankie's attention to his bruises, his solicitude for him, his handsome face so close, his warm body, and the smell of him as he leaned over Johnny. When Frankie had suddenly gone still and then leaned to put his lips to his, Johnny had not been able to stop himself. He wanted Frankie. He wanted *Frankie*. Just hours before he had concluded Frankie was not, in fact, what Lehrer had called him, a fairy. But he was. He was something anyway, something that had pushed Johnny over the edge. *How did Frankie do that?*

He glanced about the room, taking in the elegance of the furnishings, the very tastefulness of it. If he had thought about it at all, he would have predicted Frankie's rooms would run to the garishness of a bordello. He realized much of what he believed about such men, not just those who preferred other men but also gamblers, fops, the *demi-mondain*, New Orleans men in general for that matter, seemed to be turning out wrong. That made him think about other men he had known who were so inclined: Father Martin, Kurt Holtzmann, Rolf... himself?

That train of thought ended abruptly when he heard the tap at the door. "Frankie?" he called, excited and nervous.

"No, Mr. Stanley. I'm sorry to disturb you. It's Charles William."

"Oh," Johnny said disappointedly. "Come in."

The door latch turned, and the tall colored man entered. Johnny started to stand but thought better of it. He did not have to advertise his returned arousal, after all.

"No, sir, please don't rise. I came to give you a message from Mr. Deramus and to see if you would like something to drink or eat. You left your dinner early, I think?"

"Message? What message?"

Charles William cleared his throat. "Mr. Deramus extends his compliments, but regrets to say he shall not be able to join you after all. He has some business he must attend to. He invites you to join him in the saloon and has ordered a later supper for the two of you here in his rooms. He begs you to make yourself entirely at home and do whatever you wish, stay or join him."

Johnny frowned and bowed his head in disappointment. "Thank you."

Charles William hesitated, then said, "I'm sorry, Mr. Stanley. Aboard *Le Beau Soleil* Mr. Deramus's time is not his own. May I pour you a drink, get you a cigar or something to eat?"

Johnny shrugged. "Yes, I think I want a whiskey." As the manservant went to the sideboard, an idea struck Johnny. "Please, get yourself a drink as well. Stay and talk with me."

Charles William turned back and gave Johnny what for the entire world looked like an amused smile. "I thank you, sir. I must regretfully decline, however."

He set the glass of Frankie's excellent whiskey on the small round table where he had placed the bowl of warm water and towels earlier that day. He stood and waited.

Johnny gratefully took a sip of the whiskey and said, "I did not mean to be offensive. I am not accustomed to practices in the Southern states. We in Chicago are, um, more working class I'd say. There are no slaves that I have ever met, not in Chicago, that is."

"Do not worry, Mr. Stanley. I do not take offense easily. And yes, Mr. Deramus owns me. I am a slave."

Johnny asked, "I got the impression that Fra—Mr. Deramus does not agree with slavery."

Charles William cleared his throat. "That is true," he said hesitantly. "It is not as uncommon as one might suppose in the South. Especially in New Orleans."

"Please forgive me, but how did he... come by you? Did his parents...?"

Johnny saw the flicker of pain on the big man's face. "No, Mr. Deramus's father and mother both died when he was a boy, in one of the outbreaks of yellow fever. They sent him with my wife, Dominique, and me to the house on the shore of Lake Pontchartrain but stayed in the city themselves. There was no other family, so we more or less raised him ourselves."

"Oh, how terribly sad. How old was Fra—Mr. Deramus?"

"Nine years old."

Johnny sat looking at the man, who had resumed his passive demeanor. He hesitantly started, "How do you feel about... um... his... um... habits?"

Charles William looked down, frowning at Johnny's face. "I am in no position to judge Mr. Deramus."

Johnny stared openmouthed. "But isn't it a sin? To, um, lie with other men?"

Charles William appeared to be uncomfortable with the direction Johnny had taken. "Mr. Stanley, please…," he began.

Johnny was unrelenting. "Do you think a man can choose?"

Charles William responded, "Is there anything else, Mr. Stanley? May I retrieve anything from your stateroom? A change of clothing or your shaving kit perhaps?"

"No, no, I can do that. Maybe I will go and join him in the saloon." He stood. Extending his hand to the manservant, he said, "Thank you, Mr.… is it Albright?"

Charles William took his hand and shook it. "Charles William is satisfactory."

"May I ask you one more thing?" Johnny said, coloring slightly.

The manservant hesitated. "You can ask, sir."

Johnny nodded acknowledgement of the proviso. "Has Mr. Deramus ever had a… longstanding… um… friendship?" He wasn't sure if he was making himself clear.

The servant smiled quietly. "I can't answer that, Mr. Stanley. I won't betray his confidence. All I can say is that Mr. Deramus is a very good man, a kind man."

Johnny accepted the refusal graciously. "Yes, I know he is. Very good and very kind."

Charles William made a short bow. "Very good, sir," he said, smiling, and he shut the door behind him as he left.

Johnny stood where he was, unmoving. His mind was a whirlpool of thoughts and feelings. This was all so foreign to him. He had the same struggles with lust any young man would have, but how could it be directed not only at a man but a man like Frankie, a man who, with his supercilious looks and comments and his extravagant ways, he would normally dislike? "*Ein Schurke*" was what his papa would say. "A scoundrel, a rogue, a dog."

Johnny had felt liberated in Frankie's arms, but now doubt sank in. What if Frankie proved fickle? Then where would Johnny be? How would he manage his love life in the future? He suddenly felt terribly afraid. Was this really what he wanted? He supposed he could just enjoy the rest of the trip, then put it all behind him and go on as he always had. Perhaps this one fling would be enough and he could go on without another. Go on… lonely, unfulfilled, but safe.

He glanced at the bedchamber door. He thought to go in and look at the bed where Frankie had made such sweet love to him. But he decided against too much temptation. Instead, he took the decanter and glass and put them with the others. He went out the suite's door and down the promenade planning to go up the stairs to the saloon.

He smelled cigar smoke and stopped at the foot of the stairway. He looked toward a figure that stood with his back to Johnny, gazing out at the river and the shore as it slid by, the splash of the two side-wheels calming. He would know that form anywhere. Frankie. Frankie who was not detained with some business. Frankie who could have returned to his stateroom, and Johnny.

Instead of feeling abandoned, Johnny, in his tension, grasped for a chance to escape something he suddenly did not wish to face.

He turned and found his own stateroom down the same promenade. After retrieving his valise, he changed into his freshly cleaned clothing, packed the suit he had worn to dinner. Something like a quiet sob emerged from his chest. He shoved it down mercilessly, disallowing himself to think or feel anything. He simply wanted out, away. It was just too much for him, all of it.

Johnny heard the steamboat's whistle long and clear and realized *Le Beau Soleil* must be coming into some town. He had not formed an idea what he would do, but the clear, long tone made up his mind. He put on his topcoat and hat and picked up his valise.

As he reached for the door latch, the door swung in. His heart beat harder.

"Now where are you going, Mr. S?" his young roommate, Pardee, asked.

"Getting off the boat," Johnny answered in a clipped voice.

"But I thought you were going to Cairo?" The young man looked bemused.

"Changed my mind. Getting off here." He realized he had no idea where "here" was.

The fellow extended a hand. Johnny switched his valise to his left hand, accepted the hand, and shook it. "Well, Memphis is a helluva town. You make sure you spend a night or two, you hear?"

On the promenade, he gingerly glanced to see if he could get down the stairs to the main deck without Frankie seeing him. He felt both relieved and a little sad to see Frankie no longer there. He tugged his hat on tighter and dashed down the stairs.

Johnny was not the only passenger getting off at Memphis. Once on the wharf and looking about to see if any other steamboats were there, he noticed the fellow who had stopped Frankie on their way out of the grand cabin no more than an hour or so before. The man glared at him. As Johnny, his face set, passed by, the man muttered, "You'll burn in Hell, you sodomite!"

Johnny ducked his head, felt his face reddening, and hurried on.

ALMOST two months after his return to his government job in Chicago, Johnny received a much-handled envelope addressed to "Mr. John Stanley, Chicago." The stationery read "*Le Beau Soleil*" in elegant letters and showed a tiny gold sunburst. Looking around at the others in his office, he pocketed the envelope.

That night in his room, he drew out the envelope again and opened it. He instantly smelled Frankie's scent. With shaking fingers, he unfolded the single sheet of paper whose golden sunburst and lettering matched the envelope.

> I waited supper for you, but when you did not
> come, I went to bed. That young man who
> shared your stateroom told CW you
> disembarked at Memphis. I was sorry to hear
> that. I should have enjoyed being your

occasional friend, but I know you deserve better ones. I wish you joy of your life.

Your servant,

FD

Johnny folded the note again and started to slip it back into its envelope. Thinking better of it, he leaned to the fire in the grate and dropped first the envelope, and, after one last sniff of the paper, put the letter in as well.

PART II
ANTEBELLUM

CHAPTER 8

New Orleans, late January 1860

"MICK! Wait!"

Michael Murphy halted his ungainly progress up Canal Street when he heard the familiar voice. "Frankie! When did *Le Beau Soleil* get in? Aren't you a day late?"

"Two days, in fact. We had a very sad event on the way down from Cairo."

Michael frowned in fellow feeling. "Want to get a drink at the hotel?"

With Frankie's assent, they crossed Canal Street, avoiding horse carts and carriages, and made for the double doors of the St. Charles. Michael fell back to let Frankie show the way, either up to his rooms or into the bar. He kept still when he saw the latter was their destination. It seemed it was more often than not of late.

Frankie had his own table and headed straight for it. He waved two fingers to the bartender, who picked up two glasses and a bottle he took from under the bar, and met them as they were sitting. "*Merci beaucoup*, Pierre."

"So what was this terrible event that made you late?"

Frankie sighed. "It was at Louisville. You know I make it damned unattractive for slave brokers to transport coffles or even individual slaves on *Le Beau Soleil*. You also know why."

Michael accepted the glass of bourbon Frankie poured from the bottle that came from his private stock. "Well, besides your more high-toned views, you find it a messy, unpleasant, and disruptive cargo, so to speak."

"Precisely. But I can't actually refuse them. It's complicated, but once in a while a slave broker or owner is willing to pay the higher passage and cargo cost, and that's how it is." He looked around the saloon at the few other drinkers. His attention seemed to pass and come back to a single man sitting at the bar.

"So I take it you had to take some slaves aboard at Louisville?" Murphy prompted him.

Mick waited until Frankie, with apparent difficulty, turned his attention back to his story and went on. "It was actually at a tiny landing south of Louisville. I first knew something was amiss when I heard the wailing."

"Wailing?" Michael's asked, surprised. "Who was wailing?"

Frankie kept glancing across the room.

"Frankie, what's wrong?"

"What? Oh. Nothing. I just thought I saw...." He seemed to resolve to finish his story. "It was a man with a small group of slaves he wanted to bring on board. On the shore, a black man and three or four children were calling and crying to a woman who was screaming and crying herself. I generally try not to get involved with this slime, the owners and brokers I mean, but it was enough of an upset I felt I had to go down." He poured them both more whiskey. "The broker was angry that *Le Beau Soleil* has no place for chains to be fixed to the deck. That's another way I discourage transporting slaves and also Indians being relocated by railroad West from a port on the river against their will. I dealt with that fellow by acting like I don't speak English. The reason for the screaming was obvious. The woman was the wife and mother of the group on the shore. The bastard was breaking up a family."

"Oh God," Michael sympathized.

With yet another look at the man across the saloon, Frankie went on. "We had pulled away from the wharf when the woman, whose leg chain was off the coffle, suddenly got away from the broker's men and ran to the rail and jumped over. Everyone on the main deck and on shore was shrieking at the top of their lungs. I ran to the rail to see if I could snag the woman's skirts or something, but the chain on her leg was dragging her down. Then she...." Frankie stopped suddenly and he cast down his eyes. "She got caught up in the side-wheel. I screamed for the engineers to stop the boilers. But it was too late. She came up the other side, the chain caught in the paddles, and went around again. By the time the wheel stopped, what we retrieved didn't look much like a person anymore."

Michael looked around, then put his hand on Frankie's. "Good God, what a horrible thing. And with her man and children looking on." He shook his head. "How horrible."

Frankie looked up and over to the man at the bar again, his eyes haunted. "The bastard broker demanded I pay for the woman. It was my fault, you see, because I did not provide security for his cargo."

"What did you do?"

"I paid him. I had no choice."

"That took two days?" Michael shook his head.

"We had to wait for a part to fix the side-wheel."

Michael put his glass down hard on the table and made a disgusted noise. "Sweet Jesus!"

Frankie nodded grimly, then asked, "Will you excuse me a minute?" He set down his glass, left the table, and made his way to the blond man at the bar. Michael watched him.

"JOHNNY STANLEY?" Frankie said as he came to the man's side.

Johnny turned sharply, his eyes wide and face pale. "Fr-Frankie!" he stammered.

Frankie beamed at him. He grasped Johnny's hand. "Johnny, I can't say how glad I am to see you! Whatever are you doing here? Were you on *Le Beau Soleil*? I am sure I would have seen you."

Johnny looked around the saloon. He caught sight of Murphy and nodded to him as Michael saluted him with his glass. "I… I wasn't on your boat. I was on the *River Queen*." Johnny's voice was tight with reserve. "And what are you doing here?"

Frankie laughed. "I live here. No, I don't mean in New Orleans. Of course I live in the city. But I also live here, in this hotel, when it suits me. How glad I am to see you. Did you get my letter?"

Johnny frowned. "Letter?" he replied vaguely. "You wrote me a letter?" he asked, seeming to sidestep.

"Never mind. It's not important. Please come have a drink with us. You remember Michael Murphy, don't you?"

"No, I mean yes, I remember, but I can't. I have an appointment. I have to go."

Frankie sobered, looking hard into Johnny's face. He saw something like fear there but thought he also saw longing. He knew Johnny must have seen the longing in his own eyes as they gazed at each other. In a soft voice, he asked, "Are you staying at the hotel?"

Johnny did not answer. He thumped coins on the bar and grabbed his hat. He muttered, "Excuse me," and hurried out through the saloon doors. Frankie stood looking after him.

"That was the fellow you introduced me to on the levee, right?" Michael asked as Frankie rejoined him.

"Yes, Johnny Stanley. What an extraordinary thing." Frankie felt puzzled.

"What is?"

Frankie looked back and leaned in to speak in a low voice. "You remember what I told you about the fellow who stopped some asshole from attacking me?"

Michael's eyebrows shot up. "Yeah, the one who sobbed in your arms after he… well, you know?"

"*Oui*, that one."

Murphy looked at Frankie, a world-weary countenance of the old soldier deepening the lines around his mouth and eyes. "He doesn't look too happy to see you."

"No. Perhaps. I don't know."

JOHNNY heard three sharp raps at the door of his hotel room. Calling quietly, "Come in," he looked up from where he sat on his bed with his back to the headboard looking at some papers, and saw the door open and Frankie standing in the doorway looking at him.

"Johnny, may I please come in?"

Johnny saw the bouquet of flowers Frankie held in one fist, and sighed. "Yes, I suppose you can. You probably own the hotel anyway." After setting aside the papers, he threw his legs over the side of the bed. He stood and reached for his jacket, draped over a chair, and put it on. "Will you have a drink?"

Frankie shut the door behind him. He gazed at Johnny. "Well, yes, I will have whatever you have. May I sit?"

Smiling sardonically, Johnny asked, "You sure you want beer?"

Frankie looked at the tall glass of foaming amber liquid on Johnny's bed table. "Uh, no, thank you, I'll pass. Perhaps you have some wine? Or sherry?"

Johnny went to the chest of drawers and turned back. "No, but I have some whiskey in my hip flask." He lifted the silver-colored flask and shook it.

"Ah, *bien*, then I will have that, if I may."

He sat down abruptly on the chair by the door. With the flowers clutched in his hands and his hat off, and sitting stiffly, he looked like a lad come a-courtin'. When the thought struck Johnny, he paled.

"These are for you." Frankie stretched the flowers out to Johnny.

"What… what are those for?" Johnny asked, perplexed.

Frankie's face grew serious, pleading. "They are for you. Please take them. It's not easy to get that sort of thing this time of year, not even here. Please," he begged.

Johnny eyed him. "Just put them on the table there. I'll have the maid put them in water."

Johnny took a chair some space from Frankie's. His beer remained on the other side of the bed. "Here, take it," he said and leaned forward to hand Frankie the flask.

Frankie accepted the flask, putting his hand over Johnny's. Johnny froze. Frankie's eyes were riveted on his. "Johnny…." His name sounded like the soft respiration of a summer breeze.

Johnny stood up. He pulled his hand back from the flask, letting it slip to the floor where it tipped and spilled its contents on the rug. The smell of cheap whiskey filled the air. Johnny frowned at the spreading puddle. He looked back at Frankie and said, "No, Frankie. No. Not again."

Frankie leapt to his feet and took the few steps between them quickly, avoiding the flask where it lay on the rug. "Johnny, please. Hear me out." He pressed up to Johnny and put his arms around him. He leaned forward and nuzzled his face into Johnny's hair and ear. "Please. I've been so sorry about our parting. I know I handled it all quite clumsily. You must have been furious."

Johnny closed his eyes, not daring to breathe. Every part of his rigid body thrilled with the feel of Frankie's arms around him. It felt so right. It felt as if, had he died that moment, it would have been all right. "Frankie, no," he repeated. "It wasn't that."

"Can you ever forgive me, *mon ange*?"

"Please! Don't call me that. Leave me alone!" Johnny pleaded, turning his face as far away from Frankie's as he could, desperate to avoid a kiss.

Frankie dropped his arms and stepped back, looking stunned. "But… I thought…. You said…."

Johnny visibly shook. "I don't want this. Please leave." He attempted to turn a cold look on Frankie, but at the sight of the man's desolate face, he could not maintain it. "Damn it, Frankie, how can I make you understand?"

Frankie took some steps backward. He looked behind him for the chair by the door. "If I promise to stay right here and not come near you, can we just talk?" He looked back at Johnny, his dark eyes wide and desperate.

Johnny closed his own eyes, knowing he was about to make a mistake. "All right. But you must go when I tell you to. You promise? Can I even trust you?"

Frankie winced. He nodded and sat on the chair.

Johnny pulled the other chair out of Frankie's reach before sitting.

They sat in silence for several minutes. Johnny sat straight and stiff in his chair, trying not to look at Frankie, who for his part leaned forward, his elbows on his knees, his hands fidgeting with each other, and his eyes on the floor.

Finally, Frankie sat up. "Why did you leave like that?"

Johnny almost shot back, I just told you. I changed my mind.

"Why no message? I know you and Charles William talked… wait, did he say something that made you leave—"

"No!" Johnny interrupted. "No, he did not. I made up my own mind."

Frankie nodded. In a small voice, he asked, "Why?"

Johnny grew impatient. "I told you. I don't want this."

"You don't want this, what?" Frankie's eyes grew narrow and sparked. "You don't want my lips on yours? You don't want my arms around—"

"Frankie!" Johnny's voice was so sharp Frankie started. "If you talk like that, I will be forced to ask you to leave."

Frankie subsided. Another silence grew.

"This may be the right life for you. I don't know. I don't know how it can be," Johnny said at long last. "But it is not for me. I won't deny I loved… every second we spent together… but that cannot be how I live. It's not right… for me."

Frankie gazed at him, his mouth slack. He started to speak, then shook his head. He ran a finger along his black mustache. "I am so sorry."

Johnny shot, "You don't have to apologize—"

Frankie glared. "I'm not apologizing. I mean I am sorry you don't want me. Because I want you so much it hurts." He stood abruptly, and Johnny flinched back. "I thought after you left I would just go on as I had, with my little on-board dalliances, nothing that did anything more than—" He sought for the right words. "—slake my thirst. But that is not how it was. Oh, I had dalliances, but there was something missing. I couldn't understand it…." He looked hopelessly at Johnny, and Johnny closed his eyes to block out Frankie's pained expression. "For weeks when I woke up, I turned my head to see yours on the pillow beside me." He paused. "I thought… I thought I would never see you again."

Frankie turned and went to the door. He put his hand on the knob.

Johnny's eyes flew open. "Frankie!"

Frankie did not turn. "Yes?"

"I am sorry."

Frankie pulled the door toward him, went out, and shut it behind him. The thick corridor carpet prevented Johnny from hearing his retreating footsteps.

Johnny did not move for some time. He felt chilled to the bone. He finally stood and started to pace the short distance from one wall of his room to another. He kept his attention turned inward, not looking at the flowers on the table, nor at the flask on the rug, and certainly not at the chair where Frankie had sat. When the activity started to warm him and loosen his joints, something approaching coherent thought returned to his mind.

He had thought Frankie had at best dallied with him on *Le Beau Soleil*. Seeing him afterward, standing alone on the promenade—when Charles William had told Johnny he was occupied—had simply confirmed that conclusion. He honestly did not know what he would have done had he not seen Frankie there. Would he have gone to the saloon to watch him play and then gone back to his stateroom for that late supper and more lovemaking? He had worked so hard to push the events of that day out of his mind that, though the memories were coming back as starkly as if they had just happened, he could not decide.

Now his efforts to avoid Frankie, which had been as simple as taking a different riverboat on his government trips to the cities of the Mississippi River, had failed. He had not realized the St. Charles was Frankie's home on land. It did not even occur to him. Why would Frankie not live on his boat or have a family home in the city?

Johnny found himself looking up at the ceiling of his room. Frankie was not the hotel's owner, of course. Johnny had met that fellow on a past occasion and chatted with him about the fire that had destroyed the earlier building in '51. He had admired the spirit that had made the man and his investors rebuild so quickly. But Frankie no doubt had a suite on the topmost floor of lodgings. Luck had kept the two men from running into each other somewhere in the grand hotel.

Johnny let his eyes fall on the flowers Frankie had brought him. He could not help but smile. A man bringing flowers to another man. How characteristic of what Johnny believed about Frankie. Only François Deramus would behave in such a courtly way. It was more than courtly, though. It was… sweet. Charles William had been right. Frankie was a good, a kind man. A deviant, but kind.

That was the other side of what had happened in Frankie's bed. Johnny had never experienced such tenderness from another human being. Not even his mother, a practical German woman, had stroked him and spoken so lovingly to him. In spite of how awful Johnny had been to him, Frankie took care of him, reassured him, and made him feel wanted. The release he had felt with the sex had been frightening and wonderful, but it had been the caressing that had worked most of the magic on him. How he longed for that sort of bond.

He wished he could have that but avoid the temptation of Frankie's body. Could he manage that? Would Frankie be willing? Could they be companions—friends—as Frankie obviously was with Murphy, but restrain themselves from that other thing?

A thought struck Johnny. Was it possible Frankie might come to value closeness of friendship so much he could wean himself from the sin? Could it be Johnny could paradoxically be his deliverance? He certainly owed Frankie an explanation. He liked Frankie immensely. Perhaps he could be as good to Frankie, as he had been to Johnny.

FRANKIE sat within the light of one gas jet in his dressing gown, nursing a rather large brandy, when he heard the knock at his door. He frowned. The hotel staff knew better than to bother him in the evening. It could be an emergency. He glanced at the tall curtained window as if he could see *Le Beau Soleil* through the thick velvet. He put down his drink, stepped to the door, and unlocked it. Expecting a liveried hotel employee, he instead found himself looking into sheepish, pale blue eyes.

"Johnny!" He stood rooted to the spot, his eyes wide and his mouth open.

"Aren't you going to invite me in?" Johnny had a rather foolish grin on his face.

Frankie stared for another moment, then grabbed Johnny's arm and drew him in. Shutting the door, he held Johnny's upper arms in his hands and gazed at him unblinking. "What is it, Johnny?"

"I thought I owed you an explanation. I came to give it. I feel terrible that I hurt you. I didn't... I want to...."

Frankie threw his arms around Johnny. "I do too, so very much." He put his lips to Johnny's. He felt him jerk but did not want to end the kiss. He held him tighter, opened his mouth and pressed his tongue between Johnny's lips. He heard Johnny moan, then rejoiced when he relaxed and opened his mouth to Frankie's tongue....

When they pulled their faces away, they did not speak: there was no need. Frankie knew Johnny wanted him as much as he wanted Johnny. When they broke the kiss, he began to nuzzle Johnny's neck, lifting his arms so he could slide his hands under Johnny's jacket and press his palms against Johnny's chest.

Johnny's hands went to his jacket buttons. He loosed them and let Frankie push the jacket off his shoulders. It dropped to the floor, quickly joined by Frankie's dressing gown, whose belt Johnny had untied. One by one the rest came off. Waistcoats, shirts, undershirts, came off and fell on the floor. In the process, their hands had gone to suspenders and slid them off shoulders so they hung down from where they were buttoned to trousers. Johnny raised his face to the ceiling as Frankie devoured his chin, neck, and his quickly bared chest. He gasped as Frankie lightly nipped his nipples, first one and then the other.

Frankie fumbled with Johnny's fly buttons. "I'm too excited. I can't do this."

Johnny's momentary look of dismay cleared when he seemed to realize Frankie meant he could not undo the buttons. He said, "Let's just do our own." They stepped as little apart as they had to in order to reach between themselves to unbutton flies. They let their own trousers fall, then pushed down their drawers. Johnny's focus was riveted on Frankie's cock, which stood engorged and eager.

Naked, the two men reached again for each other and feasted on the feel and taste of skin, mouths, and ears. Their rigid cocks dueled as they moved to clasp and squeeze different parts of each other's bodies. As they moaned, sighed, and whispered each other's names, Johnny started to push Frankie backward. "Where is the bedroom?" he managed to ask.

Frankie reached and grabbed his hand, and turned to draw Johnny after him. "In here." He pulled Johnny across the room and through a door with an ornately carved frame. Johnny looked around the warm, dimly lit room—lit by a fireplace—just before Frankie had him sprawled across his huge canopied bed.

Frankie crawled onto the bed and over him, lying so he covered Johnny completely. He kissed and licked and sucked everything he could reach, and Johnny started to laugh with delight and put his arms around Frankie's neck—forcing Frankie to bring his face to Johnny's. They devoured each other's mouths.

THE smell of Frankie's body intoxicated Johnny. There was a spicy scent, something he obviously daubed on himself, but it was the warmth of his skin, the musky smell of his excitement that made Johnny's head reel.

Johnny felt Frankie grind his cock against Johnny's groin. The heat made Johnny buck, and he used his boxer's strength to push Frankie off him, and turn him onto his back.

Johnny gazed along Frankie's slender but muscular torso to his taut thighs and slid his palm down the middle of Frankie's chest and belly. He felt the muscles ripple under his hand. Letting his fingers fork into the black curly hair at the root of Frankie's cock, Johnny had the tip of his tongue between his teeth with concentration. He took in a sharp breath when he touched the hard tumescence of Frankie, and reached to take hold of the prick he had had in his mouth months ago. He thought he could taste Frankie's semen even now.

Johnny looked up into Frankie's eyes, marveling at the mixture of lust and warmth in them. He lay along the man, naked bodies so close. He took Frankie's face into his hands and kissed him almost chastely, their lips staying closed as they breathed in each other's breath. The kiss, so slow and delightful, was like savoring a fine wine. Frankie seemed to understand what the kiss meant, the sharing of sweet ardor rather than a frenzied plundering of each other's mouths. Johnny heard Frankie moan deeply and softly, and felt his heart swell, as did his prick. It occurred to him the two—the heart and the cock—were in concert, not at all disconnected or competing, but in a sense yoked together in making love to this lovely man he held.

With both his heart and his body, Johnny made love to Frankie.

"*Mon ange*," Frankie murmured afterward, as their gasps for breath subsided and they settled into each other's arms.

Johnny felt the warmth when Frankie pulled him into his arms and coaxed his head onto his shoulder. "Frankie," he sighed. He relaxed into the embrace without reservation.

CHAPTER 9

New Orleans, late January 1860

WITH Frankie lying with his back to him, wrapped in his arms, Johnny felt as warm and at home as he ever had in his life. The fireplace still burned on its low setting, and he could see where its light touched Frankie's cheek, ear and shoulder. Johnny kissed that shoulder and heard Frankie purr.

"Are you married?"

Johnny started at the sudden question. "No, of course not. Would I do this if I were married?"

He felt Frankie lift his shoulder in a shrug. "No need to be offended. It happens all the time."

Johnny had nothing to say about that. He supposed Frankie must be telling the truth, but he did not want any details from Frankie's own experience.

"I'm glad," Frankie said.

"That I am not married?"

"*Oui, exactement.* I want you all to myself."

Johnny smiled wryly. He did not want to ask if Frankie planned to be his alone. He did not think that sort of promise was one Frankie could keep, so he would not ask it. Instead he said, "I did not know you lived in a hotel."

Frankie rolled onto his back. "Many people in New Orleans live in hotels. Do they not in Chicago?"

Johnny shook his head. He traced the line of Frankie's jaw with his free hand. "I just thought you either lived on *Le Beau Soleil* or had a family home."

Frankie smiled impishly. In a drawl without a hint of his Creole accent he joked, "Welcome to the Deramus Plantation, suh."

Johnny eyed him for sarcasm, then concluded sarcasm was precisely what was intended. "But Charles William said you had houses here and on Lake Pontchartrain."

"We did. I sold them to raise money to buy and refurbish *Le Beau Soleil*. I make enough now that I can stay in the hotel when I want to get away from the damp."

Johnny leaned to touch his lips to Frankie's chest. He felt Frankie's hand on his hair. "Do you have any partners?"

Frankie smiled. "If you mean am I the sole owner of *Le Beau Soleil*, I am now. I had a partner, a merchant who almost lost me the *Soleil*, but I bought his share back and had Mick run him out of town."

Johnny lifted his head at the mention of Mick. "Mick? You mean Michael Murphy? How long have you known him?" He rested his chin on Frankie's shoulder so he could see his face.

"Just a few years. We met over that business with Smythe, my old partner. I hired him to find out if and what the man was up to."

Johnny hesitated. Despite his earlier resolve, he asked, "So you and Michael are just…?"

Frankie put a finger to Johnny's lips. "We are the only two people in this bed."

Johnny nodded against his shoulder. He was right, of course. Why make yourself mad with wondering? But he could not help throwing in, "Have you ever been with a woman?" He flinched when he felt Frankie's light slap on his head.

"You are a naughty boy. I may have to paddle your bum. But no, I never have. Have never wanted to. You?"

Johnny felt shy. "No. I have never been with anyone. Just you."

Frankie raised his head from the pillow to look at him, a bemused smile on his lips. "*Non, vraiment*? Only me?"

Johnny nodded.

Frankie gathered Johnny in his arms and held him tight. "I remember you said you were a virgin. I thought you just meant I was your first man. You poor sweetheart. Well, I am going to help you make up for lost time." He shifted onto his side and leaned in for a soulful kiss.

AT BREAKFAST in the St. Charles Hotel's restaurant, they found their schedules were pretty much the same. It took little persuading for Frankie to get Johnny to agree to change his return booking to *Le Beau Soleil*. When Johnny said the fare for the other boat was less, Frankie waved the concern away. "You don't have to pay to travel in my stateroom. You will be my guest."

Johnny shifted in his chair uncomfortably. "The Department pays for my travel. They won't understand why it suddenly doesn't cost them anything."

Frankie regarded him seriously. "We will have to figure something out about that. I suppose you can book passage on one of the other riverboats and just travel with me."

Johnny shrugged. "I don't know."

"Well, never mind for now. I have a big beautiful city I want to show you in the couple of days we have here. Too bad it's not Mardi Gras."

LATER, as they rode in a carriage around the city, Johnny asked, "Does Charles William stay on *Le Beau Soleil*?"

Frankie tapped on the roof of the carriage to tell the driver to stop. "No, he and Tante Dominique live in an old outbuilding of my family's city house. I negotiated that with the new owner. Now look at this! This is the Presbytere. It used to belong to the diocese, but they sold it a few years ago to the city. Isn't it magnificent? Let me show you around."

Johnny climbed out after him onto the pavement in front of a large building. "I would like to meet Dominique."

"You would? *Très bien*, we will make sure you do."

Frankie led him to the elegant building, whose front was a series of open arches leading to a gallery on the ground floor. "This was built to match the building on the other side of the cathedral, and was to be a residence for Capuchin monks. They never lived here though. You see that the windows above this gallery echo the arches. That's a mansard roof," he explained. "It slopes to the main roof and has dormer windows. The little dome at the top is beautiful, *non*?" Seeing Johnny's neck craned to look at the building's splendid architecture, Frankie's smile widened.

Johnny shaded his eyes to see the dome more clearly. "Beautiful."

"*Oui*, beautiful," Frankie echoed, but he was looking at Johnny's pale blue eyes.

They were tired and hungry by the time Frankie took Johnny down a residential lane lined with huge houses—each with a walled courtyard. Oaks and boxwoods provided shade. They went down the drive of one mansion. "This is where I grew up. I mean, except when I was at the lake house."

Johnny surveyed the huge old house. "This was your house?" he said incredulously.

Frankie nodded. "Come, the Albrights' place is around here. We can come at it directly from the lane, but because they are colored, they have to come in from the alleyway."

The little place, more than a shed but less than a house, was neat and clean, and it had what looked like well-cared-for flowerbeds that would no doubt be full of color in the spring. Neat curtains hung in the small windows. Flat stones paved the path to the front door. Frankie skipped up to the door and opened it.

"Dominique! Charles William!" he called into the unlit kitchen.

"François, *mon cher*!" came a deep, rich feminine voice from the door where a neatly dressed colored woman stood beaming. Frankie dashed up to her and put his arms around her, kissing her on the cheek.

"Step back now, boy. Let me look at you. Is that good-for-nothing husband of mine making sure you take care of yourself?"

"Who are you calling 'good for nothing,' woman?" Charles William came up behind her. Johnny saw at once that he was dressed for a nice quiet evening at home and had been reading the newspaper in his hand. "Mr. Stanley!" came Charles William's welcome. He stepped beyond his wife and Frankie and shook Johnny's hand warmly, his face lit with a genuine smile. "Dominique, come here and meet Mr. John C. Stanley."

Johnny shyly accepted Dominique's profuse welcome. He glanced up to see Frankie's face: beaming, proud. Charles William saw the expression as well and looked pleased.

Ushering them into a little parlor, the Albrights fetched coffee and brandy and some slices of a huge iced loaf.

"That's a King cake," Frankie started to explain.

"Yes, *Dreikönigskuchen...*," Johnny said, then blanched. That was the German word for the tradition.

"What is that?" Dominique asked.

Johnny stammered, "Ah, um, something a German friend of mine has with his family. I had it once when they invited me to dinner. I think it means 'three kings cake.'"

Frankie gave Johnny a curious look. "I bet the bean is long gone," he said, returning to the subject. "Wait a minute, isn't it a little early for King cake?" He looked around at Charles William and Dominique.

Dominique put her hand on Charles William's where it lay on her shoulder and looked up to where he stood behind her. "It was Three Kings' Night Sunday before last. I suppose you are going to tell me that you did not go to mass wherever you were."

Frankie quickly changed the subject. "Say, what day is Mardi Gras this year?"

Charles William answered, "Well, I think it's February 21." He looked down where a tight-lipped Dominique eyed him.

Frankie turned back to Johnny. "Can you be in New Orleans then?"

As Johnny mentally calculated his schedule, Frankie interrupted, sounding vexed. "*Merde, Le Beau Soleil* won't even be here then. We will do something on board though. I hope you can be there, Johnny."

"I don't know," Johnny said.

"Dominique, why don't you go find your Mardi Gras mask from last year to show Mr. Stanley," Charles William urged.

The woman looked at her husband. "Now, he doesn't want to see that," she protested.

Picking up on his manservant's purpose, Frankie affirmed, "Come now, Tante Dominique. I'd like to see it again as well."

"Well, all right," she said reluctantly, but with a pleased look on her face.

When she stepped out of the room, Charles William said in a soft voice, "Mr. Stanley, I am so glad to see you here with our François."

Frankie answered the unspoken question, "We ran into each other at the hotel. *Heureuse* chance."

Johnny guessed the woman was ignorant of something. He blushed. "Mr. Albright, I know that you are aware of the time I spent with Mr. Deramus on the boat. But does your wife know?"

Frankie replied, "No, Tante Dominique doesn't know about my… choice of partners."

Johnny frowned inwardly at the plural. He nodded and the other two men seemed satisfied.

A rustle of hooped skirts heralded Dominique's return with an elaborate eye mask on a lorgnette, decked with colorful feathers and glass beads. "I made it myself," Dominique admitted proudly.

"THEY are wonderful people," Johnny said of the Albrights. He noticed Frankie was looking curiously at him. "What?"

Frankie shook his head. "Nothing. I just thought you seemed embarrassed when we were talking about the King cake."

Johnny's walls went up. In a tight voice he said, "I have no idea what you are talking about." Seeing Frankie's raised brows, he went on in a more animated tone, "Where are you taking me now? I am exhausted."

Frankie leaned to whisper in his ear, "To bed." Aloud he added, "And then I will take you to Le Coq Rouge for a late supper with Mme. Antoinette."

"I definitely like the idea of bed…." Johnny was not so sure about seeing the madam again. "Frankie, may I ask you to do something for me?"

Frankie grinned. "Anything!"

"I want to spend the whole evening alone with you. I am not ready for bordellos and Mardi Gras and late suppers in public."

Frankie's eyes softened. He took Johnny's hand where it lay under the carriage blanket. "We have all the time in the world for the world. Let's spend as much time alone as we can. Who knows what the morrow may bring," he said tenderly.

AT SUPPER the next day, Frankie and Johnny sat at a corner table in a small, dark, intimate restaurant on Lafayette.

A hostile voice startled them as they laughed over a funny story Frankie had just told of his day. "So I see you two are together again."

Frankie's voice and face were blank as he looked up at Hugh Barnet. "Hello, Hugh. You know Mr. Stanley?"

Hugh leered at Johnny. "Yes, we exchanged pleasantries in Memphis."

Frankie frowned. He glanced at Johnny and found him red-faced and looking at his hands. Frankie's gaze moved back to Hugh. "What sort of pleasantries?"

"Forget it, Frankie," Johnny asked very quietly.

"Maybe you can forget it. I cannot. I am here with my wife and our dinner guests. I do not relish having them exposed to your sort."

Johnny's hand shot out to restrain Frankie, grabbing his jacket sleeve. Frankie shot him a sharp look, then said to Hugh, "Then since we were here first, I suggest you leave."

"Frankie," Johnny pleaded. "Let's just go. We're finished anyway."

Hugh smirked. "Yes, and I am sure you can think of other ways to occupy your time."

Frankie tensed again. Johnny stood and grabbed his arm and forced him out of his chair. "Let's go."

"What was that about Memphis?" Frankie asked when he and Johnny were on the pavement outside the restaurant.

"Oh, nothing. We just ran into each other on the wharf, when we got off the boat at the same time."

Frankie took Johnny's arms and stared into his face. "Johnny, I don't like this prevarication. If we are to be... friends, I want honesty between us."

Johnny's eyes flashed. "Well, I don't. I am afraid of what I will learn about you. Now get your hands off me."

Frankie was stunned to speechlessness. He dropped his arms to his side.

Johnny muttered, "I'm going back to my room. I have packing to do." He walked away toward the hotel.

"Johnny, please!"

Frankie's voice sounded forlorn, even to his ear, and Johnny turned and called to him, "Well, come along. You have packing to do too."

FRANKIE fairly bubbled with happiness escorting Johnny onto his beloved *Le Beau Soleil* and up to his stateroom. He could not stop thinking of the joy of having both his lovers at once, Johnny and the riverboat.

It brought him up short then when Johnny balked at boldly walking into his stateroom, valise in hand. "What's wrong? Did you forget something at the hotel?"

Johnny looked about for anyone who could overhear. Charles William was the only person within earshot, and he carefully averted his eyes. "You mean for me to stay with you in your rooms?" he hissed in Frankie's ear.

"*Mais oui*! Do you not want to?" Frankie caught his manservant's raised eyebrow and peered at him quizzically.

Johnny looked around once more and whispered, "If I walk into your rooms carrying my luggage, it will be obvious." When Frankie did not respond, Johnny explained. "Maybe you don't care if all the world sees, but I do."

Frankie stared another moment. "I see. What should we do?" He looked at Johnny, then to Charles William.

The latter made a quick bow. "If I may suggest, perhaps Mr. Stanley would like a stateroom of his own? From which he might visit you in yours from time to time."

Shaking his head uncertainly, Frankie said, "I will have to see if we have any spare staterooms." Another thought struck him. "But if

Johnny has a roommate, won't they notice he never sleeps in his bed?" Worried, he whispered to Johnny, "You would never want to sleep in your own bed, would you, *mon ange*?"

Johnny winced. "Don't call me that where others can hear."

Frankie's tender smile, which he'd meant to be endearing, seemed to infuriate Johnny. "I am sorry. Mr. Stanley," he added with a wicked wink.

"I may be able to arrange something, sir," Charles William offered. "In the meantime, I will take your case into your bedchamber and carry Mr. Stanley's with me. Perhaps you would like to retire to the saloon, Mr. Deramus?"

Charles William met them twenty minutes later in the Texas deck saloon. "I have made arrangements for Mr. Stanley to have a second-class stateroom but without a roommate, Mr. Deramus," he said quietly in Frankie's ear as he bowed.

"*Très bien*! Was there a completely unoccupied stateroom?" Frankie asked, grinning.

Charles William shook his head. "No, sir. But we did have a cancellation for one of the shared first-class staterooms and gave the second-class passenger that spot. He was, if I may so characterize him, very pleased."

Johnny's furrowed brow smoothed. "That's an excellent solution. Thank you, Mr. Albright. My valise is in there?"

"Yes, Mr. Stanley. I took the liberty to unpack for you and will brush down your jackets."

Solicitously Frankie asked, keeping his voice down out of consideration for Johnny, "Do you need anything from it when we go to my rooms now?"

Johnny frowned, but shook his head. "No, but let's not go in at the same time. You go and I will follow in a few minutes."

Frankie schooled his face not to show how ridiculous this all seemed to him. "Good plan." He looked up at Charles William, but the older man's expression remained carefully blank.

Frankie made his way to his rooms, frequently stopping to speak with passengers and staff. He was so delayed that Johnny came around the front of the hurricane deck promenade just as Frankie reached his own door from the opposite direction. Johnny muttered, "Damn," while Frankie smiled.

"I was delayed," he said in a sheepish tone.

Once in the sitting room with the stateroom door firmly shut and locked behind them, however, Frankie wasted no time. "Oh God, how I want you!" He took Johnny into his arms and, holding the back of his head with one palm, kissed him. When Johnny kissed back very enthusiastically, Frankie relaxed. They were back on familiar ground.

As their lips parted, Johnny gave Frankie a look of such ardor it stole Frankie's breath away. "These past few days... together," Johnny said, "have been like nothing I have ever experienced. Making... love... with you, but also all the affectionate attention you have showered on me... were like living in a dream. I imagine that soon I will wake up and find it was all just a wish fulfilled. Until then I will simply bask in the sunlight that is Frankie Deramus."

Frankie gazed into Johnny's face, drinking in every feature, but lighting at last on his shining blue eyes. "Oh Johnny..." was all he could say. He tightened his arms around Johnny and said all he felt in another deep kiss.

Frankie reveled in Johnny's enthusiastic response. *I hope neither of us ever awakes from this.*

As Frankie backed them to the bedchamber door, he said, "I don't have to make an appearance until midday. Let's use the time to best advantage." He already had Johnny's coat off and was working on his waistcoat.

JOHNNY sat stiffly in his chair at supper while Frankie made the rounds of passengers he knew by sight. He was in a quandary. He wanted nothing in the world more than to be with Frankie, but once in the public eye, he felt under scrutiny. No actually seemed to notice Johnny, though the trickle of other passengers at Frankie's table seemed to feel discomfited by Johnny's clipped, nervous responses to their polite queries. He knew he would have to get used to feeling exposed if he planned to travel on *Le Beau Soleil* in the future.

That was his quandary. As long as he remained in Frankie's company, Johnny could not happily be parted from him. He avoided examining those feelings by worrying about what it would be like to leave the boat at Cairo, as he must, and return to Chicago. Would the attachment dissipate then? Would he just go back to his government position and solitary existence? Would it be like the six months he spent between those heady days after he and Frankie had...? Would it be even harder to keep his mind on work and daily life than it had been? True, it had gotten easier as time went by to shove the memories to where they could be—almost—ignored, though his trips down river and back on other steamboats always refreshed his longing.

He worried as well that Frankie's damnable carelessness would expose them. Barnet's censure quite unnerved him. How did the man even know? Was it that easy to see? Frankie seemed unable or perhaps unwilling to be discreet, but didn't he understand how much they had to lose? How much he had to lose if their relationship was ever spoken of in the Department? The best he could hope for was scandal and dismissal. The worst... it did not bear thinking about.

Frankie came back, beaming at him, then greeted the others at his table and introduced him as if he was some prize hog Frankie was so proud of. *Madame, monsieur, may I present my magnificent pig? He took first place at the agricultural exhibition.* Johnny extended his hand to be shaken and to lift ladies' hands to his lips to kiss, all the while aware Frankie stood there, smiling. *What can these people be thinking of it?*

Frankie was no help, one time introducing him to a senator as "my particular friend, Mr. Stanley of the Department of the Treasury."

That no one seemed the least concerned finally helped Johnny relax.

When they were alone, the best chance Johnny had for talking with Frankie about it was after they made love and lay in bed in the glow of spent lust.

"Frankie, I have to ask you something," he began the last night of the trip north.

"*Oui, mon ange?*" came the sleepy response.

"Aren't you afraid... of what could happen to you?"

Frankie paused, and then his voice sounded more awake. "What could happen to me? I don't understand."

"Well, if someone found out about... you know."

Frankie got up on his elbow instantly and looked down into Johnny's face, frowning. "About... my... predilections?"

"Yes, that."

Frankie shrugged. "No, I am not worried."

Johnny looked at him incredulously. "Not... worried? But... it's against the law!"

Frankie shrugged again. "Lots of things are against the law. Prostitution, bribery, kickbacks, bigamy...."

Johnny persisted, "And people who break those laws get caught and punished."

"Not very often."

Johnny was speechless for a moment. He decided to get to the heart of the matter. "You don't worry that someone like Barnet will expose us, and we will be arrested and thrown into prison for the rest of our lives at hard labor? If we live that long." His eyes sparked.

"Now, wait, wait! I am not what you call terribly discreet, but here I lie, with you, not incarcerated—and not dead, I might add...." He leaned to nibble on Johnny's ear.

"Stop that! I'm serious."

"So am I. You have resurrected me."

Frankie's long-fingered hand sliding down Johnny's belly started some awakening of its own. "I said stop that!"

Frankie pulled back. "All right." He cleared his throat. "In my experience people are only punished for so-called criminal behavior if—"

"They get caught, I know. With you that's not much comfort."

Frankie retorted impatiently, "That is not what I was going to say. I was going to say 'if they have something the accuser wants,' and I should go on to say 'have any hope of getting it if they discredit you.' I am filthy rich, my friend, and I have big pockets, and every politician and city official in Louisiana has his hands in them. I am popular. Even someone as prominent as Barnet has no hope of getting me arrested, no less tried and punished. I know a few of his own—and Julienne's—secrets as well." He laughed derisively. "It would take nothing less than a war to ruin me."

"Well, what about me, Frankie? I'm not 'filthy rich,' as you put it, and I have little influence."

"You have plenty of influence with me…." Frankie started back on Johnny's ear.

"Would you stop that? I'm afraid, Frankie. Don't you care?"

Frankie pulled away, looking startled. "Of course I care. It frightens me how much I care. I'll keep you from harm, *mon ange*. I promise. I will try to be more discreet, for your sake."

Johnny's face softened at Frankie's genuine concern. He lifted a hand and ran a finger down the stubble on Frankie's jaw. "Thank you, Frankie."

Frankie had that wicked smirk again, however. He reached under the covers and took hold of Johnny's stiffening cock. "Besides, how could anyone ever think ill of such a fine upstanding—ow!" He flinched from the light slap to his head.

Johnny pulled his face down and kissed him.

JOHNNY turned back as he walked to the railroad station in Cairo and saw Frankie standing in front of the pilothouse on the top deck of *Le Beau Soleil*. He raised his hand to wave. He colored deeply when he saw Frankie blow him a kiss. He would miss Frankie Deramus terribly.

CHAPTER 10

Chicago, late March 1860

"STANLEY! The director wants to see you."

In his Chicago office, Johnny looked up from the reports he had been studying on efforts to consolidate railroad lines. "Thank you, Simons. Please tell the director I will be in immediately." He inked his pen and made a note on a piece of paper, stood up from his desk, and shrugged his coat more evenly on his shoulders.

"Yes, Mr. Director, you wanted me?" he asked, coming into the big office that had a view of Lake Michigan. Dirty snow covered the streets now, it being late March of a particularly cold winter.

The older man, balding and bespectacled, lifted a sheet of paper that had been folded to fit in an envelope. "I don't know if you have anything to do with this, but if you do, the government has to thank you."

Johnny smiled uncertainly and inquired, "Sir?"

"It's from a Mr.... um, François Deramus." He pronounced Frankie's name "Fran Koyz." "Owns a riverboat, I take it. It was passed along through the department in Washington."

"From D-Deramus, you say?" Johnny's heart started to thud, his face went pale, and he had to put a hand on the back of the chair that faced the desk to keep his balance.

The director noticed his hand on the back of the chair. "Yes, please, do sit down. The man is most patriotic. He has set a discounted fare for any government employee who takes his boat...." He lifted his spectacles to read the name. "Le Boo So-lale...." He looked questioningly at Johnny.

"*Le Beau Soleil*, sir. It's French for the beautiful sun."

"Ah, yes. So you do know it? What did you do to butter up this Deramus fellow?"

Johnny's pale face went beet red. "N-nothing, sir. I barely have met the man."

"Well, he says, and I quote, 'In recognition of the hard and conscientious efforts the Department of the Treasury in particular to improve transportation in the Mississippi River Valley.' Extraordinarily patriotic of him."

Johnny smiled thinly and nodded. "Indeed, sir. And this is for our department only?"

"No, no," the director's voice boomed out. "All government departments! Granted, we are among the only ones who travel up and down the river on a regular basis, but if you had any idea how much this will save us in travel expenses…."

It had been two months since Johnny had cringed at Frankie's good-bye gesture from the top deck of the riverboat. His guts had been tied up in knots trying to figure out how he would finagle to book passage on one of the most expensive of the "best boats" on the river for his upcoming trip. Damn Frankie if he did not know how to untie his guts and tie them back up again, almost in the same motion.

"So I hope when you go on Le Boo Beau Sol… you will make a point of seeking out this French fellow and thank him for us. I wonder if there is anything we should do, a thank you gift of some kind…." The director looked to Johnny for inspiration.

"Sir, I don't think that will be necessary. In fact, we should be careful not to look like we…." Johnny trailed off.

The director's eyebrows went up sharply. "Good heavens, how right you are, Stanley. No sense making it look like some sort of payoff. Can't thank you enough." He stood and shook Johnny's hand.

Leaving the director's office a few minutes later, Johnny could not help but grin. He had to hand it to Frankie. He was a clever bastard. Just so long as he didn't clever them both into prison cells.

JOHNNY grinned as he came down the wharf in Cairo and saw Frankie standing at the top of the gangway fairly dancing with his own joy at seeing him.

They shook hands, Frankie holding onto Johnny's a second or two longer than was customary. Johnny gave him a wry smile. "You sure know how to manipulate the government," he said cheerfully.

"It was nothing. Just a word in our congressman's ear and…." He made a gesture of dismissal.

"Hello, Mr. Stanley, welcome aboard." Charles William looked almost as glad to see Johnny as Frankie did. He reached for Johnny's valise. "Come this way, sir."

"Hello, Mr. Albright." Johnny smiled happily.

"Wait until you see what I've done for you." Frankie nearly laughed with pleasure.

"Oh dear. Frankie, what have you done?"

Frankie took Johnny's arm and led him up the grand staircase, following Charles William. He did not appear to notice how stiff Johnny's arm had become. On the other hand, Johnny did not pull it away.

They went up to the hurricane deck and around to the starboard side promenade, not down the port promenade to Frankie's stateroom—but they did go almost the entire length of *Le Beau Soleil*. They stopped short of the end of the promenade, and Charles William took a key from his pocket and opened the stateroom door nearest them. He handed the key to Johnny.

Frankie pushed Johnny through. "I had this stateroom built just for you. Well, for Charles William really, but for your desire for subterfuge."

Johnny automatically corrected, "Privacy."

"Privacy," Frankie made the correction. "See, come through to the bedchamber."

The stateroom was not quite the size of Frankie's, but it appeared to be as long. It looked like any of the other first-class single-occupant staterooms. When they entered the bedchamber, there was a narrow bed, a chest of drawers, and a wardrobe… and a door set in the wall. Frankie chortled. "This is Charles William's bedchamber—but this is yours." He opened the door in the wall and performed a flourish with his hand. "*Voilà*, my good man. Your bedchamber!"

Johnny stepped through the door and into Frankie's suite. "But, this is your bedchamber," he remarked.

Frankie stood next to him now, with his arm around his waist. In a soft mellow voice he answered, "It's our bedchamber now, *mon ange*."

The combination of Frankie's accustomed and most prized endearment and something Johnny could not interpret made his stomach flip. "Oh!"

Frankie turned and stared at him. "'Oh'? Is that all you can say? Isn't it clever? You can stay in here with me but come and go through the other stateroom. No one ever need know the difference."

Johnny asked, "But what about Charles William?"

"He will come through the door to my sitting room as he always has."

Johnny had come prepared to berate Frankie for his indiscretion with the government discount, but the thoughtfulness and the care Frankie had put into these preparations quite took the wind from his castigatory sail. He let himself relax and lean into Frankie's half embrace. "It's wonderful. Really wonderful."

Frankie took Johnny fully in his arms. He lifted his gaze over Johnny's shoulder and said, "I think that is all, Charles William."

Johnny could hear the smile in Charles William's voice. "Very good, sir. I will go and unpack Mr. Stanley's valise for him." He heard the connecting door close with a click.

Johnny looked deeply into Frankie's black eyes and melted into a kiss. "Frankie, you are so good to me," he murmured after their lips parted and Frankie began to lead him to the bed.

After stripping, they climbed onto the bed and interlocked arms, legs, and lips. Johnny was nose-deep in Frankie's scant chest hair when Frankie asked invitingly, "Do you want to fuck me?"

Johnny raised his head. "Fuck you? How can I do that?"

Frankie reached for a covered jar without looking. He knocked the lid off, put a finger into the jar, and brought the finger back covered with a creamy, sweet-smelling lotion. "I'll let you figure that one out, *mon ange*."

Johnny slid off Frankie to lie alongside him. He looked at the lotion on Frankie's finger, then down to his cock. He watched as Frankie reached down and rubbed the lotion all over Johnny's stiff member. Johnny jerked at the touch. He saw Frankie reach down and strain to touch his fundament with the lotion.

"It would be easier if you did this," Frankie instructed.

Johnny hesitated. "This is sodomy, I suppose. I am supposed to put my… um… in your ass?"

Frankie laughed delightedly. "'Supposed to?' I think you will find you very much want to."

Johnny looked at him quizzically. "And you want me to do it? I mean, you like it?"

"Oh yes, very much. It feels so… completing."

"But… isn't it smelly and dirty?" Johnny wrinkled his nose.

Frankie shook his head. "Not usually. And I can promise you it won't be now." He had a wicked look on his face.

Shaking his head wonderingly, Johnny took some of the lotion on his own cock and giving Frankie a questioning look, leaned to observe the crack of Frankie's ass. The touch of Johnny's hand as it made contact with Frankie's balls made Frankie sigh deeply. Johnny found Frankie's cleft and inserted his fingers, feeling for the hole. He let one finger slide in and move around to spread the cream. He realized his own breathing had become very heavy.

So was Frankie's. The touch of Johnny's fingers made him gasp and cry out.

"Now what do I do? Turn you over?"

Frankie seemed to shove the urge to laugh down hard. "You can if you want, but you don't have to. It is nicer to be face-to-face, I think. Just get between my legs and lift my ass a bit. You'll be able to… well, you know."

Johnny followed the instructions until he found himself poised with the head of his cock pressing against Frankie's tight sphincter. He bit his lower lip and pushed in, all the while watching Frankie's face. There was resistance, and then his prick slid inside. He only had a chance to see the bliss on Frankie's face and hear him moan before his own body exploded with sensation. He let out a long high cry and felt as if he would pass out.

His cock was fully enveloped in a hot, moist place that seemed to hold him and caress him. He felt the head of it gently strike the inner walls of Frankie and slide along. He could not catch his breath.

Frankie appeared to be in a state of complete sensation as Johnny's organ filled him. Johnny's eyes widened when Frankie jerked as if a jolt of energy had made his body shudder. The friction of Frankie's cock against his belly tantalized him, and he reached for and clasped it in his palm, squeezing. Johnny did not need instructions to start stroking its length.

Johnny knew his climax would not be far away. He had no volition to try to stave it off. As he thrust in and out, his rhythm grew ragged. He shoved himself in like a piston and felt the pressure building behind his cock and started to keen. He thought he could hear Frankie saying his name over and over. He felt hot fluid on his hand, and then he burst into Frankie. The hot semen seemed to bathe his cock inside Frankie's body. He lost his balance and fell forward onto Frankie, who was gasping and breathing hard. Johnny let his head settle on Frankie's sternum.

After he caught his breath, Johnny lifted his head to look into Frankie's eyes. "Why are you so good to me?" he asked. He smiled languorously.

Frankie did not open his eyes, but the corners of his lips tilted up. In a lazy voice he asked, "*I* am good to *you*? You just agreed to fuck me."

Johnny frowned. "Oh, so if I had said no, you would stop being so good to me?"

Now Frankie's eyes were open, and he stared into Johnny's face speculatively. "Of course not. Why do I need a reason, anyway? To be good to you."

"I just want to know."

"Why is anyone ever good to anyone else? Because they want to make him happy." Frankie's tone made it clear that was all the answer he thought was needed.

Johnny put his cheek back on Frankie's chest. "You do make me happy. I wish I understood how that can be. After what we just did, I shouldn't feel that way."

He felt Frankie's chest rumble with quiet laughter. "Forbidden fruit is sweet, eh?"

Johnny looked up pleadingly. "I mean it, Frankie. It isn't a joke to me. I want this, but I want it with a woman, not with a man. I don't want the fruit, as you say, to be forbidden. And don't say this isn't. You know it is."

Frankie tightened his arms around him. "I know, *mon ange*, and I can't explain it. I have never wanted anything but to love men. Where I come from, it's not accepted, but for many of us it is at least overlooked."

"But I want acceptance, not just tolerance or indulgence."

Frankie lifted his head so he could kiss Johnny's hair. "I can't promise you that, *chéri*. I can only promise that as long as you and I are together, I will do everything I can to make you happy."

LATER Johnny did bring up the discounted passage on *Le Beau Soleil*. As Frankie lay with his head on Johnny's shoulder and his arm around his middle, Johnny said, "You know, that little stunt with the fares put me in an awkward position. The director asked me—"

Frankie interrupted, laughing aloud, his eyes sparkling with mirth. "Oh no, don't tell me he asked you who you had to fuck to get the lower fares!"

Johnny realized he owed his director's fine upstanding Methodist values to the fact that he had not. "Not quite. But he did seem puzzled as to what had inspired you."

"So, what did you tell him?"

"I told him I hardly knew you."

Frankie raised his head. "You didn't."

"He just decided that you were a remarkably civic-minded man, for a Frenchman."

"Creole," Frankie automatically corrected.

WHEN the time came for them to dress for dinner, Johnny went into "his" stateroom and opened the wardrobe doors. He stood staring in at the several new suits of clothes.

"Like them?" Frankie asked from the door to the adjoining room. Leaning against the doorframe with one knee bent, he ran a finger along one side of his mustache.

"No, I don't," Johnny said flatly.

Frankie jerked upright and came to him. "Why? What's wrong? Charles William, come in here!"

The manservant came in from the sitting room. "Sir?"

"Take these out. Johnny doesn't like them."

As Charles William hesitated, Frankie looked at Johnny. "What's wrong? The style? The color?"

Johnny looked down and replied softly in an attempt to make his words for Frankie's ears only. "I don't want you buying me clothes."

"What did you say?" Frankie asked, leaning in and whispering back.

"I said I don't want you buying me clothes. Besides, how do you know they would fit me? You didn't contact my tailor in Chicago and ask him, 'My... my... whatever... needs a new set of clothes. Can you tell me his measurements?'"

Frankie and his manservant exchanged looks. He nodded to Charles William who went to the wardrobe and started to remove the suits. Frankie, with a defeated air, said in a small voice, "Will you let me give you the evening dress at least? As a welcome gift?"

Johnny pressed his lips together. "I will pay you back for it."

Frankie accepted the compromise. He murmured, "*Bien.*"

Charles William continued to remove the suits, leaving the evening suit in the wardrobe along with Johnny's clothes from the valise. "What about the other things, begging your pardon, Mr. Deramus?"

Johnny turned on Frankie, but seeing his dejection he relented. "Leave the underclothes. Those I will accept."

Frankie looked somewhat mollified. "They don't stay on you long, after all—"

"Frankie, hush!" But Charles William's posture made it very clear if he heard, he wouldn't show it.

LE BEAU SOLEIL made her stately way down and upriver several times. Sometimes Johnny and Frankie were apart for one month, sometimes two. One day in October, Frankie came up behind Johnny in their New Orleans hotel suite as he undressed. He put his arms around him and pressed his face into Johnny's neck. "I wish we did not have to be apart."

Johnny sighed and reached up to stroke Frankie's hair. He kissed his ear. "I know."

They stood like this for several moments. "What if you quit your job and came to work for me?"

Johnny stiffened, but he did not explode as he customarily would at such a possessive suggestion. "You know I can't do that," he said.

"Cannot or will not?"

Johnny turned in his arms and put his hands on Frankie's jaw, gently pushing it so Frankie's eyes met his. "Both. Frankie, I know you are accustomed to having everything you want. That's what having money does to you. But you can't own me."

"I know I don't own you," Frankie protested. "I almost wish I did."

Johnny had been picking up on Frankie's melancholy mood. "What's wrong, Frankie?" he reached to stroke Frankie's cheek, then to curl a black lock of hair around his finger.

"It's this rancor over states' rights and all. I'm afraid something will come between us."

Johnny could not deny Frankie's words spoke to something true inside himself.

"What is Mick saying now?" Johnny asked.

Frankie eyed him. "You were there. You heard him."

"You mean all that about the election? You don't seriously think that will happen, do you? I mean, Mick is a smart fellow and all, but he's not a politician."

Johnny thought back to the evening before, when he, Frankie, and Mick had met Madame Antoinette for dinner at Le Coq Rouge, her bordello. Knowing Johnny did not care to be in and among the prostitutes, both female—and male—they had eaten dinner in a private dining room. The conversation had inevitably turned to Mr. Lincoln and his sudden rise in the Republican Party.

Antoinette's customers numbered among them plenty of publicly elected local officials, not to mention out-of-state congressmen. She had listened to their mostly drunken expostulations about "that nigger-lover Lincoln." She had good reason to think the Southern states would react badly if Lincoln was elected president of the United States, and she said as much to her dinner guests.

"The no-longer-united United States," Michael Murphy commented acerbically.

"What do you mean?" Johnny asked him.

Murphy spread his hands. "You know how volatile these pro-slavery folks are. You think they will stand and smile beatifically if Lincoln—with his threat to free all the slaves—gets elected?"

Johnny scoffed. "It's all saber rattling and ruffians. Just before I left Chicago, they were talking about some rally of the Wide Awakes...," he began.

Antoinette interrupted him. "Wide Awakes? *Qu'est-ce que c'est*?" She looked at Michael.

Johnny answered her question. "Bunch of rowdies rattling swords and marching about in silly uniforms."

Frankie joked, "Sounds like fun. Maybe we should get ourselves some silly uniforms and march about."

Michael hoisted his eyebrows. "Ever heard of 'Minute Men'?"

Frankie leaned to Antoinette and jested, "We know all about 'minute' men."

Antoinette laughed. "I like them. They pay the same, but I can fit many more in with any one girl."

"Can you ever be serious?" Johnny shot at Frankie.

A chastened Frankie contrasted with the haughty Antoinette. "*Cochon*," she muttered. Frankie hid a smirk.

"It will never happen," Johnny pronounced. "People like to make noise, but it will never come to secession."

So it was Johnny who first uttered the word "secession" aloud in the company. What he did not say was that his director and the others in the Treasury were just as concerned.

"Just promise me," Frankie said now into his hair as he held him. "Promise me that if it all blows up in our faces, you will come to me."

Johnny murmured, "I promise." He let Frankie take his hand and lead him to bed.

CHAPTER 11

Le Beau Soleil, November 1860

"YOU know, it is almost *Noël*. Will you want to spend that time in Chicago with your father?" Frankie sat on the divan in his sitting room with one arm around Johnny's shoulders while the latter examined reports.

"No!" Johnny shuddered. He kept reading. Less vehemently he repeated, "No, I don't think so."

Frankie frowned at him. "Won't your father want his son with him for Noël?"

Johnny wriggled uncomfortably. "I suppose. But I would rather spend it with you."

"I could come with you to Chicago!"

The change in Johnny's demeanor was marked. "No! Absolutely not!" Shuffling his papers, he made a show of attention to his work and ignored Frankie's dismayed look.

Frankie abruptly stood and began to pace in the small space. He finally turned and asked, "Are you ashamed of me, Johnny?"

Johnny looked up at him, his eyebrows knitted. He shook his head.

"NO, OF course not," Johnny said. "I... I... just don't want to spend... Christmas where it is freezing and windy." He realized he had almost said, "*Weihnachten*."

Frankie glared at him. "It's true, isn't it? You are afraid to be seen with me. I am only *un bouffon, un paon* to you. In New Orleans you can barely stand to be seen with me. But let your father or friends see me? *Mais non. Ça, ce serait de trop!*"

Johnny got to his feet and went to him, but Frankie shook him off. "You constantly chide me for being too reckless. Has it ever occurred to you how I feel when you try to stifle me? I go my whole life being exactly who I am. People like me this way. More important, I like me this way. Then suddenly when I find someone I want to be with more than any other person in the world, I have to hide myself."

Johnny watched him as he began to pace again, gesticulating flamboyantly. "Frankie…," he began.

"I see, you want me to be your fancy man, but you don't want anyone else to know it."

Johnny frowned. Sternly, he essayed, "Frankie, please don't talk like that."

Frankie spun on him. "Don't talk like what? Like someone who cares about you, who wants you, or like some sort of… chichi man?"

"Chichi?"

Frankie leveled an icy glare on him. "You know what I mean." He mimicked his own florid gestures in an exaggerated way. He glared into Johnny's nonplussed face, turned and stalked into his bedchamber, loudly slamming and locking the door behind him.

Johnny stood stunned. He went to the door and shouted through it, "Hey, wait a minute. That's the only way I can get to my stateroom."

He heard a snort of derision followed by rapid angry French. Frankie called in English, "Then I suppose you will have to let everyone see you sneaking out of the chichi man's bedroom." Johnny heard him open the adjoining door and slam it.

He stood, unsure what to do. He turned back and sat again on the divan. Why didn't Frankie understand? Exposure was dangerous. He may have managed to steam under the bridge until now, but discovery was only a matter of time. If they went to Chicago together, it wouldn't take a particularly perceptive person to see at once what Frankie was. It would be all over the place in no time. So much for Johnny's position, his reputation.

A tap sounded on the door that led to the promenade. Johnny leaped to his feet with "And another thing…" on his lips, expecting

Frankie, but he opened the door to Charles William. "Oh, it's you. I suppose he sent you to give me a good talking to." Johnny turned and went back to the divan and threw himself down on it.

The manservant quietly shut the door behind him. He turned to regard Johnny, his posture his usual elegantly attentive demeanor. "Is there anything I can get for you, Mr. Stanley?"

Johnny shook his head. "I am quite all right the way I am."

Charles William hesitated, then asked, "Mr. Deramus is clearly angry about something, if I may say so."

Johnny shot him a look. "That is hardly any of your business, is it?" he stated imperiously.

The manservant nodded. "Yes, you are right, sir. It is not. I beg your pardon." He reached back to open the door to leave.

"No, stop. That was unfair of me. You've known Frankie all his life. Why does he act... that way? Why does he have to be such a... nancy?"

To his surprise, he heard a rumble start from Charles William's throat that slowly grew into a deep booming laugh. He turned a rueful eye on him.

"You think Mr. Deramus acts like a... nancy?" The rumble continued. "I take it you have never met any nancy boys."

Johnny glared. "Well, no. I haven't. I don't go into that part of town. I have no reason to."

Charles William cast an indulgent smile on him. "Mr. Deramus does not act like a nancy. He acts like a Creole. They would never admit it in a hundred years, but Creole people have picked up African mannerisms over the time of our close association."

"But you don't act like that."

"You haven't seen me at Mardi Gras. Most of the time I have to be very solemn and quiet. That's part of how I survive. But François doesn't have to hide to survive," he said, reverting to his master's familiar name. "He's free. And that is one thing I admire about him. I thought you did too at first."

"What's that supposed to mean?" Johnny stood, his hands in fists at his side, unsure if the man's unexpected familiarity or his intrusive comments were what riled him.

Charles William stood and gazed at him. He sighed. "If you don't need anything, Mr. Stanley, I will leave you alone."

Johnny nodded slowly.

Left alone he sat with his chin in his hands. His mind was a jumble. In part, it had been Frankie's air of devil-may-care to which he had been attracted. He was accustomed to his family's tight control of their public behavior. Of course, the first time… that had been his sheer magnetism and Johnny's own pent-up lust. But after…? It was so many things. Frankie's bottomless compassion, for one. His affectionate nature. His gentle sweetness combined with his poise, an elegant strength. Then of course, there was that he was damned good in bed.

Johnny wondered, was he trying to see Frankie in light of his family's strict limits on public shows of emotion? They did not fly into rages or pout among others, but then they also did not fly into raptures.

He remembered one time when he and Frankie were standing on the top deck of *Le Beau Soleil,* before the pilothouse, watching the sun go down over the western bank of the river. It had been so beautiful: the water so smooth, the twinkle of tiny lights from the little houses on the Missouri side. The sun, *"le beau soleil"* Frankie had said, shining through the clouds and turning them the color of flame, then of wine. Frankie had been transported with awe. Johnny had been so touched, both by the scene and by Frankie's rapture, that he had let Frankie hold him. He had glanced to make sure the pilot was not looking at them, but then he had let himself lean back against him.

Was that all it was? He tried to think of others he had met in New Orleans. Certainly Antoinette—"Tony" as Frankie called her—and her girls were like that, but you expect it of women. Well, maybe not German women. Didn't he despise Klara Holtzmann's mousiness?

The male prostitutes he met at Le Coq Rouge were like that too. Again, they were in fact "nancy boys." But other men? Not Barnet, but then Barnet was what the Creoles called *"Américain."* Murphy? Irish— they had their own extravagances. The bordello customers? There again it depended on whether they were Creole or Americans. And certainly the Creole men who were customers of the bordello were not "nancy boys." They were there to be with women.

Sitting alone, Johnny began to consider what had been behind his treatment of Frankie that afternoon. What had started it? He thought back. "Ah, *Weihnachten*... Christmas. Frankie wanted to go to Chicago for Christmas." Was he right? Was Johnny afraid to have anyone see he associated with men like Frankie, which most assuredly would make them think he was the same way?

HE HEARD someone unlock the bedchamber door from the other side. He rose and went to open the door to check and concluded it must have been the manservant: there was no one there now. Since it neared time for dinner, he went into his own stateroom and dressed in the evening attire Frankie had bought him, and that he had insisted on paying him back for. He checked his appearance in the full-length oval mirror on its stand, smoothed his hair and mustache, and went out his own door, around to the port side and down to the double doors to the grand cabin.

As soon as Johnny went in, he saw Frankie, dressed superbly as he always did for evenings, officiating where the stewards were removing the screens that set aside the "ladies' cabin" so the dining tables could be spread out and set. He watched him for a while. A steward approached Johnny, but he waved the man away.

Frankie turned and caught sight of Johnny. His face immediately lost its cheerful politeness. He averted his eyes and went back to what he had been doing. Johnny slowly walked to him and put a hand on his broad shoulder.

"Am I being inappropriate?" Frankie said in a tight voice without turning to look at Johnny.

Johnny stepped very close and said softly into his ear, "I'm sorry, Frankie. So sorry. Can we talk?"

Frankie turned. "Of course." He surveyed the progress of setting up for dinner. "Where? I suppose some place private."

Johnny shrugged. "Not necessarily private, but quiet. I have something I need to tell you that I will have enough trouble saying if we are not off by ourselves."

Frankie's eyebrows went up slowly. "What about our spot in front of the pilothouse?"

"That should do. It won't matter if Tom sees us. I just need to tell you something... about myself."

Frankie nodded and led the way.

They passed Captain Mayer on the stairs up to the Texas deck. Johnny smiled at him and said, *"Guten Abend."*

Mayer and Frankie both looked at him, puzzled. Mayer replied, *"Guten Abend, mein Herr."*

Frankie and Johnny went to their spot—a part of the deck passengers were asked to stay away from. They found two boys playing, and Frankie shooed them away. He leaned back against the railing and looked about at the quiet river, so wide here, at the other boats, mostly small, and the barges and rafts on the river, plying their way north or south. He seemed to breathe in the scene before turning and looking at Johnny.

"My name is not John Stanley," Johnny began.

Frankie drew his brows together. "Not John Stanley?"

"No, it's Johann Steinfeld."

Frankie shook his head slightly. "I don't understand. You must be. You got my letters. They were addressed to John Stanley."

Johnny looked at his feet. "I use John Stanley for my work. But that's not the name I was christened with."

"It's Johann? You are... German? Or Austrian?"

Johnny moved a little closer. "German. And it wasn't that I was ashamed of you. Well, maybe a little uncomfortable at the idea of you and your... *joie de vivre*... in my stern, colorless world. I was afraid... you would be ashamed of me."

Frankie stared openmouthed. "How could I ever be ashamed of... you? You know I think you are...." He grinned. "How would you put it, the neatest thing in two boots. I adore you. I could never be ashamed of you, *mon ange.*"

Johnny could not help but smile. "But... you don't know me."

He looked up to see one of Frankie's devilish grins. He cut off the next inevitable comment about just how intimately Frankie knew him.

"That's not what I mean. I mean… you don't know where I come from. Who my people are."

Frankie looked serious again. "But Johnny, or Johann, or whatever your name is, I don't care who they are." His voice sounded soft and tender. Johnny wanted to let Frankie gather him into his arms.

"You are wealthy. Your parents were wealthy. You are from a prominent New Orleans family. My family… they are poor German immigrants. My father came from Dresden on a ship with other refugees of the revolutions. My father was—is a baker. We live in a seedy part of town with other German trash."

Frankie took a hard grip on Johnny's arms. "You are not trash. You are my treasure. You are my wealth. I could never think of you any other way." He loosed the tight grip. "But… why do you pretend to be… not German? That was German you just spoke to Joe, *n'est-ce pas?*"

Johnny stepped back. In a stern voice he replied, "I don't want to be German. I don't want to be an immigrant's son. I don't want to be poor. I want to be an American. I mean, I want… to fit in."

Frankie's face seemed to light up from within, as if he had just had a revelation. "I see," he said. "That's why you relax a little in New Orleans. It is easier to fit in."

Johnny chuckled. "In so many ways."

They stood in the early evening light and did not speak for some time. Then Frankie said, "Let's go to our rooms. I want to hold you. There doesn't have to be any more explaining. I just want you in my arms."

In Frankie's bedchamber, Johnny met Frankie halfway in an embrace. They held each other tightly, Johnny's cheek resting on Frankie's shoulder while Frankie stroked his hair.

"Johann," Frankie breathed.

"Please don't call me that. Call me Johnny, like you always do," Johnny begged, his eyes tightly closed.

"I will, Johnny, whatever you want, *mon ange.*" Frankie's own eyes were open, his gaze on some invisible spot.

"I HAVE never seen you so solemn," Michael Murphy observed as he and Frankie sat in the sidewalk café. Michael took advantage of the fact that Johnny was at the New Orleans office of the Department of the Treasury, the official purpose of his visit, to have some time alone with Frankie.

Frankie smiled wanly. "It's just that…."

Michael knew about Johnny's revelation about his life and family in Chicago.

"I keep wondering what else he isn't telling me. I suppose he can't be a criminal. They don't hire criminals to work in the government." He had smiled at Michael's snort of derision. "I suppose he really does work for them? Besides, I'm a criminal. Why would I care? All my friends are criminals…."

"I beg your pardon!"

"*Oui*, your only crime is a crime of love." He winked at Michael.

Michael shrugged. "I'm less worried about what he hasn't told you, than what he doesn't know about himself."

"What do you mean, Mick?" Frankie interrogated, his eyes wide.

"Oh, I don't know. Forget it. But you know, I understand why he is so skittish."

Frankie seemed to let the earlier comment go. "You do? You mean about his not wanting to be exposed as, you know…."

Michael pulled his coat closer around him. "It's December, Frankie. What are we doing sitting out here?"

They were closer to Michael's rooms than the St. Charles, so they retired there. An hour later they sat sipping Michael's Irish whiskey. "So what did you mean, you understand? About Johnny's worry that he will be exposed?" Frankie asked.

Michael leaned back in his chair, crossing his long legs. He peered at the amber liquid in his glass. "I had to be completely hidden when I was in the army. Not only could I not let anyone see that I prefer men, I had to either find an excuse not to go along to brothels or I had to go along and… make do."

"So you have had women?" Frankie asked, looking genuinely interested.

"You never have?"

"Never wanted to. They just do not attract me." He gazed airily about. "So, um, how was it?"

Michael laughed. "It did the trick, but then I could do my own trick if that's what it came to. I was an officer, so I had my own tent." He sipped his whiskey and shook his head. "It… lacked something."

"I wonder what that something was." Frankie made a lewd gesture that left no doubt. He sobered. "Were there no other men—like us, I mean—*mon ami*?"

Murphy's eyes crinkled with mirth. "Oh, aye, there were. Plenty. But discretion was not enough. We couldn't even show we were interested. It was pretty miserable."

Frankie took his glass in both hands and sat forward, his forearms on his knees. "What would happen if you were found out?"

"You really don't know?" Seeing the shake of Frankie's head, he looked down. "Possibly arrest. In fact, almost certainly. Court martial. Prison. Or if the army wanted to hush things up, my being an officer and all, I might just be shipped out. You know, like they do with priests when they are… uh… discovered to be indiscreet with choirboys. Only not such a comfortable exile. That's if you are lucky."

"What do you mean?"

Michael shrugged and sighed. "Well, that was if you were caught in some public act. More likely your buddies would catch you, or your superior officer. In that case you would probably be dragged out of camp and shot or beaten to death. They would just blame it on Santa Anna."

Frankie was rigid with horror. "But… but why?"

Michael chuckled. "You are such an innocent, Frankie. You wouldn't last ten minutes outside New Orleans. Don't you realize," he continued, looking straight into his friend's eyes, "how much other men hate us?" Seeing Frankie's perplexed expression, he went on, "No, you don't. Don't you remember that man, Smythe, and how he thought he had you over that crooked deal of his? He said he knew your secret and could ruin you."

Michael recalled how the two of them had met when Frankie had sought out Michael's professional assistance over his partner's double-dealing.

"And when he said that—if you recall—I told him to go ahead and tell people? That it wasn't much of a secret?" Frankie said.

Michael laughed. "I know. And I wasn't sure if I loved you more for that insouciance or was worried that you may learn otherwise someday."

Frankie gazed at him. "You do not mean that, do you, Mick?"

"What? That I worry about you?"

"No, that you love me." Frankie searched his face.

Michael smiled ruefully. "You know we have an understanding, Frankie. Love is not what we have been about all these years." He saw Frankie's relief, with more than a little regret.

"*Bien.* And I thank you for the very fine whiskey. But I have to meet Johnny for dinner." He put down his glass and stood.

Michael unwound his long legs and stood as well. He went to Frankie and, still holding his own glass, put his arms on Frankie's shoulders, his face a mere inch or two from Frankie's. "I miss you, Frankie," he said softly.

Frankie smiled fondly and planted a light kiss on his mouth. "You know it's only Johnny now, don't you?"

"I do. And I never thought I would see the day. Do you… do you love him?"

"Yes."

"Have you told him that?"

"No. I'm afraid to." Frankie smiled ruefully. "I don't know how he would take it."

"I understand. Just remember, if anything ever goes awry, I am here."

Frankie planted his lips on Michael's and let them stay a moment longer than before. "*Merci, mon vieux.* I will remember, but it will never happen." Frankie pulled away abruptly. "I'm sorry, Mick."

"No need to be. We have that understanding, remember?"

AS HE walked the several blocks back to the hotel, Frankie thought about their conversation. It was true. He had known for a while he was in love with Johnny. It astounded him, but it also filled his heart with joy. He wondered if Johnny loved him. He wasn't even sure Johnny could admit it to himself if he did. Johnny seemed to have a manner of thinking that allowed him to make love to Frankie but somehow ignore what it said about himself. Frankie wondered sometimes if Johnny thought he would snap out of it or meet the woman of his dreams, and then what he and Frankie had felt would be no more than a memory to smile at.

Mick may have brushed it off in conversation, but Frankie knew what he thought. He recognized how blind Johnny was to what he and Frankie were coming to mean to each other. There were so many instances when *"je t'aime"* was on the tip of Frankie's tongue—in bed, when they sat companionably together, when one of those Mississippi sunsets enthralled them both—but some instinct made Frankie hold back. As he had told Mick, he feared how Johnny would react.

The first time they were separated, Frankie had not expected to see Johnny again. He had sought sexual partners on the boat and in the town, just as he had for as long as he had been an adult. After that first incredible night in his hotel room, he began to realize this thing with Johnny was different. His interest in other men had seemed to fade.

The months between their first idyll and Johnny's next trip had proved impossible for Frankie. Celibacy had never been one of his better skills. He had found other men wanting in comparison with how he saw Johnny, but when one particularly delicious musician tapped at his stateroom door and made no demur about what he had come for, Frankie had let himself go. That was, until they were in his bedchamber. As the musician reached for him, Frankie looked over his shoulder at the bed. He saw in his mind Johnny's head on the pillow. He could not bear the thought of this man's taking its place. Now that had been a scene. Frankie kicking a good-looking man out of his bed. He had never done that before in his life.

He did not tell Johnny about it. Johnny, though reluctant to accept a commitment like theirs—between men—nevertheless was jealous of any attention Frankie paid to other men. It was a conundrum quite beyond Frankie's ken.

At the elegant double doors of the St. Charles, Frankie paused and shrugged his jacket more comfortably on his shoulders. He pushed out his lower lip and smiled. He was sure it would all work out. It always did, didn't it? He made his way to the stairs and to Johnny.

CHAPTER 12

Le Beau Soleil, December 1860

WITH Frankie at another table in the grand cabin talking to a well-heeled passenger, Johnny sat contentedly at his place, having had enough meals on *Le Beau Soleil* to stop wondering if anyone was curious about him. As he finished his soup, the woman sitting next to him addressed him. She was no more than twenty-eight or thirty, not particularly pretty, nor did she play the coquette or seem a vain woman like so many of the other female passengers in first class.

"Your name is Stanley, is it not?" she asked. Her voice sounded low for a woman.

He glanced over at her. He had noticed her before on the boat as she dressed quite exotically in what must have been some Eastern style, nearly a costume, consisting of one long drape of some silk wound around and around her body and a sheer scarf that encircled her throat. He had nearly spoken to her to inquire about her clothing, but his natural shyness had stopped him.

Johnny stood and bowed. "Why yes. I am sorry, were we not properly introduced? John C. Stanley of Chicago," he replied, offering his hand. "I work for the United States Department of the Treasury."

She took his hand and shook it, her own grip firm. "Pleased to meet you. My name is Lucinda Samuels. I am traveling with my friend. We are both from Ohio."

She touched the arm of the woman sitting on her far side. Miss Samuels appealed for her friend's attention. "Dotty, this is Mr. John Stanley of Chicago. Mr. Stanley, this is my companion, Dorothy Elliston."

Dotty Elliston was slightly older than her friend and certainly more handsome. She wore more ornaments than the younger woman, but they were tasteful. "Good to meet you, Mr. Stanley," she said as he shook her hand across Lucinda. "Actually, though we have not met before, I have seen you on *Le Beau Soleil* on an earlier trip I made."

Johnny had a momentary feeling of discomfort. He always figured few travelers would be on the riverboat when he was also on it more than once. "You do look familiar, Miss Elliston."

Lucinda smiled mischievously. "That may be because she is a famous actress."

Johnny regarded the older woman curiously. "That is most interesting. I am afraid I am not much of a theatergoer though."

"But I am" came Frankie's voice from his elbow. "I saw your name on the manifest and was excited. Might this be...?" he led, looking at Lucinda Samuels as he kissed Dotty's hand.

"Watch your tie, Mr. Deramus," she replied. The stretch across both Johnny and Lucinda was enough that he was in peril of dipping his necktie into Johnny's soup. "Yes, this is Lucinda Samuels, my companion."

Frankie, tucking his tie into his waistcoat, bowed to the younger woman and took her hand to kiss. "*Enchanté*," he murmured, his eyes showing real pleasure. "I take it you have met Mr. Stanley, my own... companion?"

Johnny had not heard the term "companion" used for anyone but a younger person, usually a woman, who traveled or lived with another older person, usually a woman also. Miss Elliston certainly did not seem like someone who would need, well, companionship. And he certainly knew his and Frankie's relationship was not....

He looked at the two women with sudden realization. Lucinda appraised him, apparently approvingly. She leaned to her friend and whispered, "They are...?" And Miss Elliston nodded. Lucinda said, "How lovely! How long have you been with, um, here, Mr. Stanley?"

Johnny was almost certain she was going to ask how long he had been with Frankie. He paled a bit, but answered, with a glance at the now seated Frankie, "Ah, going on a year?"

Miss Elliston smiled. "Then you are old friends compared to Miss Samuels and me."

Lucinda nodded. "We've been together for six months."

Johnny nervously glanced at the others at their table, but they seemed oblivious. He hoped they stayed that way.

"You mentioned how you met, I think. Help my memory," Frankie invited.

"Lucinda is a talented costumer. She helped us in a production of *The Moor of Venice*. She actually knows what Othello, as a Moor, would wear, as well as Desdemona's Venetian! I was so impressed when they dressed me in my costume for the first time that I had to meet her." She reached for the woman's hand, smiling warmly. "And the rest, as they say, was history."

Lucinda smiled back. Johnny found himself thinking women could do that, show affection in public. No one would take it amiss. Just then, he felt Frankie squeeze and then drop his hand under the table. He found Frankie smiling affectionately. In spite of himself, he could not help but give him a quick return smile.

Frankie gestured to Lucinda's attire. "Is that one of your creations? It is exquisite."

"Ah yes, it's called a sari. It is an Indian woman's dress—that is, a Hindu Indian."

Her dress caught Johnny's attention. "They... um... bare their midriff?" Lucinda's skin was visible on one side between a sort of bolero blouse and the drape of the sari.

Dotty replied, "Yes, but never their legs. Isn't that curious? Here we can bare neither. Well, on stage, but rarely then either. Philistines is what I say."

"How did you meet?" Lucinda asked.

Frankie glanced at Johnny. "You might say we were riverboats that passed in the night... and collided." He looked back at the actress. "I wonder if we can prevail on you, *ma chérie*, to perform for us after dinner. Here in the grand cabin?"

"It'll cost you," the actress replied. Then she quickly added, "You must bring this lovely man to one of my performances. I should be in St. Louis in a couple—"

A loud explosion somewhere on the river ahead interrupted her response. They were south of Memphis, but only by several miles. Frankie stood up at the general uproar from the diners. He lifted his arms and stood with his palms outward. After some effort, he managed to get general silence. "Please, *mes amis*, finish your dinner. I am sure it is nothing. And I have a most splendid surprise for you after dessert." He gestured for the actress to stand and take a bow. "Miss Dotty Elliston has agreed to perform for us something from her estimable theater career."

As the commotion turned to approbation, Frankie leaned and said, "What timing. Will you excuse me? I need to go find out what that terrible noise was."

"Shall I come?" Johnny asked, starting to rise.

"No, I think it's best if we don't look like we are panicking. Stay and enjoy our lady passengers' company."

Anxiously, Johnny followed his form as Frankie, stopping to reassure people along his path, crossed the salon to the double doors to the boiler deck promenade. Johnny had trouble attending to Lucinda and Dotty's attempts to engage him in conversation. He finally made his own excuses and followed Frankie out.

He saw Frankie down on the main deck, standing with Captain Mayer and one of the pilots, Compton, looking out at the river. As soon as he peered in the direction of the other riverboat Johnny gasped. Smoke billowed out of the far side, and the boat clearly listed in that direction. When he looked back, Frankie and the pilot were no longer on the main deck, and Mayer headed quickly down the starboard side of the deck calling to crew members.

As Frankie achieved the hurricane deck, he came to where Johnny stood and stopped to speak into his ear. "Looks like one of the *Caroline*'s boilers blew up. They may be sinking. We need to get their passengers off."

Johnny shot his gaze back to the burning riverboat, the *Caroline*. "Oh my God!" he cried. He turned and followed Frankie and Compton up to the pilothouse.

"Let's see how close we can get to the *Caroline* without getting too near the flames." Frankie was talking to both pilots: Tom Rice, who Johnny knew had been on duty, and Compton, who had been in his berth until the noise of raised voices and running feet alerted him to trouble. "There will be burning material in the water on the port side."

Johnny found a place in the back of the pilothouse, no mean trick since the structure was small and mostly filled by the big spoked wheel and the three other men. Frankie and Compton were soon joined by Mayer, and all three left Rice and Johnny to go to the fore of the Texas deck promenade. Johnny watched the *Caroline* coming closer and closer, and the muscles in his shoulders and back tensed with anxiety.

He went onto the promenade when the two riverboats were a matter of yards from each other. Looking down to the main deck, he saw crew fending the other boat off with poles. In the meantime, other crew had gotten the gangway up and across to the *Caroline*. Crews on both boats were shouting back and forth, and he looked over to see Frankie coming toward him. He started to address him, but Frankie shook his head, patted Johnny's shoulder as he passed, and took the steps three at a time down to the deck below.

Before Johnny could react, Frankie dashed across the gangway. Several of *Le Beau Soleil*'s crew were already across. Frankie was talking to the captain of the *Caroline*. They appeared to be arguing vociferously. Johnny found himself muttering, "Get out of there! Do what he says."

He saw Frankie pull himself up to his full height, button his frock coat, and turn to the passengers who seemed only too willing to take orders from him. With his guidance, the crew of both vessels began to direct the passengers across to *Le Beau Soleil*.

Johnny saw Frankie's head whip around before he dashed after a well-dressed man who headed for the stairs to the boiler deck. Frankie grabbed the man's arm and used all of his might to drag him back. The task was not easy, as the man was large and strong. Frankie finally let him go and turned to a woman with two small frightened children dressed in the simple clothing of farm workers. He crouched to talk to the girls, reassuring them—Johnny was certain—and then helped their mother get them across.

The blaze spread and came through the boiler deck to burst the windows of staterooms. Johnny realized he had bitten his tongue. He kept chanting, "Frankie, get out of there!" over and over. All at once, he thought, *what am I doing here?* Then he tore down the steps and ran to the gangway.

Frankie saw him and shot, "Get out of here. Go back! The boat is sinking."

Johnny ignored him and dashed to where a woman struggled with a large, heavy carpetbag. "Forget it. Save yourself!" he shouted at her, but she would not let go. He finally grabbed the bag and threw it overboard, turned back to the woman, and bodily lifted and deposited her on the gangway. He spun to deal with the next challenge. Catching Frankie's smile, he smiled back, and got busy again.

The *Caroline* listed so much to port that *Le Beau Soleil*'s gangway was in danger of toppling off. But the passengers and crew of the *Caroline* were across, crowding into the little space the already full *Le Beau Soleil* had to offer. Frankie found Johnny's arm and propelled him to where the incline of the deck was almost too great to climb. At the last moment, Johnny saw an orange cat clinging to the deck. After scooping it up, he grabbed the gangway rail with his other arm. He made it onto the dangerously tilted gangway with Frankie and the cat. They were all safely on the deck of *Le Beau Soleil* when the gangway fell sideways and, after hitting *Le Beau Soleil*'s main deck with a deafening thwack, fell into the river while still tied to both boats.

"Cut the lines!" Frankie screamed, but it was already too late. The *Caroline*'s rising deck slowed and then lurched away. It started to sink more rapidly. One of the crew finally managed to cut the lines so the gangway flew up and followed the *Caroline* over onto its side.

The danger was not over. The pull on *Le Beau Soleil* swung it at a crazy angle, and it slewed around surprisingly smoothly. When its port side-wheel slammed into the hull of the *Caroline*, it threw everyone off their feet. Blessedly the force of the impact made *Le Beau Soleil* swing away.

After several minutes, as they anxiously watched the gap between the boats widen, the *Caroline*, with a heart-wrenching groan, went down. *Le Beau Soleil* was clear. Frankie was already off on his rounds, checking on passengers and crew alike.

FULL dark surrounded them by the time Johnny located Frankie in the captain's cabin. With no room within, he stayed near the door and listened.

Le Beau Soleil's engineer, Sullivan, was speaking. "The port wheel took the brunt. It is bent so bad it ain't gonna turn no matter what we do. We gotta replace it. No other way."

Johnny glanced at Frankie, who was nodding. "I don't see any other way. We can't just sit here, though, with all these people aboard." He chewed on his curled forefinger, thinking. "We have to get everyone we can off. *Le bon Dieu*, it will be *Noël* in a week. All these people were on their way home to celebrate with family."

Captain Mayer asked, "But where will they stay? It's too far south from Memphis and the hotels will be booked solid anyway."

"Is it?" Frankie said, looking at his captain. "Why don't we get them all to railroad stations so they can at least get home."

Compton asked, "The *Caroline*'s passengers?"

Frankie shook his head. "No, I mean, yes, the *Caroline*'s passengers but also her crew and staff, and all of our passengers as well. And while we are at it, all but a skeleton crew for *Le Beau Soleil*."

Everyone stared at him.

"Why not? What good can they do sitting here or on the bank? They may as well go home. We'll get our wheel fixed, then send for the crew we need to come back. We can steam down to New Orleans empty of passengers. Maybe we will be back by Mardi Gras."

Wide eyes shot to him, but seeing his smile, they all knew he was exaggerating. Compton spoke up, "I can stay. I don't have any family down here."

Frankie nodded, but went on, "I am sorry, but you have to stay too, Tom. If we get underway, we will need both of you pilots. And you, Joe. We won't need any staff to speak of." He looked where Charles William stood, his clothes torn and his face dirty from helping with the passengers taken aboard from the *Caroline*. "Charles William, I hate to ask you to fill in for most of the staff."

"That is fine, Mr. Deramus. There won't be many to serve. And my Dominique would want me here with you, sir."

"Johnny, it's up to you to decide what you want to do. I know you have appointments in New Orleans."

Johnny looked up. "I'll stay. I'll find some way to be useful." He caught Frankie's grateful look and smiled.

In the morning, light boats and rafts carried the passengers and some of the crew and staff over to the shore. Frankie advanced money to anyone who needed it for transport or to replace lost clothing or necessities. Johnny whispered into his ear, "Can you afford it?"

Frankie looked at him. In a low voice, he said, "No, but they can't either. I, at least, have a chance to recoup."

AFTER a full day of shifting hundreds of people and their belongings from the boat to the bank of the river—and thence to the nearest railroad stations, the whereabouts of which Johnny had been able to supply—the riverboat was eerily empty and silent. Only a handful of people still remained aboard. The captain went ashore to arrange for another riverboat to bring what they needed for the repairs. The two pilots remained, though one always slept while the other was on duty. In the final analysis, Frankie had sent the rest of the crew and staff away—save a half dozen men who could handle the bare needs of a floating hotel.

When they finally got back to their bedchamber, Frankie gave Johnny a tired but wicked look. "Well, I at least have my *cadeau de Noël*!"

Johnny looked back curiously. "You do?"

Frankie put his arms around him. "You, all to myself in this big empty boat."

Johnny grinned. "You're right! Almost private. Almost like being on an island in a mystic sea."

Frankie lifted an eyebrow. "That's very romantic."

"I know." Johnny kissed Frankie tenderly.

"But not tonight. I am asleep on my feet." Frankie drew Johnny with him to their bed. He was breathing deeply and rhythmically within minutes with his angel asleep beside him.

CHAPTER 13

Le Beau Soleil, December 1860

WAKING to the stillness, with the sound of the river flowing around the stationary riverboat at its mooring, Frankie watched the waking Johnny turn to look at him where he lay next to him. Johnny murmured, "Come here," and Frankie nestled in happily. He held Frankie in his arms, pulling him so Frankie's head fell onto Johnny's muscular shoulder. Johnny started to sing in a rich baritone.

"Come where my love lies dreaming, dreaming the hours away.

Come where my love lies dreaming, so sweetly dreaming the happy hours away."

At the beginning of the rumbling he felt in Johnny's breast, Frankie focused on the sensation. By the time the second line of verse was sung, he rose up on his elbow and gazed with wonder. "I did not know you could sing, and so beautifully! Like a choirboy, only in a man's deep voice."

Johnny's lips quirked into a sardonic smile. "I was a choirboy," he said, his tone full of bitter memories.

His puzzled response melting into realization, Frankie asked, "A priest?"

Johnny nodded. "The priest who directed the choir was all right. It's just hard for me to trust any priest after the one in the gymnasium. That is, priests who seek out work with children."

"Why do men like that have to come between us?" Frankie said bitterly.

"How did Father Martin come between us?" Johnny asked, looking genuinely uncertain.

Frankie answered immediately, "It seems as if whenever we have these beautiful, sweet moments, something reminds you of sometime you were hurt."

Johnny shook his head. "He never hurt me. I never let him get that close."

Frankie's eyes darted back to Johnny's. Unutterable sadness filled him. "Is that why you never let anyone get… close?"

Laughing, Johnny pulled Frankie tight to him. "This is not close?"

Frankie put his head back on Johnny's shoulder. He started to respond, "It will have to do," but thought better of it. He kissed the skin of Johnny's chest where his lips lay against it.

They rested together in the odd quiet of the stationary riverboat.

"You know, Johnny, it's getting harder and harder to do without you when you are in Chicago. I'm lonely without you. I can't think of anything but you. I miss your gentle blue eyes, your long eyelashes, your arms around me, waking up to find you lightly snoring on the pillow next to me. I… I hate when I wake up at night and turn to you, only to find the sheets cold and your pillow empty." He tightened inside waiting for the lecture. To his surprise, Johnny only kissed the top of his head. He went on, desperately suppressing the lump growing in his throat. "What are we going to do if… Michael is right?"

The expected question, "Right about what?" did not come. Nor did the acerbic observation, "It will never happen." Instead Frankie heard, "I don't know. I guess it depends on what exactly happens. And where we each are when it does."

Frankie bit his lower lip. He absolutely would not weep. He breathed slowly and deeply to get himself in order. "I wish you did not have to go back to Chicago."

Johnny laughed deep in his throat. "I thought you wanted me to go spend Christmas with my papa."

Frankie turned his face into Johnny's flesh to stifle a sob. He heard Johnny's quiet comforting, "Shh, *mon ange*. Shhh."

Johnny's use of Frankie's own endearment pushed Frankie over the edge. He could not stop a sob from erupting from his throat. He bit down hard on another.

Johnny was up on his elbow immediately, forcing Frankie's head up. "Frankie, you are never sad. How can you be sad?"

The question was strange and ridiculous, and Frankie felt laughter rise in his breast. "Johnny, you are so dear. I... I...." He bit off the words "love you" before he could say them. "I love how silly you can be."

Johnny gaped at him. "Silly? Me? You're the one who is silly."

"*Eh bien*, that means I am the expert. And as an expert, I deem that question quite silly."

Johnny made an exasperated noise in his throat. He pounced on Frankie and started to tickle him. "I'll show you silly!" he challenged.

Frankie stifled his screams of laughter only when Johnny's mouth came down on his hard. He soon tasted blood, whether from Johnny's lips or his own, he could not tell. His face surged up to meet the hot kisses, and his back arched as Johnny climbed atop him.

"I want to fuck you," Frankie said through clenched teeth when their mouths separated.

Stiffening, Johnny paused in his beginning thrusts to rub his hardening cock against him. "Fuck... me? You mean...?

Frankie rose, forcing Johnny's body to fall to one side. "Yes, I do. Will you let me?"

Johnny stared into Frankie's smoldering eyes. He slowly nodded. "I-I know how ecstatic it is to... be inside... you. I want that for you too. And I know how overwhelming you find being under me, and... I want that for myself. How do you want me? To lie, I mean?"

Astonished that Johnny had responded so quickly, Frankie suggested, "On... on your stomach, I think. I want to kiss and lick your backbone while I... um... ride you."

Johnny nodded. He waited until Frankie lifted from his body and carefully turned over. Frankie had already opened his jar of cream and was liberally spreading some of the sweet-scented lotion on his prick. He put his other hand down so his palm rested on the outside of Johnny's butt crack. He pressed firmly but not hard. Frankie gently kissed him on his buttocks, one and then the other.

"Tell me if anything feels wrong," Frankie said softly and waited for Johnny's nod. He reached with the greased hand and slid the fingers between Johnny's cheeks. Johnny gasped and put his face in the pillow. Frankie stopped probing.

"No, don't stop!" Johnny's voice told Frankie the sensation Johnny felt was what he wanted. He let his fingers find Johnny's hole, and he started to lubricate the opening. Johnny shuddered. Frankie slipped one finger into him. Then two. He felt Johnny go rigid, but then he relaxed.

"F-Frankie, that is so delicious. I didn't know… that place could feel so…." A low moan took the place of any further words.

Frankie began to massage Johnny's sphincter muscles, winning little gasps and shudders that made him smile with delight. He took his time, letting Johnny get used to the feel. "You have such a wonderful *derrière*." He suited his other hand's actions to his words, rubbing and squeezing Johnny's buttocks.

"Put it in, Frankie. Please. I want to feel you in me."

Johnny jumped when the head of Frankie's cock pushed hard against his hole. He seemed tense, and as Frankie pushed into him, Johnny cried out.

"Are you all right, *mon ange?*" Frankie asked in a breathless voice.

He knew Johnny was more than all right when Johnny spoke raggedly. "It's… like taking a huge mouthful of something savory and satisfying. It is comforting, fulfilling. Oh Frankie!"

Frankie slid his cock back into him. This time, he came in at a slight angle. The head of Frankie's prick touched somewhere inside his channel, and a jolt ripped through Johnny's body. Frankie saw Johnny bite the pillow hard to silence a scream.

"Let it out, Johnny. No one can hear us. No one is nearby."

He felt Johnny's balls contract and his seed course out of him onto the sheet underneath them as Frankie continued thrusting.

Frankie fell forward over Johnny, gasping. He kissed a spot between Johnny's shoulder blades, then put out his tongue and ran it up and down near the same spot. He heard when Johnny came again, delighting and wondering at the noises Johnny was making.

Frankie stayed on top of him while his prick softened and slipped out. He bit Johnny's shoulder lightly, put his mouth hard against

Johnny's back, and said something too muffled for Johnny to understand. "How I love you."

THEY had four days more to themselves. The late December cold meant they had to bundle up to spend time on the decks' promenades. They went hand in gloved hand in the dim light of the midwinter dusk. They spent time in their stateroom, whether in bed or in the sitting room, talking, reading, and enjoying the leisure and solitude.

They did have one companion. Frankie had adopted the *Caroline*'s boat cat and named him Duckie for no reason he could explain. "I like ducks" was all he would say. Though Duckie, as he had been on the other riverboat, would be on guard against mice and rats, Frankie welcomed him into the stateroom to share their time there. He curled up against Johnny on the divan, took up stretching along Frankie's legs when he sat, and more than once spent the night nestled between them.

Frankie surprised Johnny on the second evening with a candlelit dinner in the grand cabin. Only their table was set up. Charles William, who apparently had also cooked the dinner, waited on them. When the night-shift pilot came in from the side door with a violin in his hands, Johnny could not have been more surprised. Compton played exquisitely, selections from Schubert, Paganini, Vieuxtemps, and others.

When Frankie took Johnny's hand and kissed it, he quickly said, "Do not worry about Compton seeing. He is like us."

Johnny knew full well what he meant, but he asked anyway, "What do you mean, like us?"

Frankie answered in a matter-of-fact tone, "Musical, as they say in New York."

Johnny looked at Compton's violin and then at Frankie. "Musical?"

Frankie laughed. "A sodomite," he whispered.

Glancing over to the Apollo Belvedere, Frankie advanced on the statue. The fountain was off, so he could lean over the basin and snatch away the silk loincloth that hid the statue's genitals. He swung the scrap of cloth over his head. "For such a stunning man, he is not very well-endowed, is he?"

He came back to the table and made a short bow. "May I have this dance?"

Johnny hesitated but got up out of his chair. They strolled over to the open space in front of the violinist, where they stood looking at each other. "Who should lead?" Frankie asked, chuckling.

Johnny held up his arms, looking from one hand to the other. He took Frankie's left hand in his right and held it up. He reached for Frankie's right hand and put it on his waist, then did the same with his own free hand on Frankie's waist. "A compromise," he smiled. Frankie's return smile contained such sweet gratitude, Johnny laughed aloud. He prepared for the next phrase in the music, a waltz, and began.

Frankie's face was wreathed in happiness. They twirled about the floor as if men had danced like this together forever. Johnny's head swam with the joy of it. They adapted every dance to share aspects of the gentlemen's and ladies' roles. They laughed and talked, stopping to hold each other when Compton asked for a break. They then took turns dancing with Compton, Johnny providing song and Frankie humming to provide the music. From the sidelines, Charles William nodded to the music. He declined to join in on the dancing, claiming old knees.

THE fourth evening, which happened to be Christmas Eve, Johnny found Frankie in their special spot before the pilothouse. He glanced up to see Compton on duty and waved up at him. He went up to Frankie, who stood with his back to the railing watching him come, and put his arms around him and leaned full-length against him. He laid his cheek against Frankie's and sighed. "I am going to be sorry when this is all over."

Frankie wrapped his arms tight around Johnny and squeezed. "*Moi aussi*."

Kissing Frankie's ear, Johnny hummed a bar of "Come Where My Love Lies Dreaming." "I've been thinking about what you said the other morning. How you miss me when I have to be in Chicago." He tried to find the words for what he wanted to know. "Don't you have... other distractions when I am not with you?"

"Well, yes, I have businesses in the city, and of course I have several trips up and down the river on this boat."

Johnny chuckled. "You know that is not what I meant." When Frankie said nothing, he went on. "You must have... other lovers...."

"No, I do not. Not anymore. It's you now, Johnny. I don't want anyone else."

Johnny leaned away so he could look into Frankie's eyes. "Really? For how long?"

Frankie cast down his gaze. "Since just before we ran into each other in the hotel saloon."

Johnny shook his head. "But you had no reason to know you would ever see me again."

"That's true, and I am not saying I would have stayed chaste, but I lost interest in other men. It puzzled me, since you and I had been together that one time. I still looked. I still look now. But everyone I look at, I find wanting... I mean, I don't want anyone but... you."

Johnny was speechless. He stammered, "Y-you have had other men before, though."

Frankie glanced sheepishly up into Johnny's face. "Many, many men. Since I became a man myself and before that, boys like myself." He looked about as if seeking something in the sky. "Pretty much every trip, upriver and downriver, if I could find a like-minded fellow."

Johnny ventured, lifting one shoulder toward the pilothouse. "Compton?"

"No, never Compton. Just passengers. There were almost always one or two passengers."

"How could you tell? That they were likely to be interested?"

"I watched their reactions to the Apollo. In fact, I thought you reacted to the statue too. Turned out I was right. And I had... associations in New Orleans too."

"At Mme. Antoinette's, Le Coq Rouge?"

Frankie shook his head. "No, not there. I never use prostitutes."

Johnny pulled Frankie closer and put his mouth to his ear. Softly he asked, "Why?"

Frankie laughed derisively. "I don't have to. I am, as I like to say, that good."

"I should say so!" Johnny stood still and silent for some moments. "So you had... lovers in the city? Was one of them Michael?"

Frankie's voice was warm. "Yes, Mick. For years off and on, but never exclusive."

"Why not?"

"We had an understanding. Neither of us expected ever to fall in love. So we enjoyed what we had to offer to each other."

Johnny froze. "You never expected... to fall in love?" He felt Frankie chuckle, more than heard him do so. "So does that mean you think differently now?"

Frankie stiffened. He nodded against Johnny's warm cheek. "I do. Because, *mon ange*, I love you."

Johnny stepped back, breaking out of Frankie's arms. "You what?" He felt a jolt of fear.

Pain filled Frankie's face. "Is that not wonderful?"

Johnny shook his head slowly. "Men can't be in love with other men."

"Have you never heard of Hadrian and Antinous? Alexander and Hephaestion? Achilles and Patroclus? All the others throughout history?"

"They were heathens." Johnny's voice had grown cold.

"And you think it was their being heathens that made them love each other?" Frankie turned to face the railing.

"I-I don't know. I guess I always thought so. Or they just liked to make love with men. Or a man. But it wasn't real. The only true love is between a man and a woman. The rest is... just sex. Just sinning." He heard Frankie's low laugh. "You don't believe that?" Johnny challenged.

Frankie lifted his head, looking out across the river. "I don't know. That's what the priests say. All I know is that when I think of you, my heart sings. It's a thing of such beauty. It doesn't feel dirty or sinful. It feels... sublime. I cannot imagine not wanting to be with you, to grow old together, never parted. How can that be sin? That song you sing to me, the one by Stephen Foster, 'Come Where My Love Lies Dreaming'? Did you think it was about a woman? No. He wrote the music for lyrics written about him by his lover, the poet, George Cooper. I know them both. If a song like that is not about love, then I....." His voice faltered. He slowly turned to look at Johnny. "I had hoped that someday you would feel the same about me."

Johnny, Johnny, whose feelings had started to soften, felt anger flash through him. "Well, you hoped in vain." He spun on his heel and started away. He realized abruptly that he had nowhere to go. He was on a riverboat, stranded in the middle of the Mighty Mississippi. He froze in place.

From behind him, he heard Frankie say, "I need a drink." He felt him brush past and watched him head to the stairs and take them two at a time.

Compton came out of the pilothouse. "What kind of damned fool are you? Do you have any idea what you are throwing away? If I could have that man's love...."

Johnny gave the man a rough shove. "It's none of your business." He started for the steps. From downriver he heard the familiar sound of a steamboat's whistle. He was surprised to realize he recognized it. It was the *Eclipse*, the boat bringing the things and people needed to repair the side-wheel.

His heart sank. Without thinking, he continued to his and Frankie's stateroom, not bothering to use his own stateroom to pass through. He found Frankie standing dejected in the middle of the sitting room. He took him in his arms and held him tight. Frankie melted into him.

"*C'est tout*," Frankie murmured.

Johnny stroked the back of his head. "Just our time alone. We still have... all our lives."

Frankie started. He pulled back his head. "Do you mean that?"

By way of answer, Johnny put his lips to Frankie's in a long, bittersweet kiss.

CHAPTER 14

New Orleans, January 1861

"YOU won't have much choice now, I think."

Johnny looked up at Frankie and slowly nodded. "I can't believe it. I never thought they would be such fools."

The first thing they had learned as the *Eclipse* came alongside *Le Beau Soleil* was that on the 20th of December, the day after the accident, South Carolina had seceded from the United States of America.

Frankie's shoulders lifted and dropped in a profound sigh. "And from what my contacts in the governor's staff tell me, it's just a matter of days until other states join them. Mississippi is on the verge."

"Mississippi?" Johnny said incredulously. They were in the saloon at the St. Charles Hotel, sitting alone at their accustomed table, glasses of whiskey in front of them. "But what will that mean? Will there be war? Will you be able to continue on the river?"

Frankie rocked his glass in his fingers. "I don't know. But if you want to get back to Chicago, you had better do it soon. I don't think you will be able to come back." He kept his gaze off Johnny's face, appearing to fear to see agreement there.

"No, I don't mean to risk that. Is your offer still good? Of a job I mean."

Frankie's face shot up, his look of utter relief and joy radiating like a sunburst. He reached across the table with both hands and clutched Johnny's. "Oh, *mon ange!* Of course it is."

A voice at their elbows interrupted. "What's the good news? Did South Carolina change its mind and return to the Union?" Michael Murphy stood next to them, a sardonic smile on his lips. He gazed at them and then started to retreat. "I'm sorry, you two want time alone. I'll give you your privacy. We can catch each other later."

"No, Mick, stay," Frankie urged, after a glance at Johnny. "Sit and drink with us."

"Don't mind if I do. In fact, I'm paying for the next bottle." Michael turned one of the vacant chairs around and sat facing its back.

"You come into an unexpected inheritance?" Johnny asked him.

"Didn't you know? Uncle Sam was my uncle, and now he's dead...." He let it drop. "With secession panic, there are lots of people up North who want me to find out what will happen to their property. Lots of advance retainers."

"Why are you here, then?"

Michael nodded to the bartender, who had brought over the bottle and an extra glass. "Thank you, my good man." To his friends he continued, "I'm leaving by train for Jackson later. I probably won't be back until just before Mardi Gras." He looked from Frankie to Johnny. "So, John, what will you do if there's no way to get back to Chicago?"

"I'm not going back. Frankie is giving me a job expanding his businesses."

Michael looked back at Frankie with a speculative eye. "So?"

Frankie smiled back. "It's true. Of course, who knows how long any of my businesses will last?"

Murphy sipped his whiskey. "Well, Le Coq Rouge will always do a fine business. If we have soldiers here, so much the better. Same with illegal booze. Smuggling might get tougher." He glanced over as Johnny raised his eyebrows at Frankie, who chose not to respond. "As far as riverboat passengers and cargo, I suppose you could contract with whatever government we wind up with and do troop transport."

"No." Frankie was adamant. "I will not use *Le Beau Soleil* for warlike purposes."

Michael regarded him coolly. "You might not have a say in the matter."

Johnny asked, "Michael, what will you do if there is war? Will you go back into the army? If so, on which side?"

Michael shrugged. "Not sure they would take me with my leg. But I will probably go North. I don't care for the sound of an independent South."

Frankie pronounced, "Well, I would look terrible in a uniform, and besides, I'm a lover, not a fighter."

Michael quirked a smile at him. "Oh, I don't know. You are damn good at wrestling in bed…. Oh, I'm sorry. Forget I said it. I had better get my things packed and drag myself to the railroad station." He got up and turned the chair forward again. "Keep the bottle, with my compliments."

Frankie followed his form as he limped out of the saloon. "That's not like Michael. To say something like that." He put a hand on Johnny's arm. "That was a very long time ago, *mon ange*. Never again, once we met."

Johnny gazed into his glass.

WHEN they were back in Frankie's hotel room, Johnny surprised him. The door had barely shut and latched when Johnny turned back and threw himself against Frankie. He pressed him against the door, his hands pinning Frankie's shoulders, his mouth on Frankie's, and his tongue forcing its way in.

Frankie made a startled noise, but he would not protest. He responded to the kiss with both joy and intense desire. This was his Johnny at last, his to have and hold, as the marriage vow said. Making love after the commitment Johnny had made to him felt almost like a honeymoon.

"Johnny, my dearest. I am so hap—"

Johnny's lips cut off Frankie's exultation. He felt Johnny grappling with his trousers placket. Roughly undoing the buttons that attached his trousers to his suspenders, he found in his urgency he could not manipulate the buttons on Frankie's fly. Voicing his frustration, Johnny pulled the placket apart, sending two of the buttons flying, and then he pushed Frankie's trousers down along with his underdrawers. Frankie was already hard with the excitement of Johnny's onslaught.

"The bed…," Frankie began.

In a harsh voice, Johnny replied, "No. I want you here. Now. You want wrestling, then I will give you wrestling. Turn around."

Frankie surrendered. Johnny's unexpected aggression and mastery overwhelmed him. Frankie had never been anything but the initiator in sex, and not just with Johnny. Frankie was the sophisticate, the seducer, the man of experience. No one had ever called all the shots in his bed. Not even Michael.

Frankie turned toward the door. He felt Johnny pull his hips back, making it necessary for Frankie to lean and bend, his one shoulder against the door and his cheek pressed hard against it. He caught his breath, realizing what Johnny had in mind, and spread his feet apart.

Johnny made a growling noise in his throat and pressed his groin to Frankie's exposed buttocks. He leaned to kiss and then nip at Frankie's back. Frankie repressed a cry of pain. He felt Johnny's hand go around him to his almost painfully engorged cock. Johnny grabbed it and squeezed hard. This time Frankie could not push down his exclamation.

"I want you," Johnny growled.

"Yes" was all Frankie could force out of his throat.

Johnny backed up and yanked at his own trousers. Frankie looked over his shoulder and saw him grasp at his own fly and extract his prick. Turning his face to the closed door, he heard Johnny spit into his palm several times and after a moment felt him spread moisture around Frankie's hole. Almost before he could shift his buttocks to make entry more possible, Johnny had shoved himself into Frankie. Frankie made his exclamation at the pain mold into a deep throaty sound of pleasure. "Fuck me. Fuck me hard," he begged.

Johnny fucked him hard. He did not seem to notice Frankie's shoulder and chest were banging against the door. He kept pounding. Frankie wondered if anyone in the corridor would wonder at the noise of the door thumping in its frame, but then realized the two of them were making noises that should explain what was going on. He could not have cared less. His exhilaration made him drunk.

Johnny started to grunt over and over. Frankie spent as Johnny gave one last violent thrust. Then Johnny moaned, "I love you. I love you."

Gasping, Frankie echoed, "Oh, how I love you."

Johnny pushed Frankie's whole body against the door. He pressed into his back, his chin on Frankie's shoulder. Their breaths were harsh and ragged. He buried his face in Frankie's neck, nuzzled hard, and bit.

Frankie felt himself fill with light. It made him laugh and laugh, and when Johnny lifted his head to look into his face, Frankie smiled.

A smile spread across Johnny's face. "I love you, Frankie. I do. I am in love with you!"

CHRISTMAS had been subdued, but not a total loss. When they woke together in their hotel room, Johnny found Frankie grinning at him, his eyes sparkling.

"What? Oh yes, it's Christmas. *Frohe Weihnachten, Schatz*," Johnny said. He planted a kiss on Frankie's forehead and attempted to pull him close.

Frankie resisted the embrace. "*Joyeux Noël, mon ange*! I have a gift for you."

Johnny watched him climb out of bed, pad barefoot to the bureau of drawers, and bend to open one and extract something. He smiled lasciviously at the view of Frankie's bare buttocks. "I see my Christmas gift already."

Frankie turned, looking puzzled, but when Johnny gestured he looked down where Johnny indicated. "*Oui*, but first this one. *Mon Dieu*, it is cold in here." He shivered and dashed back to the bed, inserted himself under the covers, and pressed up against Johnny. "You are like a furnace. I love it." He pulled his arm out from under the blankets and presented Johnny with a small wrapped box. "*Voilà!*"

Johnny eyed the package curiously. "What is it?"

"*Eh bien*, open it!" Frankie responded, his voice tinged with impatience.

"You want me to open it?" Johnny teased, then made a sound like "oof" when Frankie punched him in the side. "All right, if you are going to get violent about it." He smiled and kissed Frankie's forehead again.

Frankie's eyes followed every move Johnny made as he untied the elaborate bow, then carefully laid the ribbon aside. The paper, an elegant paper with a shiny finish, started to come open without its silk binding. He opened it the rest of the way and held a small wooden box in his hand. "Oh, a box. How generous of you! I can keep trinkets in it."

Frankie's growl of frustration left no doubt in Johnny's mind that his teasing was no longer appreciated. "All right, all right." He opened the lid of the box and stared at its contents. "My God, Frankie. It's beautiful!"

In the box lay a silver pocket watch with an exquisite engraving of an angel, his wings and arms spread and a beatific look on his face. Johnny pushed down his first thought, that the watch must have cost Frankie a pretty penny.

"Lift the cover!" Frankie insisted.

Johnny found the tiny button below the feet of the angel and pressed, releasing the latch holding the watch closed. The cover sprung up. The inner lid was engraved simply with the words, *"Pour mon ange. FD"*

Though he felt tears beginning to fill his eyes, Johnny persisted in his joking, as much to hide his emotions as to tease Frankie. "Oh dear, it's running fast."

Frankie pushed himself up, dislodging the covers in spite of the cold. He put his hands on Johnny's chest and shook him. "*Eh bien, c'est tout!* No more jokes. I won't tolerate it." He started to tickle Johnny, who screamed with laughter and tried to wriggle free.

"Stop! Oh Frankie, please! I give up."

Frankie ceased his tickling and laid his chest on Johnny's. He gazed into Johnny's eyes. "Do you like it, *mon ange?*"

Johnny pulled his head down and kissed him long and deep. When he came up for air, he said softly, "I love it, Frankie. It's beautiful. I will never part with it." He basked in Frankie's delighted grin. "But I haven't a gift for you."

Putting his palm to Johnny's cheek to caress it, Frankie murmured, "I told you. Having you all to myself for those few days was my gift. And having you in my arms for as long as we live. I love you, Johnny."

Johnny took Frankie's hand and kissed the palm. "Thank you, Frankie."

"For the watch or for loving you?" Frankie asked quietly.

"Both," Johnny answered simply.

Frankie took the box from Johnny's hand and stretched across him to place it on Johnny's bed table. He came back to his position on top of Johnny and slowly and sweetly made love with him.

NEW ORLEANS was alive with New Year's Eve balls and parties, but Frankie and Johnny were on what they thought might be their last trip to Cairo for some time. The riverboat was full of passengers getting back to the North in anticipation of a break in transportation options. And when they set out for the trip down river, the scene was the same, only now with Southerners heading out of the North. Only a few women were among them, so the ladies' cabin was rather unpopulated. The few women were wives of men making haste to return to their businesses.

On King's Day the cooks managed several splendid "King cakes." The one made especially for Frankie's table was magnificent, with frosting dribbled over the brioche and fruit and nut filling in three colors: purple, gold, and green. "I don't think I want to know what they colored it with," Frankie laughed. Johnny found the tiny porcelain figurine in the cake and asked if it was a good luck charm. "Not really. It just means you have to provide the next King Cake."

The very next day Johnny handed Frankie a newspaper that announced Mississippi had done as expected and seceded from the Union. Over the next two days, the headlines screamed the news that Florida and Alabama had followed suit.

"Until Arkansas declares one way or another, and I think we know where it will land, we can probably still steam as far as Vicksburg."

Johnny had wired his Department that he was resigning to take a position with a private company. He received a wire in return from the director asking him if he was out of his mind with the likelihood of war. The response to Johnny's letter to his father explaining his indefinite inability to come back for a visit was a disappointed letter in German from his father. The letter entreated Johnny to think about "his family," which only meant *his father*, he shouted at the letter when he translated it to Frankie. It begged him not to betray his country.

As Johnny tore the letter into shreds and tossed them into the fireplace, Frankie asked, "Which does he mean, Germany or the United States?"

"How the hell should I know?" Johnny replied bitterly.

Frankie put his hand on Johnny's shoulder. "I am so sorry."

"There's more."

Frankie looked puzzled. "I thought you read it all to me?"

"No, not the postscript." Johnny gave Frankie a sardonic look. "Kurt Holtzmann got married."

He watched Frankie's face go from blank to dawning understanding. "Kurt? The one you saw getting his cock sucked in the alley?"

Johnny nodded.

Frankie snorted. "Well, that will end badly."

Johnny wanted to argue, to say that a man could change. He knew how Frankie would react, dismissive and even scornful. He decided it just wasn't worth arguing. He shrugged, "Perhaps."

Later in January, they were drawn to the window of their hotel room—which overlooked St. Charles Street—by the sounds of revelry.

"Which state now?" Johnny asked.

"Well, let's see," Frankie replied. He proceeded to tick off the names on his fingers. He made indistinct sounds that could have been "South Carolina, Mississippi...." and a few more, and then aloud he said, "Georgia, Texas—"

Johnny interrupted, "Oh my God." He gaped at Frankie. It's Louisiana. It's us."

With a deep sigh, Frankie said, "We no longer live in the United States of America."

Down in the street, drunken men and other lowlifes screamed and sang. When they started to fire off pistols and rifles, Johnny pulled Frankie away from the window.

"Be careful. You don't want to get shot," Johnny said. He was thoughtful, then went on, using the Creole pejorative term for many English-speaking Americans, "I guess the Kentucks don't mind."

"Creoles don't mind either, by and large. They will just have their parties indoors, and they'll be rattling sabers instead of shooting off pistols," Frankie replied.

Going to stand by the mantel, Johnny wondered, "Will anyone in New Orleans regret it? Being part of the Confederate States of America?"

"I am not sure, but...." Frankie told Johnny how he had spoken with his tailor, a middle-aged German immigrant named Auggie Schmidt. "He told me that a lot of the workers—you know, the shipyard workers and such—wouldn't mind seeing emancipation of the slaves. Whenever they try to strike for better pay or whatever, the bosses just threaten to get rid of them all and bring on slaves to take their places."

"But Schmidt's a tailor. He's not in any of those labor unions...," Johnny said doubtfully.

"Two of his brothers work on the levee. He told me one was beaten badly by a boss's goons during a strike. Schmidt told me most of the German immigrants were lying low, hoping to stay out of it."

"And the other immigrants? The Irish?"

"I doubt the Irish will be so careful."

Johnny nodded slowly. He had heard for himself the taunts of the Irish men and women who, mostly in rags, went about the city, getting in the way of the police and fire departments, though they themselves were joining the ranks of both.

OVER drinks in the St. Charles Hotel, Pierre Soulé, the richest and most influential man in New Orleans, tipped Frankie to the next development.

"We just heard from Montgomery," he began.

Frankie was, of course, well aware Montgomery was the seat of the Confederate government. He put down his drink and waited for Soulé to continue. The man, who was in control of the city machine and probably the state's as well, often knew things even the army command did not. He and Frankie were somehow distantly related, in the way all Creole families were, so he regularly met with Frankie to keep him on top of developments.

"Davis has called for all of the states to mobilize their militias," he now said.

Frankie schooled his face to remain as imperturbable as usual. "*C'est vrai?*"

Nodding, Soulé collected his walking stick and stood.

"Do we have a militia?"

Soulé stared at him a moment, bemused. Then his face cleared. "*Mais oui, mon ami.* As you imply, not much of one. But I am beyond certain that war fever shall fill their ranks." He took his hat from the waiter and put it on. He bowed slightly to Frankie and turned and walked away.

Frankie sat for some time gazing into his glass of whiskey, unable to grasp war was about to impact him and all he cared about.

Michael Murphy, back from his travels the week before Mardi Gras, told Frankie and Johnny that a former Mexican War soldier whom Michael had met briefly when fighting with Winfield Scott—an elderly man named Major General David Twiggs—was being pressured to surrender his command to the CSA. Twiggs was responsible for a great deal of the border between Texas and Mexico. "Funny," Michael commented. "I never got the impression old Twiggs was unhappy with the good old U. S. of A." Once Texas seceded, Michael said, "He probably didn't have much of a choice."

"They are not going to go through with Mardi Gras this year, are they?" Johnny asked Frankie and Michael.

The two men turned incredulous looks on him. Frankie replied, "The whole city would have to be destroyed by a hurricane before that would happen, and I doubt it would happen even then."

Michael inserted, "Fortunately Mardi Gras is in late winter or spring, and hurricane season isn't until June."

JOHNNY found his new life as Frankie's constant companion in the unfamiliar world of day-to-day New Orleans more of a challenge than he had expected. Up until now, his sojourns in Chicago had only made his time back in Frankie's arms that much more precious. Now, however, he began to realize that, although far too long, the times apart had functioned as something of a safety valve. He was amazed to realize the weeks of relatively normal life away had helped him dispel his anxiety over Frankie's frenetic and often extravagant life.

With such brief times to recapture all they had developed between them, Johnny's several visits in New Orleans had been spent closeted with Frankie—with occasional forays into society. Before, Frankie had wanted him all to himself, but now he appeared to consider them a *fait accompli*—a couple—and Frankie had begun to relax, to find a place in his accustomed life for Johnny as a fixture in his world.

Johnny anticipated life at Frankie's side would be just more and more of the same loving, sensual times, warm and passionate, with the spotlight always on himself. He could almost sing with how that made him feel. He also thought that daily life in New Orleans would be the freeing environment he had longed for all of his life. But this was not quite what he found to be the truth.

Johnny had met Frankie's various business associates and one or two acquaintances, and these were quite enough of an adjustment. Oh, Michael was a welcome part of Johnny's life, in spite of a nagging feeling that Michael had at one time been his rival for Frankie's affections. Mme. Antoinette was a less compatible associate with her persistent flirting, her outrageous behavior in public, and her intermittent and often nasty jabs at Johnny, something he could neither fathom nor respond to. When Frankie began to squire Johnny to friends' homes and to social events, Johnny felt overwhelmed by the sheer wealth he saw. He could not decide if the difference in wealth or status or some other element that appeared to set him apart, made him the object of amusement.

Frankie was oblivious. When Johnny expressed discomfort at attending a dinner party at one of his wealthy friends' homes, Frankie was clearly incredulous. "I don't understand. Don't you like my friends, *mon ange?*"

"It's not that I don't like them. It's that I don't think they like me," Johnny confessed.

Johnny expected Frankie to reassure him, but when he seemed more puzzled than concerned, and then perhaps even a little irritated, Johnny let the subject drop.

He was further dismayed when, while drinking at a hotel with three of Frankie's rich Creole friends, he leaned to Frankie's ear and said, "Frankie, can we go? I am not comfortable with the way your friends are behaving, so indiscreet." What he did not say was that Frankie was every bit as reckless, loud, outrageous, and almost provocative.

To Johnny's surprise, Frankie grew impatient. "I do wish you would get over that. You aren't among your working class Chicago Germans now."

Frankie apologized later. "I felt embarrassed. My friends were giving me looks."

Johnny gaped at him. "You should have seen the looks the other people in the bar were giving us," he retorted.

Frankie simply waved his concern away. "You will get used to it."

Johnny highly doubted that.

"Never mind. It's Mardi Gras on February 12th, early this year. I have such wonderful plans for us!"

"WE HAVE to pick up our costumes from my tailor," Frankie cheerfully informed Johnny.

"Costumes? Why do I need a costume?"

"Well, for the masquerade ball I am taking you to, for one, and everyone wears costumes during Mardi Gras—even sometimes after Lent has begun. It's part of the fun, but it also means you can be incognito. Now that has its advantages." He reached to Johnny's face and caressed his cheek.

"I don't know if I like the sound of this," Johnny breathed.

"Don't be tiresome. Nothing can go wrong," Frankie assured.

Johnny thought about it. "Where is this masquerade ball?"

"Well, as it happens, on *Le Beau Soleil*. Mam'selle Marie is hosting it. She has the best balls in New Orleans." He paused. "So to speak."

Johnny regarded his amused face with trepidation.

CHAPTER 15

New Orleans, February 1861

"WILL this Marie need us to help with decorating *Le Beau Soleil*? I suppose she has people to help her. What is she anyway, a prostitute?"

Frankie laughed aloud at Johnny's question. "No, not a prostitute. She's from one of the wealthiest Creole families in New Orleans. You've actually met her."

"I have?" Johnny could not remember many respectable women among Frankie's acquaintances. Other than Julienne Barnet, that is. "I don't suppose the Barnets will be at the ball?"

Frankie gave him a horrified look. "Oh *Mon Dieu, non.* The very idea makes my skin crawl. And it probably would make theirs do worse."

"Will Tony be there?"

Frankie shook his head. "She has her own party at Le Coq Rouge."

Johnny tried to hide his relief. However, any effort to get more information from Frankie proved fruitless. "Where are we going now?"

They left the hotel, hailed a horse-drawn cab, and started to make their way along streets already jammed with revelers. Johnny had never seen so many people in one place who were not actually marching down the street.

"My tailor, to pick up our costumes. And Michael's."

"Costumes, right," Johnny said skeptically, looking about them at all the costumes on the revelers. Since most of the people in the street—at least in this part of the city—were not the well-to-do, the costumes were more like odd mélanges of color and fabrics. "It looks like someone threw bolts of silk and boxes of feathers in the air and everyone is wearing what fell on them. Is that what we will look like?" He looked at Frankie.

"Oh no, not at all. You don't have one of the wealthier men in New Orleans as a lover and dress in rags, *mon ange*."

Johnny hissed, "Shh," and pointed to the carriage driver.

Frankie shrugged irritably.

At the tailor's shop, Johnny could not help but ask Schmidt what he thought of all the outrageousness of the day.

"Ach, since I make most of my sales for the entire year with costumes, I say, *Vive le Mardi Gras!*"

Johnny rolled his eyes when Schmidt brought out his costume. "A pirate?" he asked.

"Oh yes!" Frankie effused. There was something lewd in the sound.

Johnny soon learned why. The white canvas pants that were part of the pirate costume were almost too tight to fasten.

Frankie laughed. "If you get hard, you will burst the seams." A blue jacket and a white shirt with voluminous sleeves and plenty of lace at the front complemented the pants, and knee-high boots with heels and wide cuffs covered his legs. A wig with braids framed his now-exasperated face, and he wore a gold earring on one earlobe. "Don't forget the belt and cutlass," Frankie encouraged the tailor.

Johnny, sitting on a stool with both arms crossed over his chest and an annoyed expression, waited for Frankie to come out from behind the tailor's dressing screens.

When he did, Frankie was resplendent as a Roman general. He stood looking imperious in a white-skirted tunic with a papier-mâché breastplate painted to look like gold. His sandals were also gilded. He had a helmet with a horsehair brush and a silver-painted wooden sword at his side. He commanded, "Bow down before your emperor, Romans! You first, Antinous."

Johnny had to admit the costume suited Frankie very well. He privately thought how convenient it would be later on to lift that skirt. That made him remark, "I hope you have drawers on under that."

Frankie and the tailor exchanged amused looks.

"What is that?" Johnny asked as Schmidt handed a large box to the carriage driver.

"That's Mick's costume. He's going as Le Roi Soleil."

FRANKIE asked the carriage driver to wait while they delivered their package to Michael. With the Sun King costume tucked under his arm, Frankie dashed up the stairs to Murphy's rooms with Johnny following behind.

Michael did not answer the knock on his door. Frankie and Johnny stood on the gallery of the second floor and knocked again. They finally tried the knob and found the door was not latched. Inside, the dark apartment reeked of whiskey and… blood. Frankie called out, "Mick, where are you? Are you all right?"

Johnny found a lucifer, struck it, and lit the candles he knew were in a candelabrum on the fireplace mantel.

"Oh, *Mon Dieu*! What happened?"

Johnny turned to see Frankie kneeling next to Michael, who was stretched out in his usual chair. Michael was badly battered with one of his eyes blackened and swollen shut. He had a split lip, and blood had caked his chin and soaked the front of his shirt and coat. His clothes were filthy, as if he had rolled around in mud and worse. Although conscious, Michael slumped in his chair, his right hand hanging onto the neck of a whiskey bottle.

"Johnny, ask the carriage driver to go get Charles William at his house."

Johnny dashed out and down the stairs to where the carriage waited on the street. He gave the man a Mexican silver coin he had and the address. He ran back up the stairs to the gallery and found Frankie coming in from the bedchamber with damp towels.

"Why don't you build up that fire?" Frankie asked him. Then he went back to Michael and started cleaning the blood off his mouth and chin. Johnny had a momentary memory of the time when Frankie had ministered to his own injuries.

"Were you in a fight?" he asked Michael.

Michael responded, "After a fashion. They fought and I got hurt."

"Who?" Frankie spat.

"It's a long story. Let's say it was a tryst gone horribly wrong." Michael tried to grin, but it made his lip bleed more.

"Be quiet for now. We can get the story out of you later. Johnny, help me lift him and get him into his bed."

"I thought you'd never ask," Michael joked. His voice, Johnny noticed, was thick and his speech slurred. "Don't forget the bottle."

Johnny went to one side of Michael and Frankie to the other. They took his upper arms and lifted him as slowly as they could. Michael groaned.

"Any broken bones? Are you wounded somewhere on your body?" Frankie asked, trying to look for more blood.

"Christ, Frankie!" Johnny cried.

Johnny saw Frankie follow his look to where he had seen blood on the front edge of the upholstered chair where Michael had been sitting. Johnny leaned to look at Michael's trousers. They were darker than their usual gray in the crotch. He hissed through clenched teeth.

As they entered the bedchamber, Johnny almost let go of Michael. He had looked straight at an ambrotype photograph that was propped up against an empty liquor bottle lying on the table next to the bed. The photograph showed Frankie, lying in bed, totally naked. The bed in the photograph was their bed on *Le Beau Soleil*.

"For Christ's sake, Johnny! Be careful!"

Johnny shifted his grip and helped drag Michael to the unmade bed. He said to Frankie, "You hold him up while I get these things off him."

Frankie reached around to put his arms around Michael's body under his armpits, and Michael's head lolled forward. Johnny set about pulling off Michael's boots, then his trousers. He let out a hiss of breath as he saw Michael was not wearing any underdrawers and his backside was covered with dried blood. He glanced up at Frankie over Michael's shoulder and mouthed, "Look!" He could see as Frankie looked down that he shared Johnny's horror.

"He was raped," stated Frankie aloud.

Horrified, Johnny stared back at him. "R-raped? But how?"

Frankie put a finger to his lips and shook his head. They had to maneuver the injured man to get his coat, waistcoat, and shirt off. He was covered with bruises on his legs, his buttocks, and his upper torso.

Johnny heard the door open in the other room and Dominique's voice calling, "Frankie, are you in there?" Charles William was right behind his wife as they came through. Johnny snatched the ambrotype photograph and slid it under the bed.

"Oh sweet Mother Mary!" Dominique cried as she saw the state of the naked man whom Frankie had lowered to the bed to lay him on his back. "Do you have my basket?" she demanded of her husband.

"Yes, here it is," Charles William replied.

Dominique removed her coat and gloves, took an apron out of the basket, and tied it around her waist. "I need warm water and towels. And put some of this in the water," she instructed, handing Johnny a stoppered bottle with some dark liquid in it.

"Somebody, get my whiskey," Michael mumbled.

"I don't think so, young man. It looks like getting liquored up was the problem," started Dominique. Then she gasped and put the back of one hand to her mouth as she noticed the blood on Michael's inner thighs. "What happened to you?" She stared at the state of his body, then told Frankie and Johnny to get the towels and water.

Johnny said, "I'm sorry. The only water I could find is cold." He handed her the towels and a bowl with the water. Taking the bowl, she put some of the tincture in the water, swirled it around with her fingers, and proceeded to finish the cleaning job Frankie had started.

Sometime later, Michael lay in his bed, propped up on the pillows, clad in a mostly clean nightshirt, and looking rueful. "Get her out of here," he rasped to Frankie.

To Dominique, he expressed his gratitude in a flowery way but made it clear he wanted to rest. When she asked him if she could fetch some willow bark to ease his pain, he shook his head. "Whiskey," he said simply.

Dominique put her hands on her hips and said, "Well, I don't suppose a little will hurt him now."

Michael said, in his thickest music hall Irish brogue, "Thank ye from the bottom of me heart."

When the Albrights had gone, Frankie and Johnny came into the bedchamber and sat on either side of the bed. Michael looked sheepish. "Are you ready to tell us now?" Frankie asked gently.

Michael nodded and proceeded to tell them how he had picked up an English sailor on the street along the wharfs where the ocean steamers docked. They went into a dark passageway "to do our business," Michael said, when he found himself jumped by at least six or seven other sailors.

"You were set up," Frankie stated.

"To make a long painful story short and painful, they beat the crap out of me. 'Paddy' and 'bogtrotter' and 'you filthy Mick' weren't the only things they called me. I seem to remember something about 'buggerer,' 'bum boy,' and 'sodomite.'" He groaned as he tried to shift his position in the bed. "And that's when they pulled down my trousers and buggered me with some hard object."

Johnny stood up and backed away. "No, no!" he cried.

Mick suddenly laughed, looking from Frankie to Johnny. "Oh rich! Johnny as a pirate! And you, Frankie, as Julius Caesar!"

"Hadrian, if you please," Frankie riposted.

"I hope you did not get me a costume. I am not going anywhere tonight."

"Neither will we," Frankie assured.

"Nonsense. I will be all right. You heard Dominique. I need sleep. You two go and have fun. Are you going to Mam'selle Marie's? Of course you are. She's having the ball on your riverboat." He waved away Frankie's protestations. "Just get out of here and let me sleep."

After a pause, Frankie agreed.

Frankie asked. "How did you get home and up the stairs to the gallery?"

Michael's lips twisted. "That young English fellow, the one I picked up. He came back after the… beating, sometime later, and put my trousers back on me and got a cart. He brought me home, gave me a bottle."

"He participated in the beating?" Frankie asked.

"Aye. I asked him why he didn't stop it."

Johnny said sharply, "He was the one who set you up!"

Michael nodded. "But he apologized. He said he had to go along, or they would have accused him of being a buggerer too."

"You think he was?" Frankie asked.

"Oh, I am pretty certain. Now go give my love to Mam'selle, and let me get some sleep, for Christ's sake."

Johnny turned back once he and Frankie were about to step into the gallery. "I forgot something." He went back to Michael's bedchamber and reached under the bed. He pulled out the ambrotype photograph and looked at it for a moment. Then he put it back where it had been, propped against the bottle.

Michael eyed him warily. "Johnny, it doesn't mean a thing. He got it well over a year ago, before he even met you. I asked him for it, and I guess he probably doesn't even remember it's here. If he did, he'd have asked for it to give to you."

Johnny looked up into Michael's face. He nodded. "Mick, I am so sorry about what happened to you. I guess I knew it happened. I just never knew…."

Michael said, "He's a beautiful man, isn't he?"

Johnny nodded, turned, and left the bedchamber to follow Frankie down to the street.

THEY walked to the levee where the riverboat was moored. On the way, dozens of merrymakers jostled them. Even if they had wanted to talk, they could not have heard each other over the din. As they approached the levee, Johnny saw the costumes here were better made. He saw Red Indians and kings and queens, and a man covered in white to look like a Greek statue. He saw whores who, if anything, were in costumes that uncovered them rather than covered them. Among those engaged in amorous activities, he saw two men kissing passionately, one dressed as a harlequin and the other as a mandarin. He felt like he had slipped into one of the rings of Hell, only the other people in it were having a riotous time.

The levee had a little more space and was quieter. *Le Beau Soleil* was bright with lights, including colorful paper lanterns placed over the glass covers of the lamps.

Johnny noticed Frankie did not even look up at all the festive lights and buntings as he stepped onto the gangway. He was upset about Michael, Johnny concluded. Johnny was too.

They went to their stateroom to slip off the cloaks that obscured their costumes. Frankie turned back to Johnny and put his arms around him, his grim face nevertheless affectionate. He held Johnny tight for a moment, then let him go.

"Frankie," Johnny ventured. "Does that sort of thing happen often?"

Frankie took his hands. "It happens. Michael knew the risk he was taking."

Johnny gaped at him. This was the same Frankie who always made light of the risks he himself took with his and Johnny's safety. "Y-you aren't saying it was Mick's fault, are you?" he stammered.

Frankie frowned. "No, of course not. I was trying to reassure you. I don't want you to think that sort of thing would happen to you or me. That's a risk of anonymous dalliance or going with prostitutes. I am frankly surprised at Michael. He knows better. He must have been lonely."

Johnny thought about telling Frankie about the ambrotype photograph, about the regretful look in Michael's eyes when he had looked at it and said, "He is such a beautiful man." He wondered if Frankie knew Michael was in love with him.

"It's so overwhelming," he sighed.

Frankie kissed Johnny and released his hands. "You will be able to relax at the ball and take your mind off it. Now come along. I have been planning this evening for weeks and weeks. You don't want to disappoint me, do you, *mon ange?*" Affecting his devil-may-care smirk, he said, "Shall we go make our entrance?"

Seeing Frankie's excitement, and in spite of his trepidation, Johnny adopted his brightest smile and followed him out of the stateroom.

The moment they stepped through the double doorway of *Le Beau Soleil*'s grand cabin, conversation faltered and heads turned in their direction. Johnny was not surprised to see the richness and downright exotic quality of the costumes. A great deal of planning and money had gone into the array. There were, as far as he could tell, no two alike. Had the guests coordinated the choices? *At least*, he thought, *there would be no furious cold shoulders and spiteful remarks among the two women who both came as Marie Antoinette or Cleopatra.* Speaking of Marie Antoinette, the very lady came toward them now, complete with the tall white wig, brocaded blue silk gown with its tight waist, voluminous skirts, lace, jewels, and a remarkably uninspiring bosom.

Johnny watched her approach, her overlarge gloved hands clutching an ornate fan and her rather plain, if heavily made-up face beaming at Frankie.

"*Ma belle!*" the woman said incongruously. "Frankie, Frankie, you have outdone yourself." She looked at Johnny, gave him a scandalous up and down appraisal, and exclaimed, "Monsieur Stanley, as usual you make my heart go pitter-pat. He's beautiful, Frankie." Her voice was lower than seemed proper for a woman.

She gave Frankie her hand to kiss. "*Enchanté*," he murmured.

Johnny was surprised at the rather unladylike squeal Frankie received as his reward. He wracked his memory for any prior acquaintance with the woman.

"*Mon ange*," Frankie addressed him, "may I present Mam'selle Marie, resplendent as the heartless queen she truly is."

"You scoundrel," Marie chastised, striking Frankie's breastplate sharply with her fan. "Come, simply everyone is here. Where is the splendid Mr. Murphy? Is he not with you?"

Frankie smoothly responded, "He is, I am afraid, quite indisposed."

"Nothing too serious I hope."

"Nothing that won't heal," Frankie said, frowning as Johnny glared at him for minimizing Michael's condition.

When Marie addressed him directly, Johnny awkwardly supplied the obligatory bow and kissed her hand. She beamed. Taking Frankie's bare arm, she led him toward the others.

Following the pair into the formerly familiar room, Johnny realized with discomfort that it was full of people he could not place, thanks to their costumes. There was a Turkish pasha, an Elizabethan gentleman, a cavalier complete with cascading ringlets, a George Washington, a pharaoh, and a knight in tin armor. Others he could not identify. There were more men than women, he noticed. The latter were mostly in gowns from various eras. The most modest was an Empress Josephine, whose Empire gown did not follow feminine curves but rather tapered from broad shoulders to narrow hips. Queen Elizabeth sported a brilliant red wig studded with pearls. He thought that one over there was supposed to be Nell Gwynne, though she was rather stout to resemble the mistress of Charles II. *Ah, yes, there is Cleopatra.*

He suddenly froze. He grasped Frankie's arm and rasped into his ear, "They are all men!"

Frankie cocked an eyebrow. "But of course!"

His examination turning on Mam'selle Marie, he tried to see under the cosmetics. Slowly a face began to take shape from his recollections of Frankie's associates. "Jean-Paul," he said under his breath.

Marie was Jean-Paul Le Grand, the scion of one of the most respected and wealthiest of the Creole families. He had assumed that, as one of Frankie's regular set, Jean-Paul shared Frankie's predilections, but still, his elaborate getup and outrageous behavior shocked Johnny.

Johnny looked at Jean-Paul, puzzled. *I have met them all, or most of them. What can he mean by "of course"?* "Monsieur Le Grand?" he said aloud, without thinking.

Marie frowned. "Now that's enough of that. Frankie, spank your boy. Or better yet, let me do it."

Johnny shot a look at Frankie, who rolled his eyes. He hissed into Frankie's ear, "Can I talk to you?"

"*Mais oui, mon ange.* Please forgive us," he said to Mam'selle Marie, who looked annoyed. "My friend has the vapors." When the two of them were some feet away, Frankie asked, "What's wrong? Is it still Michael?"

"I don't understand. What is this all about? Why are they dressed as women? And why is Jean-Paul acting like that?"

Frankie chuckled. "It's a game. *Une farce.* Calm down and enjoy it."

"I can't calm down. I am terribly uncomfortable here."

Frankie sighed. "All right. Can I have a few minutes? For appearance's sake."

Johnny stared at him, annoyed at both his tone and his mention of "appearances." "I will wait over there, then," he said, gesturing vaguely away. Frankie kissed his cheek, making him flinch.

Johnny retreated. He turned and moved through the throng of people, clusters of men talking or swaying to the strains of the chamber orchestra. He caught Compton's eye. None of the musicians were in costume, and all were quite clearly men. Compton smiled and nodded. Johnny nodded back stiffly.

Closer to the fountain, several tables were set up as if for dining. Johnny found himself drawn to his own seat at his and Frankie's table as if it were a sanctuary. Glancing up at the Apollo Belvedere from his place, he squinted through the candlelight and saw that someone had festooned Apollo with a woman's wig and a frilled pink cloak. They had also draped a ribbon around the masculine figure so the bow was right above the exposed genitals.

Looking around, he started to see the couples among the ball guests. He was curious to see two elderly men sitting together holding hands, one dressed as an Old Testament prophet, the other as Henry VIII. A fragile memory surfaced, of Frankie's expressed wish that they themselves might "grow old together." *Was it this that Frankie hoped for?*

"May I have this dance?"

Johnny looked up to see Frankie smiling warmly at him, his hand extended in invitation. He nodded dumbly and rose.

Frankie drew him to where, not many weeks before, he and Johnny had danced in the near-empty grand cabin. Like their first dance there, they took their modified position, both and neither taking the man's or woman's stance. As they stepped off, Johnny heard Mam'selle Marie pipe, "Oh no fair. We have all been waiting to see which of you is the man."

Johnny recoiled. He turned an offended face to the not at all alluring Marie Antoinette. "Which of us is the man? Well, both of us, clearly. And I think it might do you all quite well to remember all of you are men."

There was a collective gasp.

Frankie took Johnny's arm and put his lips to his ear. "Johnny, please," he implored.

Johnny whipped his face to Frankie's. "Why didn't you warn me? Why didn't you tell me this ball was all men?"

The sheepish look on Frankie's face made him pale. "You did this to embarrass me. I didn't realize you could be so thoughtless, Frankie."

Squeals of "Lover's spat!" and "Trouble in paradise!" came from those nearest them.

"Do you want to leave, *mon ange*?" a clearly regretful Frankie said into Johnny's ear, almost drowned out by the laughter from the other guests.

Johnny glared back at him. "I asked if we could leave before, didn't I? What I want is to get as far away from here as possible. From you as well. I should have known you would never change. What did you call yourself, a chichi man? That's mild compared to these... these clowns."

Frankie stepped to him again and hissed, "Johnny, don't say that. These are my friends."

"I know that now. I thought your friends were men, but I see they are not. They are... freaks." After Frankie had restrained his more outrageous manner to soothe him, Johnny was unprepared for the spectacle, and hurt and embarrassed that Frankie would spring it on him without considering his feelings.

Frankie flinched as if struck in the face.

Marie barked, "At least when he is with us, he can be himself. It's only with you that he is a freak, you nancy!"

Johnny raised one hand, a gesture to ward off the growing scene, but it must have looked as if he intended to strike her. He felt Frankie grab his arm. "Don't you dare!" Frankie spat between clenched teeth. "I think you had better go. You aren't welcome here."

Johnny gave him an anguished look. "I had better go? And you are going to stay here... with them." He poured all the contempt he could into the last word.

Frankie crossed his arms over his chest and glared imperiously. Frostily he said, "At least they know me. At least they accept me. I loved you at first because you seemed to need me, my protection, my guidance. You all but broke my spirit with your disapproval of my ways. I thought lately you were coming around. You might not need my loving care anymore, and we could be two unashamed men together. But I see now that all the while I was the one who needed protection. From your high-minded, holier-than-thou condemnation."

Other guests gathered about Frankie, their looks of scorn matching his own, but Johnny only had eyes for Frankie. He gave Frankie an unbelieving look and said, too quiet to hear, "Yes, if that's what you want, I'll go."

A chorus of squeals struck his back as he turned and made his way to the double doors.

Johnny went to the stateroom he had shared with Frankie. The cat, Duckie, looked up from where he lay on the divan. Johnny went through to the bedchamber. Looking desperately at the bed, he let a sob erupt from his throat, recalling how he had lain in that bed and wept his heart out in Frankie's arms. He went through to what had been his own stateroom, stripped off his pirate costume, and retrieved his old suit from the wardrobe. Dressed, he left the room, gained the main deck, crossed the gangway onto the levee, and disappeared into the wildness of the Mardi Gras crowd.

PART III
DISSOLUTION

CHAPTER 16

New Orleans, February 13, 1861

FRANKIE made his way through the litter-strewn streets of New Orleans to Michael's rooms. It would be a day or two before city crews cleared up the leavings of a particularly frantic Mardi Gras. After all, the street cleaners had to sleep off the revels too.

This year, the threat of war had made people afraid. When people were afraid, they tried even harder to distract themselves. What better to distract one than drinking and whoring and probably more sinister activities? Or they were full of frenetic energy—waiting for the... whatever that was coming: glory, violence—and impatient to begin.

Frankie was still in parts of his Roman costume. He had set aside the helmet and the breastplate and pulled trousers up under the skirt of the tunic, a fact that made Michael laugh when Frankie came through the door and found Michael sitting in a dressing gown in his chair.

He cut off his laughter when he saw Frankie's face. "What's wrong, Frankie? Where's Johnny?"

"How the hell should I know?" Frankie snapped as he flung his cloak over a chair and then sat.

"I'm fine, thank you," Michael said ironically. "What do you mean, how the hell should you know? What happened?" When Frankie did not answer, he said, "Oh Christ, Mam'selle Marie's ball. I had a very bad feeling about that."

Frankie shot him a furious glance. "Then why didn't you say something? No, don't answer that. I think you did me a favor. Now I know how joyless the bastard is. Besides, he'll be back when he runs out of money."

Michael's voice was sharp and angry. "Now that's unfair, Frankie, and you know it. The last thing Johnny is, is mercenary." He frowned at Frankie's snort. "What do you mean, he'll be back? He's gone? Why?"

"He made a big scene at the ball. Really showed his true colors. I'm not sure I will ever live it down."

"*You* will never live it down?" Michael gaped at him.

Frankie squirmed under his astonishment. "Well, at first Marie and all were all pats on the back and little blown kisses and sympathy, but you know how those cats can be. Out came the claws, and more than one caught me by mistake as they shredded him."

Michael looked thoughtful. "So everyone was there? That must have been too much of a revelation for our Johnny."

Something in Frankie's chest caught for a moment at *our* Johnny. "Well, all his things are still in either the hotel room or the staterooms. Though, so was the costume. I can't imagine he is wandering the streets of the French Quarter in the nude."

"Might he be at the Albrights'?"

"I'm going there next." At Michael's raised eyebrow, Frankie shot, "Well I can hardly let the man lie dead in some gutter, can I?"

Belatedly, Frankie looked at Michael with concern. "How are you feeling this morning?"

"Sore. Dominique came by earlier and checked my, um, wounds, much to my great chagrin. She says the tearing is mostly external and that if I stay on a liquid diet I should heal fine." He held up his glass of whiskey. "So I'm drinking my meals." He sipped. "Frankie, do you have any idea what a prize idiot you are?"

Frankie glared. "What do you mean, I'm an idiot?"

Michael leveled an exasperated look at him. "You must have known better than to expose him to Mam'selle and her harpies."

Frankie stood up and shot back, "And you know better than to go into a dark passageway for a fuck." He was instantly sorry for his remark. "I'm sorry, Mick. You know I didn't mean that."

Michael frowned. "Oh yes, you did, and you are right. But so am I."

Frankie turned away and went to the curtained window and, brushing one panel aside, searched up and down the street. "So

Dominique came here this morning? And she didn't say anything about Johnny being over at her place?"

Michael sat examining his glass, sloshing the liquid slowly back and forth. "Not a thing."

Frankie spun. "Mick, where would he go?" His voice had a frantic sound to it, even to his own ears. There was silence between them. Frankie finally said, "Mick, if he doesn't turn up in a few days, will you help me find him?"

"No."

"What? No? Why not?" Frankie was appalled.

Frankie saw Michael wince as he shifted his weight in his chair. "Frankie, I'm leaving New Orleans."

Looking around as if he would find an answer in the room, Frankie asked, "Why? Because of... of this?"

Michael chuckled at the gesture that encompassed his groin. "This?" He shook his head. "No, it's all the saber rattling. I'm afraid if I stay, I'll get drafted into the army again. Only this time it will be the... what are they calling it now? The Confederate army. I have to get up North. I don't know if they will take me, but I'd rather fight for the United States."

Dropping into a chair, Frankie put his face in his hands. A sudden realization that he was no longer in the United States flowed over him. He looked up again at Michael. "Mick, will you go to Chicago? Will you see if Johnny went home? Will you let me know he's... all right?"

"No, Frankie, I won't. You made your bed. Now you must lie in it. Better yet, come with me. You don't want to wind up in the Confederate army either, do you?"

Frankie examined the palms of his hands. "No, and I won't. I'll refuse." Michael's chuckle grated on his nerves. "Besides, I have businesses here. And *Le Beau Soleil*."

"Frankie" came Michael's soft voice.

"*Oui?*"

"I am afraid it is no longer optional to get a brain. You have to face the facts now, Frankie. Nothing will ever be the same again. Not your businesses, not the river, not your boat, not New Orleans, and not you. Haven't Monroe and Soulé and their cronies already started in on you?"

"I don't know what you mean."

"This is their golden opportunity to make a killing. They'll find every way they can to turn this nonsense into gold. How long do you think they will let you keep *Le Beau Soleil* running?"

Frankie sat back and looked appealingly at his friend. "I don't understand what you mean."

Michael took the rest of his whiskey in one gulp and sat forward. "Well, if not legal taxes, then illegal ones, bribes, fees, tariffs. And that's before the military comes into the city. The *Soleil* is a valuable asset. The river will be a battleground. Every good-sized vessel on the river will become a battleship, so to speak."

Frankie gaped at him in indignation. "I'll ground her before I will let them take her."

Michael sighed and put a hand on Frankie's knee. "I do love you for your cockeyed optimism. Or is it naiveté?"

Scrambling to change the subject, Frankie adopted his most suggestive look. "And I always thought it was my cock. Can't we pick up where we left off, before Jo… he came along?"

Frankie looked up into an icy blue glare.

"And hear you murmur another man's name when you are in bed with me? How dare you, Frankie? I have some pride, you know." He winced in obvious pain. "I want you to leave, Frankie. Go look for Johnny. Leave me some dignity, at least."

Frankie stood, dazed, and reached for his cloak. "You will let me know before you leave the city?"

Michael, who sat with his eyes closed and his lips pursed, nodded.

"M. FRANKIE, come in. Have you seen Mr. Murphy this morning?" Dominique's caring face greeted him at the door to the Albrights' kitchen. He nodded dumbly.

Charles William stood as Frankie entered the open door. When Frankie scanned the room with a hopeless look, he said, "He's not here, Frankie."

"H-how did you know?"

Charles William went to him and put an avuncular arm around his shoulders. "Come into the parlor. Dominique, love, will you bring coffee in for Mr. Frankie?"

Depositing him in one of the armchairs in front of a small fireplace, Charles William sat on the arm of the other chair. "I went by the boat this morning to see whether your revelers burned it up. I found the pirate costume on the floor of the extra stateroom. I went to hang it up and saw that Mr. Stanley's old suit was gone. He hasn't worn that thing in months."

Frankie stared. "He took the... what about his valise?"

"It's still there. I imagine he is coming back." He paused. "That party of yours was too much for him, I suppose."

Dominique came in with a tray with cups, a coffee pot, sugar, and milk. The air was instantly full of the comforting smell of chicory. She tut-tutted as she set the tray on a small table. "Poor Mr. Stanley with all those capons dancing about."

Frankie's eyes shot to Charles William. "What...?"

"After what happened to Mr. Murphy, I had to tell her. I told her about him...."

"And I already knew about you and guessed about Mr. Stanley. I'm as good as your *maman*, Frankie. You don't think I wouldn't know my boy?"

Openmouthed, Frankie stared at her. "You knew? You never said anything."

Dominique touched his arm. "*Mon cher*, I prayed on it, and the Blessed Virgin told me to leave you to her. I don't know if you can change, but if you can, it will be her doing, not mine."

Frankie looked from Charles William to Dominique and back. "Do you think he will come back?"

The Albrights exchanged looks. "I surely hope so, Frankie," Dominique said. "I pray he does."

IN HIS hotel room that evening, Frankie stood looking out at the darkened city, trying not to keep glancing back at the empty bed. Unable to settle down, he paced, he drank, and he finally sat at his writing desk and pulled out a sheet of St. Charles Hotel stationery. He took out the quill, and after uncapping the ink well, he dipped the nib into it and began to write.

When he finished, he leaned his forehead into the hand that held the feather pen. Why did he write this letter? He could not mail it. The river was blocked; no boats would make it to Cairo. Who knew if Johnny would even be in Chicago? He bit his lower lip. How unsatisfying it was, to write and beg someone to come back when you couldn't know where he was. He had thought writing to Johnny would at least get this cramped feeling out of his breast. All it had done was make him feel the added loss of helplessness.

Sitting back in his chair, Frankie picked up the letter and read it to himself. Under the printed legend "St. Charles Hotel, New Orleans," he had written in his elegant hand:

13 February 1861

Mon ange,

I have just made the worst mistake of my entire life. You warned me. Mick warned me. Charles William warned me. Mon Dieu, even Hugh warned me, after his fashion. But would I listen? No, of course not. So full of myself, so sure of myself, I let the one thing that ever meant anything to me slip away. No, it's worse than that. I drove you away.

I can just hear you now, chiding me for being overly dramatic. "Now, Frankie," you would say, "You know you have loved many things, deeply, passionately. I am not and never could be the only thing that ever meant anything to you. Your riverboat, your city, your life. Your… friends."

But, Johnny, my love, it is only now when I have lost you that I know how little they all mean to me compared to you.

I suppose I deserve this heartache. Not so much because I pushed you into that circus last evening. That was mad. I deserve the pain for taking you for granted, for forcing you to be part of my old world, that flighty, shallow, and meaningless world. For expecting you to accept what I knew would never appeal to you. I must have thought you would frown and fuss and look cross, but you would accept it all ultimately. I would kiss the frown lines from your brow, and we would make love.

Why could I not see it through your eyes? Why could not these jaded eyes see the fear and revulsion in yours?

I am so deeply sorry for the pain I have caused you, my dearest Johnny. I will be sorry every day for the rest of my life. I will never know any joy. I have thrown your love away, something few men ever are so blessed to know.

I close my eyes and feel your lips on mine, and I cannot bear it. I know I shall never feel that benediction again.

Do please live long and be happy, Johnny. You deserve so much more than I apparently had it in me to give.

With all my love, mon ange,
Your Frankie

Frankie waved the two pages to dry the ink. Then he took one of the elegant St. Charles Hotel envelopes and folding the letter, slid it inside. On the front he wrote:

My Angel

Living in my heart

He sealed the letter and stood for some time, waving it absently in the air, staring at nothing. Then he went to the hotel room window and set the envelope on the sill. He tugged at the bottom of the window. It opened a fraction, and as he had intended it should, the breeze caught the envelope and it drifted out and away into the dark New Orleans streets.

FOR the next few days, Frankie would arrive at the riverboat only to wait around for a few minutes before going back to the hotel to see if Johnny had turned up there. By the end of February, it was clear Johnny was never coming back. Frankie spent sleepless nights staring at the empty pillow next to him in bed. He lavished so much affection on the orange tom, Duckie, that the cat stopped coming into the stateroom. He went about in a desperate state of diminishing hope.

When Michael, on his way to leave the city, came to shake his hand good-bye, he handed Frankie a large heavy envelope that Frankie did not at first recognize.

"What is it?" he asked, turning it over in his hands.

"The ambrotype photograph you gave me."

"What ambrotype photograph? Oh, that one." Frankie's lips twisted sardonically. "You don't want to keep it?"

Michael shrugged. "Not something I can really travel with, can I?"

"Probably a good thing Joh… he never saw it."

Michael put a hand on his shoulder. "He did. That day I was beat up."

"He did?" Frankie stared frantically at him. "Where was it?"

"On my bed table."

"Oh. I wonder if—" he began speculatively.

Michael interrupted him, "I don't think so. He picked it up off the floor when you left that night and set it back up on the table. It must have fallen off with the bunch of us in the room. I'm surprised it did not shatter. He looked at it and then me. I said something like, 'He's a beautiful man' and he nodded. He gave me such a look of understanding."

"Understanding?" Frankie asked, puzzled. "Understanding what?"

"Forget it. All I mean to say is that you can't deflect your own mistake onto me."

Frankie opened his mouth to protest, then dropped his head. "No, you're right."

Michael sighed. "I won't tell you to forget him. I will promise you, though, that you will soon have so much to deal with that you won't have the time or heart to dwell on it." He seemed to consider Frankie for a few moments. "You know what's different about you, Frankie?"

Frankie let a shadow of his old impish humor onto his sad face. "No, what is that, pray tell, Michael?"

He put his arms around Frankie and said, "You always hear that gamblers accept fate. You know, they win sometimes, they lose sometimes. They know that one can't win forever. But you... maybe because you were always such a good cardplayer... you never accepted defeat as a possibility. Now that it is here, you can't cope with it. I really feel for you, Frankie. It's a miserable time to find out you can't always win." Michael held him for a few minutes. "Be well, Frankie." He stepped back and offered his hand to shake. "I hope you will come to your senses and come North."

Frankie took Michael's hand, and, instead of shaking it, he brought it up and pressed the back of it to his cheek. "No, I have to stay here. What if Johnny comes back? Good-bye, Mick. I can only hope we see each other again."

Michael, looking stricken, turned and left the hotel room.

Frankie took the envelope to the fireplace. He opened it and drew out the glass ambrotype photograph. With a momentary glance, he let it slip from his fingers into the fire. He picked up the poker and smashed the glass. The fragments of image warped and became impossible to identify. It gave off an unholy stink. Frankie stepped back quickly. "Ashes to ashes, and dust to dust," he said softly, retreating from the fumes the thing seemed to cast off. Frankie's eyes stung and tears gathered at their edges. He thought those fumes may have caused it.

CHAPTER 17

New Orleans, late February 1861

FRANKIE sent for his tailor to pick up the costumes.

He winced inwardly when Schmidt asked where Frankie's "friend" was. "Traveling," he answered. He wished people would stop asking.

"Are you sure you won't want the costume for next Mardi Gras, monsieur?"

Frankie almost said *what Mardi Gras?* He stopped himself, realizing he was beginning to believe what Michael had said, that nothing would ever be the same again. Not in his life with Johnny. Not with New Orleans. Not with the entire world. Instead, he said, "*Eh bien*, charge it to my account and store it for me, would you?" The obsequious tailor grinned from ear to ear.

Frankie chanced, "Business bad?"

"*Ach, nein.* Not at all. The orders for uniforms are coming in quickly now. From both officers who want them tailor-made and the militias. My wife and sister are turning out many of those."

Frankie frowned. "It's getting serious, isn't it? People don't actually think we are going to war, do they?"

The tailor replied, "They certainly seem to hope so. I hear a lot of how we have to show those federals they cannot kick us around." He removed a grease pencil from his breast pocket, uncapped it, and wrote "F Deramus" after wiping "M Murphy" off the box with a finger.

"But I thought you were an abolitionist?" Frankie asked.

The tailor put up a belaying hand. "Don't say that, *monsieur*. People are being beaten up for less."

"*Mais non!*" Frankie protested genuinely surprised.

"*Mais oui,*" the tailor replied, grim-faced.

Frankie's circle had gone chilly with him after the Mardi Gras fiasco. He supposed it was possible he wasn't fun anymore, moping about as he did. Antoinette had to spend time with him, being his business partner, but he made sure they stayed off the topic of Johnny. Tony had heard all about the scene at the ball and had nothing but spite for Johnny, and Frankie would hear none of it.

Time spent with the Albrights proved his only refuge. He had an armchair brought over to their parlor from the *Soleil*. He sat and brooded until Charles William and his wife started to talk over and around him. He became part of the furniture.

He did not have the heart to go out with *Le Beau Soleil*, but sent Captain Mayer out with it instead. Their route was seriously curtailed now, not being able to go much farther than Vicksburg. Passenger traffic dried up gradually, so Frankie himself had little to do. The crew could handle the cargo. He continued to pay staff, though they had no role on the boat. With a small amount of money coming in, Frankie knew he would not be able to pay them forever.

Le Coq Rouge continued to do a fine business, particularly when the militiamen started to come into the city—Confederate soldiers, after a fashion, from different parts of Louisiana. But the Soulé machine ate up much of the profits with their demands for bribes and payoffs.

Although Michael had declined to go look for Johnny, Frankie was not without other resources. He remembered a man Michael sometimes called upon to help him track down information. What was his name? Baxter, Robert Baxter. Went by the nickname Bob. He tracked him down and hired him to go find whatever he could about Johnny's movements after Mardi Gras.

Baxter's initial report confirmed one fact Frankie had assumed: Johnny had left the city. He had taken the train to Monroe, Louisiana. A pocket watch Frankie had given Johnny for Christmas must have been the source of the funds for his fare. Baxter had found it pawned and redeemed it, not without a little strong-arm to make the old pawnbroker give it over. Frankie waited until Baxter had left his hotel room to flip open the case of the watch, after a sad look at the angelic figure on the silver cover. Frankie stroked the engraved words: *Pour mon ange, FD.* The corners of his lips dragging down, he recalled Johnny's words, "I will never part with it." Frankie put the watch in the back of a drawer. *With the money it got him, Johnny could have gone all the way to the moon.*

Before he left the city in late March, Michael told Frankie news had come from Texas that the General there—Twiggs, his name was—had handed the Alamo and command of all the United States forces and their armaments and ammunition over to the Confederacy. Some said he was forced to, others rather convincingly argued this was what the man wanted everyone to think. Certainly, those who were acquainted with him, who had served with him, were not fooled. Frankie was sure of that when the wires came to the hotel office announcing Twiggs had been dismissed from the army for "dishonor to the flag of the nation."

Now, word was the man was coming to New Orleans to command Confederate forces. *What forces?* Frankie shook his head. He supposed someone thought the new Confederate States of America needed some sort of standing army. Wasn't the militia enough?

Frankie soon found keeping track of all the rumors and news from the East distracted him from dwelling on his lost lover. He overheard conversations in the cafés that were as inarticulate as to purpose as they were passionate about action. He also quickly found if he asked for clarification as to what taking up arms would accomplish—since, after all, several states had already seceded and the Union was broken—all he received in response were suspicious and even hostile glares.

Frankie finally stopped asking the question.

FRANKIE sat in the hotel lobby reading the latest *Daily Picayune*. It said Abraham Lincoln was sworn in as the President of the United States on March 4. Lincoln was already the focus of secessionist rancor and the impetus for it, or so the angry Southern voices cried. The paper's editorial columns were full of heated rhetoric calling Lincoln the reason states had been forced to secede. The inauguration simply capped the dissolution of the Union.

If the war fever was bad already, the city elections in the Crescent City in the second half of March ratcheted up the rhetoric. Frankie tried with all his might to avoid exposure to them, but campaign speeches were full of the bombast over which politician was more loyal and angrier and readier to go "give those Yankees what for." However, the result of the elections depended not one whit on the matter. New Orleans was a city of patronage, of the political machine whose hands seemed ever in Frankie's pockets. Really, he mused, the only thing that had changed in years was the power of the Creole establishment had been forced to move over and let the "*Américain*" politicians share more and more of the control. No amount of marching about the streets shouting, blowing horns, rat-a-tat-tatting on drums, or fist fights would make one lick of difference. The same essential group of men was in power the day after the rigged election.

In early April, Bob Baxter told Frankie he had only been able to track Johnny to Missouri. "Nothing much is getting through anymore. I may have been able to keep after that fellow who owes you money if I'd gotten right on it after Mardi Gras...." But now railroads and river traffic were disrupted more by speculators and privateers than by any real change in government. He was sorry, but he could not get up any farther north.

Frankie, whose plan had been to give Baxter the name "Johann Steinfeld" as a last resort, kept it to himself when the detective told him even the post was cut north of the Mississippi border with Tennessee. Frankie thanked him, paid him, and went down to the hotel saloon and got very drunk.

And then the newspapers reported the beginning of the conflict: Confederate ships had fired on Fort Sumter in Charleston harbor. The anticipation had been building for several days. In fact, a Louisiana native son, General Pierre Gustave Toutant Beauregard, had the task to take down the Yankee garrison in the Southern port. It was a matter of whether the Union commander would read the writing on the wall and remove, or President Lincoln and Fort Sumter commander Major Anderson would decide to provoke the attack by refusing to surrender the fort that was clearly in Confederate territory.

In its Friday afternoon edition, the headline in the *New Orleans Daily Picayune* screamed, "Important From Charleston. Fire Opened On Fort Sumter!" It was April 12, 1861.

The crowds in the streets shrieked even louder than the headlines. Frankie was torn between staying away from the windows of his hotel room to avoid shots fired in the air in celebration or braving the crowded streets to check on *Le Beau Soleil* and the Albrights. It struck him that if he could locate one of the pilots and a couple of the boiler engineers in the chaos, he could collect Charles William and Dominique and take the steamboat out for a few days. Then he remembered the *Soleil* was not currently in port. That was one bit of good news. He could at least try to bring the Albrights to his hotel until all this blew over.

Moving about the city was easier said than done. Just getting to their little cottage through the streets was well-nigh impossible. Although General Twiggs had indeed been installed as military leader in New Orleans, the few actual troops who were in the streets were not only failing to control the violence, they were egging it on.

When Frankie finally muscled his way through, his father's old dress sword in his hand, he found the Albrights gone. There was no note. There was also no sign of violence. They must have found refuge somewhere. His conscience pricked him that he had not anticipated the need.

On an impulse, he made his way slowly to the cathedral. He stood in the back, listening to the priest intoning mass; he spotted the Albrights standing together in the colored section of the nave. He did not remain, but went desultorily out of the building without genuflecting to the Christ on the cross hanging over the altar.

He thought about going to the Barnets' big mansion in the American part of town to check on them, but figured if anyone had things well in hand, it would be Hugh. After heading back to the hotel, he loitered amid the bankers, planters, businessmen, and other city leaders in the lobby. It was there he heard Louisiana Governor Moore had issued instructions for militia units to "hold themselves in readiness for active service at a moment's call."

Frankie thought for the thousandth time about Johnny, wondering where he was, what he knew about the bombardment, what he thought about it, and what was going to happen to him now—him and Frankie—now they were no longer lovers, and officially enemies.

After climbing to his rooms in a fog of sorrow, he went to a box he kept on the bureau in his bedchamber and lifted the lid. Inside were dozens of letters from Johnny, postmarked Chicago during the period of their separations. He removed them and carried them to the fireplace, which the hotel staff had lit in anticipation of his return. He gazed at the stack of envelopes in his hand for one numb moment, then dropped them in, all at once. He saw the edges brown, curl, and then become consumed. It was only minutes until they were indistinguishable from the wood ashes.

Something in his heart let go. Johnny was gone forever. Even if he clung to the forlorn wish Johnny would want to come back, the war meant he could not, nor could Frankie go to him. Frankie could either try to enshrine the happier memories or dismiss them into oblivion forever. The former was too painful to consider. It was going to have to be the latter. He put Johnny away in the farthest reaches of his heart, turned the key, and threw it into the void.

WHEN Frankie answered a knock at his hotel suite door, he found Hugh Barnet looking grim. He looked Hugh up and down. "You always were a little toy soldier at heart, you know. Come in and let me see you by the window." He went to the big hotel room window and thrust aside the curtains.

Barnet followed him woodenly into the sitting room, obviously not enjoying the close scrutiny. He was in a skirted dark blue jacket with a double row of brass buttons; he wore sky-blue trousers, boots, and a belt. On his charcoal-gray hat was a single gold star. He was removing his white gloves.

"*Mais mon petit soldat*, I do not understand. Mardi Gras was weeks ago. Why are you still in your masquerade costume?" Frankie made a mock salute.

"As ever, you share only half your wit," Barnet replied.

Frankie raised one eyebrow at the play on words. "Not bad. So what are you? A sergeant major?"

"Major, actually. General Twiggs's staff. I see you are not in uniform." Barnet took the chair Frankie gestured him to, declining refreshment.

Frankie leaned against the fireplace mantel. "Ah, but I am, don't you see? I am a general officer in the ranks of those damned to perdition. A dressing gown and slippers are our regimentals." He made a fluid gesture. "My dear Hugh, you make it awfully easy to get a rise… I beg pardon… out of you. What do you want? I don't imagine this is a social call."

Barnet sat back and crossed one leg over the other. "No, indeed. One of my duties on Twiggs's staff is to root out malingerers, recalcitrants, and… Union sympathizers."

"And which is it you have decided I am, pray tell?"

"That is entirely up to you…."

"Well, then I choose… recalcitrant!" Frankie went to the other chair and let himself fall into it.

Barnet started to glance around. "Where is your little fancy man?"

Frankie regarded him malevolently. "Get on with what you came for, Hugh. I am not in the mood for this."

Barnet stood and walked to the mantel. "It has come to the General's notice that quite a number of the Creole gentlemen are slow to join the army or navy. There is some feeling that, since you are unlikely to be abolitionists, and therefore, not traitors, there must be some lack of a compelling reason to put on uniforms and do your part. That reason, we think, may be the old Creole and American divide. If a prominent member of the Creole community were to join up and urge his fellows to do the same…." He turned to face Frankie.

Frankie crossed one arm over his chest and, resting his other elbow on his forearm, put his chin in his hand. "Why me? I should think you would consider me the last to ask to join up."

Barnet's smile was thin and unfriendly. "I know you cannot refuse me."

"Oh, is that so? Why, Hugh, you seem to forget. It is Julienne I seduced, not you."

The mention of his wife's name caused a muscle in Barnet's jaw to twitch. "Of course," he continued, "I now know why that was impossible."

Frankie snorted derisively. "You think that because I prefer men in my life, I can't or don't want a woman?" He considered his childhood friend. "Have you told Julienne—what you believe you know about me, I mean?"

Barnet looked about airily. "You mean, have I told her how I heard you and that… fellow… rutting in your stateroom? That I heard you call out, 'Johnny! Johnny'?"

It was Frankie's turn to frown at the mention of Johnny's name. He did not respond.

"No, Frankie, I have not told her. It's not a fit matter for a gentle lady's ears. Let her continue to think you are a man."

The words, so like what Johnny had shouted at him at the masquerade made Frankie wince. He spoke tentatively. "So are you threatening to tell her if I do not play soldier with you?"

Barnet smiled smugly to himself. "No, not just her. Everyone. Life is going to become less and less private in New Orleans, my old friend. It will become more difficult to let your wealth and family protect you. I cannot have you arrested for unnatural acts of sodomy without proof, but you know it is not difficult to manufacture evidence, assuming I can't get actual proof."

Frankie's heart sank. Mick and Johnny were right. There did come a time when his devil-may-care behavior might cause him a new kind of Hell…. "Go to hell, Hugh."

"I could live with what you are so long as you stayed out of my view, but now you have something I want. I will use what I know about you and anything else to get it."

"You want me to join up and encourage the others to do the same?"

"Oh, I want more than that." He grinned at Frankie's sudden sharp attention. "I want *Le Beau Soleil*."

Frankie jumped up. "No! You will not have my boat to play war with!"

Barnet slapped his gloves on his palm. "What's to stop me?"

"I'll leave New Orleans."

"If you try, you will be arrested on some trumped-up charge. And you can't run away with the *Soleil*. There's a guard posted on the levee already. And I assume you have heard about the blockade…."

Frankie sat again and worried his index finger with his teeth. He looked up. "What blockade?"

"The Union has started to make noise about blockading Confederate ports. You don't think they'd forget about this one, do you? Some Mexican War general, Scott I think, came up with the idea, and that rail-splitter farm boy from Illinois is going along with it."

Frankie knew he had heard of a General Scott. *Was that Mick's general?* Perhaps Mick was part of the plan. He certainly knew the vulnerability of the Mississippi and this city.

Barnet went on, "Until then the privateers are having a grand old time wrecking the few ships that try to sneak up the river from the Gulf. At least our trade goods are reaching Havana. The city has to eat, after all."

Frankie pondered. It occurred to him that if he did join up, he might find a way to protect *Le Beau Soleil*. If he did not, they would most certainly take her for whatever desecrating plans they would have for her.

"Let me think about it a couple days."

"All right," Barnet agreed. He went to the door. "I have a watch on your movements. So don't try anything. Oh, and Frankie...." He put his hand on the door latch. "I know your little fancy man—how do they put it—hit the road as soon as he saw the red-blooded Southern writing on the wall. Those things never last. There is no staying power in it. No substance. You know that, don't you?" He laughed and went out the door.

AT THE levee that evening, Frankie obeyed the guard's command to halt. "Roland, is that you?" he called to the man, who was dressed in the dark blue uniform of one of the Creole soldiers. "So you joined up?"

"That's Private Roland Messier to you, Monsieur Deramus. I see you aren't in uniform." He waited for Frankie's excuses, then getting nothing, said, "My orders are to keep you and everyone else off this boat."

Frankie sighed. "Do you think I can steam away all alone? It takes at least a pilot and two engineers even to take a riverboat out of its mooring." He reached out and put a hand on the soldier's arm. "Don't you remember when your papa was sick and I made sure you all had money to buy bread? Come on, I want to get something out of my stateroom."

Roland glanced about to see if they were being observed. "*D'accord,*" he said. "But you better not be up to anything."

Frankie slipped aboard in the growing twilight and went up the grand staircase. He trailed his hand possessively along the railing as he went down the promenade to the grand cabin. After opening one of the double doors, he went in, then shut them behind him. In the dark, he could make out dim shapes, but they were all on the far side of the room. Glancing to his left, he thought he could tell that the ladies' cabin screens were down, though the divans and chairs along the walls were in place, and a few of the dining tables. He went to them, navigating by memory, until he stood at the two chairs he and... someone... had used for meals. Frankie looked over at the Apollo Belvedere. Its white marble seemed iridescent. The fountain was turned off. The loincloth was in place, he noted with wry amusement. He wished he had more light so he could see the fleur-de-lis and sunburst design of the ornaments in the tall cabin. He looked up, pleased to see that the lights of the city still shone through the skylight.

Going out into the evening air on the promenade, he wondered where the other man was who guarded the boat when it was at its mooring. He went up the stairs to the hurricane deck. He could not bring himself to go into his stateroom. Instead he took the last flight up to the Texas deck. The saloon door was locked. He had the key, but he did not bother to unlock it and go in. Instead, he strolled about the promenade. He was startled when he suddenly saw Compton at the pilothouse, coming out with a valise of some sort. "Clarence," he called.

"Mr. Deramus, I didn't know you were aboard. It is good to see you." Clarence Compton strode forward, his hand out in greeting and a wide smile on his face. "I was just... well... leaving."

Frankie caught the hesitation. "Leaving? You mean leaving, not just going home for the night." His voice betrayed his resignation.

Clarence nodded. "This war is going to be terrible. I have to get home to Indiana, if I can. I should have gone by now. You know Tom joined up, don't you?"

Nodding, Frankie said, "Yes, he's to be a pilot on a rammer, I hear. You don't want to do the same?"

"Naw, I grew up in Indiana. My folks are buried there. It's home, I guess. I suppose if I join up, it will be from my home state."

"You'll join the Federal Army?"

Compton lowered his chin and shrugged.

"Captain Mayer hasn't gone too, has he?" Frankie cleared his throat, waiting for the bad news.

"Not as far as I know. What's going to happen to you, Frankie? Will you try to follow Mr. Sta—will you go up North? Or will you stay here?"

In the light from the street lamps, Frankie saw the real concern on Compton's face. He reached out one hand to run it along the railing next to where he stood. "I was born and raised here. My family goes back to the last century. No, I have nothing up North. And I really only ever had one love, you know."

Compton did not hesitate. "*Le Beau Soleil*."

Frankie's heart screamed, *Liar*, but he nodded. "I have to stay with her, to protect her."

"Will they let you keep her?"

Frankie let out a long breath. "I don't know. I just don't know."

Compton nodded several times in understanding. "Well, Frankie, I guess it's good-bye." He took Frankie's hand and shook it. "Look after yourself, Frankie. They say this will all be over within a year. If I come out of it, I'll come back and…."

Frankie gave him a sardonic grin. "See if I come out of it too?"

It was so quiet after Compton's footsteps on the flights of stairs faded that Frankie could hear some exchange of conversation from where the guard had been standing. He ignored it. He went to the spot before the pilothouse that had become so special a place for Johnny and him. He stood at the rail and looked out across the river at the lights on the opposite bank. He leaned his forearms on the railing and put his face in his hands. He bit down hard to keep sound from issuing from his mouth as he felt the anguish gather in a huge ball in his chest, hot and red and intensely painful, threatening to burst out through his head. He could not entirely stifle the low sound of his moaning.

"Monsieur Deramus?"

Frankie recognized Charles William's voice. He turned and put his face on Charles William's broad chest. Long arms came around him and held him, as comforting as they had been when he was a little child. The deep baritone crooned, "There, there, it will be all right. Uncle Charles will make it all right."

Frankie did not weep. He stood with his arms bent against his chest and his hands in tight fists. He kept his face in his manservant's chest, his head bent way down. He held himself stock-still, terrified to move.

As the terror slowly ebbed, he put his face to the side, letting his cheek rest on Charles William's shoulder. "They are going to take it all away from me, Charles William. They are going to take the *Soleil*. They are making me join the army. I've lost… lost everything."

"Hey, what are you two doing?"

Frankie and his servant sprang apart.

"You weren't kissing, were you? I heard about you." It wasn't Roland but a scraggly American in some other uniform.

Frankie straightened up and shook his shoulders to make his coat fall correctly. "We were not!"

Charles William looked down and shook his head.

"What are you doing up here, boy?" the man, whose voice broadcast Kentucky, demanded.

"He's my servant," Frankie said haughtily. "I brought him on to carry out some personal items."

The soldier grinned, showing two missing teeth in the front of his mouth. "Well, all righty then, you and your boy mosey on down off this boat. I don't know how you got on here—"

Frankie's fury burst forth. "I own this boat."

"You do?" It was said more like a dubious statement than an actual question. "Well, you get along now anyway. Nobody's supposed to be here. Captain's orders."

Frankie thought about demanding the name of the man and his captain, but he felt a weak tug at his sleeve. "All right. I will go for now. But you'll hear better in the morning."

He let Charles William fade back to walk behind him as he went to the stairs and down them, his head high with forced pride.

CHAPTER 18

New Orleans, May 1861

"SO YOU decided to do the right thing?"

Frankie would have liked to slap the smugness from Hugh Barnet's face. "I think you made it abundantly clear that this is the only possible thing to do."

Barnet remained smug. "I would suggest you show a little more enthusiasm if you want to get along in the Confederate Army. Or are you going to be in the navy?"

Frankie wanted to respond, *What navy?* but restrained himself. "Why, Major, I will serve where I can be the most useful."

Barnet offered up a triumphant smile. "That's more like it. I'll take you to the major who can get you squared away." He gestured for Frankie to follow him into the headquarters.

"Frankie!"

As Julienne Barnet came forward beaming with pleasure, Frankie caught the annoyed look on her husband's face. He took her gloved hand and brought it to his lips. "Madame Barnet, this is a distinct pleasure."

"Julienne, my love, I have persuaded Deramus here to show some pluck and patriotism. He is joining up"

"I had no doubt about that. And he will be so dashing in his uniform. I cannot wait to see it. You will come to the supper on Saturday, will you not?" Julienne simpered.

"My dear, I am so sorry. Mr. Deramus will be far too busy getting settled into his new duties to gallivant," Hugh said before Frankie could even open his mouth.

Julienne's brow creased into a frown. "Don't be a bore, Hugh. You know the supper is all part of the war effort. Really, I should think you would be more sensible of my contribution to that… and to your career."

Frankie quickly put in, "Madame, I am in no doubt that the good major is simply predicting the inevitable. I imagine that I will be up to my ears in learning my new duties."

He could not tell whether Hugh found the support more annoying than if he had played the flirt.

Julienne's nose was elevated as she answered with a pretty pout, "He is still invited, Hugh. Don't make me speak to the general."

Frankie suddenly turned as if his attention had been snatched away by something and he could not possibly have heard her last few words. He pointed to a man who was approaching the door of the headquarters building. "Is that not Hercule LaPorte?"

Barnet looked up from where he had been furiously whispering to his wife. "Why yes, and he is the major you will need to speak with. I beg your indulgence, madame, but I need to flag him down for Deramus." He stepped away and called to the man.

"If I possibly can, I shall be at your supper. At your house at the usual time on Saturday?" He kissed her hand again, bowed, and watched her turn reluctantly away.

"Come along, Deramus. The major can see you now." Barnet also turned to watch Julienne—all hoopskirts, flounces and parasol—cross the street and catch up with her friends on the sidewalk.

Frankie followed the two men into the building, glad they could not see his wry smile. Hercule LaPorte was an old acquaintance. In fact, he was usually at Mam'selle Marie's masquerades. He had not been there this year, but that just meant Hercule had heard whatever stories were circulating about the scene with his friend secondhand. Besides, Frankie had never known Hercule to be petty.

LaPorte took them down a short corridor to a door he pushed open and stepped through. "*Bienvenue*, François. Take a seat. Thank you, Barnet, for convincing him to enlist."

In other words, good-bye, Hugh, Frankie thought. The two officers saluted each other and with some murmur of pleasantries, Barnet took his leave. "Charming fellow," Frankie said indolently.

LaPorte took the seat behind his desk while Frankie found a place to lean his walking stick, removed his hat, and sat on the chair indicated. "You are old friends, I believe?"

"We grew up together."

LaPorte's cocked eyebrow told Frankie he had gotten the impression that "friends" would not reflect the relationship accurately. He went on, "Well, past associations are best left in the past." He gave Frankie a significant look.

"*Je comprends*. You can count on that." He sighed. "I suppose that as of now I will have to start saluting him and calling him 'sir.'"

"You were always a thoroughly courteous man. The 'sir' should not bother you."

Frankie thought, *but now it will be a pretense of respect, not simply politesse*. Aloud he said, "So, Major, what do I need to do now? See my tailor, I suppose." He suddenly realized he was going to have to drop his languid demeanor and be more... well, military. He sat up straight.

LaPorte looked like he had been thinking along similar lines. "Well, yes, but first we have to figure out which uniform to have Schmidt make for you, *n'est-ce pas?*" He sat back in his chair, crossed one arm over his chest resplendent with brass buttons and other insignia, resting his other elbow on it, and considered Frankie. "Did you have anything in mind?"

Frankie knew full well no matter what he had in mind, it was unlikely to be the outcome of this meeting. "Barnet... excuse me, Major Barnet said there was a need for someone to encourage other Creole gentleman to do their duty to the Confederacy."

LaPorte chuckled. "He did, did he? I should think my presence in this capacity would give the lie to that. Besides, Soulé has taken care of that need."

Frankie looked down with a bemused expression. "I see."

LaPorte suggested, "You have *Le Beau Soleil*, so you are fit for navy service, I suppose."

Frankie interrupted, "But Barnet—" Then the riverboat was mentioned.

"Don't tell me Barnet has promised something else, something regarding *Le Beau Soleil*?"

Frankie shook his head. "He just used it as a threat. Implied that if I did not 'do my duty' the army or navy will confiscate her."

Lowering his arms, LaPorte frowned. "You realize that will happen anyway."

Trying to hide dismay, Frankie urged, "Is there nothing I can do to prevent that? I am simply afraid of losing my livelihood after the war."

"Understandable concern, Deramus, but much worse sacrifices are being made by men who have decided to serve the Southern cause." He thought a moment. "You know, President Davis is offering letters of mark and reprisal for privateers...."

Frankie shook his head. "It's not that I don't want to serve. It's that I would rather not risk my boat in battle situations."

LaPorte shrugged. "The best I can promise is to try to channel the *Soleil*'s use away from actual battle. But it won't be up to me, you realize."

Frankie considered this. "I am not a sailor or engineer. I don't know how I can be of any use to the navy. Do you?"

LaPorte shook his head. "No, though we can talk to whomever they assign to be commander of naval forces on the Mississippi. Can you navigate?"

Frankie essayed a smile. "In social circles, *mais oui*." The major's frown made him realize he was being flippant again. "No, sir, I cannot pilot. The two pilots who worked for me have both... been placed."

He wasn't sure if Compton had had time to get out of New Orleans yet. Then, a thought struck him. "I believe my captain, Josef Mayer, has not made up his mind what to do yet. I can ask him to stay with the *Soleil* in the army or navy's service."

The man at the desk smiled sardonically. "Well, that will be up to the army or navy, but I think I can make a case for his knowing the boat and the river better than anyone the service can supply. I remember it's quite capacious. Lots of cargo and passenger space?"

Frankie nodded hopefully.

"I should think it would be better used for cargo and troop transport, then. It would not do well as a rammer."

Frankie knew about the rammers. Tom Rice, one of the former pilots on *Le Beau Soleil*, had told him he was to pilot the *Magnolia Queen*, which was to be a rammer.

The *Queen*, like most of them, was a privateer—also a steam-driven side-wheeler like the *Soleil*, but skimpy on main deck space and low in the water. The privateers were hardening their bows with steel, so they could steam up to both merchant and military vessels and sink them by ramming through their hulls. The response was making existing ships ironclad, but it would be a while before most could be refitted, either on the Federal or the Confederate side.

"I agree." Frankie thought hard. He hated the idea of hundreds of soldiers picking at the gold leaf on the doorways and pissing in the fountain, but perhaps he could make sure the impact would not be devastation. "The staterooms would do well for officers. There are quite a few." He put out a tentative feeler. "Would I... will I lose ownership entirely?"

LaPorte waved one hand dismissively. "I shouldn't think so. If you insist on gouging the government for its use, then you might."

"But if I don't, if I offer the *Soleil*'s use during the war as part of my... contribution to the cause of liberty...?"

The major shrugged. "I can't guarantee it, but that ought to ameliorate things considerably. But that only takes care of *Le Beau Soleil*. What about you? Let me think...." He stood and moved around to the front of the desk and leaned back against it. "You are primarily an entertainer. I hope that is not insulting?"

Frankie waved a hand in dismissal. "Not at all. Besides being a wealthy man with interests in numerous businesses, I make most of my money as the star attraction, I suppose you could say, of taking passage upriver and back. But I doubt you have positions for gamblers."

"No," LaPorte answered, stretching out the word. "But you must be able to get into a man's head and anticipate his actions. Maybe even influence them."

Frankie nodded slowly.

The major stood and went to sit behind his desk once again. He opened a side drawer and drew out some papers. "I think you might be particularly useful in intelligence." He took a pen from an inkwell and dipped it. "That is, if you are loyal." Hesitating, he asked, "You do have slaves, don't you?"

Frankie thought of the Albrights and their official status as his property in spite of his own wishes that he did not have to own them. He answered with ease, "Yes."

"And you harbor no sympathies for the North."

Frankie could look LaPorte in the eye and state firmly, "I am first and foremost a proud citizen of New Orleans and the great state of Louisiana. I would never take any action to harm my beloved homeland. You know that I am a man of honor. I may be a less than stellar citizen, but I am no traitor to my people, my country."

Hercule LaPorte, Major, Army of the Confederate States of America, smiled. "We understand each other perfectly." He started to write on the papers. "Of course, you won't be called an intelligence officer. That spooks everyone. You will be in communications." He continued to write. At a pause, he looked up with a knowing smile. "What rank?"

Frankie was clueless at first what the major meant by the look. Then it came to him. "How much is a major?"

LaPorte smiled. "You'd like that wouldn't you, not having to say 'sir' to Barnet. Believe me, I would too. But that might be pushing it. Captain. Be extraordinary and you may find yourself promoted." He scribbled more on the document, turned it, and pointed to where Frankie should sign.

Picking up the pen and dipping it into the ink, Frankie said— probably for the last time for a long time to come—exactly what came into his head. "Being extraordinary is what I do best."

NOT only could Frankie find the time to attend Julienne's supper, he was instructed to do so by his superior officer, Colonel. J. Davidson Brownworth.

"May as well start getting to know people. I know you are already familiar with most or perhaps all of the local society, but there are lots of new people, like me. Have you been introduced to the general yet?"

Frankie, still not in his final full uniform, had started to fit in with the way things were done in the command. "Not really, sir. Just to salute and be acknowledged. He's… older than I expected."

Brownworth was a solemn, middle-aged man, easy to work with because he was simple, clear, direct, and reasonable. "He's over seventy. I know that much. And I don't think he is well. But he handled that business with Texas pretty well, if you ask me."

"Yes, sir."

"Twiggs will be at the Barnets' supper. I'll make sure you get properly introduced."

"Will you be there, sir?"

Brownworth responded, "Yes, I will." His voice communicated disinclination, but Frankie did not know if it was for suppers in general or for this one in particular. "Will your uniform be ready?"

"No, sir. I'm sorry."

"Well, I'll get my lieutenant to go light a fire under your tailor—Schmidt isn't it? This is important."

Frankie made a shallow bow. "Thank you, Colonel."

THANKS to his colonel's efforts, Frankie was in full dress uniform when he arrived at the Barnets' lovely house in the Faubourg St. Mary. It was an old house, but not a longtime family estate, since Hugh's father had bought it when he and his young family came to New Orleans from North Carolina. Old Mr. Barnet had three or four plantations, so he had parked his seven-year-old son, his wife, and two younger daughters, along with their slaves, in the city while he went from his sugar plantation to his cotton plantation and on to a second sugar plantation, all located up the river in Louisiana and Mississippi. The old man was dead now, his daughters married and moved away from New Orleans, but Mrs. Barnet still lived in the house; she was quite deaf and becoming addled in her old age. The butler was an octoroon fellow rumored to be old Mr. Barnet's son by a *placée*, a free woman of color he set up in a nice little house on Rue Burgundy. Hugh probably had more half brothers and sisters up on the plantations. As far as Frankie knew, Hugh himself had never gone into the practice of keeping a colored mistress. He and Julienne did not have any children either.

"Colonel Brownworth! Captain Deramus! I am so happy you were both able to come to my party."

Julienne was resplendent in the latest style of gown—peach silk, full hoopskirt, and crazy with ruffles and lace. She had a confection of white feathers in her hair. Hugh Barnet stood at her side in full dress uniform.

While the colonel and Frankie each kissed Julienne's gloved hand, Hugh said, "I see you are well and truly with us now, Captain. Communications, I see."

Frankie saluted. "That's right, sir."

Julienne fawned over Frankie. "You look splendid, Frankie, or do I have to call you 'Captain' now? Doesn't he look splendid, Hugh?"

"We have other guests, my dear," Hugh admonished.

"Ah, there's General Twiggs right now." Frankie's colonel nodded in the direction of an old man who sat looking sleepy in a big chair by the fire in the parlor. Approaching the old man, he said in a slightly raised volume, "Excuse me, General, may I introduce my new captain, François Deramus."

Frankie saluted the old man, who flapped a hand at his brow as a return salute. He looked up and asked in a gruff voice, "Deramus, you say? Is that a French name?"

Frankie offered a gracious bow. "Creole French, sir."

"So you must be a native of New Orleans."

"I am indeed, sir."

Twiggs gestured toward the two empty chairs near him. "I am from Georgia, m'self. Been in Texas a while. The Confederacy needed me, so here I am."

Brownworth smiled broadly. "Yes, sir, most certainly. May I get you some punch, General? Or something to eat?"

The General made a vague circular gesture in the air and said, "Yes, find me a stiff whiskey, will you?" He turned back to Frankie. "So, what sort of work were you in before this folderol started? Or were you a soldier? In the Mexican War, though perhaps you are too young."

Frankie made sure his voice was loud and his English precise. "I own a riverboat and did transport, sir. I have never been a soldier, but a good friend of mine, a Michael Murphy, served with you, I understand."

Twiggs eyes lit up. "Mick Murphy? Knew him well, poor fellow. Nasty wound laid him up for quite a while. So he is still around?"

Frankie chatted with Twiggs about Mick and the Mexican War for several minutes. When Brownworth came back with the general's whiskey, he seemed glad to see him animated. "Beg pardon, General, but I hate to take the captain away. I have some office business I need to discuss with him."

The general reached out a hand to Frankie, who shook it. "Call of duty, I know. Just be sure to stop back later, young man. It was good to hear that Mick Murphy found a new line of business. Hope he finds Old Fuss and Feathers in the pink."

Walking away, the colonel asked, "Mick Murphy off to serve with Winfield Scott? He someone you know, Murphy I mean?"

"Yes, sir. He went North. He was from somewhere up there. Boston or some such place. A private investigator, confidential agent now. Or he was. That is how we met. I hired him to look into a business matter for me."

The colonel introduced Frankie all around, taking time when he could to make discreet comments about this businessman, that officer, and ask questions about local politicians.

They overheard a heated discussion. One man expressed great frustration over the refitting of ships in New Orleans shipyards. "The Yankees are on their way now to blockade our shipping or worse. I tell you, we have to stop dillydallying about, getting the warships *Mississippi* and *Louisiana* ready to fight."

"Now Stevenson, you don't think our ships and our privateers can't handle a puny little Federal navy, do you?" scoffed another man in a fine civilian topcoat.

The angry man, dressed in a civilian ship's captain's uniform, responded, "Mark my words, Lincoln may be a country boy, but he's no fool. And he knows the big rivers. He was even here in the city, or so I heard. He knows that if the North can cut us in half at the Mississippi, the jig is up." He made a rude gesture of dismissal at the answering laughter from his audience and stomped away.

Frankie thought he knew this man. "Colonel, is that Capt. John Stevenson, the man building the *Manassas*?"

"That's the man. Hell if I understand how you can pour all that iron into the water and it still floats. But what the Secret Service is starting to hear, is that he's right. I wouldn't be surprised if his *Manassas* is the first submarine boat in the CSA." He looked at Frankie. "But he's from here. You didn't know him?"

"Only to nod on the street, sir. He's a very serious man."

Brownworth chuckled. "And you aren't?"

Frankie smiled sardonically. "I used to be a great deal less serious than I am now, sir."

CHAPTER 19

New Orleans, late May 1861

"I AM beyond endurance with this issue," the choleric Captain Stevenson said as he addressed the command officers at headquarters a few days later. "In fact, I have found it necessary to write to President Davis about it."

The high ranking naval officers sat together, their lips tightly compressed and their gazes on the tabletop before them.

Stevenson lifted a sheet of paper and read from his letter:

> We have no time, place, or means, to build an effective navy. Our ports are, or soon will be, all blockaded. On land, we do not fear Lincoln, but what shall we do to cripple him at sea? In this emergency, and seeing that he is arming many poorly adapted vessels, I have two months past been entirely engaged in perfecting plans by which I could so alter and adapt some of our heavy and powerful tow-boats on the Mississippi as to make them comparatively safe against the heaviest guns afloat, and by preparing their bow in a peculiar manner, as my plans and model will show, render them capable of sinking by collision the heaviest vessels ever built.

He looked about at the assemblage with an expression of injured dignity. "And now, as we have been brought together to discuss this blockade, whereof I wrote is a fact. The *USS Brooklyn* may have grounded herself a couple of times, but her captain managed to blockade the mouth of the river anyway. Are we going to get those ships ready to fight or is it too late?"

"Aw, Jack, will you give it a rest?" came a fractious plea from one of the naval command.

Frankie leaned to Brownworth. "So I heard the boats from northern ports were all impounded a couple days ago. At least that means we can use them."

He had been relieved to hear this news because it meant he might have some leeway in controlling the disposition of *Le Beau Soleil*. As it was, his old and new connections among the military staff had let him establish Josef Mayer as her official captain. He had had less success obtaining control over her furnishings. Barnet had kicked up a fuss when Frankie had tried, and as LaPorte had explained, "He had a point, Deramus. You are too unknown a quantity yet. Letting you have access to the riverboat has the potential for damage or subversion. Be patient. I will make sure your recommendations are followed. And everything in your personal stateroom will be packed up and stored." He cleared his throat and continued in a quieter voice, "If there's anything sensitive, of a private nature… I can see to it someone safe…."

"No, Major, that won't be necessary. Anything like that, if it even exists, is in a safe place. But I very much thank you for your discretion."

In fact, Frankie, having destroyed the nude ambrotype photograph of himself, had thereafter done the same with the letters from Johnny that he had in his possession. He had only gifts, innocuous, with the exception of the watch, and that he had placed with his gold in the hotel safe.

The bitter wrangling went on around them. Brownworth said, "And I heard one of the privateers, Calhoun, has three vessels he captured coming upriver. Must have gotten them underway before the Brooklyn blockaded the river."

Frankie chewed on his lower lip. "Then, if I may ask, sir, what next?"

The colonel shrugged. "I suppose the Federals will try to blockade up north. There won't be anything going out of or into New Orleans. Stevenson's right about the building and refitting of the ships. Typical Southern leisurely work. Sorry, not to impugn our Southern ways, but we don't seem to know how to get things done like they do in the North. Anyway, it remains to be seen what will happen if there is no shipping of supplies other than back and forth along the river to Tennessee and Missouri."

Frankie shook his head. "New Orleans is a perfect port, but not if the river is blockaded. We aren't equipped for overland transportation. We have never needed to be." He added a quick, "Sir."

As Frankie went about his duties, primarily consisting of meeting with representatives of the many civic groups, going back and forth to outlying forts like St. Philip and Jackson, and simply keeping his ears open, he started to feel the lack of a love life. He knew his disinclination after his breakup with Johnny would not last forever. His heart may have been frozen, but his cock was quite aware of the attractive men around him. He previously had an extraordinarily active intimate life until he met Johnny. The times they had been apart between Johnny's travels up and down the river had taught Frankie some discipline. But all he really had now was self-pleasuring, and too often that brought back painful longings for what he would never have again. In addition, he knew Barnet, or Barnet's own network of unofficial spies, had an eye on his activities. He could not risk a liaison right now, even if he wanted to risk the emotional complication, which he did not. A veiled suggestion to LaPorte had been quashed immediately. LaPorte was having none of it. Frankie let it drop and did not pick it up again. "Frankie," LaPorte had commented simply, "you are going to have to put that on hold for some time. You don't want something to develop within the staff and you never know who is bankrolling anyone you could hire."

Frankie had started to protest, as he always had, that he had no use for lovers for hire, but he instantly thought, *I'd be lucky to have that now*. So loneliness and frustration, something he had little experience with, became the mode of his existence.

THE blockade of all access from the Gulf of Mexico to the Mississippi brought about deprivations almost at once, yet people in the city remained boisterously in support of the Confederacy and the war. The first recruitment efforts were staggeringly successful. Frankie was surprised when some of his own friends signed up, including Jean-Paul LeGrand, known in some circles as "Mam'selle Marie." Frankie was on hand when "Marie" and a few of the others who had been at the ball left the city, resplendent in uniforms of the best fabrics, with gold braid and rich leathers and a sporting air about them. He kept his opinions about their romantic notions of war to himself.

Then those early recruits sent to fight in Virginia and other parts of the young Confederacy started to come back with terrible wounds and horror stories. Many, many others never came back at all. They lay far from home in graves their mothers, wives, and sweethearts would never see.

The mood in the city may have changed, but it was toward an even more frantic and angry support of the war. Now it was no longer, "Those Yankee bastards want to tell us what we can and cannot do!" but rather, "Those Yankee bastards killed Sam or Pierre or Nate!" The few men who survived death but came back maimed, missing arms or legs, or gone blind, were daily reminders of the war. Frankie was not immune. He heard with bitterness of the death at Ball's Bluff, Virginia, of Etienne Culaliene, an artistic young man he had known and who had briefly been his lover years before. Deep inside he blamed the foolishness of war, though so much personal grief inclined him to agree that Yankees were savages. He tried not to think of one particular Yankee.

Dominique appeared to have trouble believing in the danger, but Charles William was grim. He knew young colored men were beaten up for no other reason than they were an ostensible object of the Yankees' crusade.

Frankie weighed his options for the Albrights. If it were only Charles William, he could install him permanently as his body servant. All the officers had them and most of those servants were colored. But there was Dominique. How could he protect her? He decided to talk it over with them. He found with chagrin they had already discussed the matter and come to conclusions of their own: they simply did not wish to be separated. Any suggestion Frankie made, they vetoed. They would stay in their little house. Charles William would valet his master, as always, but would go home every night he could, as before. If anything, the fact that Frankie was in the city all the time now meant the Albrights had more time together.

"What about going up North?" Frankie suggested.

Dominique responded, "And leave you alone?"

Frankie was speechless. He had not considered their affection for him would be part of any equation. "Frankie, you are like our son. The fact that I can say those words to a white man is more a reflection on you than on me. What kind of mother would abandon her boy?"

Frankie knew lots of white "boys" whose mothers all but shoved them into the army to get rid of them, or went somewhere where they felt safer and left their boys and their husbands to fend for themselves.

The other people who began to behave in unexpected ways were the huge population of immigrants in New Orleans. As supplies became scarcer, these families suffered disproportionately. Frankie was in an ideal position to monitor this atmosphere in his capacity as "Captain Big Ears," whose very responsibility was to learn what he could, however he could. Whether he reported all to his commanding officer was at his discretion, or so he liked to think.

After two waves of enlistment fever were over, the pressure was on for every man to join up. Many of the immigrants held back from joining because they were the sole breadwinners for their families and could not see themselves supporting them on the sometimes-unreliable soldier's pay. Though they were not rabid abolitionists by and large, they had so little stake in slavery and its specious benefits that the jingoistic fervor of the native-born did not outweigh simple pragmatism. But when the thugs went about their enclaves—whether as street gangs or actually organized by politicians—and beat up these men or threatened their families, the Helmuts and Paddies and Ginos started joining up too.

A factor that made Frankie's life more difficult—in spite of the healing effect of the passing of time—was increased exposure not only to Hugh Barnet, but also to his wife, Julienne. She was about headquarters constantly, ostensibly delivering sweets her cook had made, but which she acted as if she herself had labored over. She used her visits to flirt with senior staff and to wheedle favors for herself and her husband.

Julienne took the opportunity and implicit invitation to visit Frankie in the office he shared with his own colonel, to sit in the chair by his desk and whisper gossip she had heard about this man or that, on the pretense she was helping him do his duty as an intelligence officer. If Brownworth was not present, she sat closer, touched Frankie at every opportunity, and made such outrageously suggestive hints that, rather than tempting him, caused him to have to struggle not to laugh. He was sure her husband had been truthful when he had said he never shared overhearing Frankie at lovemaking, for nothing in her demeanor spoke of surprise or curiosity or even the challenge he knew some women regarded men who preferred other men as.

Her confidences about the traitorous—or at least questionable—people she reported to Frankie to help with his duties as an intelligence officer were starting to wear on him. He was relieved when Brownworth never asked him to report any "unnatural behavior or tendencies" he became aware of. Frankie had quite expected it and had steeled himself to clandestinely protect others like himself. He imagined Brownworth's failure to assign such an endeavor probably came from the man's seeming lack of awareness of men who loved other men. In any case, Frankie was never forced to deal with the topic. He wondered if Hugh Barnet ever tried to insinuate the need for vigilance in this area, but if he did, Brownworth—bless his sheltered soul—seemed unable or unwilling to take the hints.

Frankie could not help but be puzzled over Hugh's unpredictable behavior where Frankie was concerned. They had started out as friends, the two boys and Julienne as constant companions—as much as Julienne's mother and governess would countenance. There was always a tacit expectation she and Frankie would marry someday, being good little Creoles and both from well-off families. But of course, Frankie had no interest in Julienne as anything but a friend. She finally accepted Hugh's oft-repeated proposal when it was clear Frankie was not going to make one.

Frankie, Hugh's best man at the wedding, began right away to notice the marriage was not a happy one. He had no idea why. Frankie had in the meantime become fully in control of his inheritance with his majority and sold his parents' two houses to buy and refurbish what he always called his "true love," *Le Beau Soleil*. Julienne started in on him whenever he was within reach, in spite of his obvious indifference. He wondered if Hugh had been a romantic disappointment for Julienne, or if there was some other tension between the Barnets. They had no children: if that was the bone of contention, Frankie imagined it must be in their minds that Hugh was the one at fault. He could not understand how Julienne would come to that conclusion, but perhaps she had, and Hugh either resented this or accepted it with all the unmanning implications it brought. Or, Frankie considered, perhaps Hugh was impotent. He did not know.

Then there was the evening when Hugh, coming back early from a business trip, had walked in on what he had seized upon as Frankie's attempted seduction of Julienne. In fact it was quite the opposite. Julienne had invited Frankie over for dinner on the pretense others would be there as well. In fact the dinner, intimate and dimly candlelit, was for the two of them. Frankie had tried to leave when he realized this, but she had thrown one of her tantrums, weeping and saying he simply could not be so heartless as to leave her all alone in that great big house. Hugh's mother was upstairs, in her invalid bed, but poor Julienne could not cope with that. She finally threw herself at him, and he was on the verge of telling her why he would never be her lover when Hugh came home. In his understandable outrage, Hugh had tried to call Frankie out, but Frankie was not someone who considered dueling healthy, so he let Hugh gain the upper hand, the moral victory.

Frankie was entirely baffled by Hugh's behavior since he had discovered Frankie could not, and would not, have tried to seduce Julienne. Shouldn't that have made Hugh relax, knowing he had never been at risk of cuckolding? Frankie knew men like Hugh despised men who engaged in unnatural acts. That would explain part of the antagonism, but Hugh still bridled when Julienne all but stripped Frankie every chance she got. How was that Frankie's fault?

Now, he waited for Hugh to expose him. Barnet obviously resented how quickly Frankie had become a success in the army. Maj.

Barnet was not so popular with his superiors. In fact, when they could, people avoided him and Julienne. It had occurred to Frankie finally that Hugh, though a twit, was no fool. He knew no one would ever take his side against Frankie. No one liked or valued Hugh, and everyone from Twiggs down liked and valued Frankie.

CHAPTER 20

New Orleans, September 1861

IN LATE September, the songwriter Harry McCarthy was to hold a concert in New Orleans featuring his new song, "The Bonnie Blue Flag," which had become an unofficial Confederate anthem.

When Hugh Barnet came to him with his hat in his hand and an obsequious demeanor, Frankie knew his childhood chum needed a favor. He gestured Hugh to the chair by his desk, sat back with his legs crossed and his hands clasped behind his head, and waited.

"You know about that concert?" Hugh began tentatively.

Frankie was tempted to play dumb, but baiting Hugh had lost all its luster of late. "You mean Harry McCarthy?"

"Yes, are you going?"

Hesitating, Frankie shook his head. "Not planning on it. Too much work."

Barnet grimaced. "Well, it's just that… Julienne wants to go."

Frowning, Frankie asked, "Well, can't you take her?"

"Of course, but her cousin, Georgiana, will be in town, and Julienne asked me to ask you to escort her." He looked at Frankie appealingly.

Hugh winced as Frankie's boots hit the floor with a loud protest. "Oh for God's sake, Hugh. Grow some—" He was about to say "balls" but instead inserted "spine." Even that was a mistake. "I'm sorry," he said to Hugh's scowl. "You know I won't want to go to a concert with that twittering little bird, Georgiana. Can't you get someone else?"

Hugh twisted his hat with its one star in his hands. "She says it has to be you."

"Who says it has to be me?" Frankie saw from the look on Hugh's face that it was Julienne who had insisted. "Oh, I see."

Hugh's glower deepened. Clearly he could guess what Frankie was thinking, that Julienne was using Georgiana as the excuse to go to the concert… with Frankie. Frankie felt a twinge of compassion for the man. "Well, all right. I'll come to your house with a carriage before the concert. Do you want me to get the tickets?"

Hugh stood and glared. "That won't be necessary. Julienne already bought them."

Frankie's right eyebrow went up, but he said nothing as Hugh stiffly turned and left his office.

Frankie sat back again and sighed deeply. Why did he care how Hugh felt? Hugh had made that bed with Julienne and he could lie in it. He certainly would not hesitate to make Frankie's life a living hell if he could. This "command performance" was a case in point. So why did Frankie go along with it? It was no longer fear of exposure. He was making sure whatever Hugh thought he had on Frankie, he never got anything more. Frankie's love life was nonexistent as a result.

He thought back to when he, Julienne and Hugh had been childhood friends. What had he seen in them, these children who turned into such unpleasant adults? Frankie knew he himself had been a lonely boy. He had never felt like he fit in with the others, something he came to understand when he began to mature sexually. He simply did not in fact fit in. He was different. For some years his only friends were Hugh and Julienne.

Hugh seemed as lonely as he, but it was not, as he first hoped, for the same reason. He could only speculate on what had made Hugh so unhappy. The boy had never divulged his own troubles. Was it his family? Being new to the society of the other children in New Orleans when his family first moved here? Was it something else? He and Frankie had become fast friends almost at once, but now Frankie thought it may have been no more than they were all each other had.

Their one thing in common was Julienne. Her mother and Frankie's had been close friends. Their mothers had had plans for their marriage as long ago as when they were toddlers. It was Frankie who had first introduced Hugh to the pretty little girl. It was obvious Hugh was instantly smitten. Like Frankie, who had been instantly smitten with Hugh. Frankie could not help but shudder now, thinking, *mon Dieu, the man had been my first love*. What a thought.

Julienne, for her part, had never been any different than she was now: vain, selfish, fickle. She had treated Frankie as her own property even then, and that was part of the reason for this "invitation." Part, but not all. She had always been a shameless flirt. Naively he had thought marriage to Hugh would simmer her down, but whether the marriage could ever have done that, he could not guess. She wanted him, he knew. Wanted him desperately. Hugh would always be a fallback, and she treated him that way. No wonder Hugh hated him.

Frankie's thoughts were drawn back to one afternoon in Julienne's garden when she had suddenly turned to him after he had repulsed one of her none-too-subtle advances not long before she had accepted Hugh's proposal. She glared at him, her fists on her hips. "What is it, Frankie? Is it me you find so unappealing or all women?"

Frankie went pale. "I… I don't know what you mean, Julienne."

She glared at him a few more moments, then stamped one foot in frustration. "Don't make me say it. I have never seen you… show any interest, not only in me but any of my friends." She had turned her face, but now glanced back at him. "Or are you only interested in…?"

Frankie cringed inwardly, waiting for Julienne to ask him if he preferred boys.

To his relief, she said instead, "Women of a lower sort? Why would that stop you from marrying a respectable girl and settling down? I know you men have to have your dalliances. But you will need children, Frankie." She moved to him and pressed herself against him. "Why can't I provide you with those children?"

It was then Frankie saw his way out of the situation. In a mock mournful voice, he said, "*Mais, ma chère*, you know my only love is *Le Beau Soleil*. It would be unfair, nay, unchivalrous to expect a woman to play second fiddle to a boat."

Yes, Frankie knew he had been Julienne's first choice. Perhaps that was the reason for his compassion for Hugh. He folded when Julienne had Hugh's balls tightly in her grasp. Perhaps Frankie could imagine what it would have been like if he had done what was expected of him and married her. Perhaps he blamed himself for leaving a scorned woman to say yes to Hugh.

"*Merde*," he said to himself, straightening in his chair. He would go to the concert, do his escort duty, then find somewhere else to be whenever Hugh or Julienne came around wanting something from him.

ON HIS way in a rented carriage to pick up the Barnets and Georgiana, Frankie noticed a lot of people milling about the streets. He frowned. Disturbances had become commonplace as economic conditions worsened, but this one had a different feeling. The groups of people seemed to be a mix of "Kentucks," poor Irish, and the assortment of ruffians who appeared to thrive in these times of fear and want. But the makeup of the crowd was not what was amiss to Frankie's mind. He could not put a finger on what was wrong. He had heard nothing about a gathering in his snooping about, so he dismissed his wariness as groundless.

The Barnets' colored butler opened the door when Frankie arrived as promised. "Well, Mr. Frankie, right on time, as usual. It's good to see you, sir."

Frankie smiled and nodded, handing the man his hat and gloves. "Good to see you, too, James. How are Minnie and the children?"

"They are all well, Mr. Frankie. Thank you for asking, sir. The major and Madame and their guest are waiting in the parlor."

Julienne was beaming when James introduced Frankie as "Monsieur Deramus."

Frankie went to her, took her hand, and kissed it. "*Enchanté*, Julienne. Astonishingly lovely, as always. Hello, Major. And this can't be little George, can it?" He went to Julienne's cousin and kissed her hand. "*Mais non*, it cannot be. She is a knobby-kneed tomboy. This is a beautiful woman."

Georgiana, a spinster at twenty-five, was far from ugly, but she was not a beauty. She grew radiant from his praise, which even Frankie had to admit made almost any woman beautiful. She hardly resembled Julienne, being much shorter, skinnier, and without the feminine curves. Her pale brown hair and gray eyes had the same dull look to him they had always had. "Not the shiniest coin in the collection plate" was how Tante Dominique had put it.

Georgiana was, however, gorgeous in a gown that looked vaguely familiar to Frankie—no doubt one of Julienne's, taken in and shortened. The neckline that was de rigueur for an evening gown had little to justify it. There were Julienne's gems too. But as was always the case with any woman who accompanied Mme. Barnet to a public event, there was something missing beyond the lack of true charm. Julienne, posing as benefactor, always made sure she was the beauty in the room.

"Mademoiselle, that gown could not possibly look so lovely on anyone but you," Frankie complimented smoothly. He caught Hugh's smirk and Julienne's affront out of the corner of his eye as Georgiana giggled happily.

Their wraps fetched by James, each woman took one of the men's arms. Of course, Julienne took Frankie's, pressing his arm tight into her bust and wriggling against him. He hoped this was not going to be the pattern for the whole evening. When they got to the hired carriage, he helped her mount the step, but then turned to make a big show of helping Georgiana up and sliding in beside her.

Their box at the Academy was excellent; it was certainly chosen for everyone to see them, not so much for them to hear the orchestra. The women, with their wide skirts, sat closer to the rail, the men behind and slightly to the outer sides of the box. Julienne preened for the rest of the audience in the first-tier boxes while Georgiana simpered over Frankie's courtly attentions. Hugh seemed content to watch Frankie make a fool of himself, that was, until Julienne recommenced making a fool of him.

Julienne alternately leaned over the rail to look at, or rather to be seen by others in the audience, and leaned behind Georgiana to touch Frankie's knee with her outstretched hand. She made clever remarks, laughed at them, and pouted prettily at him.

He was noticing Georgiana's discomfort. She sat and spread out her wide hoopskirts, accepting Frankie's hand on her elbow; then she glanced down at the neckline of her bodice. Frankie could see the tops of her breasts where the bodice pulled away thanks to its stiffness. Glancing up at Frankie, she colored deeply, although he had quickly looked away. He had removed her short cloak gallantly, but now wished he had not. She reached for it, pulled it around her shoulders and tugged it close to her chest.

Frankie sat in his own cushioned chair and looked at Julienne. Her amused smirk faded quickly as he glared at her. He knew she had engineered the embarrassment, and he loathed her for it at that moment. He said loud enough for them all to hear, "It is rather chilly in here, isn't it? Are you warm enough, my dear Georgiana? Would you like my cloak?"

Her tight shake of the head showed she was both grateful for his consideration and also more than a little chagrined he had guessed her discomfort. He sighed inwardly. One never knew precisely the right thing to do. He cringed as he remembered the things he had said to Johnny at the masquerade. Of all the things he believed about himself, gaucheness was not one he had recognized.

Frankie looked over the audience as it waited for the concert to begin. The Academy of Music was packed with soldiers. Frankie had seen them in the city, recruits from Louisiana, Arkansas, and Texas who were about to be deployed in Virginia. They were restless and full of anticipation, waiting for the author of the new lyrics to an old Irish song, and they were not to be disappointed.

Applause filled the hall when Harry McCarthy came to the conductor's podium and bowed. The orchestra was heavy on winds and brass—almost but not quite a military band. The first tune was a mellow Stephen Foster piece, luckily not "Come Where My Love Lies Dreaming," and Frankie was glad of the need to be quiet and listen.

He let his mind wander, catching himself when he realized he was imagining himself in the grand cabin listening to musicians perform after an evening supper. He could almost feel Johnny's hand in his, hidden under the drape of the tablecloth. He jerked himself back to the present. He glanced around and caught sight of a man he did not know who was sitting in the orchestra playing an oboe. He was strikingly good-looking. He had a full head of curly dark hair, green eyes, finely sculpted cheekbones and red lips. He had what had come to be called "Byronic" good looks. Frankie scanned every bit of him he could see from where his seat gave him a tolerable view. He pursed his lips, then put out the tip of his tongue to moisten them. He ran one index finger along his moustache as he savored the view. He absently put out the tip of his tongue to wet his lips.

He happened to look over to catch Hugh scowling at him. The man mouthed something that might have been "deviant." Frankie closed his eyes, and wanted to get up and leave. But he couldn't. So he kept his eyes closed and tried to focus on the music.

During the brief intermission, Frankie volunteered to get cups of punch for them all. As he returned to where the ladies were now standing alone, he found Hugh sailing to cut him off.

"I saw you ogling that musician. Can't you keep it in your pants, you scoundrel?" Hugh demanded.

Frankie considered him, rehearsed maybe a dozen ripostes involving the lack of anything in Hugh's pants, then sighed and carried the cups over to the two women.

Finally the excruciating evening was almost at its end. In the audience, Frankie watched as McCarthy, dressed in full Confederate uniform with pack and rifle came out on the stage. Frankie breathed, "*Mon Dieu*," as he glanced over at the rows and rows of soldiers. What decorum they had exhibited during the concert was coming apart. They cheered McCarthy wildly as he came onto the stage. They burst out gleefully when he began to sing the words to his new song, "The Bonnie Blue Flag." When he started into the chorus, the whole group of soldiers sang along, growing more and more exuberant.

"Hurrah! Hurrah!

For Southern rights, hurrah!

Hurrah for the Bonnie Blue Flag that bears a single star."

At one point a woman ran in from the wings with a blue flag with a white star and threw her arms around McCarthy, appearing to hang on him weeping. If the uniform and song had the soldiers in a riotous mood, this little melodrama made them jump up and shout. Frankie saw even McCarthy looked nervous, and the singer tried to slow the fever down. Nevertheless, the soldiers, who might be facing death in Virginia, would not quiet down. Frankie started to become concerned for his party's safety.

Frankie sat forward, ready to spring into action, as one of the men sitting with the Texas Rangers kept shouting the chorus even though it was over. A policeman in the hall tried to calm him, and the man struck him in the face for his trouble. More police rushed in to subdue the man, and his fellow Rangers, unwilling to let their comrade be abused, joined in to what became a general brawl.

Frankie turned to face Hugh. With one mind, they took the arms of their ladies and slowly but firmly led them out to the lobby, while most of the others in the audience sat trying to decide what was happening.

Frankie led the Barnets and Georgiana through a door to a long dark hallway, then into the wings on either side of the stage. He pulled Georgiana along behind him into a narrow hallway perpendicular to the back wall of the theater. He heard Julienne's loud protest, "Hugh! Stop pulling at me. My skirt is caught." Frankie heard fabric tear, Julienne's anguished cry, and Hugh's dark scolding demands.

Frankie looked back at Georgiana. She had gathered up her hoopskirts as best she could, uncovering her pantaloons and petticoats on one side. She gave him a sheepish look. He smiled warmly at her, and said, "Brave girl." She nodded grimly.

Seeing the numeral "1" on the farthest dressing room door, he reached and found the doorknob, twisted it, and pushed back the door into the dark room. He called, "This way, in here!" He would not have told them how he knew of the small door that led out of the main dressing room. He raised one wistful eyebrow, remembering that actor he had had a liaison with, right there in the man's dressing room. The door, camouflaged with draperies, was how he had sneaked in to see the fellow. He found the door again, opened it very carefully, and peeked out.

"It's clear. Come quickly. Julienne, be quiet or they'll notice us." He grasped the crying woman's arm and pulled her through the door, then reached back through to take Georgiana by the hand and guide her through. Hugh followed.

They were in an alleyway behind the theater. Hugh said, "Ladies, cover your jewels. You don't want this mob to see them."

Frankie drew off his cloak and threw it around Georgiana's shoulders. He put his arm around her and held her tight against him. He saw Hugh follow suit with his wife.

Their route proved clear, but they could hear shouts that lessened in volume as they headed for the Garden District. Frankie had no reason to chide Hugh for his use of the word "mob." For all he knew, the soldiers had spread the brawl to the streets. He knew they'd better get away.

Once back at the Barnet house, the women went into the parlor, where they each promptly sat and started to cry. Hugh barked orders at a dismayed James to lock up the house tight, let no one in, and to get the women's maids to help them upstairs.

Frankie went into the parlor and stood helpless, looking at the two women's distress. Julienne's skirt was torn; the part that hung loose was muddy and stained. Her delicate buttoned boots were caked with mud as well. She still had Hugh's cloak, but it fell off her shoulders as she raised her arms to Frankie. Her face was pale and tear-stained, and her hair was a disaster. "Oh François, *mon cher*, you saved us from those awful Kentucks!"

"Oh I don't know," he said sardonically. "They weren't 'Kentucks.' They were from all over, including here. Violence is not limited in its accent."

He ignored Julienne's entreating arms and went to sit next to Georgiana. He took his handkerchief out of his pocket and began to dab at her face. He made comforting noises. "There, there, *ma chérie*, it is all right. You are safe. You were a very brave girl." She nodded dumbly and tried a small smile. She glanced up when Julienne made a protesting huff.

"Wasn't I a brave girl as well?"

"I couldn't tell with all the whining and complaining you were doing," Frankie retorted.

"Hugh, are you going to let him talk to me like that?" Julienne cried, as Hugh came into the parlor.

Hugh stopped and looked at her, then glanced at Frankie. To her he said, "Yes, I think I will." He grinned at Frankie's approving look.

In spite of the affront, Julienne tried to detain Frankie as he went to leave. She hung on him, shameless in front of her cousin and husband, until he peeled her hands from the lapels of his uniform tunic and roughly shoved her away.

He hastened through the nightmare streets to the Albrights', where he found them sitting by their fire, ignorant of the mayhem in the Latin Quarter. Their faces reflected shock as he recounted the evening's events. He shepherded them into their bedroom, then sat with his service pistol in his hand and watched out through a window all the rest of that night. As he looked out on the empty street, worried about the *Soleil*, he wondered at the sudden burst of laughter and marveled at the power of a simple unsophisticated song to spark violence. He wished with all his heart he had not bowed to Hugh's blackmail and enlisted. He could have taken the Albrights away somewhere—anywhere— where they might be safe. But in uniform, he was stuck in the city. A civilian could leave. An officer could not desert. Frankie put his face in his hands for a few minutes and, silently as he could so he would not disturb Charles William and Dominique, let the grief and despair spill out of him.

Frankie and the Albrights had stayed safe through the night. He learned the next day that, while disturbing, the riot had been more or less contained. He wondered if future disturbances would turn out so benignly.

General Twiggs had grown increasingly infirm, and that September he requested replacement and got his request approved. Frankie was confident the new general would be as approving of him as Twiggs had been. It turned out better even than he could have hoped.

CHAPTER 21

New Orleans, October 1861

MAJOR GENERAL Mansfield Lovell was by no means a likeable fellow. A former soldier and a businessman in New York City who had enlisted with the Confederate Army, he was vain, bombastic, outlandish, and entirely corrupt. He was also incompetent. Frankie curried immediate favor by inviting Lovell to *Le Beau Soleil* for a cruise about the river and Lake Pontchartrain.

The riverboat was a shadow of its former self, with the exquisite and opulent décor stripped or covered up. The shipment of cargo by less dependable roustabouts meant not only the main but other decks were in deplorable condition. The troops who were transported had destroyed the carpeting in the grand cabin. The skylight with its exquisite stained glass was cracked and broken in places. The staterooms smelled of human bodies and urine and the public areas of expectorated tobacco. But it was still a magnificent vessel with a smooth ride and lots of perfect vistas.

Lovell was a peacock. He liked to parade about the city with his stirrups so long he stood rather than propped his feet in them. That was how he arrived at *Le Beau Soleil* the first time. Instead of dismounting and using the gangway to board, the man stepped from his horse to the deck, much to the delight of the crowds of townspeople who always came to the levee to watch him and his antics. You had to give Lovell one quality: he was clearly fond of his horse. He could be seen stroking its neck, talking to it, even kissing its nose.

It grated on Frankie to give the man his own stateroom, with all the memories that kept Frankie out of it, but it was the only choice. On the cruise, he made sure Lovell had lots of the best food and whiskey. He let him win at poker, showed him the house he had grown up in—a house that said all that was needed about the privilege of his own background—and generally impressed Lovell immensely.

Frankie noticed how Lovell and the politicians in the city he had kept happy with bribes were two of a kind.

Frankie was promoted, as LaPorte had predicted and Brownworth promised. He was a major now. His new responsibilities included long stays at Forts Jackson and St. Philip. He was communications officer with Col. Edward Higgins, the forts' commander.

Frankie had a surprise when he visited his tailor, Auggie Schmidt, to have his major's uniform fitted. He noticed right away Schmidt was uncommunicative and tense. Frankie finally asked him if something was the matter. Schmidt temporized and dragged his feet, but he finally told Frankie he could not serve him anymore.

"But why?" Frankie asked, dismayed.

"Monsieur, it is because you have always been such a decent gentleman to me that I feel I can share this with you. It is your position in… I know it is called 'communications' but no one is unaware that it is really intelligence. You are a spy. People are suspicious of any contact I have with you, monsieur."

His brows knitted, Frankie asked, "But I have never tried to worm gossip out of you or insinuated myself into confidences you might not be willing to share with me."

"I know that, Monsieur Deramus, but it's the others. They don't trust me. They are sure I am telling you… well, whatever they might not want you to know."

"Do they not understand that it is not the men in my office who are going about using strong-arm tactics to intimidate them, but street gangs in someone's pay doing it? We 'spies,' as you call me, have bigger catfish to fry." He was thinking of the numerous acts of sabotage of the shipbuilding projects and how they were related to labor disputes. Then he realized how thin the line could be perceived to be.

Schmidt spread his hands. "I am sorry, monsieur, but I have to think of my family. And my position in the community."

From this Frankie knew what he was already beginning to recognize: the working class people of the Crescent City were growing restive. There were matters that affected them directly. He was beginning to think they impacted the large proportion of the enlisted men at the two forts as well. Virtually all of them came from the immigrant communities of New Orleans. He wanted to tell Schmidt not to worry, that he would use his position to prevent anything untoward from happening to them or… because of them. He kept his silence, however, because he knew he could not guarantee his protection.

By Christmas, one of the bleakest the Crescent City had seen, deprivations were becoming critical. There was no currency. Although first the state and then New Orleans had issued their own, it ultimately came down to the merchants themselves to issue their own "money." It was what people called a "shinplaster" and was a cross between scrip and a credit account, with less value than whatever the issuer demanded in exchange. The scrip was flimsy and smelly from all the handling by grocers and butchers. There was nothing to buy for Christmas anyway. Most people were barely managing to keep any food on their tables.

Frankie watched the decline, feeling torn that he was provided for, not only by his position in the army but also what little of his own money he could hang onto. He was being loaded with largesse from Le Coq Rouge, but he tried to use that charitably whenever he could. Antoinette joked with him that he was depriving her of potential employees when the women he helped did not have to turn to the streets for the food they could get from men who themselves had little money.

Frankie's attorney, an older man named Joshua Levy, helped him arrange his businesses as trusts to protect what little he had left. The hardest part was deciding for what or whom the trust existed. The Albrights could not legally inherit, be the beneficiaries of, or even administer any trust. He and Levy finally hit upon the creation of a corporation with arcane purposes, with Captain Mayer as the trustee. Frankie would have to trust Mayer to make sure the Albrights could count on some sort of protection should Frankie die. He was safe in New Orleans, but he knew he could be sent to a battle zone, and Frankie had no reason to think he was invulnerable. If the Yankees won, the Albrights would be freed, but if the South and slavery continued, they were at risk of being sold. So he made them part of the property that would affix to the corporation, their new legal owner. In the meantime, he removed some of the gold he had in the hotel vault and asked Charles William to hide it in some secure and unguessable place. He put Johnny's watch with it.

Frankie did continue to meet with Mme. Antoinette as co-owner of the brothel, Le Coq Rouge. His own abstinence was beginning to wear on him, and not really intending to pay for a prostitute for the first time in his life, he glanced idly about for a fellow he had always found attractive—a young Creole named Louis-Bertrand. When he did not see him for several visits at a time, he asked about for him.

"Tony, that nice young fellow you used to try to throw at me, what was his name? I haven't seen him for a while. Did he join up?"

Her face was grim when she replied. "*Le pauvre*, he was attacked in the street for not being in uniform. They tore up his pretty face. We had to let him go."

Frankie was furious. "How could you do that? He's been a good employee for years!"

She adopted her haughtiest look. "That was the other thing. He was no longer a young man. His usefulness as a whore was long finished." She flinched as he leapt up and looked as if to slap her.

"Where did he go?" Frankie demanded.

"How should I know?" the madam protested. "Try the docks."

Frankie made one detour in his search for the young man. He went to Levy and set in motion the sale of his interests in the brothel. "Sell it for half its worth, but make sure neither Mme. Antoinette nor any of her associates, public or clandestine, get their hands on it. I have one proviso, no matter who buys my share: they have to provide some sort of position of a permanent nature for a fellow named Louis-Bertrand—I don't know his surname—who used to be employed at Le Coq Rouge. It has to be something he agrees to, not mucking out the privies or anything like that."

Levy took notes and had Frankie sign some documents he drew up. "I can see, monsieur, that you are quite agitated. May I ask where you are going now?"

Frankie frowned. "To look for Louis-Bertrand."

"Sir, if you find him, will you ask him to see me at his earliest convenience?"

Having assured the attorney he would pass on the message, Frankie headed for the district along the river where many of the seediest brothels and taverns could be found. It was an extremely dangerous area, ruled even more tyrannically by gangs of rowdies. He knew he was risking everything even by asking around for where Louis-Bertrand might be found, but he had to find him. He felt responsible; his imperfect involvement in Le Coq Rouge had made him unaware of what was going on there.

He could not find anyone who would disclose which brothel Louis-Bertrand might be working in. He made the rounds of the taverns, earning some lupine smiles from the bullyboys who either worked in them or hung around. He finally found his quarry, slipping behind a cheap curtain with a very drunk and unpleasant-looking man, at a particularly smoky and noisome shack that had no name as far as he could tell.

Frankie waited for the whore to return from wherever he had taken the man. Seeing Louis-Bertrand again horrified Frankie. That formerly remarkable face was unrecognizable. Frankie had known him by his shape, though he was thinner now, and by his voice, though it was different too—whining, wheedling, coaxing.

"Louis-Bertrand," he said as the man looked up and recognized him.

"M. Deramus, how in hell…," he said, looking both relieved and anxious. "Why would you come here?" His tone said, "You could have anyone and anything!"

"Come with me. You don't have a procurer, I hope?"

"No, monsieur. None will take me on. You know I got sacked from Le Coq Rouge?" He followed Frankie out of the tavern to drunken cheers of "Louise has a rich soldier boy!"

When Frankie and Louis-Bertrand arrived at Frankie's hotel room, Frankie was muttering, "Damned if I will let them tell me what to do," and realizing that letting "them" tell him what to do was getting to be a habit.

Louis-Bertrand pressed himself up against Frankie once they were inside and the door was closed and locked. "Do you want to fuck me or have me suck your cock?"

Frankie put his hands on the man's arms and pushed him away. "Let's get you a bath and see if anything I have will fit you."

Louis-Bertrand tried to look seductive. "I am sure I can manage anything you have. Mouth or asshole, it will fit."

Frankie ordered a bath after closing the young man in his bedchamber. He also ordered coffee, sandwiches, and brandy. He hoped the waiter was not one of Barnet's spies.

Louis-Bertrand was naked when Frankie himself brought in the coffee, brandy, and food. "Get this dressing gown on. They are bringing the bath," Frankie commanded irritably.

As he watched Louis-Bertrand devour the food and coffee, which was liberally laced with the brandy, it came to Frankie like a slap in the face how much New Orleans had changed in a few months. He realized that in spite of all his duties to be aware of the thoughts and doings of his fellow citizens, he really had not seen the underlying truth. New Orleans had become a place where no one ever smiled or laughed, not merrily at any rate. People were dying—if not all of them in their bodies, certainly all of them in their souls. He thought something he would never have said aloud: that perhaps it would be best if the Yankees came. They couldn't do any worse for the city, or could they?

Once Louis-Bertrand had eaten and drunk and had his bath, Frankie showed him a suit of clothes he thought would fit him. It was one of Johnny's. He thought, *so there was a good reason not to burn it after all.* "I think this will fit you well enough," he said aloud.

Louis-Bertrand gazed long at Frankie and asked, "*Je ne comprends pas*, why are you doing this? Don't you want to go to bed?"

Frankie took a breath and answered, "No. I just want to help you."

To Frankie's horror, Louis-Bertrand looked crestfallen. "It's my face, isn't it? You can't stand to look at me." Tears began to pour out of his eyes. One of those eyes had a drooping lid, and the tears ran down cheeks both broken and scarred.

Frankie stepped forward and took the man in his arms. "No, I promise you it's not that. It's just that...." He felt Louis-Bertrand put his face on Frankie's shoulder, and he stroked the damp hair and the man's back. He crooned comforting words. The memory of another weeping man in his arms cut him to the core. He maneuvered Louis-Bertrand's head so they were face-to-face and kissed him gently on his lips, feeling how they depressed inward over missing teeth. "Come here," he said.

He drew Louis-Bertrand to his bed. Kicking off his shoes, Frankie climbed onto the bed and held open his arms. The young man, still weeping, climbed on after him but stayed on his knees. He reached for the waist of Frankie's trousers.

"No, please. Just lie down. I know you can't help it, but I really don't need a disease. We can rest and hold each other."

Louis-Bertrand nodded silently and with an air of resignation. He lay down along Frankie's body and, as Frankie expected, soon fell asleep. They lay with Frankie's arms around him, Frankie crooning quietly, stroking his back and hair. It felt so good to have a man in his arms in bed again. Frankie finally went to sleep and slept more deeply and dreamlessly than he had in months.

When he awoke, Louis-Bertrand was gone. The suit was gone too, as was the money he had set out with a note and Levy's address. Louis-Bertrand had taken a single flower from the arrangement in Frankie's sitting room and laid it on the empty pillow. Frankie allowed himself some tears before he got up and put his public face back on.

He fully expected a visit from a smug and triumphant Barnet for several days after, but no threat ever came. It appeared his good deed would go unpunished.

MANY wondered what would take place on Mardi Gras on March 4. After the extremes—even for Carnival—of the last year, where the rowdiness made headlines in newspapers as far away as Atlanta and Charleston, the mood was so somber and the scarcity so severe that all waited to hear what the Mistick Krewe of Comus, the Anglo-American organizer of Mardi Gras festivities, would decree. On the first day of March, the *New Orleans Daily Picayune* had the answer.

Frankie read the notice aloud to Charles William and Dominique.

To Ye Mystic Krewe—

GREETINGS!

WHEREAS, War has cast its gloom over our happy homes and care usurped the place where joy is wont to hold its sway. Now, therefore, do I deeply sympathizing with the general anxiety, deem it proper to withhold your Annual Festival in this goodly Crescent City and by this proclamation do command no assemblage of the

-MYSTICK KREWE-

Given under my hand this, the 1st day of March A.D. 1862.

COMUS

Frankie raised his eyebrows. "I seem to remember a time when the Church declared Carnival, not a bunch of upriver hooligans."

Charles William shook his head. "Now, Mr. Deramus, don't we have enough division already?"

"Well, the Good Lord knows this town can do with a day of prayer instead of profligacy," Dominique proclaimed.

Remembering the events of Mardi Gras last year, Frankie was more inclined to bless the decision than he was willing to admit. "Poor Mam'selle Marie. It would have been her night to shine if she were not at the front playing soldier boy. But I know several of the men at headquarters who would be chary about attending this year anyway." *Including me*, he thought.

FRANKIE spent days at a time at Fort St. Philip checking out intelligence that Brownworth had passed on. There was some sort of conspiracy involving enlisted men there. Most of the brass, both at headquarters and at the Fort, dismissed it as absurd. Brownworth was not so cocky. Naturally pragmatic, he told Frankie the immigrant soldiers who made up the garrison both there and at Fort Jackson were accustomed to simply laying down their tools and refusing to work at the shipyards and elsewhere if they had grievances. It was largely these strikes for better pay that kept the two great ironclads from being completed, he said.

"And the strikers blame the navy, rightly so since Hollins has done everything he can to make sure the pay is on time, but what can he do when no pay comes in from the War Department?"

Frankie nodded. "I know the admiral has had to borrow money himself to pay the men. He touched me up for a substantial sum. But how does that affect the forts?"

Brownworth's grim face matched his voice. "If they will stop work on warships during a war, knowing as they must that failure could threaten their own families, what's to stop them simply refusing to fight?"

Frankie gaped at his colonel. "You think they might mutiny? That's... that's treason!"

Brownworth said in a low voice, "And as big a catastrophe for themselves as for the Confederacy. See if you can do anything to steer the St. Phillip garrison away from such a move, will you?"

Frankie did what he could. Before he left, he visited his former tailor and told him to let anyone he knew who had friends at the forts to tell them if they had mutinous plans, to think twice.

At Fort St. Philip he tried to talk to the officer in charge when the overall commander was at his headquarters at Fort Jackson, but he might as well have talked to a brick wall. He found talking with the sergeants as difficult—their protestations in their many foreign accents not all that convincing—but he could only hope they would take his advisories back to the men.

IN EARLY April, news came that nearly broke the spirits of everyone in New Orleans. The last group of recruits sent from New Orleans had been so young, so determined, so solemnly brave when they paraded down St. Charles Street accompanied by the cheers and tears not only of their loved ones, but of those back from earlier battles who were leaning on crutches or standing with an empty sleeve pinned to their chests. A band played "Listen to the Mockingbird," and people along the parade route reached to touch the boys' sleeves. If there was any man left in the city not in uniform, he stayed out of sight on that day.

Frankie had stood with Hugh Barnet and watched the boys march by, neither speaking. Each was lost in thought, each more worn and aged by the year that had passed since Fort Sumter. Both Hugh and Frankie now had gray at their temples. Gray peppered Frankie's thin, elegant mustache as well, and Hugh had grown a beard like Lovell's, itself sporting a shock of gray in the middle under his lower lip. They eyed each other and walked off in opposite directions once the street was clearing.

On a stormy April 6th, the wires carried news that had all the church bells ringing. New Orleans's own "cavalier," the dashing Albert Sidney Johnston, and General Beauregard had surprised federal troops under Ulysses Grant and were poised for a stupendous victory. No one danced in the streets, but the few people who ventured out smiled cheerfully and hopefully at each other. Frankie, at headquarters, was as glued to the telegraphers' table as everyone else. They waited nervously—the room becoming thick with cigar smoke—for more news. They learned the storm had knocked out communications for a time. Then when the dots and dashes recommenced, the victory was announced but with a heavy price: Johnston had been killed. Now the church bells tolled for the local hero.

The officers either went home to their families, if they had them in New Orleans, or headed to the St. Charles Hotel for a night of drinking. Though they could hope for news of a stunning victory at— what was the place in Tennessee called? Pittsburg Landing?—it was hard to accept the death of someone so admired, so full of life and optimism.

The next day another blow came on top of the ill news of Johnston's death. The wire told the assembled officers that in fact the day before, the reported victory had been turned on its head. The Confederates were in retreat. At a place called Shiloh, they made a stand and were torn to pieces. The Army of the Mississippi, which contained those boys from the Crescent City, faced the worst onslaught of musketry anyone had ever known—so the wire said. Frankie found himself grinding his teeth as he stood frozen, listening to the voice of the officer who took the telegrapher's copy and read it aloud.

By the morning of the eighth, the city got the butcher's bill. Nearly two thousand men had been killed, another one thousand captured, and over eight thousand were wounded, and that was just Confederates. The list of the dead, including Johnston, filtered in, and many homes were shut up and deep in mourning.

LaPorte and Frankie lifted glasses of whiskey in the former's office. "To Jean-Paul LeGrand," LaPorte said softly.

Frankie bowed his head, then lifting his chin breathed, "To Mam'selle Marie. I hope wherever you are, they put you in charge of the masquerade ball."

A tremendous crowd gathered to see those men who accompanied Johnston's casket home. If the City of New Orleans had any spirit left, it was all but broken.

The news that Admiral David Farragut was on his way up the Delta with battleships and mortar barges to capture New Orleans crushed any hope that remained.

Frankie took the first opportunity he had to head for the Albrights' little house. He sat unblinking as Dominique and her husband prayed. In the morning, he would take a steamer to Fort St. Philip to help the garrison there face bombardment from the Federal onslaught.

CHAPTER 22

Fort St. Philip, outside New Orleans, April 1862

FRANKIE did not want to leave the city for his duty at Fort St. Philip. He tried to console himself that unless and until the Yankee flagship got past the forts nothing would happen. He imagined General Lovell was still defending his conviction that if the Federal forces were coming at all, they would come overland from the north. He hoped the man was right.

He knew from many past visits, both Forts Jackson and St. Phillip were stoutly built. Their stone and brick walls were many feet thick, and each had well-placed gun batteries. In addition, they were stocked with weeks and weeks of supplies. How any siege could break either of them was unimaginable. That was why they were there, why they had been so successful in the past wars, and reinforced by order of Andrew Jackson himself.

Entering at the sally port of St. Philip, Frankie tried not to register his irritation that the man who commanded both forts was on hand to greet him. Colonel Edward Higgins was a hardheaded, arrogant bastard who got on Frankie's nerves. He suspected Higgins was not terribly fond of him either. Frankie had hoped to arrive while Higgins was where he should be, at Fort Jackson oppressing everyone there. While Frankie was not impressed with the fellow who had usual command of the fort on the eastern bank of the river, he could usually get his work done by avoiding him.

Frankie saluted Higgins. "Good to see you, General," he offered politely.

"So Lovell doesn't think I can handle a few Yankee boats?" Higgins came out of his metaphorical corner swinging.

"No, sir. I mean, that is not what I have been sent for. General Lovell knows you are more than competent to address the challenge, sir." Frankie thought the two men could be bookends of abusive arrogance.

"Then what is your message?"

Frankie bit his mental lip. "General Lovell sends his compliments and asks if Fort St. Philip is in need of anything, and that I may be allowed to remain and observe any coming action."

Higgins's harrumph was delivered perfectly. "We have what we need, and you can do as you please. Just don't get in the way. And you say St. Philip. What about Fort Jackson? No message for that facility?"

"I believe, sir, that someone else has been dispatched to report to you there. I thank you for your courtesy, sir. I will see if I am billeted in the same quarters as usual."

"Well, if you can tolerate all these dagos, heinies, Polaks, and worse yet these goddamned micks, all I can say is, good luck to you, Frenchie."

That answers my question about morale, Frankie thought. He saluted the man and thanked him.

Higgins had already shifted his attention to a return across river to Fort Jackson. Frankie thanked his lucky stars and headed into the officers' mess to find Dan Singleton.

Dan was an affable fellow with whom Frankie had formed a friendship on his many visits to the fort over the past few months. He was from Alabama, a planter's youngest son with a penchant for music. He played the banjo and was quite popular with his troops, who knew him as Major Dan.

"Frankie Deramus, as I live and breathe. Come to rescue us from the evil Yankees? Did you see Higgins?" Dan extended a hand in greeting.

"I had that distinct pleasure, Dan. I'm here to get a feel for morale and that sort of thing. You know." Frankie had always been able to talk about military concerns with Dan Singleton.

"Let's get some coffee and talk, shall we?"

The officers' mess was essentially deserted at that time of day, so Frankie and Dan could talk at ease. "I don't know, Frankie," Singleton drawled. "There's something afoot. I don't know anything concrete, but every so often I catch one of the enlisted men looking at me like he is measuring me for a pine box. Not outright insolent, but there's tarnish on that respect."

Frankie nodded. "I've been picking up on some undercurrent in the city too. People are jumpy, though whether that's having no food, no jobs, the wolf being at the door, or just that nobody's getting any, I can't say."

Dan chuckled. "Well I have food and a job, and I feel pretty safe behind these here walls, but I sure as hell ain't getting any."

Frankie lifted his cup in salute. "Here's to an end to the war so we can both get some."

Dan shrugged. "At least in the city you have the brothels."

"Too risky. You never know what the girls are picking up from the soldiers." Seeing Dan's nod, he went on. "You know about the Club of Lincoln." It was a statement, not an inquiry.

"Abolitionists and such?"

"I am not sure if that's who they are or even if they exist. You never know if it's some fool wanting to look like a big man either by claiming to be dangerous or wanting to uncover a threat to the safety of the city. Those powder magazine explosions and some of the shipyard sabotage were damn serious, but as to who is responsible...." Frankie shrugged eloquently.

"So why are you here, Frankie?" As usual, Dan came to the point swiftly.

Frankie smiled wanly. "I am not sure how I am going to manage this, but I'm supposed to quell any temptation to... mutiny."

Dan's eyebrows shot up so high they all but flew off his forehead. "Mutiny?" he whispered hoarsely.

"There's been talk that a lot of the immigrant enlisted don't want the Yankees prevented from taking New Orleans."

Dan scratched his head. "I suppose that's possible. If it is true, I expect most of it is at Jackson. We are a smaller garrison."

Frankie sat back. "True, but the men here have cousins and brothers and the like over there. If you know of any enlisted who seem to have frequent communications with friends and family in the Fort Jackson garrison, I'd like a nudge in his direction, if you think it would do any good."

Dan put out his lower lip in consideration and nodded. "Can't hurt. Who's your counterpart at Fort Jackson? Not the same fellow as usual, I hope."

Frankie winced. "Afraid so. Barnet."

"Oh Lord." Dan shook his head.

"Indeed. The way Higgins goes on about dagos and the like, it would be no wonder if the men hated him. And Barnet could rival Higgins for his contempt for immigrants. Maybe you can get away with that off on some plantation where you'll never meet one, but New Orleans is absolutely replete with people from other countries."

Dan grumbled, "Heaven help us."

FRANKIE spent a couple of days at the fort, making it appear that he was inspecting gun emplacements and putting himself in a position where enlisted men could share their fears and worries with him. It was useless, as he knew it would be. He was everything the men weren't: wealthy—or had been; a New Orleans native; an officer; and an intelligence officer, as they all knew, whether or not that was what he was officially called.

Dan managed to find a likely conduit for whatever Frankie wanted to communicate: a middle-aged corporal of Sicilian extraction, a scholar of some kind named Giuseppe Maniscalco who had joined the army when he was fired from his position at the College of the Immaculate Conception where he taught classics. Frankie was able to engage the man's interest by talking about Greco-Roman sculpture—mentioning the Belvedere statue, which was now in storage with the other decorations from *Le Beau Soleil*. Maniscalco expressed interest in seeing the reproduction, and Frankie promised if they ever got out of the war, he would make sure he had the chance.

In a lull in the conversation, Frankie idly observed, "It looks like the Yankees might be the next owners of the Apollo. Unless Lovell can keep them out of New Orleans, that is."

Maniscalco kept silent.

"So long as they take good care of it. It really isn't worth that much. It's mostly sentimental to me." Frankie looked about the stout walls of the section of the fort where they had taken up strolling. "They can't get past the forts. But Lovell, General Lovell, I mean, thinks they will come by land anyway."

Maniscalco nodded sagely, still silent.

Frankie went on, almost as if he was talking to himself. "I expect he's right, and though I would never say this to him or any of his cronies, I think there's not much we can do to stop them. I mean, Davis and the army moved most of our boys up the Tennessee and all."

He stopped where he stood and waited until the other man paused and turned. Looking Maniscalco straight in the eye, Frankie said to him, "I sure would hate to see any officers or enlisted men hurt in some sort of hasty action… you know, here in the fort."

Maniscalco gazed at him for a few moments, then turned and walked away calmly.

That's about all I can do, Frankie thought. Let them know we suspect.

He met up with Dan in his office and answered his friend's inquisitive look with a shrug. "I planted some seeds, that's all. I hope it got across that if there was trouble stirring, it might be as well to put a cap on it. It's no wonder the soldiers are agitated."

Dan gestured to the chair next to the desk, and Frankie sat.

"Any news?" Frankie asked. Frankie wanted to know more about the Yankee ships coming up the river from the Gulf.

"Yeah, they should be here sometime tomorrow," Dan told him.

"Truly? That was fast. I assume all is in readiness."

"Yes, and we have scouts out who can alert us. There's really nothing more we can do than wait and be vigilant." He looked consideringly at Frankie. "Want to have some supper? You know I do sketches of the fort and the men. I'd like your opinion, the opinion of a cultured man."

"Flattery will get you anywhere. I would be honored."

In Dan's quarters, they ate a relaxed meal, going easy on the wine with hostilities so close at hand. Frankie looked up with interest as Dan retrieved his sketchbooks.

"Clear off those dishes and put them outside the door, if you would. My orderly will gather them."

At Dan's invitation, Frankie picked up his chair and brought it around to Dan's side of the table. The sketches turned out to be pencil and charcoal. As Dan flipped through the pages, which were protected with a very thin tissue between them, Frankie saw quite faithful representations of the fort's buildings and fortifications. But it was the portraits of the men, singly and in groups, that really caught Frankie's eye. Dan had them standing on guard, slouching against walls, sitting in their mess playing cards, dancing together while a man played a fiddle. There was even an amusing one of a fellow who was looking at the remains of one of the mass of mosquitoes, which plagued everyone, in his palm.

"You have a skill at bringing out the individual. It's almost like you can read their minds." Frankie flipped back a couple of pages. "That one looks like he's enjoying the piss he's taking. And this one"—he went on, flipping another couple of pages—"looks like he's had about as much staring out at miles of swamp as he can take."

Dan's smile showed his pleasure at Frankie's astute observations and the praise. "I had quite a few that I did at Fort Jackson a month or so ago. Higgins saw them and confiscated them. He burned the whole pad right in front of me and accused me of sedition." At Frankie's openmouthed look, Dan explained, "Conditions are not optimal here, but Fort Jackson is a hellhole. The moat around it is a cesspool and breeds mosquitoes the size of wrens. The place stinks all the time. I don't know why, maybe it's the orientation on the bluff, but it's actually hotter and muggier there than here. The men are crowded in more. It's no wonder they have so much desertion in spite of how far a man would have to go through alligator-infested swamp to get anywhere. And the officers are largely cut from Higgins's cloth. I'm surprised no officers have been shot." He looked up at Frankie. "I guess you are right. That is mutiny, if it happens."

Frankie chuckled. "Lovell refused to issue ammunition to one of the militias south of here. He said he did not trust them not to kill their officers."

Dan picked up another sketchbook and started flipping through it. It was more of the same, with several still lifes in addition. He flipped one page to reveal a sketch of a young man in the nude, his back and buttocks to the artist, and the most remarkable look on his face as he looked back over his shoulder—a look that was knowing, inviting. Dan quickly flipped the page to the next drawing.

Frankie shot out his hand and stopped Dan from completing his move. He searched Dan's eyes.

Dan looked chagrined and his cheeks blossomed with color. He looked at Frankie's hand where it was still on his, then looked straight into Frankie's eyes.

Frankie leaned toward him and put his lips to Dan's. Dan was still for a few moments, but then he kissed back. Frankie prodded his mouth open with his tongue. The kiss that started out tentative quickly became intense. The two stood as if on cue and feverishly began to reach for the fastenings of each other's uniforms. Frankie got Dan's collar open and sunk his face into his neck and collarbone, tasting the sweat and breathing in the masculine scent.

Dan gasped, "Wait!"

Frankie was relieved when all the man did was go over to the door of his quarters and lock it. "Bless the need for keeping records under lock and key." He was back in a flash into Frankie's heated embrace. He started to push Frankie to his small camp bed.

"Let's get these clothes off now so we waste no time."

They stood ripping off their own uniforms while looking at each other hungrily. Completely naked, they fell together on the camp bed, stifling their cries and moans as best they could.

Dan was not a skinny man. He was not exactly stout, but he was solidly and squatly built. He appeared to be used to taking the lead, maneuvering Frankie onto his back under him. He held Frankie's shoulders against the cot and assaulted him with his mouth, kissing, licking, tasting, and nipping everything he could reach. All Frankie could do was lie back and take it. It had been so long.

When Dan's face made it back up to Frankie's, Frankie raised his head and bit Dan's chin. Dan let out a gulp of excitement. He pushed Frankie's legs far apart with one knee, positioned himself between them, and with no preamble, thrust himself inside. The small amount of pain merely intensified Frankie's pleasure. He was fully engorged, straining, and the assault on his balls and prostate threatened to send him over the edge. He gritted his teeth and tried to call back his climax.

Dan's climax—as Frankie could gauge by the hard and heavy thrusting, which became more rapid but also more ragged, and by Dan's hard bites on his chest and arms—was also near.

"I need… something… in my mouth." Frankie begged, knowing he would not be able to keep quiet.

Dan, without breaking stride, found a handkerchief somewhere within reach and pushed it into Frankie's mouth. The moment it was in, Frankie let go, a long low moan rising in pitch from his throat. Almost at the same time Dan started to grunt. As he spent inside Frankie, the air hissed through his clenched teeth like steam from a boiler valve. He collapsed on Frankie. They lay gasping and unable to think, much less move or speak.

They did not talk about what happened, but wasted no time better-employed in touches, kisses, and licking sweat off each other. Dan, when he could move at all, got up on his knees and proceeded to clean Frankie's seed from his belly where it had shot and lay puddled. They made love again, once they were rested enough, and this time it was almost as intense. They fell asleep spooned together in the narrow bed.

In the morning, the sound of a hard rap on the door and a man's shout awakened Frankie. He opened his eyes to find Dan already dressing. "Good morning, Major."

Dan looked around and smiled. He saw Frankie's quizzical look. "The ships are—"

Just as he said it the first blasts came.

ACHIEVING the ramparts beside Dan, Frankie looked down to see a long line of Union vessels coming two by two up the passage. There were barges armed with mortars, then a host of ships of various types, a chain stretched across the waterway the only barrier to their progress to Frankie's city.

The garrison at Fort St. Philip watched the bombardment of Fort Jackson. Frankie stood with Dan on the ramparts, using spyglasses to monitor the damage.

When the first shells landed in the moat of the fort across the river, an immense plume of filthy water flew up, then drained away almost as quickly. They did not see any channels letting the moat water trickle away. "Dear God, it's breached the wall under the level of the moat. It's flowing inside."

Frankie looked at Dan and cringed. "And I've been there, so my guess is that the swamp water will follow the moat water."

The walls of both forts took plenty of hits. Frankie started to grow accustomed to the shrill whistle and boom of shells not far from where he stood. The smoke made his eyes and throat smart. His head ached constantly. Though the shelling died back at night, there was no rest. Repairs had to be looked to. Meals were taken on the fly. Dan and Frankie had no more chances to make love.

"Where are the gun boats? Ours, I mean," Dan asked no one in particular, his voice full of frustration and anger.

"What boats?" Frankie responded unhelpfully.

Dan gaped at him. "What do you mean?"

Frankie sighed. Coming closer to Dan so he could be heard in the din, he shouted, "Hollins was up at Memphis with most of the so-called fleet when I left the city to come here. There were only three gunboats at New Orleans."

Dan shook his head, uncomprehending. "Which ones? The *Louisiana*? The *Mississippi*?"

"If the *Louisiana* shows up, she won't have been completed, and I think the *Mississippi* is far behind her in schedule. The only gun boats I saw in port were the *Manassas*—which at least is ironclad—a rammer, and two others."

The forts, of course, were firing back and having some success. If morale had been bad before, the hopelessness and sheer tedium of neither side making headway chipped away at it further. Still, driven by Dan Singleton's hearty shouts of encouragement, the return fire and rebuilding continued.

Wooden structures did not stand up to the bombardment, of course. Shells crashed through the roofs of the buildings and set them on fire. The smoke billowed up over at Fort Jackson. In no time,

Frankie saw that every wooden building and platform was now simply ashes.

On what was to prove the last night of the battle, a shout came up from the lookouts. Frankie and Dan, having coffee with other officers who were not directly involved in battle and repair, leaped to their feet. A lieutenant dashed in. "The ships! They must have broken the chain across the river. They are passing through on the way up the river!"

"Goddamned sneaky bastards!" Dan exclaimed. He, Frankie, and several officers ran to the parapets to see a double line of ships heading past both their fort and Fort Jackson—the ones on their side firing at them, the ones on the other side firing at Fort Jackson. The shells were not doing much damage. The commanders ordered return fire that proved even less effective. Only one Northern ship was hit and damaged, but a cheer rang out anyway, the men slapping each other on their backs and smiling and laughing. "Got one!"

The ineffectual fire back and forth went on until dawn, by which time all but three of the Yankee vessels had passed by both forts. Of the three remaining, one was the ship a shell had disabled and the other two turned back as soon as it was light enough they could easily be seen. The whole night had been like a phantasm: the dark, the smoke obscuring what was happening and making any flashes of light from explosions more insubstantial and eerie.

"They're on their way to New Orleans," Dan said simply.

In that general direction, Frankie and he heard the scattered sound of guns. "Someone's firing on someone," Frankie commented acerbically. "I'd better get back to headquarters somehow."

Dan reached over and squeezed his shoulder. "You look after yourself, Frankie. God only knows where and if we'll meet again."

Frankie put a hand over Dan's where it stayed on his shoulder. "Thank you, Dan."

Singleton smiled, saluted, and turned back to the parapet.

CHAPTER 23

New Orleans, April 24, 1862

IT TOOK Frankie all that day to make his way on foot, by boat, and finally a stolen horse, back to New Orleans. Through the growing darkness, he could see the light of fires burning. "*Mon Dieu*, they bombarded the city."

As he approached, it slowly dawned on him that none of the city's buildings were aflame. The fires were coming from the levee. He pushed his horse harder, his heart thudding in his breast. He knew with a certainty it must be the people of the city, if not the army itself, burning all the boats in their moorings to prevent them from falling into the hands of the enemy. Long before he reached the levee tears streamed from his eyes. It was the smoke, yes, but it was also knowing what he would find.

He leaped off the horse when he got to where *Le Beau Soleil* was moored. All he could do was stand and stare helplessly. Most of his beautiful riverboat—the boat he had sold off his patrimony to buy and refurbish, the boat he had spent so much loving care on, his pride and joy, his true love… and the site of all his memories of those first times with Johnny—was already consumed by fire. He could smell the spirits used to accelerate the burning. In the aft, he could see the curtains burning in stateroom windows. The boilers exploded, and *Le Beau Soleil* listed to one side. Glass was bursting. The liquor bottles in the saloon were bursting. The very bones of the beautiful bit of heaven on the river groaned and wailed.

He heard the roar of flames, the pop of smoldering coals, and then a sound that tore at his heart. It began as a squeal, like a pig being spitted alive. That turned into a groan, and finally he saw it. The gilded sunburst on the grille between the smokestacks was twisting away, the grille already warped and breaking, and he watched with horror as the solemn face of Sol turned black, warped, and then, with a resounding crash, fell.

Frankie sank to his knees and covered his face with his hands. It was beyond understanding. The focus, in one way or another, of his entire adult life and all that mattered to him in it, was gone. He was too paralyzed to form coherent thought; this was probably the only thing keeping him from springing forward into the inferno to die with all his dreams. "Johnny," he croaked through his smoke-choked throat.

He felt something brush him. Instinctively he reached out and felt a cat push his head into his palm. Once the familiar feeling registered, he turned his eyes. "Duckie!" he breathed gratefully. He gathered up the mouser in his arms and buried his face in its neck. Rather than struggling, Duckie settled into his embrace and purred.

A shout directly behind him startled him out of his catatonic state. "Stop that nigger!"

He jumped up, looking around frantically. "Charles William?" he called. He saw three white men chasing a black man along the levee. He could see, even in the changeable light of the burning boats all along the water, that the man they were chasing was a much smaller man than Charles William and ran too fast and too agilely to be an older man. He reached for his pistol but realized the four were far too distant for him to effect any rescue.

He put his pistol arm back around the cat and turned to the boat in time to hear something inside crash through a deck to a lower one. He held the cat to his face, noticing its fur was wet with his own tears. He allowed one single sob to erupt from his chest. "*Adieu, mon cœur,*" he breathed.

Holding Duckie in his arms, he turned and made his way through the chaos, terrified at what he would find when he reached the Albrights' cottage.

His fist was poised in the air when the door opened. Dominique flew out and gathered him to her. She was weeping. "Frankie, Frankie, thank God Almighty, you are here." She broke the embrace to look at him. Duckie took the opportunity to leap down and run into the open door. "Are you all right? Are you hurt?"

Frankie looked over her shoulder. "I am fine, but where is Charles William?"

A hoarse voice called from the parlor, "I'm here, Frankie." It was a strained voice, tinged with pain. He grasped Dominique's hand and pulled her along after him through the kitchen and into the parlor.

Charles William was lying on a daybed in the parlor that usually had Dominique's yarn and sewing projects stacked on it. He was propped up on three or more pillows, his face haggard, and he was covered with a quilt. Frankie rushed to him, dropping Dominique's hand and going to his knees beside him. "Uncle Charles, what happened?" he cried, feeling for the older man's hand under the quilt.

"Frankie, *Le Beau Soleil…*," Charles William began.

"I know. I went there when I saw the flames were coming from the levee. She's gone. She's finished. Everything in her is all burned up." He put his face down onto Charles William's chest. He raised it quickly again. "Are you hurt? What happened?"

Dominique had gone to get tea. Charles William put his hand on Frankie's hair. "I went down to see what was happening. There were all these rumors about the Yankees in the river. As I was going down there, some militiamen ran by. I shouted, 'What's happening?' and someone turned and said, 'We gotta torch the boats.'"

Frankie listened to the rest of story with his head lying on Charles William's chest. The sound of his deep voice reminded Frankie of a steadily running engine, like the boilers on *Le Beau Soleil*. "One of the militiamen turned and saw me. He told me to go home, that I wasn't safe. That made another man turn. He almost stopped and came over to me, looking fit to thrash someone, anyone, preferably a Yankee or a colored, I would guess. I let them go but followed them. I got to the levee as some men were pouring some kind of fuel oil or something that smelled really strong, more than liquor, on the decks of the riverboats and other boats there. Then they started tossing in torches. I knew why they were doing it. They had to, Frankie. They had to."

Frankie nodded, not lifting his head from the older man's chest.

"Someone spotted me standing there and yelled, 'Get the nigger. It's their fault the damned Yankee bastards are here.' He and several men came after me. They knocked me down, then started to wale on me. I don't know why they stopped, but they did after only a few blows. After a while, I felt someone pull me up by my arms. Two men put my arms around their necks and said, 'Where can we take you, Dad?'" I never saw their faces. I never knew if they were black or colored or white or purple. Maybe they were angels. Anyway they brought me home."

Dominique had come back in, and Frankie heard her shudder, causing the teacups on her tray to rattle. He looked up again. "But how are you injured?"

"Just bruised, Frankie. I checked him over," Dominique reassured. "Now come have some tea."

Frankie slowly stood. He let his arms hang at his sides. "No, I have to go. I can't stay in New Orleans. But I can't leave you here alone."

Charles William said, "We will be all right. Don't you need to get to headquarters? I think all the troops have gone. I haven't seen a soldier on the street for two days. I heard that Lovell sent them north…"

"He did what?" Frankie was astonished.

Dominique answered, "Yes, they've been heading north for a couple days. But last we heard, the general was still here." She had set the tray down, and now she came to take Frankie's arm. "Is it true, François, *mon cher*? Are the Yankees here? Are they in charge of the city?"

He turned and took her by her shoulders. "I don't know for sure, but it would only be a matter of time." He glanced over at Charles William and then back. "You are free. The Yankees have freed the slaves everywhere they've taken back."

She put a hand to his cheek. "Frankie, son, you freed us long ago."

He took the hand and kissed the palm. "I am going to have to leave now. If I stay, they will put me in prison. I set up a trust with Levy." He looked at Charles William lying in the daybed. "You know Levy, the attorney. He has my money tied up. Captain Mayer is the trustee. He will see to it you have what you need. Please stay indoors for now. Don't venture out for at least a few days. It won't be safe until the Yankees are in control. God, how I hate to leave you. You are all I have left."

He put his arms around Dominique and held her, then went over to the older man and touched his cheek. "Was life ever cheerful and peaceful? Or was that some sort of dream?"

Frankie blinked away a tear.

THE rumors were right. Lovell had sent his troops by railroad north into the interior of the state, to Camp Moore. He and several members of his headquarters staff were still in the city. Frankie found LaPorte mopping his face with a crumpled handkerchief.

"Deramus! Where in Hell have you been?"

"I was at Fort St. Philip on assignment. I just got back. Is there coffee or whiskey or anything?" Frankie strolled in purposefully.

"*Oui*, over there. At the fort, were you? Any sign of... of mutiny?" LaPorte followed him to a desk where a pot of coffee and tin cups sat.

"Mutiny? No, why?"

"Fort Jackson... hundreds of them just refused to fight the Yankees. They held guns on their officers. A bunch. Over two hundred left in the night. They locked the St. Mary's artillery men out of the fort and seized control."

Frankie looked hard at the man. "How do you know all this?"

"Barnet was there. He told us. Higgins is fit to be tied. Lovell's raging."

Just then a sound came to back up his assertion. General Mansfield Lovell was in his office screaming at someone, every fifth word an oath or obscenity.

"Where's Barnet now?"

"In there," the major said significantly.

The door of the office flew open. Hugh Barnet came out, his face white. He glared at LaPorte and Frankie. Then he put on his hat and went through the room to the front door, flung it open, and left.

Frankie ran after him, catching him by the arm just outside the door. He asked with a single word, "Julienne?"

Barnet gawked at him, then shook his head to shake out the confusion. "I'm going home to see how she is. Can you come with me?"

"Hugh, I want to, but I have to report in."

Frankie knew his anguish must be clear on his face. Hugh nodded. He put his hand on Frankie's shoulder. "Frankie, the riverboat...."

"I know."

"I'm sorry."

"Go see to your wife. And, Hugh...," Frankie said, as Hugh turned to go. "There was nothing you could do."

Whether he referred to the mutiny or Julienne or *Le Beau Soleil*, he did not say, but Hugh nodded gratefully, turned, and fled.

IN THE morning, the city was far from quiet; the sounds were of marching feet and chanting, "Long live Jeff Davis!"—over and over, growing louder, then going away as the crowd headed toward City Hall.

Lovell was behind closed doors in his office. Frankie had now heard what little was known of the past few days. Brownworth had come in and received Frankie's report on the situation at Fort St. Philip. Then he had told Frankie more about the mutiny at Fort Jackson. There was not much more than he had heard from LaPorte, but he learned that after they had sailed into New Orleans, the Yankees had sunk or crippled all the boats and ships sent to meet and repel them. The *Louisiana* had indeed been launched, but when her engines proved too weak to propel her, she became a stationery gunship. She was useless until the Yankee ships came into range. She did not do any damage at all to them, and in the final moments, she was scuttled to keep her out of enemy hands. "You should have heard it," said Lovell. "When she came into view, the people along the levee started to cheer. Then they must have seen she was on fire. They groaned in a mass then started to weep and cry. There was violence on the levee, horrible to see. Fires. I think the soul of the city died that moment."

The door from outside flew open, and a man in a business suit ran in. "I got a message for the general! It's from the mayor and them Yankees!"

Lovell must have heard the man's shout because his office door opened. He stood in the doorway. "What does that lily-livered mayor want?"

The man stood in front of the general. "The Yankees demanded he surrender the city. He said he couldn't, that you are the military authority and you have to do it."

"Balls. I'm not going to. You go back and tell Monroe he can take his precious city and shove it up his shithole." The general started to turn.

"It ain't so much the mayor, General. It's the Yankees. The commander, Farragut, sent his representatives, and they want to talk to you," the man said, a shrill note in his voice.

"God damn it. All right." Lovell looked around at the men assembled in the room. "Brownworth, Deramus, come with me."

They found the general's beloved horse and two other horses ready for them when they got outside. There was a squad of soldiers. The general seemed inclined to take his time, but the distance was not far enough to really delay much. It was a miserable ride, however, with the rain pouring down and the drawn and waterlogged faces of the people who watched them ride by.

As he entered the mayor's suite of offices in City Hall, Frankie surveyed the group of men. He knew the mayor, Monroe, as well as Pierre Soulé, along with a few political hacks on Monroe's payroll. He looked at the Yankee navy men. He was not introduced to them, but when he glanced at another man, this one dressed in a Union officer's uniform, he had to suppress a shout of joy. Michael Murphy stood there, trying to suppress his own look of pleasure.

Frankie was glad when Monroe and Soulé took the two Yankee naval officers and General Lovell into Monroe's office and left the rest in the outer room. He glanced around and drifted slowly toward Mick.

Mick, for his part, had gone to a window and stood with his back to Frankie. He was in a colonel's uniform.

"Scowl at me," Murphy said, when Frankie stood next to him to look out the window.

Frankie gave him a haughty look of disdain. "Blue belly," he muttered. He saw Mick unsuccessfully trying to keep the end of his lips from turning up.

In a whisper, he asked, "But why? I am sure everyone recognizes you. You used to live here, after all."

"How are you, Frankie?" Michael said as quietly as he could. "I see you joined up, Major?"

"How did you come to be here?" Frankie could not wait to ask.

"Well, Winfield Scott was the author of the blockade, and he asked me to go with Farragut and Porter to see how it was coming along. So you are on Lovell's staff?"

Frankie nodded. "And I can't believe my luck to be here with him to see you. Mick, I have a favor I need to ask."

Michael glanced over briefly. "Anything."

Frankie allowed himself a smile. "That's only if you are going to stay in New Orleans...." He gave Mick a quick look and saw the brisk nod.

"Look after the Albrights, won't you? I have money in trust with Joe Mayer, but if you tell him I asked you to keep an eye on everyone...."

"Frankie, you know I will, and I would have even if we had not had this chance to talk."

They and everyone else looked over at the door to the mayor's office at the sound of Lovell's shouted, "I will not, sir!"

Frankie chewed his lower lip. "He'll be leaving in a moment. We don't have much time. I can't say where we will go now. But I want to say thank you."

Mick looked over, and the look in his eyes was so full of affection Frankie almost reached out to touch his hand.

"Did he ever come back?" Michael asked.

"No, he did not." Frankie's voice was a mixture of bitterness, regret, and pain.

"I'm sorry, Frankie."

Lovell threw the door open and stepped quickly into the room. "Deramus, Brownworth, we're getting out of here."

Frankie felt Michael's quick touch on his shoulder as he turned to follow. He nodded and, putting on his hat, followed Lovell and Brownworth out of the building.

PART IV
RECONSTRUCTION

CHAPTER 24

On the White River, Arkansas, May 1862

"THANKS, Abe." Johnny Stanley took the tin mug of coffee from the private. Johnny had been standing by their shared tent listening to a growing commotion over by the river. "Why don't you go see what all the excitement is about?"

"Yes, corporal," the skinny young man replied, and with a salute, he set off with his long awkward lope.

Johnny moved to a log near their fire and sat. Watching Abe's retreating form, he smiled thinly. The young man, a boy, really, at nineteen, had attached himself to Johnny after Pea Ridge, insisting on tending to him like an unofficial servant, doing all for him, including cooking, building fires, taking care of every little thing Johnny could want. In return, Johnny watched out for Abe, heading off the bullies who picked on him, acting as a deterrent not only because he outranked them but because, as he learned later, they knew he was a boxer, and as a result, a favorite with the senior officers who pitted him against rival officers' fighters.

Johnny had first found Abe standing, shaking and weeping, covered from head to toe with pig shit. "What the hell happened to you, Private?" Johnny demanded. When the shivering man did not reply, Johnny looked around and thought he saw a couple of soldiers fleeing, all the while sniggering with contempt. He looked back at the filthy man and said, "Come with me. We'll get you cleaned up."

Johnny took him back to his own campfire and told him to strip. He kept his eyes averted and said, "Go wash up in the creek." After retrieving a blanket from his tent, he went over to where the fellow had sat down in the running water to scrub at himself. "Good thing it's starting out to be a warm spring, eh, private?" he asked. "What's your name, soldier?"

The boy peered up at Johnny through long sandy eyelashes and answered shyly, "Private Abraham Pollard, Corporal."

"Well, Private Abraham Pollard, how'd you come to be covered with pig shit?"

"I-I'd rather not say, Corporal. It's shameful."

"Them boys were teasing you about something?" Johnny saw he would not get much more of an answer and shook his head. "Well, Abe, you are going to have to wrap up in this blanket until we can get your uniform clean and dry. I don't know how long that will take. It's not *that* warm a day."

No one in Abe's unit must have missed him, since no one ever came to take him back. Johnny guessed the other soldiers were as glad to see the tail end of him, and it may have been that his lieutenant was one of the ones who hadn't made it back from Pea Ridge. He decided to say nothing, even after he overheard some of the boys in one unit call Abe "Abe Stinkin'." It was not long before Johnny guessed why the boy had been targeted. The adoring looks Abe sent his way told the tale. Johnny knew he should send the boy away or at least make it quite clear he wasn't interested in any messing around, but Johnny's empathy kept him from taking any such action. The boy was pretty nice to have around. Having anyone at all around was pretty nice.

Johnny was not what one would call a popular fellow, at least as far as the rank and file or his fellow noncoms were concerned. Even the officers only spent what time they had to with him, related either to duty or the regular boxing competitions the command wanted set up. Johnny recognized his brief period of being relaxed and cheerful around Frankie Deramus may as well have never occurred. He knew he was back to his dour, humorless, and now rather biting self, but knowing that was how he was seen, Johnny used the image to keep others away. That's how he got away with keeping Abe close by. No one shared Johnny's campfire, much less his tent.

"Corporal Stanley! It's good news, Corporal! New Orleans fell!" Abe dashed up, then stood grinning at Johnny. His smile faltered at Johnny's grave demeanor. "What's wrong, Corporal? Ain't that good news?"

Johnny poured the dregs of his coffee into the fire and set down the mug. "Yeah, I suppose it is. I can't help but wonder…."

"You know some folks there, Corporal?" Abe asked, standing uncomfortably watching Johnny.

Johnny nodded. "Before the war."

Abe shuffled his feet anxiously. "I'm sorry, Corporal. Do you want me to find out more?"

"Naw," Johnny said. "The Mississippi's been locked up in the North, and I expect the generals want both ends capped. Looks like they got that now."

"Can I do anything for you, Corporal?" Abe asked softly.

"No, Private, but thanks. Just clean up this camp a bit. I hear we are moving more toward Little Rock in the morning, if the Rebs will let us." He looked up questioningly when Abe didn't move. "What is it, boy?"

Looking around as if trying to find something in the piney woods not far away, Abe asked Johnny, "Them Rebs. Do you think they will keep shooting at us?"

Johnny chuckled a little derisively. "Well, yeah! We're at war, boy."

"I mean, not like in battle, but sneaking up, raids and such."

Johnny stood up and put a hand on Abe's shoulder. "I expect so. Mostly the pickets will stop them though, so don't go worrying it to death."

"All right, Corporal." Abe essayed a smile and salute. He took off his kepi to run the fingers of one hand through his dirty, greasy yellow hair, then put the cap back on and turned to get to work.

Johnny wandered off on his own, heedless of any threat from raiders hiding in the woods. He could not help but think about his friends in New Orleans. Michael Murphy, the Albrights, and, most of all, Frankie. What would happen to them all, now that New Orleans was in Union hands? What, for that matter, had become of them all in the more than a year since he had seen them?

More than a year? Johnny could not quite fathom it had been so long since he had left the Crescent City with little more than the clothes on his back and the money from pawning Frankie's watch. He winced at the memory of standing in the pawnshop and handing over the silver pocket watch to the old man who owned the shop. The man had read the inscription inside, *For mon ange. FD.* "Someone is sweet on someone else, I see." At Johnny's quick look of anger, the man had seemed to subside. "No questions asked. That's what the sign says," he assured, pointing to a notice on the wall behind him. Johnny supposed the man thought he had stolen the watch. That was probably why he got so much less than the watch was worth. It was enough to get him on a train north. That was all he cared about. All he cared about… then.

All he cared about now, or so he thought. Then why had hearing about the capture of New Orleans made his heart go heavy? That was all done now, out of his life, no longer weighing on him. Wasn't it?

Back at the campfire when the day started to fade into twilight, Johnny sat, glum, while Abe chattered away about where the company would march next. He recounted the news and rumors he picked up, that the draught animals were weakening with so little fodder, that some said Rebs were keeping the supply lines from St. Louis unreliable, that they might have to break off the march General Sam Curtis planned to Little Rock.

When Johnny sat mute, Abe changed topics. "How come you joined the regular army, Corporal? Why not just volunteer, like lots of the others? You could have signed on for three months, then gone home to your family. If you don't mind me asking." He quickly added, "Corporal."

Looking up at him, Johnny tried a smile. He reached out and tousled Abe's lank hair. "I told you. I don't have any family."

"But why did you join for the long term, Corporal?"

Johnny scratched his unshaven chin. "I didn't have a thing. I needed a job. I didn't really have any prospects, so I figured, get a job where they don't just put you to work. They clothe you, feed you, tell you where to go and where to stop. It sounded pretty damn good at the time. Now you," Johnny said with emphasis. What he thought but did not say was he feared his defection to the South would tag him as a traitor or a spy if he tried to use his old government contacts. "You are the one that puzzles me. You don't seem cut out for this life, no siree.

Why did you join up? You should be in school or back in the bosom of your mama and papa and sisters and brothers."

Abe never talked about his life before he and Johnny had met. Johnny kept prodding, but was nevertheless surprised when a subdued Abe shared, "They threw me out. I had nowhere to go, Corporal, like you."

"They what?" shot an incensed Johnny. "Why?" He saw Abe's head duck further, and he thought he might know why a sweet young boy like Abe might suddenly be cast out by his simple, God-fearing family. "Never mind. Doesn't matter."

They sat in silence. Johnny had left his own home and family voluntarily. *Both of them*, he now said solemnly to himself. He'd met other soldiers who did not appear to be among those excitedly dashing off to war and adventure but kept their business to themselves, whether they were like Abe, cast out, or were escaping debt, were wanted by the authorities, or for all he knew, some might have even been sent to enlist so they could spy on troop movements for the Confederacy.

Like Kurt Holtzmann. Now that had been a surprise, running into Klara's brother in training camp. They had stared at each other uncomfortably for several minutes, then Kurt relented and came to shake Johnny's hand. "Great to see someone from the old neighborhood. Weren't you Klara's young man?" Johnny was not sure if Kurt really had such a fuzzy memory of him or was pretending. He invited him to get a beer.

They sat silently for some time, when Johnny asked, "So, my papa said you got married."

The look on Kurt's face did not bode good news. He grimaced, all the while nodding. "*Ja*, I did. Marthe Steuben, do you remember her? Pretty little thing."

"I remember," Johnny said. He laughed. "The little girl who used to make you help her carry around all those dolls?"

Kurt laughed. "That's the one. I guess she figured all that made me a good candidate for fathering a bunch of babies."

In spite of a reserved look in Kurt's eye, Johnny asked, "Well, did it?"

Kurt looked grim. "*Nein.*" He took a long draught of his beer and emptied the glass. He brought it down hard on the table to signal his demand for another glass. "*Nein,* that did not work out. I… I wasn't… ready… for marriage, I guess. Things did not work out for Marthe and me. She moved back in with her family." He looked up into Johnny's eyes. He seemed thoughtful, questioning. "Wait a minute. I remember you. You were that kid who always followed me and Rolf… You saw us."

Johnny froze, guessing where this remembrance was going. "Kurt…," he began, attempting to caution Kurt.

"Hansi, you knew, didn't you. And you understood. You wanted…." He suddenly reached out and clutched Johnny's arm. "Can we…? It's been so long!"

Johnny jerked back. "No, Kurt, no."

Kurt gazed at him pleadingly. "Why not, Johnny? No one needs to find out."

Johnny stared hard into Kurt's eyes. "You're married. It would be wrong."

He was startled when Kurt let out a loud laugh. "Wrong? That would be the least of it, that I am married. It's no marriage, and besides, we are talking about a lot more than my having a fling with some little doxie. I want—"

Johnny stood, slamming a fist down on the table, and shouted, "No, Kurt!" He quickly glanced around at the faces that stared, drawn by the loud voices and rancor. "I'm going." He strode to the hat stand to fetch his cap and slammed out the door. He glanced back briefly through the dirty window to where a candle shed light on Kurt Holztmann's miserable face.

Afterward Johnny had remembered how, when Frankie had listened to Johnny read his papa's letter, he had said, "That won't end well." Johnny had protested that men could change, they could have a normal life if they tried. Perhaps Frankie had been right. Maybe men who love men can't change like that. Maybe he himself…. He did not want to go on with that thought, but over and over he had found himself looking at, and enjoying, his fellow recruits. He could not remember a single instance where he had felt the same attraction for a woman. He did not understand it, but it must be his nature. He concluded the only thing he could do about it was not act on the attraction, to live like a priest. That thought made Johnny snort derisively. *As if priests resisted temptation.*

Johnny's better education than most of the other recruits soon came to the attention of his superiors. Despite only being in the army a few months, Johnny had been promoted to corporal. He soon found himself moving about to serve the commanders of different command tents, and it was through this exposure that Johnny's experience as a boxer came to light. The result of these two qualifications, his intelligence and his pummeling fists, was that Johnny never seemed to stay with one assignment for long. That suited him fine.

Back in their tent, Johnny awoke to the whimpering sound that meant Abe was dreaming about Pea Ridge. If he let Abe go on dreaming, he would awake with a scream and go on screaming until someone came and shouted at them both, "You wanna tell all the Rebs where we are?" He definitely did not want any Rebs finding them, so he got up and moved the short distance to the place where Abe lay twisting and turning on his blanket. Johnny gathered him up in his arms and squeezed him tight, murmuring, "Shhh shhh, it's all right now. It's over. You're safe."

Abe calmed slowly, his whimpering easing off, and he stilled as he fell into more peaceful sleep.

Johnny couldn't blame Abe for his nightmares. His own first experience of battle had surprised him, not for the noise and blood, but for how quickly his training kicked in. They had taught the recruits well, not only parading them endlessly, but instilling in them a sort of mindless instinct to follow orders, like some kind of automatons. The drill sergeants followed up by exposing them to the noise and smell of gunfire, making them go through mock battles until they dreamed nothing but battle. When Johnny saw his first action, he instantly recognized the purpose of all that drilling. When the real Rebs, in this case the Missouri State Guard, were shooting at him and the artillery shells were hitting, making soil and plants and body parts shoot up into the sky only to fall back on the advancing soldiers, he found he did not have to think to know what to do. Johnny had been a private then, forced into the front row of soldiers, another standing right behind him with his own gun resting on Johnny's shoulder. The firing pin was not even two inches from his ear, and for the first weeks in battle training, Johnny was stone deaf in that ear. That came in handy in real battle. It made it less overwhelming, though it also kept the soldiers from hearing the enemy no longer was shooting and the sergeants were shouting "Cease fire!"

That was one of the first things he noticed at Wilson's Creek: it wasn't as overwhelmingly loud as he had thought. He knew it was the training and also being deafened. If he had ever thought the first blasts would cause him to turn and run away, it proved quite the opposite. He started firing, advancing, not stopping, unable to stop, unable to hear that shots only came from the Union troops and a cease-fire had been called.

The thing he could not have expected, had not been trained for, was the smell. The acrid sulfurous odor of the gunpowder was only overcome by worse—blood of course, but also piss and shit. After the fighting at Wilson's Creek, he found he had wet his own trousers. All around him fallen and wounded messmates smelled of their own shit. A violent death always made the sphincter muscles go slack. *A degrading bit of glory*, he thought.

Even more unexpected was that the commander of the Union forces, General Lyon, was killed. If a general could be killed in Johnny's first battle, then anyone could. It chilled Johnny, however, to realize death seemed as good a future as any. It was at that moment he knew he had ruined his life by abandoning Frankie. Even if Frankie was selfish and unreasonable, at least he had made Johnny feel like life was worth living.

If Wilson's Creek was bad that past August, Pea Ridge was worse by far. The battle took place in early March, when General Sam Curtis had his troops pursue the trounced Missouri Guard into the northern part of Arkansas. They entrenched at a stream called Little Sugar Creek. Johnny was part of Brigadier General Franz Sigel's heavily German immigrant troops. Sigel, a fine-looking, tall man with sharp cheekbones and a neat black beard and moustache, a German immigrant himself, had his nose out of joint for being passed over for Curtis, who would command all the divisions. Johnny heard from others of Sigel's men that the general resented being passed over and it seemed to Johnny this caused him to make decisions he would have called bold, but instead proved hasty. He advanced his troops too fast and too far.

That day Sigel proceeded to lead his troop of Illinois men on the trail of a chimera, heading one direction, then retracing their steps and even splitting up for no apparent reason. At one point Johnny's band was captured by Confederate soldiers, who threatened and taunted the Union men. Sigel's chance detour happened to cross their path, so Johnny was among those prisoners who were rescued. That was at least one happy happenstance, though the debacle left many good men dead on both sides of the conflict. But that was war, and the fighting was not over even for that day.

Johnny had little memory of the rest of March 8, 1862. He had reason to be thankful for the rote responses he learned in training. With a vague sense of artillery explosions and musket and rifle fire, he went through the motions.

The humiliation of Sigel's last decision to chase phantom Rebs north to Missouri where he said they had retreated meant Sigel's men, including Johnny, arrived some time after the rest of the army knew victory. Johnny ignored the catcalls and insults as he fell on the ground back at the main camp and slept where he fell.

JOHNNY learned from Abe that the battle had been even worse for him. Abe was deployed with an artillery corps under an officer named Bussey. When they were ordered to start firing on the Confederates who were moving across a large farm, they were routed, and Abe managed to escape as the Rebs captured all four cannons. He and a couple of other soldiers made it through woods to the west, where they found soldiers from Iowa. Believing they were more or less out of danger, they were suddenly attacked by Cherokee Indians fighting for the Confederacy. Abe shook with horror as he saw that the Cherokee showed wounded Union soldiers no mercy. Abe only avoided being murdered by hiding himself under other fallen soldiers. He felt the blood from one man, whose scalp had been taken, dripping down on his head for what felt like an eternity.

The scenes played over and over in Abe's dreams, so he told Johnny.

Tonight as Johnny lay next to Abe, he felt the steady deep breaths that meant the man was asleep. He let his own thoughts drift to New Orleans and Frankie. It was only a couple of months between that awful masquerade ball and the beginning of the war in earnest. The riverboat traffic was cut even before that, with the country divided in two. So Johnny knew that part of Frankie's business was curtailed for the remainder of the war. Frankie, however, was not dependent solely on the *Soleil* for his livelihood. He seemed to have numerous, and not particularly legitimate, enterprises, some of which no doubt prospered during wartime. Brothels certainly flourished. Illegal trade and smuggling did as well. No doubt Frankie was making money hand over fist now. Maybe Michael had taken Johnny's place in Frankie's bed. That would be good, since Johnny knew Michael was hopelessly in love with Frankie. Perhaps Johnny's departure had been for the best.

But oh, how he missed Frankie. As time went by and he faced the somber matters that accompanied battle, Johnny began to mostly remember the good times. He recalled the fun they had, the cozy moments, but more than anything, both the playful and the intensely exciting times in Frankie's bed. In *their* bed.

Johnny was startled awake by the feel of a hand on the trouser cloth over his cock. "What? What are you doing?"

Abe was awake. "I want you, Johnny," he murmured. He took Johnny's hand and put it on his own erection. There was no barrier between the skin of Johnny's palm and the slender but rigid organ. "You were moaning and your prick was hard. It is what I have wanted, to be with you."

Loneliness, need for comfort, and undeniable desire overcame both Abe and Johnny. The latter felt himself surrender to the ardent attentions of the young man. He grasped Abe's hard cock and began to stroke it, then pump it. He put his lips to Abe's as much to quiet him as to suck the sweet nectar of his lips. Abe spent quite quickly, writhing in Johnny's strong arms. When he was still, Johnny moved over him. He used some of Abe's own semen to slick his own now-throbbing cock, leaned over him, lifted and spread Abe's legs, and slowly and gently entered him. Abe's breath caught, a squeak of discomfort, but then the small noise opened out into a deep moan of pleasure as Johnny's cock slid into that tight place. Johnny matched him sound for sound. He felt the slip and slide of his member in Abe's hot center. When, with a guttural sound, he spent his seed into Abe, he felt a poignant thrill that was almost pain in his heart. He bit down on an utterance, *Frankie....*

After that night, Johnny and Abe made love in their tent in the dark, forgetting sometimes to be quiet. If anyone heard, if anyone knew what the sounds of passion signified, no one said a thing. Those who remained alive knew better than to begrudge anyone a fleeting connection.

Now the two men sharing both campfire and blankets found a peace together. Johnny came to treasure the sweet smiles with which Abe gifted him.

A weary Johnny went with the Union forces to Helena, Arkansas, which they took, creating yet another Union port on the Mississippi River.

Johnny's hope that he and Abe would be posted to the garrison holding Helena was not to be. The two men followed their general back north to Missouri. A new general from Illinois, a Ulysses S. Grant, came to lead the Army of the Tennessee, and Johnny and Abe became part of that great force. By December, they were traveling south again into Mississippi. The goal of both the Army and Navy was the fortress port of Vicksburg—Vicksburg and virtual control of the mighty Mississippi River.

Johnny and Abe shared a comradely existence on long days of marching here and there, and other long days of sitting in camp, uncomfortable in filthy clothing and bored out of their minds. Johnny enjoyed Abe's simple acceptance of whatever came his way. He did not spend any thought on what would ultimately become of them. He took it one day at a time, laughed at Abe's stories, and delighted in the sights along the way and holding Abe tight at night in the privacy of their tent. Johnny found himself relaxing as he became aware there were more "couples" or at least coupling in camp. He thought, *You can't face what we are facing, death one day, boredom the next, without seeking solace of some kind.* No one pointed out what was going on. They ignored it. Johnny was as discreet as ever, but he took a sort of comfort from knowing he was not entirely alone in his affection for another man.

IT WAS during one of the many battles that contributed to the capture of Vicksburg that Johnny suddenly noticed Abe was no longer in the line of troops behind him. He had tried to keep an eye on the boy, but it was mostly Abe who stuck to him and never let Johnny out of his sight. Johnny could not break off the charge to go look for what had happened to Abe. He bit his lip with the worry but pushed on as he must. He glanced about when he could, hoping to see Abe back in the ranks, but his dread grew when he never found Abe, looking to Johnny, as he usually did, for reassurance in the fight.

When the Rebels were beaten back and on the run, Johnny tried to find Abe. He went to each of his troops and asked if anyone had seen the boy. Most of the men shook their heads, too weary and drained to do much more than sit where they had stood when the battle ended. When he approached the sergeant, the man likewise shook his head, but he gripped Johnny's arm and gave him a look of sympathy. "I'm sure the lad is all right. He just got separated from the others. You'll find him."

Johnny gave the man a sharp look, part suspicion, part gratitude, then nodded and went on looking.

And although Johnny did find Abe, he was not all right. Johnny found him crumpled like a ragdoll in his own blood. When with a groan Johnny turned him on his back, he saw the boy's belly had been blown away. Reaching down to close the open, staring eyes, Johnny put the back of his hand to his mouth to stifle a sob. He straightened, took the boy's body in his arms, and walked stiffly to where the Union dead were being buried in a single shallow grave. He stood silent as he watched the clods of earth fall from shovels onto the bodies. Then he turned and faced the next battle with a piece of his heart missing.

Those few of his division of regulars who survived the taking of Vicksburg were slated to be posted on provost duty in New Orleans. Unable to face returning to the Crescent City, Johnny applied for a transfer and was granted it. It seemed his skill with a rifle had been noted. A certain Colonel David Kincaid, leader of a special band of sharpshooters, was recruiting. Instead of using New Orleans as their base, as the rest of the regiment would, Kincaid's band would travel all through the region, from Tennessee to Arkansas, from Mississippi to Louisiana, wherever they were needed. No roots, no longstanding connections, nothing to distract Johnny from his only purpose: kill or get killed.

CHAPTER 25

Western bank of the Mississippi, Louisiana, April 1, 1865

LIEUTENANT JOHNNY STANLEY squinted along his rifle's sight at the riverboat passing slowly downriver. Over the heads of the line of Union soldiers who made up his squad, he could see right away she was not *Le Beau Soleil*. She was too small. She was much older, but then, he realized, *Le Beau Soleil* would be a wreck herself by now anyway, more than four years since he saw her last. *When would that have been*, he wondered. Mardi Gras, that awful masquerade, in February 1861. It was April 1865 now. He could not believe he was still alive. He wondered if Frankie was alive too.

Colonel David Kincaid slid up alongside him. "Like all the others, a fortress made of cotton bales. But can you get a clear shot at the pilot?"

Johnny hesitated a moment, thinking, "What if that's Tom Rice or Clarence Compton?" He felt Kincaid's eyes on him. "Yes, sir, I think I can." He sighted along the barrel to the open door of the pilothouse. He could see a man standing in front of the big wheel. He carefully pulled the rifle's trigger. As the reverberating echo of the shot rang across the river, he saw the man fall. Johnny watched as others suddenly appeared, pointing rifles at the western bank of the river but unable to see where the shot had come from.

The rest of the small squad of Union soldiers selected their own targets and fired almost immediately after Johnny's shot. None of these bullets seemed to reach their desired targets as the men who had appeared on the decks dove behind the cotton bales that lined the decks specifically for that purpose.

"That's all we can do for now, boys," Kincaid called quietly. "Move back."

Johnny and the others followed Kincaid's lead and, crouching, moved backward from the slight rise that had been their emplacement. It was a long, exhausting duty, lying in wait for riverboats and other vessels going upriver or down, but it was important work that discouraged traffic in the corridor.

Back at their small camp in the patch of woods, Kincaid came over to Johnny and squatted next to where he sat on a log. "So what was that all about, Lieutenant?"

"Sir?" Johnny looked blankly at his colonel, a fine-looking, tall man with reddish hair and a handlebar mustache.

"You hesitated before you fired. Why?"

Johnny shrugged. Kincaid's blue eyes drove a hole through his face. "I thought the pilot had moved out of the shot, that's all."

The colonel picked up a blade of grass, stuck it in his mouth, and started to chew on the stem. He continued to squint at Johnny. Finally, he nodded and made a low bark of laughter. He stood and moved away from Johnny.

One of the enlisted men watched Kincaid go and then wandered over to sit next to Johnny on the log. "He got a bug up his butt about something, sir?" Private Alexander Hogan, "Lex" to his friends, was a scruffy fellow in an oft-patched uniform and boots whose soles had to be tied on with string at the toe.

"Nothing, Lex. Just shooting the breeze."

"Well all righty, then. That was some good shootin' back there, sir." Lex, who was from Upstate New York, had been a store clerk in a rural town. He was one of the assortment of men from different units and different states who made up this small band of sharpshooters and scouts.

Johnny said, "Yeah. You would have done as well."

Lex gave him a gap-toothed grin. "Why, thank you, sir. I used to do target shooting back home with the boys. Was the best one at it then. 'Course, now I'm with a whole bunch of sharpshooters." He gave Johnny a considering look. "You're regular army, sir, right?"

"Yeah, I joined up in Illinois before war was declared."

Lex shrugged. "Guess you got caught up when the war started, sir?"

"Oh, I knew what was coming. I knew what I was signing up for."

"What was you in Illinois, if I can ask, sir?"

Johnny twisted to look directly at the young man. "What is this, twenty questions? I didn't have any job. So I got one. I became a soldier."

Lex grimaced at the comment about his questions. "Sorry, sir. They always said I had an inquisitive nature." He chuckled.

Johnny playfully punched him on the arm. "And that ain't a bad thing, boy. Now do me a favor and piss off, would you?" He grinned to let Lex see he was joking.

"Yeah, sir, thank you, sir." He got up and started to walk away, then stopped. "One more question, sir?" he asked.

Johnny sighed. "Are you going to ask me if the war is ever going to end?" He saw Lex's nod. "How the hell should I know? Do I look like General Grant?"

When Lex had gone away, he tossed the remains of his cold tin mug of coffee into the fire and heard it hiss. He sat with his arms on his knees and the mug dangling from one finger. He knew others were sure the war would end by Christmas. It got to be a joke: "Which Christmas?" Four had come and gone, '61, '62, '63, '64. It felt like more. The North was steadily pushing the South back. They had Vicksburg and New Orleans, so the river was sewed up, save for this short stretch. The sharpshooters' job was to disrupt what little river traffic was left: supplies, troop transport, whatever.

That was one thing, he reflected, when you were fighting in the infantry. They shot at you; you shot at them. You knew what units they were in, what states they came from most of the time, letting yourself imagine you couldn't possibly know the man you had just shot. Not that Johnny felt all right about all the killing. It wasn't true you got inured to it. You had no choice.

When he had joined the elite corps of sharpshooters, all that had changed. You were relieved of the constant stench and gore of battle. But you also did not have to choose whether to shoot or be shot. The man you had in your sights did not even know you were there. You saw him, but he never saw you. You could be shooting at anyone, at a stranger, someone you had met, someone from any state, someone who was fighting because he believed in the rightness of slavery or was defending his beloved South. Even though he was removed from his target, Johnny felt more like a killer than when he was running with the infantry into a bloody field. That was a brawl. This was nothing but murder.

Johnny had always been able to build a wall around his feelings. At least, he had tried to. All that time he had fought to convince himself that he was a normal man, or later that he was involved with one particular man but could eventually get over that, find a girl and get married and be the man he was sure he could be. So when he had to fight, he built a wall around those feelings of guilt. It was harder now, with being a sharpshooter, and though he could still build a wall, the walls weren't so strong. They tended to crumble.

Crumble, like that other wall. He knew he was not a normal man now. That wall could only keep his mind off his attraction to other men. He could not hide it from himself anymore. Johnny wondered if this was the same with being a sniper. He couldn't pretend anymore that he would settle down and marry, and he also could not pretend he wasn't killing in cold blood. He tried not to think about what his remaining life could be like. Maybe if he was lucky, he would be killed before the war was over. Then he would not have to face any more facts about himself.

Seeing the riverboat…. *What was it about this one that stirred so many miserable thoughts and memories?* He glanced over to where Colonel Kincaid was berating one of the privates for some infraction or another. He liked Kincaid. He was firm but fair. He took care of his men. He only got on your butt if you deserved it. And he had been right to question Johnny about his hesitation at the river.

Johnny had hesitated. Recognition that the man in his sights was a real person had burst through his carefully built wall. Yeah, it could have been Rice or Compton or another of the riverboat pilots he had met when he was with…. Even if it was not, he knew full well there was not this one enemy, one monolithic Rebel, dumb as a box of rocks, mean and nasty and immoral, hating the North and Lincoln and coloreds. He wasn't sure if his experience in New Orleans would have been repeated in other Southern states, but at least in the cities it must have. Wherever there was a working class, there would be people who not only had no vested interest in the institution of slavery but also were threatened by it. And there were good people, thoughtful people, and compassionate people like Frankie.

Frankie. The name had slipped out of its hiding place into his consciousness. He saw the man's affectionate smile. Then the smile changed to the hauteur and hurt he had seen on it when Johnny had shouted those things at Frankie at the masquerade. He knew he should be angry that the man had sprung such a terrible surprise on him. He certainly had been when it had happened and for some time after. Now he wasn't so certain he had a right to be that furious. Frankie could be reckless and thoughtless, but he was never cruel or vindictive. Johnny knew in his heart of hearts he had thrown away one of those once-in-a-lifetime chances for happiness when, on that dreadful night, he had stepped off the main deck of *Le Beau Soleil* onto the levee. He knew he had let fear and confusion and his constant desire to be someone he was not take him off the riverboat and out of Frankie's life… and arms.

Johnny was knocked out of his reverie by one of the other men putting his two fingers in his mouth and giving a whistle. "Move out," called Kincaid. Johnny looked about and realized that while he had sat, lost in memory, the others had put out the campfires and camouflaged any sign they had made camp there. He got up, took a leak on the former perimeter of the camp, tucked himself back in, picked up his kit, and followed the ragtag unit off into the woods.

"God damned mosquitoes," one man complained.

"It's all these here swamps. They breed in 'em," another man said.

"I hate swamps. They are smelly and full of alligators."

"I wish the mosquitoes would bite the alligators instead of us," a third man threw in.

"I wish the alligators would bite the mosquitoes… and leave us alone." This remark won the speaker a round of chuckles.

Kincaid's voice spat, "Pipe down. We don't need some Rebel scouts picking up on where we are."

Johnny thought, I think that burst of gunfire took care of that already.

That same day, north and east of Ferriday, Louisiana

"YOU hear gunfire?"

Regimental Operations Officer Major Hugh Barnet had come into Frankie's tent while he was holding up a fragment of mirror and attempting to shave in the dim light.

"God damn it, Hugh, are you trying to make me cut my own throat? Don't answer that," he quickly added. He took his filthy shaving towel and wiped the last of the soap from his chin. "Yeah, I heard it. We must be nearer the river here than we thought."

He actually had been perfectly aware of how close to the river they were: not that far north and east of Ferriday, Louisiana. After spending years traveling up and down the Mississippi, he knew every smell it gave off, not all of them pleasant but every last one of them sweet to his nostrils.

Barnet came closer.

Frankie winced at the alcohol smell that was perennially on Barnet's breath these days. He knew why the man drank. Julienne was long gone. Not as long gone as Johnny, but Hugh took it as hard. She had utterly refused to leave New Orleans when the Yankees came. As far as either of them knew, she was still there. Knowing Julienne, she wasn't playing the faithful Southern wife and waiting for her dear noble husband to come back from the war. Neither Hugh nor Frankie would have laid odds on it. In fact, Frankie rather assumed she would have taken up with some Yankee senior officer. She probably had a couple of little Yankees hanging on to her skirts now. What would happen when, or if, Hugh came marching home?

"Well, that's what we're here for. To track down what the Yankees are up to and deal with the snipers on the river." He turned and bodily pushed Barnet out the flap of the tent. "Now come along. We have been summoned to General Beadle's command post."

Beadle was a small man with a full beard, who tried to look as much like his hero Stonewall Jackson as he could. He was not a personable man; he held himself aloof from even his highest-ranking staff officers. He was always prim and neat and straight-backed, sitting or standing. He ignored the two officers' salutes and kept examining a map he had unrolled on his desk. He had the corners held down with a pistol, a small cannonball he seemed to regard as a relic or lucky charm, a bottle of brandy, and his own elbow. He did not invite them to partake of the brandy.

Frankie and Barnet stood at attention, waiting. Frankie noticed the major was starting to tip toward him. He reached out to push him upright with a finger but snatched his hand back instantly when Beadle finally looked up.

"Colonel Deramus, Major Barnet. I suppose you heard the gunfire from north-northeast? Stand easy, for Christ's sake." He leveled a gimlet eye on them both.

"Yes, sir. We did, sir," Frankie answered for them both. "Snipers, I suppose, sir."

"Don't know. That's why I sent for you. I want you to take a half dozen or so men and scout it out. Find the shooters and get what you can from them. We need to clear the area of snipers, but we also need to know what the Yankees are up to on this side of the river."

He pointed to the map. "Here's our camp. We think the snipers may be about here."

Frankie and Hugh peered down. "That looks right to me, sir," Barnet said.

"I want you to be out by afternoon. Reconnoiter the riverbank, then see what you can find north from there." He traced the route with his finger.

The two officers said, more or less in unison, "Yes, sir." They waited.

Beadle had stood up, letting the corner of the map he had held down with his elbow jump and curl almost to the middle. He went over to a table and picked up a glass. Turning back, he seemed surprised to see them. "You still here. Well, off with you." He made a sweeping motion with his free hand.

Outside the command tent, Frankie asked, "Whom shall we take with us?"

Frankie was a Secret Service officer now, while Barnet's gaffe way back in 1862 and the mutiny at Fort Jackson had gotten Barnet transferred out to an infantry command. They were often paired on these small missions, going out to interrogate Union officers captured by other units. It could be a supremely distasteful job: when the officers were wounded, it was Barnet's job to have them shot. Frankie's was to get what he could out of the men through any means he could manage. It was an unholy marriage, what with Frankie's reluctant manipulation and Barnet's obvious pleasure in seeing the wounded officers shot. But it was an arranged marriage, so to speak, and neither had any choice in the pairing.

They moved out an hour later. Going slowly and as quietly as they could, they followed faint trails east until they could sense the river, wide at this point. Natchez lay across the river just to the south. Between Union-held Vicksburg and Union-held New Orleans, an astounded Frankie felt caught in a vise. They reached the bank of the river. While Frankie and Barnet and three of their men waited, the rest scouted north and south along the river to look for signs of enemy snipers.

Frankie's eyes were hooded as he looked out from under his hat at the river. He could picture the area where he now stood as it would look from the Texas deck of *Le Beau Soleil*. He shook his head so slightly no one could have seen it. He knew full well that every spring the river changed, widened, narrowed, opened new channels, never the same shape or direction. The spot he rested on now could easily have been half a mile inland when he last steamed by. He judged this was more likely than the opposite possibility that the spot used to be some way into the river. The foliage around him was too well established to have been river bottom that recently.

Frankie sighed. Was there anything left of the river he had loved so well and so long? For that matter, was there anything left of the South he had lived in all his life? He supposed the war would be over within the next few months, if it lasted that long. Assuming he could go home to New Orleans, that no prison sentence awaited him as an officer in the defeated Confederate military, would it even still be there? Since the Yankees had taken the city in April '62, there had been no news whatsoever. He supposed Michael Murphy was still in the city, out of combat situations, but were the Albrights all right? They were all he had, they and Mick. Once Johnny....

He let out another sigh. Johnny. It was more than four years now. Why did he still feel it, the pain, the hurt, the... love? What had it been about Johnny, of all the people he had known, that had written him so indelibly on Frankie's heart and soul? "*Mon ange...*," he murmured. He put his palm to the spot over his inside breast pocket and felt the watch where it lay next to his heart. For all he knew, Johnny really was an angel now, gone, but never to be forgotten.

He heard the shuffle of dried leaves as Barnet sidled over to him. "Old times, eh, Frankie?" Barnet said companionably.

Frankie nodded. "Brings it all back," he said, falling back on cliché, always safer with Hugh.

They stood in silence for some minutes.

Their quiet was interrupted when Barnet sighed. "Almost over, you think? What do you think will happen to us?"

Frankie raised an amused eyebrow. "Us? You and me? The Confederacy? The South?"

"Oh, I suppose I mean those of us who were in the army. They can hardly put us all in prisons, can they?"

Frankie frowned. "I most certainly hope not. I should not like to be in a military prison. Nor any other."

Barnet gave him one of those knowing looks that Frankie wanted to slap off his face. "Oh, I just bet you wouldn't."

Frankie glared at the supercilious bastard who would take any opportunity, any discreet opportunity, to insinuate this or that about his sex life. "You don't think it would happen to you, I suppose?" Frankie turned and walked quickly away from Barnet.

It was ironic. He used to be rather frank, or at least unconcerned about who knew of his preference for men. Barnet was one person with whom he was cagey, perhaps because he knew instinctively the man would needle him about it relentlessly, if not worse. He had never really believed Hugh would turn him in for unnatural acts of sodomy against the law of the Great State of Louisiana. He did not think it was out of friendship nor loyalty nor simple decency. He did not think Hugh had the balls.

Frankie halted some twenty yards from where Barnet stood. He looked out over the river, noting how empty it was. There was a time when it was like a goddamned parade, both directions, with steamboats, barges, keelboats, rafts, and heaven knows what else, arks for all he knew. All he could see right now was a snag of tree limbs floating slowly downriver. The blockade had slowed river traffic down considerably. Now a combination of the wrecked economy hereabouts and the threat of snipers on both banks had it almost unused.

Frankie smiled self-deprecatingly at a fancy that his own life was like the river. It used to be full of everything he could want. Lovers, laughter, adventure, fun, riches, and then Johnny. Much of that was gone and not likely to hit the river steaming again. He had had brief flings over the years, starting with that fellow at the fort, what was his name? *Dan. That was it. Quite a good fuck.* Now the flings were further apart. He supposed Hugh was the solitary snag floating by. He chuckled at his weak witticism.

"Ho, Major!" he heard. It was Yeager, one of the scouts who had gone north along the river.

"Barnet," he called to get the major's attention. He waited while Yeager and Barnet converged on him almost simultaneously.

"Sirs, Wittkamp spotted a small band of riflemen about seven miles upriver. He's keeping an eye on them while I report."

Barnet took charge. "Yeager, you stay here and wait for the other scouts, then join us." He whistled and made an expansive scooping motion with his right arm, summoning the other soldiers. "We'll find Wittkamp and take care of these Yankee bastards."

The soldiers hurried to catch up and follow. When they were far enough ahead, Frankie said peevishly, "Now, Hugh, remember. Tell your men to wait until we tell them to shoot. I don't want to lose another ranking officer again."

Barnet glared at him. "You do your job, and I'll do mine."

"It's both our jobs to capture officers alive. Dead officers can't tell us what they know."

Barnet scowled.

THEY found Wittkamp crouched on a rise and crept forward to see what he saw. They could hear their men coming up stealthily behind them. Frankie gestured back at them to make them stop. Wittkamp pointed a long arm toward motion in the distant woods.

Frankie and Barnet took out their spyglasses and trained them on the spot. All Frankie could see at first were branches and shrubs shaking, but there was no wind. At first, he saw only green, but then a more solid green showed between the variegated green of leaves. He knew it was what was called "rifle green" for the Union sharpshooters who wore that uniform.

"I see them," he said.

He gestured to Barnet to look the way Frankie was looking. He managed to train his own glass on the spot. "She-it!" he hissed.

Something seemed wrong to Frankie. It wasn't what the Yankees were doing. They were just scouting a possible campsite. He could see a couple of officers, or so he guessed from their uniforms and the fact they seemed to be directing the activity rather than participating. He wasn't sure of their relative ranks. But they were snipers, all right. Every one of them had a rifle of the type used by sharpshooters.

But Frankie could not decide what seemed out of place. Was the set of that one's shoulders familiar? *Ridiculous*, he thought. You'd think after all these years he would stop seeing Johnny everywhere he turned.

Barnet had gone back to organize the ambush. He tried to hiss back at him to remember… but he sighed. It wouldn't do any good anyway.

CHAPTER 26

Later that day, west bank of the Mississippi, Louisiana

THE light was failing, but it was too early for the campfire to make silhouettes of the forms seated around it. One of the men was squatting by it stirring something in a pot. Another played a harmonica, a tune Frankie recognized as "Lorena."

The picket, a man whose shoes were tied together with muddy string, lay behind them now, his throat cut, having never heard the soldier Barnet sent to silence him.

Back in the darkness a good way from the little campfire, Frankie tried to catch Barnet's eye, to communicate the importance of preserving the officers for information. But Barnet had moved out of Frankie's sight. He sighed, waiting for the signal. He thought, *Les pauvres, they must be dead on their feet to be so easily taken.*

He did not hear the signal when Barnet gave it, but obviously, the rest of the Rebel soldiers did, for with a bloodcurdling scream, they came at the men in the camp from all sides. The Yankees didn't have a chance to snatch their guns and defend themselves. They were shot as they jerked up to stand.

Frankie screamed, "The officers!" knowing full well he could not be heard over the explosion of gunfire. He dashed forward, a second after the rest of the band converged on the campsite. He finally spotted Barnet, who had a colonel on the ground, holding his gun on him. The man lay on his back, his hands up and empty, a developing bruise under his chin from Barnet's rifle butt.

The other Rebel soldiers milled about the bodies, prodding them with boot toes and their rifle barrels. None of the Yankees stirred. They were all dead. Frankie exchanged cold looks with the Yankee colonel, then went over to where a lieutenant lay on his back. "God damn it," he muttered. *Dead.* He went over to the body to strip it of its pistol and look for any papers before the man's blood soaked them. He knelt and reached for the sidearm, then for the collar buttons of the man's uniform tunic.

He froze. It couldn't be. The moment he recognized Johnny's face, he saw movement so slight only he could have seen it. "Johnny!" he allowed to slip out under his breath. He fell on his knees by Johnny's side and reached to his throat to feel for a pulse. It was there and strong. He was alive. He frantically started loosening buttons and straps to give him air and noticed as Johnny's head fell sideways there was blood on the back of it and on a gnarled tree root where he must have struck it. He was only alive because he had been knocked out so the soldiers did not bother to shoot him. Officer or not, wounded men were shot. There was no way to deal with them, no way to take them back to camp as prisoners. Frankie put his hands palms down on Johnny's chest and said an Ave as quickly as he could.

"What's the problem?" Barnet was behind Frankie, peering through the gloom. "He not dead?"

Frankie thought fast. "No, but I thought he was reaching for his pistol, so I grabbed it. I think he's unconscious."

Barnet turned his head and spat on the ground. "Wittkamp, get over here. We got a wounded man."

The muscularly built private stepped over to the wounded lieutenant and started to raise his rifle to shoot him. "Stop. It's an officer. I can interrogate him when he comes to."

Wittkamp looked at Barnet, who shrugged. "All right, Zeke. Maybe later."

Barnet directed his men in the disposal of the bodies. Bender guarded the colonel, who had been trussed like a pig and now sat watching their every move from under bushy red eyebrows. Frankie was aware of the man's glare as Frankie examined Johnny's body.

Frankie lifted Johnny to inspect his wound. The gash was bad enough to knock him out and was bleeding like mad as scalp wounds do. Frankie retrieved his handkerchief and held it folded into a compress against the wound, his palm cradling the back of Johnny's head. With his other hand, Frankie searched for gunshot wounds. He found none, at least none fresh. He noticed how well developed Johnny still was, perhaps more so, as if he had resumed his boxing.

"Johnny, *mon ange,* what has become of you all these years?"

At the sound of his name, Johnny's eyelids fluttered. Ice-blue eyes tried to focus on the face of the man who held him. "Frankie," he breathed. He smiled contentedly, then lost consciousness again.

Barnet had come back over and stood behind Johnny, peering at him. "He said your name. How could he know your name?"

"He didn't say my name. Maybe he said 'Yankee.' I don't know."

Barnet appeared not to recognize Johnny. He had only seen him a few times, and his alcohol-riddled brain probably had more than a few holes in it. When Barnet turned away, Frankie quickly made the sign of the cross, something he had not done since he was a boy.

The men cleaned up the campsite and settled down to use it themselves. Frankie had some of them improvise a lean-to where he could sit with the two prisoners. He took care that they built it just big enough for him, the seated colonel, and the prone Johnny, no room for an inquisitive Barnet to insinuate himself. He sat, ostensibly interrogating the colonel, who said his name was David Kincaid and told Frankie his rank and unit. That was all. Kincaid was hard as steel. He was not going to divulge any intelligence without some serious persuasion.

Frankie nodded when Kincaid told him Johnny's name and details. He felt Kincaid's gaze on him. "So, is he badly wounded?" the man asked.

"A bump on the head. He should come out of it soon."

Frankie gently lifted Johnny's head and dribbled some water from his canteen into his mouth.

"You're being awfully gentle with him, Colonel."

Frankie took his eyes away from Johnny's face long enough to glance up at the man with the intensely penetrating blue stare. "He... he reminds me of someone. Someone I used to... know."

Kincaid seemed satisfied with the response. "Yeah, he has that kind of face. Good man, Stanley. Steady, reliable. Quite the marksman."

Frankie looked up with a glimmer in his eye. "Really? Fancy that. Never would have suspected." He realized his slip and started to try to explain it, but the other man did not seem to catch it.

Another dribble of water brought Johnny around, sputtering. "Hey, stop that. You trying to drown me?" He shook his head, winced, and then looked about. "Sir?" he said to Kincaid, then followed his colonel's gaze to Frankie. He looked at Frankie's face, and his mouth dropped open and his eyes widened. He started to form the letter F with his lips.

"Lieutenant Colonel François Deramus of the Secret Service. You are my prisoner, Lieutenant Stanley. I suggest you rest easy for now. Don't talk."

"But... how?"

"Hush now. Be an angel and sleep."

It was an odd thing to say, but he knew enough about Yankees to know they thought Rebs were either overly sentimental or downright pig stupid. Kincaid did give him a puzzled glance, but he made nothing further of it.

"Getting anything out of them?" Barnet's voice came from the direction of the campfire.

"Not much," Frankie called. "The usual."

"That lieutenant come around yet?"

"*Oui*, but only for a moment. I suggest we get some sleep. Maybe I can get down to some serious questioning in the morning."

He heard a shout from some distance away. He thought he heard a scuffle, then raised voices.

"Let me go!"

"Shut up, you goddamned Yankee!" a Southern voice snapped.

Another called, "Major Barnet, we got us another one."

Frankie heard Kincaid whisper, "Eames, shit."

Frankie got up and went to where two of the soldiers held a Yankee corporal between them. Barnet walked up to the group and pointed his pistol point-blank at the man's nose.

"Where'd you come from, Yank?" he demanded.

The man, who looked hardly more than a boy, said nothing. The smell of urine came from where he had pissed himself.

Kincaid called over from the lean-to. "He was our other picket."

Barnet looked back. "How do I know there aren't more or that this boy didn't send for help?"

The look on Kincaid's face was ironic. "You don't."

Barnet gazed at him for a moment or two, then turned back to Eames. He put back the safety on the pistol and fired straight into the young man's forehead.

Frankie flinched. He had seen this time and again. It disgusted him, but he knew he was feeling it more than usual because of Johnny. He was not going to let this happen to Johnny.

Through the rest of the night, Frankie sat and watched Johnny sleep. He took Johnny's hand and held it under his own bent leg so it would not be visible. Johnny stirred several times but did not fully wake. When he could be sure Kincaid slept, his broad back to them, and no one outside the lean-to was looking, he leaned down and gently kissed Johnny's lips. "I have missed you so much, my love," he said with nothing more than his breath.

He did not dare hope. He had seen the slight smile when Johnny recognized him. But a fully conscious Johnny might not be so pleased to see him. He knew any doubt he had ever had that he would draw Johnny into his arms and never let him go again was cleared up. His Johnny, his angel, his love was here, and if they both died now, at least he held Johnny's hand in his.

He must have fallen asleep, for when he opened his eyes, he saw Johnny's puzzled look as he stared into Frankie's face. They were no longer holding hands. Frankie looked over to where Kincaid had slept, but his spot was empty. He started up.

"They took him so he could piss," Johnny explained. "I have to too. They said I could go next." After a pause, he said to Frankie in a considering voice, "It's gone gray."

"What has?"

"Your mustache. And you have streaks of it in your hair. It makes me realize how long it has been since I saw you last."

Frankie looked away. "Four years. More. Too… too long." He looked back at the prone man. "Johnny, how I have missed you."

Johnny's anguished look was all the answer he got as the soldiers brought Kincaid back and roughly threw him on the ground. They reached for Johnny. "No, I'll take care of it."

Frankie got to his feet and offered an arm to Johnny. "Can you stand?"

"I think so." Between them, they managed to get him to his feet. He was unsteady but could manage one foot after another. Frankie took him out a bit farther than he needed to.

Frankie held Johnny around his waist, savoring the fondly remembered feel of the man. He asked, "Can you manage your fly?"

Johnny nodded and unbuttoned himself. Frankie politely looked away while Johnny relieved himself. He waited until Johnny was buttoning his trousers again and looked to see him staring back with a bitter expression. "What?"

"You never lost a chance to look at my dick before," Johnny commented acerbically.

Frankie frowned. "I… I…."

Johnny gave him an amused smile. "Not so smooth a talker anymore, eh, Frankie?"

Frankie said in a low voice, "I'm so sorry, Johnny."

"Sorry? About what?" Johnny frowned.

Frankie looked down at his shoes. "Everything."

"Everything? All of it?"

Seeing Johnny's skeptical look, Frankie hastily corrected, "No, not everything. Not the good times. Not for loving you. For all the thoughtless things I did to hurt you." He dropped his gaze again to keep from seeing Johnny's reaction.

Surprisingly what he heard was a soft, "I hurt you too."

When he looked up, though, Johnny was staring off to one side, looking impatient.

"We had better get back." Frankie maneuvered Johnny back to the lean-to and lowered him gently into place.

"So now what?" Barnet asked as Frankie approached him.

"I'll interrogate the colonel now. I don't think the lieutenant would survive the trip back to camp. Let's spend another night here and then take him and the colonel back in the morning."

Barnet eyed him suspiciously. "You seem almost solicitous with these two. Why, Frankie?"

"I don't know what you are talking about, Hugh. You suspect everyone and everything since Julienne…." Frankie shut up as Barnet's fist grabbed the front of his collar and squeezed.

"You just goddamn keep your mouth shut, you nancy."

Frankie glared at him. "Major, you forget yourself. Attacking an officer, especially one of superior rank, is a serious offense." He jerked his tunic from Barnet's hands.

"What are you going to do about it?" Barnet snarled.

Frankie let his dark eyes burn into the man. "Whatever I think is right, Major. You are interfering with Secret Service investigations. Do you think you will get away with that? Like it or not, Hugh, you have to do as I say when it comes to the prisoners. If you cross me, I will in fact have you arrested."

Barnet's lip curled. "You just try it, you nancy."

Frankie shrugged. "If you are willing to take the risk, then so am I."

Barnet turned away, shooting a fierce glare at the soldiers who were gawping at their two officers. He barked, "You got nothing better to do than stand there?" The two men scattered with a muttered "Yes, sir."

CHAPTER 27

Northeastern Louisiana, April 3, 1865

"LOOK, Colonel, I don't want to explain this, but tonight I am going to get you two out of here."

"What? I don't understand. Why would you do that?" Kincaid whispered.

"I said I don't want to explain. Just go along. I assume you don't have any objections?" Frankie said.

Kincaid looked to Johnny to see his reaction. The apparent lack of one confused him further. "You already knew about this, Lieutenant?"

Johnny shook his head. "Not specifically, sir, but I am not surprised."

"You trust this Reb?"

Johnny's smile was almost amused. "No, I don't, but if he says he will help us escape, I believe him."

Frankie nodded silently.

Kincaid scratched his head. "Well, I'll be." He looked back at Frankie. "Well, I don't get it, but I'm not about to miss this chance. What do you want us to do?" He looked around again.

"Not 'us.' Just you. It's not going to be easy." Frankie grimaced. "Major Barnet will expect me to… ah… interrogate… you both. That's how I usually get information out of prisoners when they prove intractable… under duress."

"Torture?" Johnny asked, his eyes wide with dismay. "That's not something I can imagine about you—"

"I'm an intelligence officer. I used to win a subject's confidence. But that's when I was with people who were ostensibly loyal to the Confederacy. Once we started capturing Yankees, that all changed."

Johnny's face clearly showed anger and confusion. "I can't believe it," he said, turning his back to Frankie.

Frankie tried to control his anguish and saw Kincaid frowning as he looked at Frankie. "I don't know what is going on here, and I don't like it. There's something between you two that I can't even begin to guess at. I mean, you seem to know each other. I suppose it must have been in New Orleans. Johnny has told me he lived there for a couple of months before the war. But just knowing each other... wouldn't cause such... I don't know... disbelief? Johnny, I insist you tell me."

Johnny remained silent.

Frankie's heart was chill in his chest. How could he possibly explain to Johnny what he had had to do and how he had come to live with the knowledge of what he was capable of? Clinging to a shred of hope that if he could get Johnny out of this, the man would at least let him explain, he thought he might have a chance to melt his cool disdain. With the revelation that he had to... torture men to get information, he saw his hope dashed to hell.

"Like I said, Barnet will expect something. If we don't make it convincing, he will be suspicious and keep closer tabs on you, maybe even take control into his own hands. You saw how quick to shoot a man he is."

"What do you mean, 'convincing'? You aren't really going to torture me?" Kincaid glared.

Frankie's eyes were on Johnny's back. "I have already told Barnet that the lieutenant is in no condition to travel and that any torture would probably kill him. So we are staying here tonight, then heading to camp in the morning. That doesn't affect you, though, Kincaid. As I said, he will expect some... ah... efforts to get you to talk."

"What if he talks, without coercion? He could make things up."

Kincaid shook his head. "He wouldn't believe it, I can tell."

Frankie cast him a grateful look. "But I might be able to convince him if it sounds like you gave it up under duress."

Kincaid nodded slowly. "I have to talk to my lieutenant about this. Can you step away a minute?"

"*Mais oui*," Frankie replied without hesitation. He got to his feet, glanced first at Johnny and then out into the camp. He bowed his head and walked toward the campfire.

JOHNNY watched Frankie move away out of earshot. *I don't know him. No matter how we left things I could not have imagined he could be... a torturer....* Johnny's thoughts were chaotic, desperately trying to find some way to match the man he had loved to this—what could he call it but cold and unfeeling?—man. But no, even now he could not dismiss the fleeting looks of hope and then despair, of love and then regret he saw in Frankie's eyes. He shook his head in complete confusion as Kincaid came closer to whisper to him.

Kincaid immediately grasped Johnny's arm and pulled him closer to rasp in his ear. "Look, Stanley, I don't know what's going on here between you. It worries the shit out of me. But I can tell you aren't going to tell me. What I wonder, though, is whether we really can trust this Frenchie. He said it himself, he used to get information by getting people's confidence. Couldn't he be doing that now as well? Trying to look like he's on our side only to trick us into telling him something we don't want him to know?"

Johnny shook his head. Unwilling to look Kincaid in the eye, he said, a hint of sorrow in his voice, "Before I heard about the torture, I would have said no, this... fellow would not do that. I'm not so sure now. I never saw that in him... I don't think so, anyway."

Kincaid conceded, "War does terrible things to a man. But it means he was capable of it before... before whenever... when you knew him. It might have taken war to bring it out. But the point is, do we do what he asks?"

Johnny shrugged, reaching to pull out some bits of scrub from the floor of the lean-to. "Honestly, I don't know what else we can do. Maybe we should go along but be extra careful what we give up, what we say." Not focusing on anything, he stared off into the distance. "I...

I don't know him anymore. But I think we can trust him in this instance."

"All right, Lieutenant. I won't trust him, but I do trust you. If you say give it a chance, that's what we'll do. What choice do we have?"

The colonel looked over at Frankie who stood, having poured himself some coffee from the pot on the fire. Frankie caught his eye and raised one eyebrow. Kincaid gave a slight but stern nod.

Frankie gestured to someone out of Kincaid's sight. When he returned, a grim look on his face, he had the muscular private with him. Kincaid shot a wary look at Johnny.

"HELP me get them up, Wittkamp." Frankie made sure he had hold of Johnny so the broad-shouldered young man would go to Kincaid.

Kincaid winced as the man jerked him upright by his tied arms. He scowled at Frankie, baring his teeth at him.

"Let's use that tree." Frankie indicated a stout pine in a slight clearing nearby. He propelled Johnny to another smaller tree and let him down to sit at its base. He whispered, "Don't worry. I will handle this as best I can."

Wittkamp turned Kincaid so he faced the pine. Frankie joined them and unbuttoned Kincaid's tunic and pulled it off his shoulders so it bunched where his wrists were tied. The private produced a knife, cut the bonds, and pulled off the tunic. Frankie had the man's shirt off and was holding Kincaid's wrists. Wittkamp, clearly following an accustomed procedure, went around the other side of the tree, took Kincaid's hands, and tied them so the Yankee hugged the tree tightly. His cheek was against the rough bark.

"Watch the lieutenant. Don't let him get up." Wittkamp went to stand near Johnny.

Frankie took a deep but silent breath, his shoulders rising only to fall again. He drew a knife from his belt. He went close to Kincaid's ear and rasped into it "Now, Yankee, I assure you I will get out of you what you have so far refused to give me. You know what I want. You Yankees think you have beat us, but we Southerners have reserves of strength and determination you Yankees will never guess at. We can get the information any number of ways, but it will go a lot easier on you and your lieutenant there if you give it to me now."

"You can go to the Devil, Reb," the colonel growled.

Frankie glanced over at Johnny and saw he was looking away. "Wittkamp, grab him and make him watch."

Frankie started to pace back and forth behind Kincaid, close enough that his tunic brushed Kincaid's bare back. He played with the knife, turning it and testing the blade. He suddenly shouted right in Kincaid's ear, "Where is the rest of your unit?" He jerked the point of his knife up so fast Kincaid flinched. Instead the knife stopped short of where his cheekbone had been. Frankie continued to shout, to make quick violent moves toward his prisoner.

"Private, come over here. I want you to punch this yellow bastard in the kidneys."

Wittkamp stalked over and stood behind Kincaid. He pulled back one arm and brought it forward. Kincaid cried out even though the blow never followed through.

Wittkamp laughed and stepped back.

Frankie took his place. "A blow like that can do a lot of damage. And it hurts and doesn't stop hurting." He leaned in and whispered, "Make this look good."

Wittkamp went back over to the other side of the tree and leered menacingly at Johnny. His attention distracted, Kincaid did not see Frankie pull back his own arm and jab into his kidney. He did not hit hard, but Kincaid was surprised enough to gasp as if he had. Frankie followed up the blow with two more. Kincaid had caught on now and howled with simulated pain.

Frankie ran the tip of his knife down the middle of Kincaid's back. His victim clenched his teeth and closed his eyes tight as if waiting for the blade to cut into him. Frankie started to shout again, the same words over and over, "Give me what I want, you shit-assed Yankee!"

He flung the knife away. "That not enough?" He pulled his pistol from his belt. "Maybe you would like some of this instead." He put the barrel of the gun to Kincaid's temple and thumbed back the lever. He shouted, "What'll it be?" He let Kincaid see his furious face, then pulled the trigger. Just as the shot rang out Frankie pointed the gun up so the bullet went up into the tree. Leaves and twigs rained down on him.

"I missed. I won't miss again!" He cocked the gun again and pushed the barrel into Kincaid's cheek. "Well? Nothing? All right, if that's what you want." He made as to fire again, but stopped before he pulled the trigger, at the same moment screaming, "Bang!" into Kincaid's ear.

Frankie shot again. This time Kincaid screamed as if he had taken a superficial wound.

Johnny struggled with his bonds. "You goddamned cocksucking bastard!" he shrieked.

Wittkamp, without orders, kicked him hard in the side. He fell over gasping.

Kincaid heard Frankie's hiss of surprise and dismay. "That's enough!" Frankie screamed. "Go get my other pistol."

Wittkamp, looking more resentful than chastened, looked from Johnny to Frankie and ran off.

Frankie went to Johnny. "Play along, you fool. Don't make this harder than it is."

Johnny twisted into a sitting position with Frankie's help and looked at Kincaid. The colonel nodded at his defiant look. "It's all right. He hasn't hurt me."

Frankie stalked back to Kincaid. "Shut up there, bluebelly. I don't want to hear from you unless you have some information for me."

"Give me that," Frankie yelled at the private when he came back with the pistol. "Get him back up." He gestured at Johnny.

In Kincaid's ear, he said menacingly. "You think I don't mean it, don't you? You think I am going to keep missing, that this is all a bluff. You think your information is too valuable for me to kill you? Even if that was true, and it's not, I would really enjoy putting a bullet in your goddamned head. The only good Yankee is a dead Yankee."

He went over to where Wittkamp held Johnny upright and grabbed the prisoner's arm. He dragged him roughly over to Kincaid. "I am getting anxious to kill a Yankee. What if I do this little one?"

Kincaid called out, "No, goddamn you. No!"

Frankie let a grin of triumph show on his face. "Fond of this little one, are you?"

He started to drag Johnny around to where Kincaid could not see the two of them. He held him still and shouted, "So is he your sweetheart? Maybe he wants your rod in his mouth, eh? Let's see if this will do in a pinch." He pretended to shove the barrel of the pistol in Johnny's mouth, but actually had it against his cheek pointing to the side. "Make a noise like your mouth is full," he instructed Johnny.

Johnny tried to say "No, stop! I'll talk!" as if the gun was actually preventing him from talking. Then Frankie pulled the trigger. The shot rang out. Johnny fell to the ground.

Kincaid screamed, "God damn you. I'll talk, you son of a bitch."

"That's more like it." Frankie holstered the pistol and came over to Kincaid. "Spill it." He listened as Kincaid, doing an admirable job of looking stricken, gave him the information that Frankie assumed the colonel and Johnny had cooked up.

Frankie turned to see Johnny struggling up onto his knees. Beyond him stood Barnet.

"That sure was easy," the man said thickly. "How come you didn't have Wittkamp do the punching? You never hit the prisoners yourself."

Frankie felt his stomach lurch. Barnet was more observant than he had given him credit for. "You mind your own duties, Major," he snapped. "Don't push me."

Barnet did not look chastened. He looked at Johnny for a long moment. He narrowed his eyes. "There's something out of place here. I don't know what it is, but I'm going to find out."

Frankie pushed past him.

"So what did he have?" Barnet insisted, grasping Frankie's arm to stop him.

"His encampment is upriver about twenty miles, twenty-two hundred infantry, sharpshooters, and cavalry. Two hundred sharpshooters. They are tasked with taking down any troop transport they see on the river and any offshoots. His squad was detailed to go the farthest south. Pretty much what we thought."

Barnet observed, "So, maybe eight hundred to a thousand and several dozen sharpshooters? Cavalry?"

"Not likely any cavalry. They always exaggerate, even under duress."

Wittkamp cut down the colonel, who had managed to piss himself on cue. He dragged him past the officers. "Do I kill him now, Colonel?"

Frankie said, "No!" a little too vehemently.

Barnet eyed him. "Why not? You got what you wanted from him. Time to get out of here and report."

"I want to take them to camp. I think there is more that can be extracted there." Frankie glared into Barnet's face.

Barnet frowned. He gestured with his head to Wittkamp. "All right, Zeke. Make sure they are secure and stow 'em back where you got 'em." He turned back to Frankie. "I want a word with you, Deramus."

"I have work to do. Maybe later," Frankie shot back bitterly. He brushed off his tunic and stalked away.

FRANKIE strolled up to Private Bender where he stood guard at the camp's edge. "All quiet, Private?"

"Yeah, sir. Nothing doing. Can't sleep?"

"You know I'm restless the night after a good interrogation. Gets the blood flowing, I guess. Barnet asleep?"

"As far as I know, sir," Bender replied.

Frankie looked about him. He sidled up confidentially to the private. "You know, Bender, I know a secret."

Bender's face brightened. "Really, sir? Who about? The major?"

Frankie hesitated. He took out a thin cigar and used a cutter to snip off the end. "Oh, you want one of these?" he asked the private.

"Yeah, sure, sir." He eyed Frankie warily but took the cigar and accepted a light from the lucifer Frankie struck against his own boot.

"Well, I suppose you could say it's about the major. But it's about you mostly."

Bender pulled on the cigar, then looked sharply at Frankie. "About me, sir?" he asked anxiously.

"You and the major's wife," Frankie replied coolly. "And what you two were doing that one Sunday afternoon before we left New Orleans."

Bender stared warily at Frankie. "I don't know what you are talking about, sir." He added, "That was years ago."

Frankie gave him an amused look. "Which is it? No, no need to answer that. It doesn't really matter, does it? The only thing that matters is that the major thinks it's true. And I think you know the major would believe anything like that."

Bender almost dropped the cigar. Frankie took it out of his hand and put it back into the man's mouth. "Wh-what are you saying, sir?"

"I'm saying," Frankie drawled, "that unless you do something for me, I will tell Barnet what you and Julienne were doing that afternoon. And I will suggest that you spent many more afternoons together that way."

Bender swallowed hard. "He'll kill me."

"I expect he will."

Bender pleaded, "What do you want, sir?"

Frankie looked around. He sighed. "I want you to let me knock you out."

"Now, sir?"

"Yes."

"Or you will tell the major about me and his wife?"

"Yes."

Bender looked away. Sweat clearly had broken out on his brow. "Can't I pretend to be out, sir?"

"No, but I'll try not to do any permanent damage."

"All right, sir, but can I ask what you're doing?"

"No."

Bender slumped. He let Frankie take the cigar, then his rifle. He held his breath as Frankie went around behind him and raised the rifle butt.

Bender dropped to the ground. Frankie stubbed out the cigar on a rock and stowed it in Bender's pocket. He gestured behind himself, and Kincaid and Johnny came forth. "Let's get out of here quick."

He gave his second pistol to Kincaid and Bender's rifle to Johnny. He gestured away from the camp. "Just hightail it, *mes amis*."

CHAPTER 28

Northeastern Louisiana, April 4, 1865

THEY walked quickly to make as little noise as possible, then broke into a run when they were well out of earshot. Once or twice one of them tripped on a tree root or rock and went sprawling in the leaves and other detritus on the ground. They crossed cleared fields, ran in tiny creeks, cut across small woods while trying not to fall into swampy spots, and skirted any sign of habitation. In the first light, they slowed to drink water from a stream and get their breath.

Frankie thought they still had hours of daylight, but he could see his companions were as exhausted as he. Johnny called, "Colonel Kincaid, sir. We gotta rest."

Kincaid slowed his pace and came to a halt, turning back to where Johnny stood behind him. Frankie stooped over with his hands on his knees, breathing hard.

Kincaid looked about. "Yeah," he finally said. "If we can get a little rest, we'll be in lots better shape to fight should those Rebs catch up with us."

Frankie watched Kincaid go over to a tree and put his back to it, sliding down until he sat at the base. Turning so he faced away from the Yankee colonel, Frankie stepped closer to Johnny and spoke quietly. "Johnny, I want to talk to you."

Johnny said, "So, talk."

Frowning, Frankie went on after a pause. "I want to talk to you alone."

"You have something to say that you can't say in front of him?"

Looking away with a pained grimace, Frankie replied, "Of course I do. We have to deal with what happened, to explain…." When Johnny started to answer, he went on, "To tell you how deeply sorry I have been that I hurt you. God damn it, Johnny. I saved your lives. Don't you owe me something for that?"

Johnny would not look up at him now but rather turned and stood staring off into the woods. "I don't know. I don't think Kincaid would be all right with our going off together."

Frankie stared at him. "Just for a few minutes. I beg you."

Johnny shrugged. "What do you want?"

"I want you to send Kincaid away. Give you and me some time to talk. I want some time alone with you."

Johnny's eyes flicked over to Frankie. For a heartbeat it looked as if he might assent, but instead he shook his head. "You know I couldn't do that, even if I wanted to. Kincaid would never go along with that. Ignoring orders is… is *desertion*. I could be hanged or shot for that."

Frankie chuckled unpleasantly. "Oh, don't worry. I know what happens to people who desert."

With a strange look, Johnny said, "You deserted."

"That's right. Just now I have nothing to lose. If you won't let me talk to you, then what does it matter? If you will give me a chance, then we can leave together after I have my say. I'll let you take me prisoner."

"How can I trust you?" Johnny said.

Frankie could only shake his head.

Irritation crossed Johnny's averted face. "No, Frankie. No. It's too late."

Frankie's expression became desperate. He chewed on the knuckle of his forefinger. He glanced at Johnny, then at Kincaid, who sat with his head back and his eyes closed. Frankie sighed, drawing out his pistol. He cocked it and said, "Give me your rifle."

Johnny turned at the sound of the hammer of the pistol being cocked. He found Frankie glaring at him, the pistol in his right hand pointing directly at Johnny's chest.

"I said give me your rifle," Frankie said angrily. "If you don't, I will kill Kincaid."

Frankie reached to the rifle's shoulder strap and tugged. Johnny let him take the weapon, raising his hands in a gesture of compliance.

"Kincaid!" Frankie shouted. "No fast moves. I want you to stand up slowly. I have my pistol on Stanley, and I won't hesitate to shoot him dead right here and now."

Kincaid had opened his eyes at the sound of the hammer. His own pistol was in his belt holster, and he had to stand to pull it out. He saw Frankie holding both of the other weapons and froze. "All right, Reb. Hold on there. Don't shoot him."

Johnny looked from one man to the other. "Frankie, what the hell are you doing? Kincaid, he is bluffing. He would never shoot me."

Frankie laughed grimly. "You don't think so? I haven't been that man for years, the one who would've thought twice. You saw what I've turned into. And you did me terribly wrong once. I have a private score to settle with you."

"He means it, Lieutenant. I can see that with my own eyes." Kincaid was standing, his hands out away from his body. "What do you want, Deramus?"

Frankie was surprised after all the blows his heart had taken over the last years he could feel the pain of it breaking now, worse than ever. He had to breathe several times before he could make words issue from his throat. "I want you to take out your pistol, very slowly, and very carefully, with your thumb and forefinger. You understand?"

"Frankie, I beg you. Don't do this," Johnny pleaded.

Frankie rasped, "I begged and you refused. Why should I listen to you now?"

Kincaid had slowly and carefully drawn out his pistol and stood holding it away from his body as Frankie had instructed.

"Now, show me the hammer." Frankie was able to see the gun was not ready to fire. "All right, now toss it over here. No tricks. *Comprenez-vous*?"

"Yeah, I get you." Kincaid drew back his arm and then swung it forward and loosed the pistol. It sailed through the space between the two colonels and landed at Frankie's feet. "Now what, Reb?"

Silently and warily, Frankie bent his knees and reached for the pistol. He snagged it and stood up. The rifle strung over his shoulder, he juggled the two pistols so he could open the cylinder and let the bullets fall out. He did this deftly, catching the bullets and keeping an eye on Johnny at the same time. He lifted the pistol and threw it overhand as hard as he could into the thicket of trees. Then he took the handful of bullets and threw them in the opposite direction. He could see both Kincaid and Johnny carefully tracked where the gun and bullets appeared to land. "Take out all your ammunition," he ordered Kincaid.

Out of the corner of one eye, Frankie could see Johnny was shaking his head, trying to communicate with his colonel. When Kincaid had pulled his hands out of his tunic and trouser pockets and displayed a couple handfuls of bullets, Frankie ordered him, "Now throw them in that direction, hard as you can." He indicated behind Kincaid with his own pistol.

Kincaid complied.

"Now if you think that leaving a few in your trousers will help you, you are mistaken. Take them off."

Kincaid shrugged and began to unbutton his fly. He reached under his tunic and undid his suspenders. He let his trousers fall and gather at his feet. He stepped out of them and, with some difficulty, pulled them off over his boots. "I suppose you want me to take off my boots as well?"

"Not necessary," Frankie replied. "Leave your trousers on the ground, then turn around and hightail it as fast as you can in that direction." This time he indicated Kincaid should veer between the two directions the bullets had taken. "Keep running. I know you will try to come back, and I will watch for you. If you want Stanley to live, then you will run far and fast."

Kincaid stood in his tunic and underdrawers. He gazed at Johnny. "Johnny, I'm sorry. I don't know what this lunatic is playing at. But I gotta do what he says."

Johnny scowled. "I know. You gotta. Don't worry about me. I can handle myself. And I don't believe this guy is capable of shooting me. Go. Get to Vicksburg. I'll find my way there somehow."

Kincaid looked at his trousers on the ground, then at the two men facing him. He seemed about to say something, but instead, he made a frustrated sound, turned, took one last look over his shoulder at Johnny, then started to run away. He kept going until he was well out of sight of Frankie.

When he could no longer see the Yankee colonel, Frankie turned and looked back at Johnny. "Now we go in that direction." He pointed to the opposite of the direction Kincaid had taken.

"So you aren't going to keep a lookout for him at all," Johnny said sardonically.

"No, but he doesn't know that. Get moving." Frankie made an impatient shooing gesture with the pistol that was still in his hand.

THEY walked quickly for somewhere between one to two hours, then Frankie called a halt, holstered his pistol, and handed Johnny back his rifle. He stood looking at Johnny with his hands on his hips. "This could have all gone more smoothly if you'd come willingly."

Openmouthed, Johnny stared at Frankie. "That was playacting? I guess I somehow knew. I didn't think you could shoot me."

Frankie gave him a twisted smile. "And why do you think that is?"

Johnny looked flustered. "I know you still love me. In spite of everything. In fact, this hostage charade is a way to protect me. If I run off now, no one will believe I deserted. I wish you didn't have to scare the shit out of me and Kincaid doing it."

"Johnny, I tried to get you to come with me... but you're right, that would have been desertion. I could hardly say 'go along with this' and trust you. You would have warned Kincaid. In fact, you tried to, even with a gun pointing at you." His stern face softened. "Johnny, I just wanted a chance to talk things over."

"There is nothing to say."

Sucking in a sharp gulp of air, Frankie put his hands out to Johnny, palms up. "Please!" he entreated.

Johnny glared. "Well, all right."

JOHNNY knew what he should be doing at that very moment was getting away. Whether he would shoot Frankie first, well, he wasn't going to think about that. He knew why he stayed instead.

From the moment he had seen that riverboat on the Mississippi, it had all started coming back. His life with Frankie. The good times. The heady headlong times with sensations and emotions he had never felt before. He could feel those loving arms around him, taste Frankie's kisses, hear him say *mon ange*. The only thing that kept Johnny from breaking down under all the memories was his complete belief it was all over, long gone, and never to be regained.

He could barely recall the moment when he had come around with Frankie's joyful but anxious face above him. He had an impression of waking to a familiar comfort. He had only had a chance to smile and say his lover's name before he drifted into unconsciousness.

Then in the morning, he had awakened to feel Frankie holding his hand in the lean-to. He had been horrified to find himself a captive. He glanced over at Kincaid and realized that he and the other officer were now prisoners of a Rebel band. He pulled his hand away from Frankie's, taking care to not wake him. Kincaid was awake, and they spoke so quietly even the soldiers guarding them did not look over.

When Frankie awoke, Johnny saw the hope and fear in his eyes. He longed to assuage the pain in them. But the happy memories had been pushed aside by the bad ones, magnified by four long years of war. This was Frankie, his Frankie, yes, but besides being the man who broke his heart at Mardi Gras, he was an enemy. All those years, he had imagined Frankie as he had been on *Le Beau Soleil*. He saw him suave, mirthful, seductive, and a civilian. Seeing him now in an officer's uniform and with the insignia of the Secret Service, all he could see was a Reb.

Frankie had tried to thaw him, but it had not worked. There was too much conditioning, too much habit. Then came the revelation

Frankie was responsible for interrogating Yankee officers and using whatever cruel means he had to in order to gain the intelligence he needed. Johnny was aghast. Even though Frankie had explained the torture of Kincaid was a sham, Johnny could not keep from remembering the cruel accusations Frankie had made at Mam'selle Marie's masquerade. He remembered Kincaid's remark that if the man could be cruel now, he must always have had it in him.

The stunt Frankie pulled when he disarmed Johnny and Kincaid and took Johnny away at gunpoint. That cinched it. Frankie was up to something, something downright diabolical. When Johnny had told Kincaid the Rebel officer was bluffing, he had half believed it, as a lingering memory reasserted itself, a memory of a man who would not even defend himself against another gambler's attack. His mind was in a whirl.

"Here?" Johnny asked, indicating a fallen log.

Frankie did not answer at first. He looked about. "I don't know. I want to make sure Kincaid can't come upon us."

Johnny smirked. "So you realize that? That my colonel wouldn't go off and leave me?"

Frankie glared. "Like you left me once?" He shook his head. "No, forget it, I didn't mean that. I am not thinking clearly. Yes, let's talk here. I wish we had a third, so he could keep watch. Don't say it."

Johnny said, "All right, Frankie. Have your say so we can get out of here." He realized he had said "we" and meant it.

They sat some distance apart on the moss-covered log. Johnny watched Frankie as he sat with his arms on his knees, looking miserably at the ground between his feet. After a while, it became apparent Frankie could not think how to begin. Something in Johnny made him speak first.

"Frankie, why did you spring that masquerade on me? I didn't even know such things existed. I had a hard enough time reconciling in my mind that two men could have… what we had. Not just the fucking but the love. I had come to realize that I was truly in love with you. Then you dashed all my faith in that with those… those clowns."

Frankie did not look up. He smiled painfully and shook his head. "You know, I don't entirely know. I know now, of course, that I deserved your scorn and anger. But I swear I was not intentionally cruel. Just horribly and fatally stupid. Stupid. I have regretted it every single waking hour of my life since. I mean, I threw you away, Johnny. The best thing that ever happened to me. My angel. I threw you away. If I was not stupid, I must have been mad." His voice had taken on a shrill, disbelieving note.

Johnny regarded him, frowning. "You were many things, Frankie, but you were never a stupid man."

Frankie glanced sideways at him. "No? Mick asked me the morning after you left if I had any idea what a prize idiot I was."

"He said that?"

"Oh yes. He said that he knew the masquerade was a mistake, that you would take one look at 'Mam'selle's harpies,' as he called them and run screaming away as far as you could."

Johnny rested his forearms on his own knees and nodded. "Had he told you that before?"

Frankie made a disgusted noise and cast down his gaze again. "He said he tried. I don't remember. I asked him if he would go look for you. He said he was done cleaning up my messes."

Looking over at him, Johnny commented, "Well, that wasn't fair. I don't remember his ever having to clean up a mess for you. In fact—" He stopped what he was going to say. Instead, he asked, "How is Mick?" He was remembering Mick's injury on Mardi Gras.

Frankie did not raise his eyes. He made a dismissive gesture with his right hand. "Oh, he left soon after. Went north."

"Then you were alone." Johnny's voice was thoughtful. He sat up and looked at Frankie. "Why did you join up?" He indicated Frankie's uniform with a tilt of his chin. "I thought you were a lover, not a fighter."

Frankie laughed, a harsh sound. "Not much of either, as it turns out. I had to. Barnet threatened to reveal what he had heard outside my stateroom that… that wonderful afternoon. With you."

Johnny regarded him speculatively. "And you thought anyone would believe him?"

Frankie cast deeply sorrowful eyes at him. "How could I risk it? I couldn't. I couldn't risk his telling even Julienne."

Johnny's eyes widened. "He hadn't already told her?" Seeing Frankie's shake of the head, he went on. "And you didn't want her to know? It would have stopped the incessant flirting, wouldn't it?"

"Not for certain. Some women consider a man... like me a challenge. And honestly, I could not have borne her scorn. I can't explain it."

Johnny frowned at his former lover. "I still don't understand. The torture. I can't imagine that you of all people are capable of that."

Frankie's eyebrows went up. "Imagine how surprised *I* was," he said ironically, revealing a little of his old humor. "I was given no other choice. That was my assignment. I didn't want to do it. Do you really think I could have avoided it if it was a choice? It was killing me. Where do you think the gray came from?" he asked, flicking hair from his temple with a finger.

Johnny winced. Like being a sniper, I suppose.

They sat in silence for some time. The sight of Frankie's pain started to erode the barrier around Johnny's heart. He got up suddenly.

"We should go," Frankie said forlornly, standing also.

Johnny went to him and put a hand on his cheek. "Frankie, I am sorry. It was a bad thing all around. The past four years have changed us both. I can't promise anything. There is too much muddy water under this bridge. But we do need to talk. Just not here, not now."

Frankie stared into Johnny's face, his dark eyes with their fringe of dark lashes full of surprise. "J—"

His words were cut off with Johnny's lips on his: soft, tender, but promising nothing. Frankie was too surprised to react. Johnny pulled away and put on his hat. "Let's make some tracks, all right?"

Frankie nodded dumbly and followed him off into the woods.

CHAPTER 29

Northeastern Louisiana, April 6, 1865

"GOD damn it!" Frankie swore, chilled to the bone from the soaking rain. "Can't see ten feet for the rain. If we're not careful, we'll find ourselves knee-deep in alligators."

They tracked as close to due north as they could, skirting the swamp, trying to stay to higher ground, and getting soaked to the skin with every shower that came along. The going was slow, no matter how they went. The day after they'd sent Kincaid on his puzzled way, the rain came down in a steady downpour.

Johnny said, "We have to find some shelter from the worst of it." He peered as best he could through the murk. "I thought I saw something…."

Frankie followed his pointing finger. "What is it?"

They had to brush aside sodden branches and squeeze through bushes that left their trousers even wetter than they had been. When they emerged into a narrowly cleared spot, they came on a shape that Frankie decided was highly reminiscent of a structure. "*Mon Dieu*, I can't believe it," Frankie said.

"It's an old cabin, I think," said Johnny. "Looks like my Uncle Curly's shack, the way it fell in. Most of one side collapsed, but there looks to be enough of the opposite wall to hold up what's left of the roof. I doubt it's very dry in there. And it could fall in on us…."

"Right now, I'd rather be under cover and let it fall on my head and kill me. Better make sure there's no one and nothing in there with the same idea." Frankie drew his pistol from under his cloak. "I expect of our two weapons this one has a better chance of its powder being dry."

"You can always hold it to its head and yell bang!"

Frankie glared angrily, then was discouraged to receive only a twisted smirk from Johnny.

He directed Johnny to take a position outside what might at some time have been a door but was no more than a misshapen doorway now. Johnny placed his back to the crumbling wall of the cabin, holding his rifle ready, and nodded to Frankie.

Frankie cocked the pistol, took a deep breath, and dashed inside the cabin screaming like a banshee. It was dark, but all seemed still. It was dead cold, with no signs of human or even animal occupation, except for the aroma of mouse piss. Frankie stopped screaming and called, "It's clear."

Johnny came in behind him, saying, "Well, damn. Good enough."

Frankie lowered his pistol and stood looking about. It was dim inside, but several chinks in the logs let in enough light to make out what a wreck it was in the cabin. The roof was mostly intact if not where it was supposed to be. Enough of it still rested on beams above an old fireplace that either of them could easily stand upright. Something squeaked and leapt out of the doorway behind him.

"I would rather not stop moving north, but while it is raining so hard, I don't see we have a choice. But we better not chance a fire." Frankie went to a relatively dry spot against the more vertical of the walls and said, "Here, we can sit here. It looks dry."

"You sit there. This is fine for me." That end of the far wall seemed to be standing well enough for Johnny's taste. He crossed the weed-grown dirt floor of the cabin and sank to his rump with his back to the old logs.

Frankie hid his dismay, not difficult in the gloom, and slid down the same way Johnny had. "Do you want my cloak?"

"Keep it" was the simple, chilly answer.

They sat in silence. The chill soaked into their wet clothing, making them shiver. Frankie sat glumly listening to the rain on the roof and the trees outside. He was startled when, finally, Johnny broke the silence.

"You said you have nothing, no one. Whatever happened to Charles William and Aunt Dominique?" Johnny asked.

Frankie had been sitting with his knees up and his forehead resting on them, miserably following the events of the past few days and pondering where they inevitably would lead. "I haven't seen them since... well, in three years. Since the Yankees... you... captured New Orleans."

Johnny did not reply right away. Then Frankie heard him say softly, "I guess they are freed now."

"I suppose so. Murphy said he would look out for them."

"Murphy? When did he say that? You said he went north."

"Yes, he did. He left right after... well, right after. To go see if he could get back in the army. He was with Farragut and Butler when they came to New Orleans. He was in uniform, but I couldn't tell if he was actually in the army again. He came with the navy," Frankie clarified.

"And you saw him?"

"*Oui*, they demanded Lovell surrender. I was there. We left for Fort Monroe right after."

Johnny nodded, the movement of his head just visible to Frankie. "How about Mayer, Rice, and Compton?"

Frankie chuckled. "I don't really know. I haven't seen Rice and Compton since Sumter or shortly after. Rice joined the blockade-runners. Compton went home to Indiana. Mayer was still there, in New Orleans, but I don't know what he did after the capture."

"Wouldn't he stay with *Le Beau Soleil*?"

After a brief silence, Frankie said in a flat voice, "There is no *Le Beau Soleil* anymore."

Johnny's voice communicated his shock. "What? What happened?"

"Someone burned up all the boats on the levee so Farragut wouldn't get them."

"You hadn't taken her out of port? To safety?" Johnny sounded incredulous.

"I had no options, Johnny. The military took her. I did everything I could to protect her. I wasn't even there when they started the fires. Charles William was, though...." His voice fell off.

THE immensity of the loss Frankie had sustained overwhelmed Johnny. Johnny could not answer. The emotions rushed in, tightening his throat. He finally managed, "Was he hurt?"

"Yes, but not too badly. And you won't believe it. The cat was all right."

Johnny's face spread in a long-unaccustomed smile. "Duckie? What about the others? Like Hugh's wife? Or the 'girls,' as you put it?"

Frankie sighed. "I can't tell you about Julienne. She remained in New Orleans, much to Barnet's distress. After that, who knows? Hugh doesn't. As for Mam'selle Marie and the others, I only know that Jean-Paul was killed at Manassas."

Johnny stared openmouthed. "She was, I mean, he was? He joined up?"

"Oh, he was one of the first. Enlistment fever." He paused, then went on, "You would not have recognized New Orleans. It was the worst I'd ever seen, even worse than when the fever went through. By the end, no one had work, there were gangs of thugs roaming the streets, and the merchants were so busy speculating there was practically no food, nor anything else." He paused. "I take that back. Tony was making money hand over fist. Do you remember Louis-Bertrand? From Le Coq Rouge?"

"Yeah, vaguely. One of the... um... men prostitutes."

"*Oui*, he got beat up really badly. Disfigured. Tony let him go."

"She did? Was it like... Murphy, when the English sailors beat him up? Because he was... you know...."

He heard Frankie's deep sigh. "No, it was because he was out of uniform. By then, they were beating up anyone who hadn't joined the army or who said he was not a native Louisianan, or who they just wanted to beat up. Several were lynched, both white and colored. Antoinette let Louis-Bertrand go because he wasn't pretty anymore." Frankie's voice was bitter. "I found him in some hellhole of a tavern turning tricks for the worthless scrip the merchants issued."

Johnny felt the old twinge of jealousy. He shook his head vigorously to clear the odd emotion. "You found him? What do you mean, you found him?"

"I got him his job back, after a fashion. It's a long story. I sold my part of the bordello for a song to get one over on Tony and made one condition of the sale that Louis-Bertrand had to have some sort of position if he wanted it. I gave him some money."

Johnny was silent for a while. "I'm glad you had… someone… to be with."

"Who?" Frankie's voice was sharp. "Louis-Bertrand? Johnny, I did not sleep with him. You know I never used prostitutes."

Johnny felt his heart lighten and rebuked himself as much for that as for his jealousy a moment before. "So unless Charles William and Dominique are still alive, you truly don't have anyone or anything to go home to. Murphy, I suppose."

Frankie did not answer.

They sat for a while longer. Finally Frankie cleared his throat. "What about you?"

"What do you mean, what about me?"

"Did you ever marry the girl in Chicago? I don't remember her name."

Johnny laughed aloud, surprising both of them. "Klara. No. I don't know how she managed it, since she wrote the letter to Johann Steinfeld, but she told me my papa was dead. He died a year and a half ago. And no, there is no one. Not anymore, anyway."

He realized he could not really leave it at that. "Frankie, when I left New Orleans, I… I did not want to believe I was… you know… like you. But being around other men in the army, I could not long ignore that I was attracted to certain men and never to women. I finally had to accept what I tried so hard to ignore. I am not normal. I never was, and I never will be."

Frankie was still for a while. "Did you ever act on that attraction?"

"Yeah, once. Abe. He was killed at Vicksburg. You?"

"A few times. Anonymous sex or as good as. There was never anyone… like you, Johnny. I still love you. Even though I lost you. I threw you away."

Johnny sat stunned. Frankie had lost the riverboat, his business interests, perhaps even his little family of Charles William and Dominique. Now he had given up his beloved city. By saving him and

Colonel Kincaid, Frankie was more than just a deserter. He was a traitor. If he ran, he faced a life of wandering, but more likely he would wind up in a prison camp for Confederate officers.

"My God, Frankie, it's all gone. And Mick always said, everyone did, that *Le Beau Soleil* was your true love."

Almost too quietly to hear, Frankie said, "That was what I told everyone, including myself."

Johnny nodded, then replied, "I knew I desired you, but I did not realize I was actually in love with you until almost the last. I think I fell in love with you the first time I saw that smile of yours. It radiated. Full of warmth and mirth. I don't really remember, but I think that is what I caught a glimpse of when I first came around in the lean-to. I haven't seen it since. I suppose the war took that from you."

Johnny heard Frankie stir. "The war? That's not what took it from me. It was you. You took it with you when you left me. I doubt I ever really smiled again."

Johnny froze. "I... I took it from you?"

Frankie's disgust was apparent in his tone. "I know I made a serious mistake making you face the world that seemed so innocuous to me, just '*les jeunes filles*.' But right after what happened to Mick. And those awful things we said to each other. Mick really let me know what an ass I had been. I threw you away. And with you went any joy I ever knew in my life."

Johnny slowly got to his knees. "Dear Frankie," he said with a voice full of anguish. Getting to his feet, he went over to slide down next to him. He put one arm around his shoulders and drew him to rest his head on his chest. "I am so sorry. I didn't realize."

FRANKIE dared not let himself believe the man he had loved so long and so deeply now held him. He looked up and into the dim topography of Johnny's face. "Johnny?"

They drew together and kissed, a long tender kiss that slowly turned more intimate. Johnny pushed his tongue between Frankie's lips and along his teeth. Frankie's delicious mouth opened to let Johnny in. Johnny snaked his arms around Frankie's neck and held him in place. They kissed long and started to explore with their frozen hands. Frankie felt the chill fingers Johnny wove into his hair, the hair with the streaks of gray at the temple. He buried his own cold hands into the open collar of Johnny's soaked tunic, over his shirt so he wouldn't make him jump when the icy cold touched his skin.

He drew away only so he could kiss and nuzzle Johnny's face, his hair, his ear, and finally his throat. Johnny said, "You know, I judged you for torturing men, but I am a hypocrite. I was a sniper. I killed people who did not even know I was there, who had no chance to defend themselves. How can I act like I'm any better than you are? Like Kincaid said to me, war makes a man do terrible things."

Frankie crooned into his ear, "*Oh, mon pauvre, mon ange.*"

"Frankie, is it possible? Can we be together somehow? I do love you so dearly. You are everything to me."

Frankie pulled his face away and stared into what he could see of Johnny's. He said, "Somehow, some way. I don't know how. I don't know where or when. But if I know you love me, as I love you, I will be as happy as I can be."

Johnny sat up and put his hands firmly on Frankie's shoulders. He pushed him back until Frankie lay along the wall. Johnny leaned over him, his side on the dirt floor, one leg reaching across Frankie's and his torso covering him. He leaned his face over, and found there was just enough light for him to see Frankie's face. Johnny traced his mustache, his jawline, then cupped Frankie's cheek with his free hand. He leaned in with his eyes open and glowing with love and desire, and he sank into a kiss of such sweetness.

Johnny reached for his own buttons and started to undo them, first his tunic and then his trousers. Johnny pushed the clothing away to bare what was directly underneath. He felt Frankie's hands started on his own clothing, and it was not long before they could feel chest against chest and belly against belly. Johnny put his hands down to engulf and hold Frankie's hard cock.

Frankie gasped. "Here, up on our knees. I want it to be together."

Johnny hesitated, then understood. He maneuvered off Frankie and helped him sit up and then rise to his knees. They knelt with their bare chests and abdomens pressed hard together, their pricks rubbing. They wrapped arms around each other and devoured lips, mouths, faces, shoulders, ears. Johnny leaned to kiss and lick each of Frankie's nipples, letting his hands slide down and into his dropping trousers to cup and squeeze an ass cheek.

Johnny felt Frankie grind his cock and belly against him. Frankie's hands worked in between them to grasp both of their cocks. He held them both, stroking evenly and tenderly up and down.

Johnny buried his face in Frankie's neck and groaned with pleasure. He bit Frankie's neck, then used his tongue to soothe where his teeth had caused some pain. When he did that, Frankie thrust his hips hard against him. His head went back, allowing Johnny more license to kiss, lick, and bite his bare throat. The sounds coming from Frankie's throat were animal.

They began to rock their hips, their breaths in rhythm with their thrusts. As their passion built and the pressure began in their groins, their rhythm became erratic. They called each other's names over and over, then exploded almost at the same second, their combined seed mixing together, its consistency blending to make one dripping puddle that ran down both their bellies into their loosened trousers. They held each other hard, gasping and moaning, until the mutual shaking slowed.

Johnny grabbed a handful of dead leaves that had blown into the little cabin and cleaned spunk off their bellies. He looked down where the fluid had collected in the crotch of their trousers and said, "Oh." That set Frankie off laughing, something that always drew Johnny in the past. Johnny's own laughter bubbled up from his chest. They reached down to pull up their trousers.

"It's not like they were dry before," Frankie managed between laughs.

"Don't button them completely. I think we will want them open again in a little while." Johnny grabbed Frankie and pushed him down again onto the floor. He reached for Frankie's wool cloak and draped it over his own shoulders so when he lay down on him it covered them both. He put his face down on Frankie's shoulder and sighed.

"Sing to me," Johnny begged.

"I haven't sung a word since... well, since." He was quiet a moment and then began to sing, "Come where my love lies dreaming...."

"Maybe I should do the singing," Johnny chuckled, putting a finger to his lover's lips. "I forgot what a terrible voice you have."

Frankie placed a firm hand on Johnny's cheek. "No, don't forget. Remember it all."

Nodding, Johnny leaned in for a kiss.

CHAPTER 30

Northeastern Louisiana, April 8, 1865

THOUGH the rain finally eased and stopped, it was too dark to risk stumbling into swampland, so Frankie and Johnny, still anxious about being followed and surprised, remained in the fallen cabin. They lay under Frankie's cloak, warm in each other's arms. Whatever was to come, the two tried hard to savor the night of closeness. They slept intermittently, the cold making it hard to stay asleep, but they put wakeful time to good use. Kisses, stroking, making love in gentle, loving ways resealed a bond torn apart by a less perfect union.

Frankie took advantage of the growing light of dawn to examine and kiss every scar Johnny had gotten in battle. He murmured his dismay when Johnny accounted for each scar's origin. "The only scars I have are on my heart," Frankie said melodramatically.

"I will do everything I can to heal those scars. It's the least I can do since I inflicted most of them."

"No, not most. Just the first and deepest. And they are already healing."

They came together and made love slowly, almost sadly.

"I THINK I might be able to get us a rabbit or the like for breakfast," Johnny finally suggested, sitting up and pulling his shirt and tunic shut to button it.

"Do you think we can risk a fire?" Frankie asked.

Johnny shrugged, pulling on his boots over the socks he had never taken off, though they were damp from the rain and wet ground.

"If we wait until I have the rabbit cleaned and ready to cook, it won't be lit long enough to alert anyone unless they are practically on our doorstep."

"All right, I'll lay a fire, then, if I can find any dry wood." Frankie sat up and stretched.

Johnny gazed at his mostly bare chest. "God, Frankie, you are so beautiful."

Frankie looked up and returned Johnny's gaze. "I was thinking how glad I was that when I woke up it was not a wonderful dream." He reached to stroke his lover's jawline. "I love you, Johnny. I have since we met and never stopped."

Johnny took the hand, smiled, and placed a kiss in the palm. "We will find a way to make this work, I promise."

Their moistening eyes stayed on each other's. Then Johnny got up, reached for his rifle, and blew a kiss. After looking out the open doorway and seeing no threat, he headed out into the early morning chill.

Frankie pulled on his shirt and tunic and made sure his trouser buttons were secure. He got into his own boots and rose. He noticed some small scraps of wood someone had put, who knows when, near the little musty fireplace. Everything smelled of mouse piss and mildew. He built a small fire, only stopping short of lighting it, waiting for Johnny's return.

He went out to relieve himself and stood contentedly surveying the little clearing where their haven stood on the verge of total collapse. In this humid climate anything built but not maintained could disappear into the undergrowth in a matter of years. He smiled to himself, finding it hard to believe he and Johnny had managed to make it up between them.

He heard a familiar click and whirled to find Colonel David Kincaid pointing straight at his heart the pistol Frankie had thrown. Frankie put up his hands.

"I don't understand," the Yankee colonel said. "I saw Johnny head off into the woods with his rifle. And here you are unarmed. What's going on?"

Frankie shrugged. "*Je ne comprends pas*," he responded unhelpfully.

"Well, don't that just beat the Dutch. You are a funny fellow, Deramus. Maybe Stanley was right, you are a little mad. Certainly nothing you have done has made a lick of sense."

Frankie said nothing. He watched Kincaid watch him. He thought of calling out to Johnny. That would assuage Kincaid. After all, he and Johnny had had their chance to be together. He had determined the only choice was to give himself up to the Yankees. It was the only way to protect Johnny. If he ran, Johnny would insist on coming with him. If he could slip away, it just meant there would be no definite end to the separation. If he was taken into custody, he knew that the day he was released from the military prison, he would find Johnny outside the gate waiting for him.

Kincaid was at a loss at his silence. He finally said, "So you won't mind if my lieutenant and I tie you up and take you to Vicksburg as our prisoner? Only we aren't going to help you escape."

Frankie had no time to answer. He heard a gunshot and saw Kincaid fall to the ground. When he raised his eyes, he saw Hugh Barnet holding a smoking pistol.

"You helped them escape? That's what I suspected, but Bender insisted it was the Yankee colonel here who knocked him out. Now why would Bender say that?"

Frankie's lips thinned in a bitterly amused smile. "Oh, something I said I'd tell you, about him and Juli—" The blow of the pistol on his cheek interrupted his words.

"You can't resist it, can you? I am going to enjoy killing you. As a traitor as it happens. I'm surprised at you, Frankie. You should have been long gone by now. I suppose you and your sweetheart couldn't wait to do whatever disgusting things you do. Lucky I came along or this one would have caught you at it." He prodded Kincaid's body with his boot toe.

Frankie lifted his hands and bowed his head. "Good morning, Hugh. I'm unarmed. Go ahead and check."

Keeping the pistol trained on him, Barnet stepped forward and patted Frankie's waist and chest. He stepped back.

"Where's your fancy man?"

Frankie gave a profound sigh. "Left. He overpowered me and took off and left me alone here."

Barnet's lips quirked in a derisive grin. "Oh, I don't think so. That asinine smile on your face a minute ago gives the lie to that."

"I am glad he got away. That's all." Frankie knew Barnet did not believe him, but all he could do was try.

Barnet looked around. "He inside there?" He gestured to the cabin with a tilt of his head.

"Look for yourself."

"Oh, I will, but first I tie you up." He grappled with a length of rope he had attached to his belt, keeping his pistol raised. He tossed the rope to Frankie. "Put that rope around yourself and that tree. Tie it tight, and no funny business."

Frankie went over to the tree, put his back to it and reached one hand behind him with the rope, grabbing it with his other. He pulled it tight and tied it.

"One more time around." Watching him, Barnet finally was satisfied with the knots and holstered his pistol. He went to Frankie. "Put your arms around the tree behind you." Frankie complied, feeling the loose ends of the rope being pulled around his wrists and tied tightly.

"What are you going to do with me?" he asked as Barnet, the pistol again in his hand, came around in front of Frankie.

"Hmm, I think I will kill you. Same thing I did with that bluebelly colonel you freed." He gave a short, harsh bark of a laugh and went to the side of the doorway. Holding his pistol ready, he stood in the doorway and waved the pistol right and left. "Empty. Well I better get on with it. Your sweetheart may be back soon."

Frankie wanted to beg Hugh not to hurt Johnny if he confronted him, but he knew it would only encourage the man to do just that. He hoped Johnny, having heard the shot that killed Kincaid, would be careful coming to investigate. Or if Johnny took off, and he vainly hoped he had, that Barnet, after killing Frankie, would return to camp.

Grinning, Barnet asked, "Any last requests I can gleefully refuse?"

"*Oui*, there is. Something that has puzzled me for years."

Barnet's face was a picture of both anxiety and curiosity. "Yes, what's that?"

As he looked around, Frankie managed to appear to be searching for words. "I know why you hated me before. You thought I seduced Julienne. So why weren't you happy to find out that I had no interest in her, in any woman?"

"You admit it, then? That you are a sodomite?" Barnet was surprised.

"Why not?" Frankie said offhandedly. "I'll die the way I lived."

He shrugged at Barnet's triumphant "and go straight to hell." Barnet apparently decided to enlighten Frankie. "Well, you see, my wife miscarried a child. I knew it wasn't mine, so I thought it was yours. When it turned out it couldn't be you, besides being utterly disgusted with filth like you, I realized it had to be someone else. Someone I could not even guess."

Frankie wanted to make a comment about Julienne's frequently warmed bed and the likelihood almost anyone could have fathered that child, but he saw no point in applying accelerant to the man's ire.

He closed his eyes as Barnet lifted the pistol so it rested on his temple. "Your hand is shaking," he observed. "Too long without a drink?"

"Yeah, damn you." Barnet pulled back the safety.

Frankie whispered, "Johnny, I love you."

He heard the shot so close to his ear it deafened him on that side. It sounded like two shots, and what's more he felt no blow where the bullet should have entered. Perhaps you didn't. Perhaps you went straight to hell. He could still feel the ropes. He moaned, thinking, *So I'll be tied up like this for all eternity.*

He heard Johnny's voice. "Frankie, are you hurt?" His eyes shot open. With one ear deaf, he thought the sound had come from his left side, but there was Johnny's stricken face looking straight into his, Johnny's hands holding his cheeks.

"Barnet?" he choked.

"Dead."

Frankie looked down to see Barnet lying full-length on the ground on his side, the smoking pistol inches from his hand. His eyes were wide open and staring.

Johnny was staring at the other body. His voice broke as he said, "And Kincaid. Barnet killed him. Who got here first?"

"Kincaid. He was about to take me prisoner. Then Barnet showed up and rescued me, after a fashion." He grimaced. "Untie me," Frankie said.

Too anxious to take the time, Johnny used his knife to cut the rope around Frankie's wrists. He came around again as Frankie rubbed where the rope had been too tight. "I had this feeling I should turn around and come back. I saw him tie you up. I thought I was too late when he fired. Thank God I fired a second before. But I don't see any blood on you. Did he miss?"

Frankie put his hand to his temple and felt for moisture. "You saved my life. Your shot made him miss his."

Johnny put his arms around Frankie and held him tight. Frankie leaned into the embrace. "I was afraid you would come back and not see him, and he would kill you. I tried to tell him you had taken off. But I don't think he believed it."

They stood holding each other.

"What are we going to do with them?" Johnny's miserable voice was in Frankie's ear.

"I don't know what we can do. We could bury them, or at least Kincaid. He deserves at least that much respect."

Johnny let out a long breath. "Better not. I doubt Barnet was alone. Someone may have heard those shots. We have to get out of here."

Frankie hesitated. He looked around the small clearing, then at the falling-down shack. "I can't do that. We can't leave people who once cared about us to the elements."

"People?" Johnny asked incredulously. "You mean Barnet? After all he has done to you?"

Giving Johnny a shrug and a twisted smile, Frankie explained, "He was a friend once. In fact, he was my first secret love. I have to honor that."

Johnny eyed him for several moments, then inquired, "Well, then, what do you suggest? We have nothing but our two hands and our knives to dig with. Even covering them up with dirt would take a long time. We don't have that."

Walking over to the cabin, Frankie looked at the joint of the one more or less standing wall and the precariously leaning perpendicular one. "Do you think the two of us could knock this thing down?"

Johnny looked up from gazing at Kincaid's body. His eyes were lit with hope. "Yes, I am sure we can!" He came over to inspect the same joint Frankie had and nodded assuredly. "Yes, I know we can."

"Let's drag them both in here, then."

All too used to dragging the bodies of soldiers to burial, they went to Kincaid's, and while Johnny reached under him and supported his shoulders, Frankie took his feet. They carried him solemnly to the door of the cabin and laid him inside.

Johnny asked, "You sure about this?" when they had returned to Barnet's body.

Frankie simply nodded and leaned to take his boyhood friend's feet.

When both bodies were laid out in the cabin, they looked at each other. "Now what?" Johnny asked.

Frankie looked at a loss for words. "I don't know. Do you remember anything from the Mass for the dead?"

Putting his bent forefinger to his lips, Johnny considered. "But neither of us is a priest. Is it all right to say even part of a Mass over them?"

"Somehow, impersonating priests seems the least of our sins. What can it hurt?"

Johnny eyed his lover. "I suppose. And when is prayer ever wrong?"

Resisting the urge to reply, when it is for something God won't like, Frankie removed his hat and took a reverent position, his feet apart, hands clasped before him, and his head bowed. "Go ahead."

Johnny stared at him for a moment, then, removing his own cap, took a similar stance. "Hmm, let me see. Being a choirboy might actually come in handy."

Frankie waited while Johnny tried to recall the words of the Mass. In fact, Johnny was composing himself, looking at his colonel's body.

> *Requiem aeternam dona eis, Domine.*
> *Et lux perpetua luceat eis.*
> *Si iniquitates observaveris, Domine: Domine, quis*
> *sustinebit?*

Johnny took a deep breath and repeated the prayer in English.

> *Out of the depths have I cried unto thee, O Lord:*
> *Lord, hear my voice.*
> *Eternal rest grant unto them, O Lord,*
> *and let perpetual light shine upon them.*
> *If thou, Lord, shouldst mark iniquities, O Lord,*
> *who shall stand?*
> *But there is forgiveness with thee: because of thy*
> *law I wait for thee, O Lord.*
> *My soul waiteth on his word: my soul hopeth in*
> *the Lord.*
> *From the morning watch even until night let*
> *Israel hope in the Lord:*
> *For with the Lord is mercy, and with him is*
> *plentiful redemption.*
> *And he shall redeem Israel, from all his iniquities.*
> *Eternal rest give to them, O Lord.*
> *And let perpetual light shine upon them.*
> *If thou, O Lord, wilt mark iniquities, Lord, who*
> *shall stand it?*

Frankie murmured "Amen" when it sounded like Johnny was finished.

But Johnny was not finished. He looked at Kincaid's dead face and went on, "Colonel... David, you were my friend as well as my commanding officer. You knew how I hated the war and what we did, but you also knew our duty. I don't know if you ever quite convinced me of that duty, but I trusted you and trusted in your belief in it. I am the cause of your death, I know it, and I never will be able to reconcile myself to that, but what's done is done, and I will seek forgiveness." He held up his hand when he felt Frankie move to reassure him. "No, Barnet may have killed him, but it was trying to rescue me that brought him to this point. I'll have to atone for this death. No matter how I come to see what you and I are to each other, I will never be able to talk myself into thinking even that was worth this good man's death." He made the sign of the cross over his chest.

Frankie stood staring at him. Even in the dim light of the cabin's interior he could see the pain etched on his face. He wanted to go to Johnny, but he knew this was not the time. He turned back to Barnet's lifeless corpse.

"I have it easy, *mon ami*. Either you or Johnny had to die, and even if I did not love him with all my soul, he so deserves to live more than you did. God forgive me, but I can't see it any other way. I'm sorry, Hugh. I once cared deeply for you. You had my heart in your possession, though you never knew it. I won't bear any blame for what you became. I don't know what was to blame. Maybe nothing. But I do wish with all my soul that you and I could have ended well. That is the regret I will take to my own grave. *Adieu, mon ami*."

After a few moments passed, they stirred as one and went outside the cabin. As Johnny inspected the joining of the walls again, Frankie observed, "Rather ironic."

Looking up at him with mild irritation, Johnny asked, "What? Putting them in there together?"

"*Non*," Frankie breathed. "That we sanctified the place twice, once with our love for each other and once out of love for them."

Johnny turned a solemn face away from him. He cleared his throat and said, "Go over there and wait until I say, then push with all your might."

Taking position, Frankie waited. Johnny showed him where to put his hands and waited for him to copy when he put his knee into the job as well. "Try to rock it back and forth. Its own weight will take over."

Frankie sighed, "Hopefully not back over onto us."

They applied themselves with all their combined might. Frankie was stronger now from the years constantly on the move finding and interrogating Yankee officers. He was able to give effort almost equal to Johnny's boxer's strength.

At first the leaning wall did not seem to react to the pressure, but all at once there was a groan of timbers, muffled by the dampness that had soaked into it. The wall began to rock ever so slightly. It seemed to come close to toppling.

"Stop a minute," Johnny commanded. He stepped back and put the sole of his right boot on the wall. "Try this," he said.

Between them Frankie and Johnny were able to rock the wall more forcefully. Suddenly there was a creaking that grew ever louder, and the wall, the separate logs twisting out of alignment, toppled forward and buried both the two bodies and everything else the little cabin had contained.

They stood and stared at the wreckage. They murmured "Amen" almost simultaneously.

Now Frankie came to Johnny and folded him in his arms. He put his face on his damp shoulder. "*Mon ange*," he said softly.

Johnny reached up to stroke his cheek with his calloused fingers. He cocked his own head and first kissed and then rubbed his cheek on Frankie's hair.

"We'd better get out of here," Johnny said.

In concert they donned their hats, picked up their weapons, and without a look back took off at a trot.

THEY stood on the bank of the huge river, fearing the separation they would undergo on the other side. Johnny knew the signal for drawing a transport boat over to pick him up, this time with a Rebel officer as a prisoner. They had plenty of time to wait and plenty of time to talk over what they would do when they reached Vicksburg.

The Yankees had taken Vicksburg long ago. From its levee, boats of all kinds traveled the Mississippi and its tributary rivers. It was Johnny's base of operations.

Johnny tried to convince Frankie to flee rather than be taken prisoner. Frankie would not budge. "I want to know you and I will find each other again after this war is over."

Johnny sat and turned his hat around and around in his hands. "So I am going to lose Kincaid and now you. I start to see what it's all been like for you, losing everyone you care for."

"Not everyone," Frankie said softly. "So long as I know you love me, I have all I need in the world."

Johnny opened his mouth to continue arguing.

Frankie put his arms around him, holding him tight. "*Tais-toi, mon ange.* I love you with all my heart. Just hold me." He took Johnny's arm and drew him to the base of a tree where he pulled him down to lie. They lay quietly in each other's arms. Gradually they started to stroke and touch each other. Slowly they began to make love. It was gentle, tender, even sweet. They finally lay asleep, naked together, on the bluff that looked out on the Mississippi River. They kept each other warm in the April night.

With morning light, they dressed and resignedly went to the bank. Johnny watched for a transport.

"There's one. A riverboat." Johnny had his hand over his eyes to shade them from the glare.

Frankie barely looked up. He nodded silently.

"We gotta do this. If you won't run, then I have to take you in. I will tell them what you did for Kincaid and me. Maybe they will have some sort of prisoner exchange and you can go back to, well, wherever you have to go." He stared at Frankie, who had taken a seat on a fallen log.

"I hope not," Frankie responded.

Puzzled, Johnny asked, "Why not?"

Frankie turned a baleful eye on Johnny. "If they exchange me, I'll be court-martialed. If I'm lucky."

"Oh, yeah."

"Better truss me up," Frankie said, holding out his hands to tie.

Johnny morosely took out the bit of rope he had removed from Frankie when he had found him tied to the tree. It had been Barnet's rope, Barnet, whose body lay with his enemy's in their rustic tomb now. He tied Frankie's wrists now, but Frankie stopped him. "Do it right," Frankie said. Johnny frowned at him, removed the rope and replaced it tighter.

Johnny stood over him when he had finished. "I love you, goddamn you."

Frankie looked up, a wry smile on his lips. "And I love you too, *mon ange*."

Johnny made the signal to attract the boat. It slowly steamed over to where they waited.

AT HEADQUARTERS in Vicksburg, Frankie sat dejectedly in the reception room while Johnny paced furiously.

"They're running about like chickens with their heads cut off. I can't seem to get anyone to stop long enough to tell me what to do with you." It was true. No one seemed to be at their proper stations, except for the stone-faced guard at the door of the main building in the Union fortification. That fellow was not saying a word. Frankie had to stifle a laugh watching Johnny all but kick the man trying to get a reaction from him. They had given up and walked straight through the door and into a tiny, empty office, totally unchallenged.

Frankie asked, "But weren't you stationed here in Vicksburg?"

Johnny nodded. "Officially, yes, but our company of sharpshooters was pretty much on its own. We came in to report and get supplies, then headed out again on assignment. I never really got to know the place."

At one point, they heard voices raised somewhere. Frankie could not tell the tenor of the shouts, whether condemnatory or celebratory. Johnny wanted to go find out, but Frankie balked. "Let's stay here. At least we can be alone and together for a few more minutes."

"For what good it does us," Johnny fretted.

A clerk of some sort popped his head in the front door and gaped at them. "What are you two doing here?"

Johnny walked to the man quickly. "I've been here for over an hour waiting for someone to come in. I have a prisoner."

"You have a what?" the man said, giving Frankie a blank look. "Oh, are you here for the prisoner exchange?"

Frankie and Johnny chorused, "Yes."

"Well, there's no one here to deal with you. But if you see Colonel Pitcairn, tell him he is wanted at the general's residence."

Johnny started to protest, but the man was gone. He turned to look at Frankie, who shrugged.

Nearly a half hour later, a colonel came out of an inner office. He abruptly asked, "Who are you waiting for, Lieutenant?"

"Anyone!" Johnny replied, exasperated. "Sir," he quickly added.

The colonel looked at Frankie. "Why are you here, Colonel?"

"He took me prisoner," Frankie replied, nodding to Johnny.

"Are you mad?" the man asked Johnny.

Frankie was about to ask the man if his name was Pitcairn when the man ducked back into the door.

"That's it!" Johnny cried. "Come on." He reached for Frankie's arm.

"Why are you in such a hurry?" Frankie's expression showed the amusement he was beginning to feel.

"This is hard enough to do. I want it over with."

Frankie let Johnny pull him up and out of the building. As they passed the unmoving and unblinking guard, Johnny spat. "Some way to run an army. We won't beat the Rebels. We'll make them wait forever."

He was startled to hear Frankie chuckling at his side. He arched an eyebrow at him. "What's so funny?"

Frankie shook his head. "I was just thinking, who do I have to fuck to be imprisoned around here?"

They spotted a harried clerk walking toward them. "Hey, you, Corporal! Stop a minute," Johnny barked.

The flustered corporal saw Johnny's rank, stopped where he was, and saluted. "Sir!"

"What the hell is going on here? Where is everyone? The Rebs about to attack or something?" Johnny stood glaring at the clerk.

"N-no, sir. I mean, didn't you hear? The war is over. Came over the wire this morning. Lee surrendered to Grant." He allowed himself a smile. "It's over. We can go home now."

Frankie shook his head. "Lee can't do that. I mean, he can surrender to Grant, but that doesn't mean the war is over. That's up to each state."

The corporal shrugged. "I don't know, uh, sir," he said, eyeing Frankie's uniform. "You are probably right, but everyone says it's as good as over." He waved the papers he was carrying. "Got it right here. They've already sent messages to the Confederate prisons to release Yankee prisoners. They are going to send them here to Vicksburg to exchange for Reb prisoners up North."

"Well, I'll be shot for shit." Johnny put his hands on his hips and stood looking distracted.

Frankie looked as confused. "If the war is over, will they not want to take me prisoner?"

The clerk shrugged. "Hell if I know, sir. I suppose you should go see the provost." He muttered something about having to deliver the messages and, after a perfunctory salute, turned and dashed away.

"Hellfire and damnation," Johnny breathed.

"Your language has certainly gotten more colorful," Frankie observed. "Now what? I suppose they keep provosts near the stockade in Union forts too."

Johnny frowned. "Yes, I suppose they must." He looked about. "Over there, I suppose."

Frankie pretended his wrists were shackled and said, "Time to take in the prisoner."

Johnny took Frankie's arm. "Let's go see what the provost says."

Solemnly the two headed in the direction of the stockade. When they arrived, they saw a small group of Union soldiers gathered about, talking to each other. The men eyed Frankie warily as they looked up at his and Johnny's approach. Then they saw Johnny was an officer and stood to attention and saluted.

"Where can we find the provost?" Johnny asked, returning the salute.

One of the soldiers pointed at the door to the apparent stockade. "Major Graham's office is in there, sir."

Johnny thanked the man and led Frankie over to the door. "Here goes. You sure about this?"

"*Oui*, let's get it over with."

Johnny opened the door into what proved to be a tiny room full of furniture, mostly a desk and several chairs and a cabinet of some type. The top of the desk, behind which a harried-looking man sat, was a confusion of papers in stacks and spread out across it. Johnny stood at attention and saluted, while Frankie stood dejected.

"Begging your pardon, sir. I have a prisoner...," he began, but stopped when the major interrupted him.

"A prisoner?" the major shouted. "Fine time to bring in a prisoner. Who are you anyway?" The major was an older man, white haired and clean-shaven. He glared at first Johnny and then Frankie through wire-rimmed glasses. His face was ruddy with irritation. "Well, speak up!"

"Lieutenant John C. Stanley, sir. This is Colonel François Deramus of the Confederate Secret Service."

The major glared at Frankie. "Guess the secret is out, eh? There is no more Confederacy. Didn't you hear?"

Johnny, who had removed his cap when he entered the room, twisted it in his hands. "Yes, sir, we just did."

"Where'd you come from, son?" In spite of the use of the word "son," nothing about the major bespoke friendliness, nor paternal feeling.

Johnny replied, "My unit was across the river. This Confederate officer had captured my colonel, David Kincaid, sir, and then helped us escape. He surrendered to me."

"He did? Why did he do that? Extraordinary." The major did not wait for an answer. "Well, what do you want me to do with the lunatic, Lieutenant Stanley?"

Johnny glanced at a bemused Frankie, then turned back to the major. "Take him prisoner, sir?" he asked doubtfully.

The major sat back and laced his fingers behind his head. "Now why would I want to do a thing like that?"

Johnny could no longer think of an answer. "Sir?"

"Well, I mean, son, that the war is over. Good as. Why would I want to put him in there?" he went on, gesturing to the stockade door. "I'd just have to feed him, then arrange transport for him to the prison at Rock Island, and then they would turn around and send him back, and I'd have to feed him again."

Johnny stood utterly still and silent. He finally asked, "What do you want me to do with him, then, sir?"

The major barked, "Well, you imbecile. What do you want to do with him?"

Johnny blushed when he heard a quiet snort from Frankie's direction. "I don't know, sir."

"Oh for Christ's sake. Let him loose."

Johnny peered at him. "Just like that, sir?"

The major relented. He sat straight again and said, "Well, I suppose not. We need to do something official. And he probably shouldn't be seen in uniform."

Frankie finally spoke up. "I'm sorry, sir, but if I am out of uniform, might I not be taken for a spy?"

Graham made a disgusted noise. "How can you spy for a country that no longer exists?"

For once Frankie had nothing to say.

"Ah, well, here's what we will do. I'll make you swear an oath, write out some sort of pass, and you two can get the hell out of my way and let me get some work done." He gave Johnny an imperious look. "That good enough for you, Lieutenant?"

"What oath?" Frankie asked.

"How the hell should I know? I'll make something up. Smithers!" Graham shouted.

The soldier who had directed Johnny to the major's office came to the door and stood at attention. "Yes, sir?"

The major stood up. "Come in here and write this down." He cleared his throat. When the soldier had located a blank sheet of paper and dipped a quill into the inkstand on the major's desk, the older man began, "I... what did you say your name was, boy?"

Frankie leaned to the soldier and said, "François Deramus, Colonel, Confederate Secret Service."

The soldier looked up at him. "Fran... swah? How do you spell that?"

Frankie spelled it out. He added, "Put a little hook on the bottom of the C."

"Like this?"

Johnny almost chuckled this time. The major, however, was not amused. "That's enough. Here, let me go on." He cleared his throat again. "I... all that... do hereby swear not to take arms against the government of the United States of America either now or at any time in the future. So help me God." He leaned to the soldier. "That ought to do. You got that, Smithers?"

"Y-yes, sir, just about." He finished the document and picked it up and waved it in the air to dry the ink.

"Now you sign it," the major said to Frankie.

Frankie took the quill from the soldier and leaned to sign the oath. "So help me God," he read aloud.

He and Johnny exchanged hopeful looks. "And the pass, sir?" Johnny asked the major.

"Smithers can take care of that. He's been signing my name on all types of stuff for months. You all just go on and let me get back to work."

As the three saluted and headed for the door, the major spoke again. "And good luck to you, fellows. We are all going to need it."

Outside the office, Smithers asked them to wait for him while he prepared the documents.

Once he was out of earshot, Frankie purred to Johnny, "When you stand up like that and salute and say 'sir,' it makes my heart go pitter-pat… and other parts of me too."

Johnny smiled and laughed. "Well, that was easier than I thought. Now what do we do?"

Frankie looked about. "I suppose we could find a telegraph office and wire Mick that we are on our way home."

With a happy face, Johnny said, "Home. That sounds so wonderful. But I am already home. I'm with you, aren't I?"

Frankie gazed at him. "If you are going to say lovely things like that, better make sure we are alone or I won't be responsible for my behavior."

Johnny smiled fondly back at him. "We will have a whole lifetime for that."

Frankie risked a squeeze of Johnny's arm. "So we shall, *mon ange*."

EPILOGUE

MY NAME is Michael Murphy.

I was present when Union naval authorities demanded the surrender of New Orleans in April 1862. I cannot tell you how surprised I was to see my old friend, Frankie Deramus, come into Mayor Monroe's office with General Lovell's party. I also cannot say how pleased. Those few minutes we had to talk as privately as we could manage were something, anyway. I could only hope then that I would see him again.

As soon as the surrender was settled a few days later, I sought out the Albrights. They were as happy to see me as I was to see them. Charles William was scuffed up but seemed to be healing from a beating he had gotten.

"You realize now you are both free," I said to him and Mrs. Albright.

Charles William smiled that quiet smile of his and replied, "Mr. Murphy, we've been 'free' for a long time."

Mrs. Albright was worried about what they would do. "Can we stay in this house?" she asked.

They already knew Frankie had made some provision for them. I had seen Joe Mayer about the trust. It seemed it was entirely in his hands, so we had gone to the lawyer, Levy, and he had me put on the papers as the trustee. This was necessary because officially Mayer, though a civilian, was on shaky ground with the Union authorities. I was technically also a civilian, but I was attached to those same authorities so would have a rock-hard handle on the funds. I got along better than most with General Ben Butler too, so I was confident any arrangements I made would be left alone. I hired the Albrights "on paper," as they say.

Then all we could do was sit out the war and hope the Union's victory would be assured. We could not know what happened to Frankie. There was no effective communication between the armies' personnel.

New Orleans was already a shabby version of what it had been before Fort Sumter. While food and other supplies began again to come into the city and the rowdies who had terrorized everyone were long gone, there was a despairing air among most of the citizens. They could not be blamed. Their men were still at war and with the very people they had to deal with as captors now. While the abolitionists and others in jail for sedition came out and returned to their families, the recalcitrant from among the city fathers took their place. Butler was not a polished fellow by any means. He's what they call a political general, often rough-hewn even for a Northerner. These Southern ladies and gentlemen, including the Creoles, found his directness intolerable.

The only groups that seemed content were the Germans and Irish and other immigrants. Not all of them. Hell, there were even loyal colored who joined the Confederate army, though they were never permitted to fight. There were immigrants as hostile to us. But when jobs started coming back to the shipyard and the warehouses, their acceptance increased.

Many of the city's prominent families found ways to get around the need for permits to travel. Frankly, I don't think Butler, and later General Banks, minded some of those shrill wives thinking they had gotten one over on us.

As a result of these flights, however, Frankie's family's city home came on the market. I remember his telling me he had sold it and the lake house to finance his late lamented *Le Beau Soleil*. When the next owners left without government permission, the house was confiscated from them. I used some of the trust Frankie had set up to buy it for him. Charles William and his wife moved in as caretakers, and I moved into their cottage and set up my confidential agency office in the parlor.

The Crescent City may never be the same again, I am afraid, but at least it will soon have one of its old residents back. I just got a wire from Frankie via Vicksburg, letting me know he would be back in town soon. Glory of glories, and I would not have credited the news if I had not read the wire myself, Johnny Stanley was with him! I went straight to the telegraph office and sent the two of them a message that I was still here, the Albrights were fine, and I had a place for them to live when they were ready to be settled. I can't wait to see them and hear their stories.

Then I sent a boy to Auggie Schmidt's tailor shop to order new clothes for both of them.

I expect the two men who arrive will not be the two I knew once. That will be sad in some way, since Frankie was always such a free soul. I can only hope Johnny will be more at peace with himself and Frankie. I knew the moment I met Johnny, all those years ago on the levee, that Frankie was falling in love with him and that he could not help but come to feel the same way. How with all the horror of the war that pitted brother against brother these two dear lovers could find their way back to each other... well, that's a blessing if I ever heard one. There must be hope for the human race yet.

HISTORICAL
NOTES

NEEDLESS to say the main characters in this novel are fictional. It may interest readers to know that I originally decided to write this novel about thirty-five years ago when I saw the surname "Deramus" on some document. I said to myself, then and there, "Someday I am going to write a novel about a riverboat gambler named Deramus."

Many of the historical figures have received dramatic touch-ups, but their characters were much as I have illustrated. There are quite a few firsthand accounts of New Orleans in the first couple of years of the Civil War, most of which were available on the Amazon Kindle Keyboard, which meant I, who am too visually impaired to read print, was able to listen to them with text-to-speech.

All of the dramatic events are factual, from the death of Albert Sidney Johnson to the sabotage of the New Orleans shipyards to the riot at the concert hall. The wonderful book *Mutiny at Fort Jackson* by Michael D. Pierson tells the story of the immigrant population's dissatisfaction with conditions in 1861-62 New Orleans. I was only too happy to give Hugh Barnet a part in it all falling apart the way it did.

Not familiar with the Creoles? They were descendants of the original French and Spanish settlers of the Mississippi River delta. They had a distinct culture that began to erode as "Americans" from such places as Kentucky began to dominate in terms of population. You can learn a lot about the Creoles in George Washington Cable's books. Creoles should not be confused with Cajuns, whose name came from "Acadians," the Francophone exiles from the Canadian Maritime Provinces in the late eighteenth century.

I want to share with you some of the history that not everyone may know about New Orleans in the 1850s and 1860s. It was a remarkably diverse city, for one. Not only had Americans, or "Kentucks" as many called them, crowded out the old Creole families we are so romantically familiar with, but immigrants from Europe, many fleeing from failed revolutions and the Great Hunger in Ireland in the late 1840s, had helped make New Orleans the sixth-largest city in the United States. In fact, the city had the highest Jewish population of any city in America, including New York and Chicago. These immigrants came from all classes, but a good portion were working class. Socialism was not a new thing. Even Abraham Lincoln held views that supported the concept of strong labor unions and workers' rights.

The result of this immigration to New Orleans was that this city in particular was unlike the South as a whole. Its racial, political, social and religious makeup was unique. In general, people in the secessionist states were quite loyal to the Confederacy, whether or not they were sufficiently rich to have a stake in the institution of slavery. However, the immigrants who had come to Louisiana in the past twenty years found that not only war, but slave labor itself, impeded their dreams and ambitions. When the shipbuilding unions threatened to strike for better pay, the boss simply shrugged and said, "We can get slaves. We don't have to pay them at all and they can't strike."

So when conditions at Fort Jackson were at their worst and the ray of light in the form of Farragut's ships came in sight, the largest mutiny in the history of the Confederacy took place. The very next day Farragut obtained the surrender of the City of New Orleans to the Union Navy.

I have not shied away from using the terms related to ethnicity and race that the average person would have used all along the Mississippi River at the time. Anyone who thinks a novelist who puts the word "nigger" in a bigoted character's mouth also uses the term himself doesn't get it. Historical fiction is full of outmoded conventions offensive in our day and age. To be realistic and accurate the novelist must use the terminology of the day as much as he possibly can.

And that leads to attitudes toward same-sex desire. Under the Napoleonic Code, which until the Louisiana Purchase in 1804 was in force in Louisiana, there was no law against what the laws usually call "sodomy." Laws enacted after the Louisiana Purchase by the United States in 1804 made both anal and oral sex a criminal act, and the punishment was a life sentence at hard labor. [*The Sensibilities of our Forefathers: The History of Sodomy Laws in the United States— Louisiana*, by George Painter, published in Gay & Lesbian Archives of the Pacific Northwest at http://www.glapn.org/sodomylaws/ sensibilities/louisiana.htm.]

In Frankie and Johnny's lifetime, the practice would remain a criminal offense. However it is generally known that arrests did not necessarily mean trials and trials did not mean convictions. I have always maintained that class has more to do with who would be punished for sodomy. As a rich, influential man from an old family, François Deramus was highly unlikely to be arrested for sodomy. There were many homosexual men who were celebrities or at least prominent at the time. The poet Walt Whitman, for one, and President James Buchanan and his partner, Rufus King, for two more. The songwriter Stephen Foster was what we would now call gay.

It would not be a life of open liberties. Frankie got away with being as "out" as I portray him because he was good at playing a role and had politicians eating out of his hand. You simply are not going to send the police to arrest someone who is a major contributor to your political ambitions. "Mam'selle Marie" and the others were much the same. Those who insist "But it was against the law!" need to remember that a lot of lawbreaking went on under our noses then, as it does now. Prostitution was widespread and whores mostly untouched by police… well, unless the policeman wanted something.

It is a professional and personal mission for me to encourage historical novelists to write intelligent tales of what life for a same-sex-desiring person might have been like throughout human history. GLBT history is thin for the same reason women, racial and ethnic and religious minorities, the lower classes, and people with disabilities have been left out of historical records. This is termed "erasure." But certainly there were GLBT people for all the time people have existed and some of them must have found each other, fallen in love, and made lives together. I mean, really, how are you going to stop people from falling in love?

I welcome comments and questions. You can find me with no trouble by writing to christopherhmoss@gmail.com. I am also the editor of Our Story: GLBTQ Historical Fiction at http://www.glbtbookshelf.com, that treasure trove established and run by prolific gay novelist Mel Keegan.

Frankie and Johnny do make it back to New Orleans, I assure you. Their story is far from over. Stay tuned, as they say, for further novels starring Frankie Deramus, Johnny Stanley, and Michael Murphy, along with the Albrights and Duckie!

Your servant, Mesdames et Messieurs,
Christopher Hawthorne Moss
Seattle, Washington State

CHRISTOPHER HAWTHORNE MOSS wrote his first short story when he was seven and has spent some of the happiest hours of his life fully involved with his colorful, passionate, and often humorous characters. Moss spent some time away from fiction, writing content for websites before his first book came out under the name Nan Hawthorne in 1991. He has since become a novelist and is a prolific and popular blogger, an editor for Wilde Oats and the GLBT Bookshelf, where you can find his short stories and thoughtful and expert book reviews. He lives in the Pacific Northwest with his partner of over thirty years and four doted-upon cats. He owns Shield-wall Productions at http://www.shield-wall.com. He welcomes comments from readers sent to christopher hmoss@gmail.com and can be found on Facebook and Twitter.

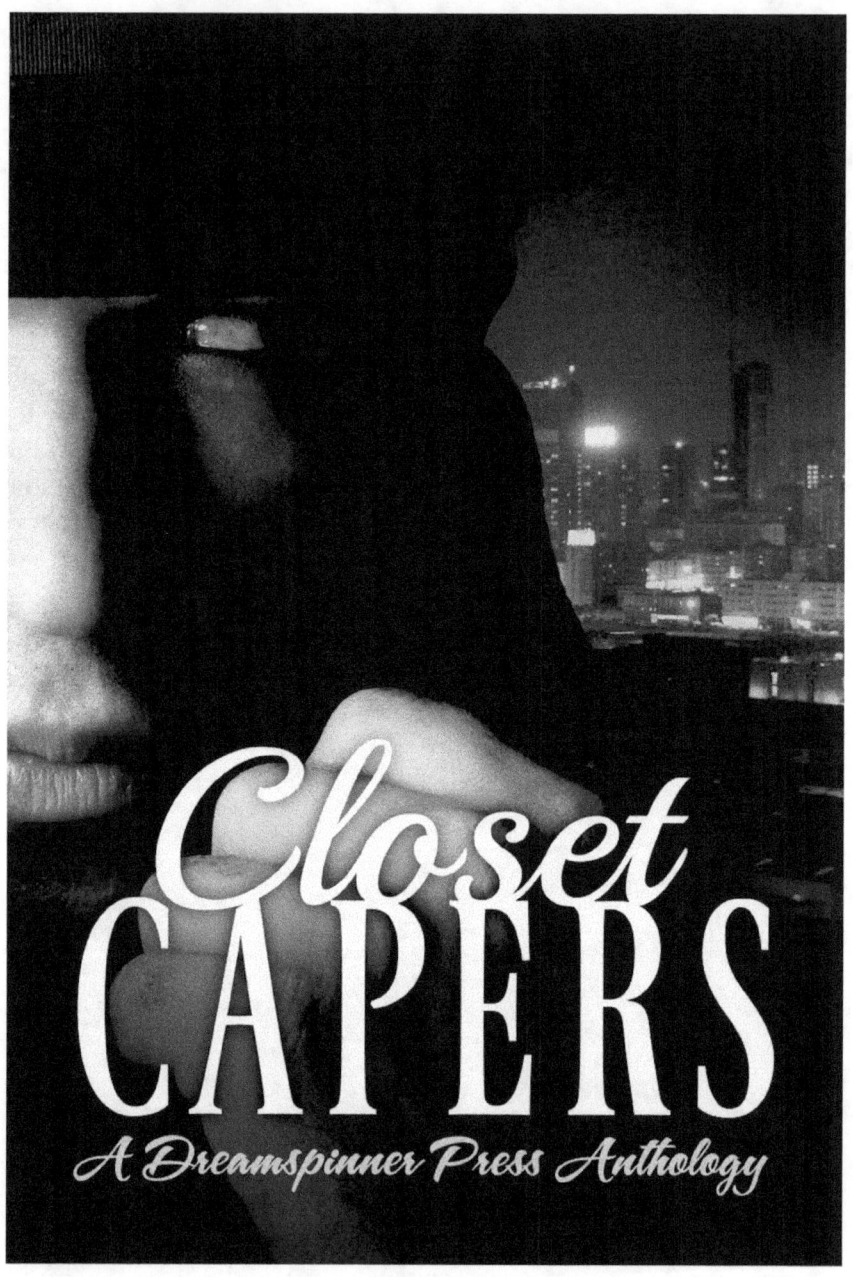

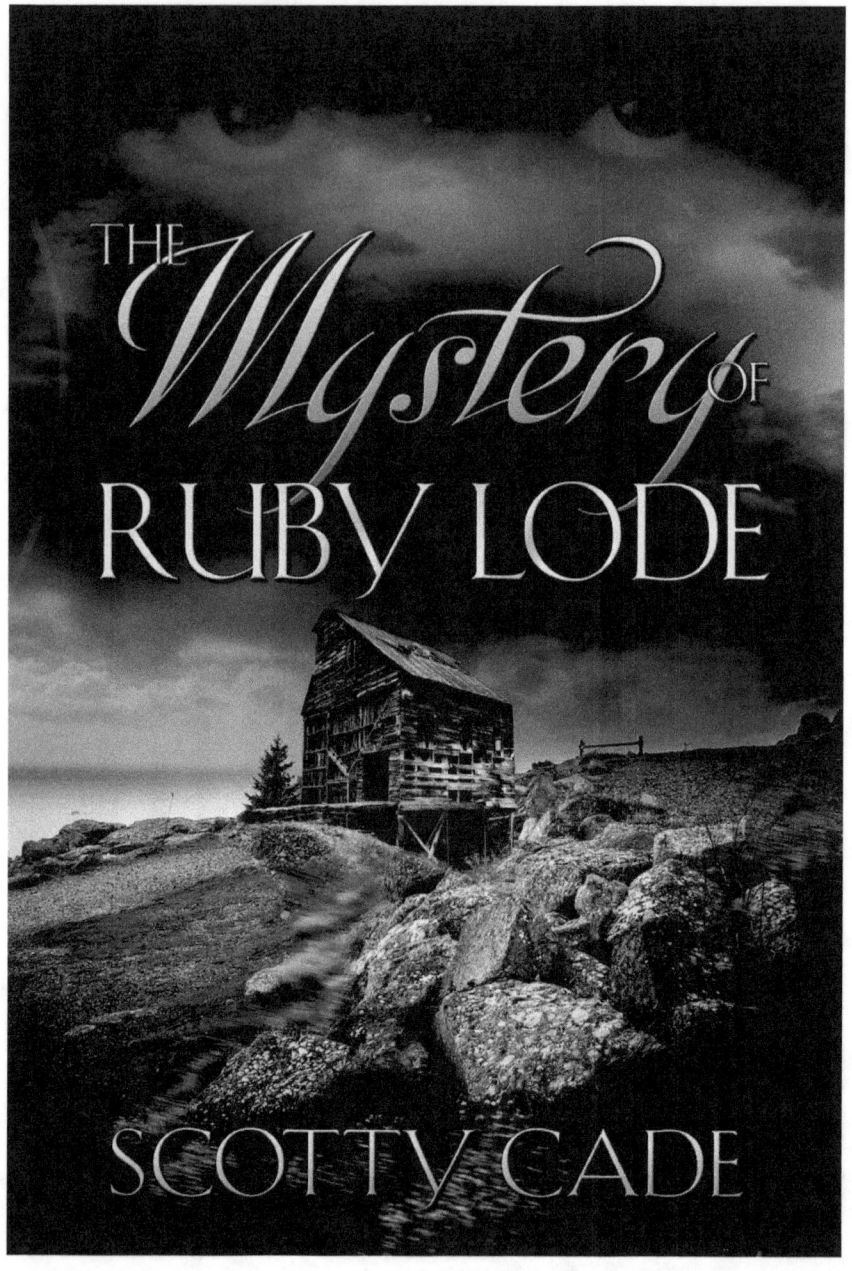

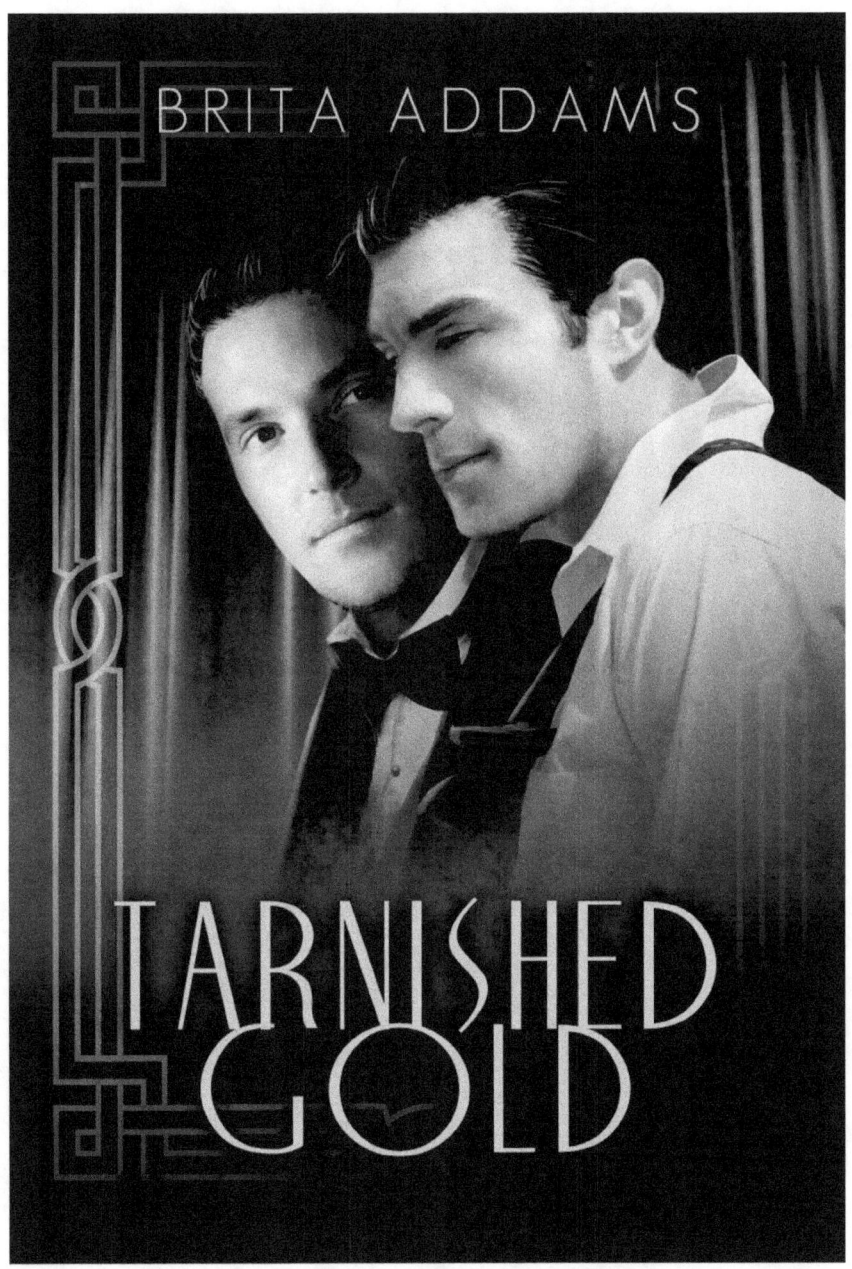

www.ingramcontent.com/pod-product-compliance
Lightning Source LLC
Chambersburg PA
CBHW050033030726
47506CB00001B/257